THE
OTHERING

❧

BLAIR MacKENZIE BLAKE

First privately published by the author in an edition of 200 copies in 2018. A limited second edition was published in 2019.

Printed in the United States of America.

The author would like to thank Greg 'Daily Grail' Taylor for his editing and typesetting services, Joseph Nagy for the cover layout, and LaraLee for proofreading, as well as for her suggestions, most of which didn't fall on deaf ears.

TREASURIA PUBLISHING

CONTENTS

CHAPTER I
CORNPOCALYPSE

My eyes twitched as the dark mask of our Siamese cat rubbed against my face.

Usually this was my first wake-up call, but I had been so excited waiting for the morning to arrive that no exuberant nuzzling or squeaky chattering was needed. Already dressed in my school clothes, I raised my head from the pillow and noticed a prismatic streak cast by the sun on the decorative beige cover. A smile spread across my face. Unclouded skies meant that the daring scheme concocted by my friends and I during our last sleepover would soon be set in motion.

Burnt toast wafted from the kitchen as Zuzulia's tail friskily slapped my face. Soon, my mom would tap on the door and tell me that it was time to get up. To which I always replied that I needed five more minutes of sleep. She would be in for a surprise on my favorite day of the year. In five minutes I would be on my bicycle heading towards the meeting place.

My favorite day of the year was called, "Addison's Day", though you wouldn't find it marked on any calendar or listed in any farmer's almanac. It was a day that existed between days, one might say. On Addison's Day I could do whatever I wanted without having to worry about getting punished. There was only one rule. Under no circumstance could I catch a glimpse of the day's 'other' date, such as printed on mom's refrigerator calendar or in the newspaper spread out on the breakfast table. And, I re-minded myself, not on my friend Ollie's new Day & Date Timex wristwatch. These were to be avoided at all costs.

Now where did Zuzu disappear to, I wondered? She had just shifted position and was motoring with a throaty rumble. I rubbed my forehead while trying to think more clearly. Sud-denly I realized that those dreams had tricked me again. This time they seemed even more real. Not allowing myself to get too rankled, I smacked my pillow and threw back the covers. Climbing out of bed, I quickly laced up my high-top Keds and grabbed my crumpled black windbreaker. Swapping it for the right colored one, I quietly walked out of the room and tiptoed down the hallway.

"Oh, you're already up and dressed." My mother seemed be-fuddled while putting together my school lunch in the kitchen. "Well, your breakfast is waiting. Cheerios without milk — blah! — and fresh cantaloupe that you like."

"I'm doing this school thing for extra credit — so I don't have time for anything today," I said, using what I figured would be the most believable of several lies that I had thought up to get out of having breakfast this morning, especially a slimy, over-ripe melon.

"Well, at least have a slice of toast. You need to put something in your system," she said while handing me my paper lunch sack, anticipating that I wasn't exactly champing at the bit for her scraped offering.

"Sit down and have a bowl of Cheerios, mister, or we'll stop buying them," I heard my dad say with a raised voice from the table in the family room.

Mom leaned out of the kitchen. "Addison has a school project. I'll pour the cereal back into the box and give the cantaloupe to the Johnsons' Pinscher."

While she was distracted, I quietly opened the broom closet and quickly pulled out several brown grocery bags, tucking them under my arm before heading towards the back door.

"Hey, where are you taking my Schnucks bags?"

Pretending that I didn't hear her, I opened the door and slipped away.

Minutes later, I was pedaling a green Schwinn Stingray as fast as I could on a crushed gravel road. The bike's front basket might not have been cool, but it was functional, especially when spending most of the day transporting grocery bags filled to the brim with shelled field corn. This might not sound like the greatest day of the year, but the 'corning' preparation process was nearly complete and the best part was soon to come.

I didn't care if anyone on my block noticed that I was heading in the opposite direction of my elementary school. Someone like Elmer Griesedieck, who I waved at while he was busy raking autumn leaves into tidy piles by the curb. To all appearances, I was just another twelve-year-old kid in brown corduroy pants and an olive-green windbreaker (the best camouflage that I could come up with) heading to the five-and-dime in Podunk. Our neighbor in the flannel shirt had no clue that I was playing hooky. Even less so that later that night I was going to dress in black clothing and unleash hell on the unsuspecting town folk, starting with that dickhead who put a caramel-covered onion into my trick-or-treat sack last Halloween.

Soon, my classmates would be raising their hands and droning "Here" as our strict, grey-bobbed 6th grade teacher, Mrs. Rutledge, took roll call. As she crept between the small desks with her infamous yardstick knuckler, waiting for me to show up tardy with a pathetic excuse, I would be at the rendez-vous point meeting my two best friends, who were also ditching school on Addison's Day. (Though, of course, they didn't know about this loophole in the multiverse.) This was one day that I would not be standing naked to the world at the chalkboard, subjected to the old prune cake's verbal humiliation while at-tempting to diagram sentences.

Clicking the bike's 3-speed "stik-shift", I whished through the acrid bluish haze of more burning curbside leaves. A few cardinals flitted from branch to branch in a front yard – just like those that I had passed seconds ago darting from limb to limb in a similar-looking tree. Similar? Oddly similar, I often thought. In fact, at times, the surroundings appeared so alike that it was like being in a *Flintstones* cartoon, where the exact same background scenery repeated over and over again. But, that's how it was living in a typical small midwestern town in the late 1960s.

Passing the last vacant lot before crossing into a subdivision where most of the streets were blacktopped, I leaned forward from the silver-glow bucket-style saddle, firmly grabbed the but-terfly bars and pedaled my flashy green machine even harder.

Having crossed a blighted field, I was the first to arrive be-hind the town's convenience store. Feeling a little apprehensive, I hopped off my bike and rested it on the kickstand. After a few minutes spent watching for Bosworth's squad car, my second best friend showed up, pulling a wheelie on his 5-speed Red Apple Krate. With its small mag-sprocket front wheel, spiffy

racing stripes and excess of chrome; Ollie's new prized possession was clearly the winner as far as our bikes went.

"Tell me you're not wearing the new Timex?" I asked while
keeping my eyes fixed on my grubby sneakers.

"No, fucktard, but I should have," he spluttered. As was usually the case, Ollie had a giant SweeTart candy disk wedged in
his mouth, which he pulled out to reveal a bloody tongue.

"Faaaark, said the crow," he uttered while touching one of
the sores on his gums.

Blood as red as his shiny Apple Krate trickled down his chin.

"When are you going to realize, Spitzer, that all giant
SweeTarts want to kill you?"

The most recent attempt occurred on the very first day of
school. While sucking on one of the jumbo tablets, during a daring maneuver to flip it over with his tongue, it got lodged in his
throat. As Ollie's face started to turn various shades of purple,
Rutledge realized that something was blocking his air passage.
After attempting to dislodge the tangy behemoth by smacking
him on the back of the head, the old battle-axe jammed her
wrinkled, liver-spotted fingers into his mouth and somehow
managed to wrench it free. With a look of utter disgust, she held
the saliva-dripping hunk of grape flavored candy up high for the
entire class to see. What made the whole episode even stranger,
was that just prior to his choking, Rutledge had used her favorite
expression, "Wake up and die right" when Ollie appeared to not
be paying attention.

Shortly afterwards, our strict disciplinarian principal mer-
cilessly paddled Ollie's "Fruit of the Loom"-clad behind with a
large hickory board. This wasn't the 'Board of Education' stock
model of "Applied Psychology" that most grammar schools used
for corporal punishment. It was a paddle known as the "Bottom

Burner", on which several holes had been drilled to reduce wind resistance. I almost felt sorry for Spitzer that day, even though he had actually lucked out. In the bottom drawer of the bald fart's desk, placed in a velvet-lined box, was the exotic Bubinga "Whammer" that was used when some poor kid was told to slide down his cotton briefs.

My jaw tightened just thinking about the hunched fossil in musty tweed that walked briskly down the crowded hallway with his talons ready to clench the back of the neck of any child that he deemed to be out of line. I tried to imagine what might happen if we got caught, but quickly blotted from my mind such an improbable scenario. With the Day & Date Timex left back in Ollie's bedroom (as I had instructed him to do so), there was nothing to be worried about.

Ollie had a habit of closing his eyes before turning into a top of the line wisenheimer. I wasn't sure what made the kid with the puffy cheeks and shock of blond hair such a smart aleck, but he had paid for it numerous times with a split-open lip or bruised eye socket.

"Any trouser chili for your first time skipping?" He shouted the last word while sniffing at the light breeze.

"Yeah, grab some Saltines and help yourself," I shot back.

Sifting through a handful of coins and metal washers that he pulled from his pocket, Ollie found a tarnished 1950 Franklin Half Dollar and proudly held it up for me to check out.

"Somebody's lucky day," he said with a fiendish grin.

Ollie was also quite the prankster. One of his favorite tricks was to steal coins from his father's valuable collection, which he glued to sidewalks where excited passersby would reach down to pocket.

Because he applied a strong adhesive to the back of the coin, most of the 'fortunate' finders were unable to budge them as he watched with fits of giggles. Ollie's new favorite place to pull such a cruel prank was the thrift shop on the 'wrong side of the tracks', where those looking for hand-me-downs would go to great lengths to attempt to pry a silver dollar loose.

"Where's Kelby? Did that burr-head chicken out? He's probably at his desk with his sharpened pencil at the ready," Ollie sneered before easing the giant SweeTart back into his contorted mouth.

"Here he comes," I pointed excitedly.

The sight of my best friend (more like a brother, actually) approaching through the dusty field on his sparkling purple chopper was a huge relief. Otherwise, I would have been stuck all day with the Ollie-mouth. While only yards away, Kelby started pedaling wildly before jamming on the brakes in order to stop with an impressive skid.

"Let's do it exactly like the plan," he reminded us with his characteristic 'Don't screw things up!' look. "Bosworth will be making his morning rounds soon."

Inside the "Short Stop", our eyes were glued to the ticking timer dial while gathered around a large stainless steel toaster oven whose heating device emitted a mysterious radiance. According to the directions, the frozen hamburgers in cellophane wrappers would be ready in a few minutes.

From the stockroom a male voice shouted, "Floor's slippery when it's wetted!"

"Nestor's back there with a boner," Ollie laughed while banging the countertop machine with his palm. "Whimpy says, cook me up a hamburger, and I will gladly pay you on Thursday."

"It will be Thursday before it's done," Kelby joked while looking around for a wall clock. "Where's your Timex, Spitzer?"

"What did one burger say to the other burger in the washroom?" Ollie elbowed me.

"I mustard," he answered before we had time to say anything.

Kelby looked at me for an explanation for this lame attempt at a joke.

"I musTURD," Ollie corrected himself; pushing me into the industrial toaster as if it were my fault that he had flubbed the punch line.

"Did you hear the one about the burger that couldn't stop making jokes? It was on a roll," he chuckled to himself in a last-ditch-effort to get us to laugh.

A narrow face full of acne appeared at the counter. The gangly figure's nametag said NESTOR, and using this as a badge of authority he summoned us to where he was leaning on a mop.

"What are you Romper Room rejects doing here on a school day?"

"I have the mumps," I said while pointing to my crotch.

A deafening buzz let us know that our burgers were finally ready. Racing back to the "atomic stove", I pulled open its hinged cover and gazed at the thermal infrared reflected on the burgers' translucent covering. Being in a hurry, all three of us burned our fingertips while attempting to remove the steaming cello-wrappers.

Once unwrapped, I ravenously bit off a mouthful without blowing. With faux char marks, the soy-extended beef under its seeded crown had all the makings for a truly unforgettable breakfast.

"Mine sucks," Ollie complained to Nestor... "But if it had pickles it would be DILL-icous."

"I'd think about laughing at your corny jokes, shit-spitter, but my throat is a little... horse." Nestor's eyes grew comically large as he gestured to Ollie's half-eaten burger.

Having wolfed down mine, I grabbed a large bag of our favorite "Ozark Country Style" BBQ potato chips from the rack along with a few "Chick-O-Sticks" from the cardboard display. While paying for this, Nestor leaned over the cash register and said in a teasing sing-song voice, "Not-so Bright's gonna get a butt-full of Bubinga."

Outside, my friend with the pocketful of slugs was having trouble defrauding the humming vending machine. Frustrated, he stuffed another quarter-sized metal washer into the slot and selected his choice, waiting for the tumbling soda can. Any metal alloy that tricked vending machines into dispensing their product fascinated Ollie, and he had more of these in his pockets than genuine coins. Many were common punchouts that he had found in the alley near the machine shop or knockouts from electrical junction boxes, but he also had some penny planchets and foreign currency. However, none of these were working in the Short Stop's brand new Pepsi machine. Evidently, the coin-op companies were being more proactive with their security measures, so Ollie had to resort to pounding like a madman on the select tabs. After monkeying with the coin return device and kicking both sides, he finally gave up and unplugged the thing.

Kelby jokingly had a solution for Ollie's latest failing.

"Go buy a quart of soda and then ask Nestor for three large cups of ice for free."

Kelby was the smartest kid in school and better than the rest of us at every sport. He was also lucky. The other day he had won the prized German-made "Joseph's Coat Swirl" that my dad had given to me when I was younger. This happened while we were playing bridgeboard "keepsies." The wooden board held by Kelby contained seven different sized cutouts along one edge, and I felt that I could easily shoot my colorful marble through the larger sixth archway. In doing so, I would win his "Cornhusk Swirl" – a honey-yellow beauty that I always wanted.

My shot seemed to be perfectly on target, but the marble stopped just short of the arch. Losing the valuable "Joseph's Coat" to Kelby was the one thing that I could never tell my father, especially after the big deal that he made about it being hand-crafted before entrusting me with it.

With his well-scrubbed mug and short burr haircut, parents thought that Kelby was a model kid. But, behind his shy exterior and Honor Roll marks, he could be deceptively mischievous. He wasn't afraid to engage in a little devilry, so long as it was well planned out and involved some creativity. He would be more reluctant to swipe a penny jawbreaker from the Ben Franklin 5-10 than he would be to steal gold fillings from his dentist's safe during a midnight heist.

A '58 Chevy Apache pickup with a patchwork of paint, primer and bare metal pulled up with a loud rumble. Inside, the driver glared at us with a non-filter Kool dangling from his mouth. When he climbed out, I recognized him to be a local troublemaker named Chooch. He had a ruddy, pitted complexion with dirty blonde hair that nearly reached his waist. His wiry frame was sinewy and strong as revealed by a faded denim jacket whose sleeves he had cut off.

While strutting to the door in skin-tight indigo jeans, his head bobbed as if to some loud rhythm in his head. As he was about to pull open the door, he paused to pick up something that he spotted on the pavement. It was the Franklin Half Dollar that had been glued there with Ollie's powerful bonding agent. Making things worse, I saw that the high-school tuff was missing a couple of fingers as he struggled to lift it. "What the hell?" I heard him mumble.

When I saw Ollie shut his eyes, I knew that we were dead meat.

"Finders keepers – losers weepers," he smirked.

Chooch turned towards us while brushing back greasy blonde strands.

"Which one of you ass-clowns glued this here?" he calmly asked.

To my surprise, Ollie fessed up right away.

"Sorry, it was meant for Nestor in there. He gypped me with a re-freeze."

"You chewed one of those rubber things from the cooker?"

Chooch stood up and walked over to us with his head still wobbling as if to some crazy beat. Instead of backing away, we stood there as if we were glued to the spot with Ollie's epoxy. Flicking the sparkling shower of his cigarette butt at Ollie's red Chucks, I tried not to cough from his thick mentholated exhale. While leaning inches away from my friend's face, he pulled out a switchblade from his back pocket and clicked it in front of Ollie's shocked expression.

"Tell me you're not dumb enough to bring a Chick-O-Stick to a knife fight?" Chooch bobbed his head while pointing the blade at the sugary orange rod of peanut butter and toasted coconut that Ollie had been in the process of unwrapping.

He then looked at me while spinning the weapon in the palm of his good hand.

"Is your father Mr. Albright, the history teacher?"

"Yeah, at the High School," I nodded.

Chooch proudly showed me where a couple of his digits had been severed; smiling with tobacco-stained teeth while also displaying what remained of a terribly mangled thumb.

"That putz flunked me before I dropped out because I didn't know that Lincoln's mother died of poisoned milk or something. That's cool, though. I crushed my thumb while punching in the machine shop, and then got de-gloved here due to… tangentially moving parts. There are going to be hazards in metal fabrication, but that place was grossly negligent with their workplace safety regulations. So, check it out… my new Bonneville."

He pointed to a brand new Triumph motorcycle that was haphazardly chained in the bed of the beater Apache pickup.

"My settlement was over a thousand dollars. Make sure you tell old chalkie that."

Ollie pulled a metal disk out of his jingling pocket.

"Yeah, I know that place," he told Chooch. "Found lots of your slugs in the alley."

"So, you try to gyp the machine with metal washers, but glue half dollars to the concrete? Your parents threw away the boy and raised the foreskin," Chooch laughed while shaking his head.

Shoving the closed switchblade back into his pocket, he gestured for me to follow him over to his old Chevy. Leaning over the rusted bed, he pulled out three shiny gold cans of "Stag" beer.

"Do you butt guppies need some beer?"

Without hesitation, I accepted the beers and quickly dropped them inside a grocery bag. He tossed me an extra one before heading back to the store with his wildly jouncing head. Kicking the stuck half dollar with his biker boot, he abruptly whirled around and jerked out the flick knife.

"Who just said Mooch said that Cherrie is muddin' in a stripper's pit?"

As he took a couple of steps towards us, the guy who inhaled too many welding fumes appeared to come unhinged. Before we had time to react, he stopped dead in his tracks and flashed a big smile full of discolored teeth.

With most of our supplies procured, we struck off across the wide-open field and ducked into the closest neighborhood so as not to be detected by Bosworth. We were heading to our fort on the outskirts of town. Though it had served as our base of operations for several years, the hideout was really just a small clearing in the woods. There wasn't even a tree house.

Passing the last address in the neighborhood, we could hear the banging of hammers as houses were being framed on large dirt plots where a new subdivision was being built. A pudgy yokel on a backhoe waved at us, and then did a double take. At the end of a gravel and oil stretch, we stopped and walked our bikes up a small bluff.

Soon we were in the woods.

It was just a short ride to the clearing on a path carpeted with shriveled burgundy leaves. Other than a couple of small piles of white crusted dog crap, the place looked undisturbed.

After moving a dark blanket onto which Ollie had painstakingly glued various shades of autumn leaves, we brushed back a layer of fetid dirt to reveal a plywood board that functioned as the lid for our secret hiding spot. This was a small square pit that we had dug and lined with carefully measured pieces of Styrofoam cut from cheap disposable ice chests.

Lifting the plywood cover to retrieve our stash, the first thing visible was a piece of ruled notebook paper that had a handwritten curse scrawled by Kelby after being inspired by a late night television "Bijou Theater" horror movie. The magic marker malediction contained a warning of the terrible consequences that would befall any would-be thief.

The cache was a couple of burlap sacks filled with corn kernels that were dried to a pebble-like hardness. Beneath this was an assortment of grain-belt beers – Colt-45, Stag and Falstaff – that we had managed to accumulate over the course of weeks. There was also a set of olive-drab walkie-talkies, a half pack of Kool cigarettes and some wrapped snack cakes that Ollie had bragged about getting for a five-finger-discount at the local "Tomboy" market.

As Kelby transferred the grain corn into the Schnucks bags, Ollie and I checked the walkie-talkies. I pressed one tightly against my ear and was about to test it when I felt something crawling on my face. I slapped my cheek repeatedly until I noticed a brown insect with forceps-like pinchers wriggling on the ground. Examining the unit, I was shocked to see that it was teaming with earwigs. Revolted, I dropped the slithering nest onto the ground, unable to take my eyes off those pouring out of the earpiece. I felt a tickling sensation in my right external ear canal. Realizing that it might be one of the slimy little things burrowing, I immediately stuck my index finger in as far as I could, hoping to crush it before it got too far along. Unable to feel anything, I withdrew my finger and examined the tip for any smushed remains.

"Pincher bugs in the walkie-talkies!" I shouted.

Ollie checked his unit's earpiece – shaking it hard – but no fast-moving insects exited.

"Don't worry about one getting in your ear," Ollie said… "Unless it tunnels into your brain and the pain is terrible… before it crawls out the other ear. But if it lays its eggs inside… well, then you probably should worry… before you go insane… after all the babies are hatched."

"That's true, Addison," Kelby nodded… "When you're five years old."

According to Kelby's calculations we didn't have enough of the really loud corn – the "Hubb's Stubs" – and if we really wanted to make an impression on our neighbor's aluminum siding and picture windows, we would need to, once again, raid the nearby farmer's field. Risking getting caught in the stalks, or, even worse, having our flesh riddled with burning rock salt was one thing; once we had snatched enough husks, we would still have to remove the tough kernels from the cobs. Deciding that it was worth taking the chance, we grabbed the empty burlap sacks and headed into the autumn foliage towards Hubb Ohlendorf's field. One thing was for sure: Knowing damn well about the local corning custom in these parts, the farmer would be on the lookout for kids like us trespassing on his property.

After trudging through a stretch of forest for about twenty minutes, we emerged onto a ploughed track that surrounded the highly prized 'loud corn'. Motioning for us to stop and be quiet, Kelby scanned the immediate surroundings. With no sign of the farmer, he gave the 'all clear' sign, after which we made a mad dash into the rustling yellowed stalks.

While filling our sacks with the stunted ears, we listened for any signs of danger, such as the crunch of footsteps or racking of a shotgun. All seemed good, and we were nearly finished when, suddenly, from out of nowhere, a Porter Wagoner song blasting at full volume scared the wits out of us. Catching the glint of a massive John Deere tractor parked amongst the dense corn stalks, I expected at any minute to see a muzzle flash and feel the sting of rock salt.

Having the presence of mind to hold onto our sacks, we ran as fast as we could on the rough earth between the crops. Without any warning, Kelby abruptly turned and began running cross row.

I followed the best that I could, but after losing sight of him and Ollie, I turned and continued down the parallel rows. When I eventually reached the edge of the field, I wasn't sure where I was. After catching my breath, I climbed over a rickety fence and made a beeline for a stand of partially denuded trees.

Scrambling between some decayed logs, I continued up the gently sloping ground, pushing back snapping branches until I reached an opening. Looking around for the others, I cautiously approached a rotting picket fence that bordered a small cemetery nestled between cornfields.

Parked on the withered grass within my range of view was a funny looking old black hearse. Not far away, a couple of men were filling in an open burial plot with dirt scooped from a wheelbarrow. Curiously, for a freshly dug grave, I noticed that the headstone was weathered from the passing years – similar to the others around it. With their backs turned to me, I saw that the two men with shovels were dressed exactly alike and that their motions while tossing dirt were perfectly in sync. Unlike their ordinary work clothes, the man watching this odd unison was impeccably dressed in an all black suit and sporting a black German-style fedora hat.

Running around in the "Indian Summer" weather had made me thirsty. Thinking there might be a garden hose on the grounds, I decided to climb over the fence. Almost immediately after setting foot inside the graveyard, I felt a strange tingling sensation.

Moving slowly along an overgrown shady walkway, the pigments of autumn made the cemetery even more somber. There were no cardinals, no squirrels... and no flowers. Sneaking between worn headstones with shriveled climbing ivy, I saw that the peculiar funerary markings were marred with spray-painted graffiti. This and other evidence of vandalism, including mossy broken statuary, was most likely the work of thrill-seeking teenagers. Though I longed for water, something – perhaps those interred in this secluded, unkempt place, I reckoned with a nervous chuckle – compelled me to take a closer look at the tomb inscriptions. Beneath the Masonic-esque symbols on one faded slab were the crudely marked words:

BEWARE MOLEWHISKER THE BODY SNATCHER

With electrified needles still pricking my entire body, I sidled over to another marker whose greyish tones had been defaced with:

NO CORPSE STEW HERE UNHOLY MOLEY

Sitting on top of a chipped marble headstone was an empty bottle of "Coon Hollow" bourbon.

Encircled by painted greenish flames, the bleached graffiti on the memorial next to this was harder to make out, but appeared to read:

MAXX HELL FOR THE WILL O' THE WISPS

While resting for a minute on an eroded mourning chair, withered leaves tumbled from branches. The prickling sensation coursing through my body intensified. I must be dehydrated, I figured. That, or the infrared-heated refrozen horseflesh had got me feeling weird. Of course, I also thought about an earwig squirming inside my brain.

I gazed down at tadpoles flitting in a stagnant puddle. While fixated on them, passing clouds obscured the sun. It felt like there was a sharp drop in the air pressure – similar to the changing weather conditions before the tornado warning sounds. I also had this overwhelming feeling of heaviness – like when I was younger and mom bundled me up in a thermal coat on a frigid winter's day. What was happening here? The place was going nuts. I needed to leave...

Just as I was about to take off, the sunlight returned, causing a prismatic sheen in the small pool of rainwater where tadpoles darted about. Watching the dark squiggles, my mind started drifting until my body was jolted by a sharp, quick tremor. I inhaled forcefully. With this, my strange physical sensations changed again. The vibrations ceased, as did the heaviness. I felt a pleasant tingle rising up my spine. A warm, cozy feeling enveloped me, and I saw the sepulchral hues with exceptional clarity.

An instant later, this vivid awareness was both confusing and alarming. Did this sudden uncanny perception mean that I was at death's door? About to join the lingering spirits that haunted the environs, I half-joked, hoping to lighten my nerves. I felt myself starting to panic. I didn't want my lifeless body to be found slumped over a stone chair while holding a burlap sack full of field corn. (On Addison's Day!) How could I not have felt the sharp fangs of a venomous copperhead while clambering over deadfall? Or was it the bite of a fiddleback spider that I didn't feel while reaching around inside the dark hiding place?

As my anxiety increased, I watched with fascination as the dark shape on the ground moved along with my body motions. While doing so, a second dark outline appeared beside it.

"Pretending to be alive, are you?" an irritated gravelly voice asked.

I jumped from the rough seat and turned to see an elderly visage glowering at me from under the brim of a black fedora. It was the man in the suit from the newly dug burial plot – his gaunt frame now leaning on a fancy walking stick.

Although I refrained from looking directly at the bitter disposition etched on his face, the one thing that I couldn't help but notice was the curly black whisker – well over an inch long – that protruded from a rather ordinary mole on his chin. Perhaps this was the reason for my initial impression that there was something odd about his facial structure.

Slightly taller than average height, the old fellow was attired in a tailored black suit with a silver-grey cravat necktie. Jutting from the breast pocket was a mauve silk handkerchief. His black slacks were perfectly pressed right down to polished oxford shoes. I noticed that the stylish black fedora had a faint black rosette, but quickly averted my gaze from the quizzical dark blue eyes that scrutinized my adolescent features.

"I was just looking for a hose to get a drink of water," I said as my heart pounded faster.

Though he was dressed like the scion of a Teutonic family, he spoke with a raspy midwest twang that was better suited for a local yokel in faded bib overalls and an oil-smudged John Deere cap.

"First bell rang... and the second bell – the tardy bell – it rung, too, but where's the dick-sneeze who's supposed to be sitting at his desk? Dontcha' know that truant officer – Millard – casts a wide net for boys without a proper dismissal slip. You think you snookered 'em all until you get yourself a good whooping with the strap."

"It's Addison's Day," I mumbled, forgetting that I wasn't supposed to tell anyone.

"Got a cocklebur on your tongue? It's mostaccioli day," he said while stroking the dangling whisker.

"Today?" I asked.

"Newspaper lunch menu said mostaccioli hot dish in the school cafeteria –"

"I always brown bag my lunch unless it's –"

"I don't care if you eat Elmer's paste with a piddly wooden stick. I'm telling you that The Spectrum said it was mostaccioli when it yoosta be Johnny Marzetti."

With his thin venous hand, he pounded the walking stick against some shriveled leaves. While clenching the ornate handled crutch, I noticed that, although his clothes were immaculate, his fingernails were as dirty as those of a backwoods cornbilly.

"Y'aint causing trouble I hope," he asked while gesturing to the bulging cloth sack.

"Just some corn," I said.

"Boy-oh-boy, you'd better watch out for that farmer – Ohlendorf – sittin' on his butt beard in that air conditioned tractor listening to the warbling of that pompadour twiddlefuck… lesson you want a barrel full of crow shot in the hind-quarters."

He spat a missile of tobacco juice and nodded to the brown splotch on the ground.

"Pardon my expectoration. A nasty compulsion, I'm sure we can all agree."

"What?"

"What?" he mocked my cracking larynx.

"You're gonna make quite an impact on society with that string of F's as red as a peckerwood's barn paint," he spat again while repeatedly tapping the walking stick's exquisite workmanship.

"Nobody gets F's anymore. We get U's – for Unsatisfactory," I corrected him.

"Unsatisfactory? Yep, now that's what I'm worried about, son. Do you know why there's a fence here?.. Because people are dying to get in." He said this so straight-faced that it took me a while to realize that he was intentionally making a bad joke.

"Tell that to those niblets watchin' from yonder with chiggers on their schniggles."

Unable to break my gaze away from his unsettling eyes, I slowly edged backwards. Seeing how he knew the name of the truant officer, I thought that it might be best to make a run for it before he asked me what my last name was. Grabbing the burlap tightly, I glanced over at the narrow walkway… and took off towards the fence.

"Skedaddle!" I heard him shout.

Once over the fence and a safe distance away, I paused to get my bearings. While doing so, I saw an old cast-iron well spigot whose flaking red paint was covered with bird droppings. I could hardly believe my eyes. What was it doing here in the middle of nowhere? I pumped the squeaky handle. Nothing. I pumped it again and water began to gush out. Bending down, I let the cold, clear stream pour into my wide-open mouth. It was delicious – better than any carnival soda pop that I'd ever drank.

After having more than my fill, I wiped my face and once again took stock of the surroundings. Unsure which way to go, I started off on a rutted track that skirted yet another cornfield.

Rounding a corner between rows, I was met with a bizarre sight. Before its gaudy coloration registered in my brain, there was a loud rustling sound as Kelby and Ollie jumped out of the stalks, hoping to scare the crap out of me. Instead, I let out a burst of laughter while pointing at the scarecrow propped up near the corn. The decoy that had been placed there to frighten away crows had its shabby farmer clothes replaced with a frilly pink ballerina's tutu. Its stitched mouth was smeared with thick red lipstick and long fake lashes accentuated charcoal button eyes. There was a bright blue ribbon in its locks of golden straw hair, and the hayman was holding a large rainbow pinwheel lollypop on which a few flies were crawling. Evidently, some high-school 'cow-tipper' types had really outdone themselves.

"Give me a quarter if I take a lick?" Ollie asked.

"No way," I said while still chuckling at the ridiculous look-ing thing.

"How about a dime?"

Before we had a chance to respond, the crazy ass leaned over and stuck out his eroded tongue. While holding out his palm, he took a big lick, causing flies to scatter from the multicolored swirls.

"Okay, you each owe me a dime."

"Who was that old codger?" Kelby asked.

As I was about to tell him what happened, Ollie interrupted me with a finger-wagging warning. "So, I'll bet you think you have an excuse for missing school by saying that you were at a funeral. Won't work, dumbass."

I didn't know if it was the cold well water or what, but my anxiety subsided. Instead of concern, I looked even more forward to executing our well-thought-out plan. Sure, there had been a few unexpected snags – just hiccups, really – from which we came out unscathed (thanks to Addison's Day). We just need-ed to hike back to the fort so we could shuck the newly obtained husks and remove the dried grain.

With high-fives all around, we set off towards the woods…

"Mole whisker!" Ollie uttered while de-husking. "Do you know who that was? Maxx the Molewhisker. The body snatcher. If Kelby and I weren't around, you'd be tonight's supper."

"He's just a poor old scrounger that smells like garbage cans," Kelby said, downplaying the cannibal notion. "People here make fun of him because he used to be an undertaker and because he's a curmudgeon. And, because of his mole whisker."

"He's a cannibal, Kelby. Just like those in National Geo-graphic – only without stupid bones in his nose. The creep adds people meat to cans of Dinty-Moore stew. Ask anyone."

"Done with my corn," I announced while shaking the filled burlap sack.

Over the past couple of years we had perfected a technique to make the process of removing the hard kernels from the cob both faster and less painful. The trick was in the opposing twisting motion employed after loosening the stubborn higher pieces with one's thumbs. When done correctly, the corn fell easily into our opened sacks.

A few minutes later the others were finished with theirs. After increasing our stash, we leaned against a tree trunk and dug into our school lunch bags.

"What do you got in yours?" Ollie asked.

Holding the closed brown paper bag to my forehead, I pretended to be the turbaned soothsayer, "Carnac the Magnificent." "Deviled Ham, Graham crackers… and a tangerine."

"What about those cocoa deathbricks your mother makes?"

I closed my eyes again and held up the bag, pretending it was now much heavier.

"Yes, no-bake cookies, too – says Carnac the Magnificent."

"Save 'em for tonight," Ollie said, half-seriously. "In case we run into a situation where we need some heavy artillery. Hey, give me some of those fuckin' Hillbillies," he said while motioning to the bag of Ozark BBQ potato chips that Kelby had just ripped open. "I gotta have something to go with my baby franks and musTURD sammich."

With his hands in position to catch the bag, Ollie wrinkled his nose as if reacting to a bad smell.

"And you're gonna be Sugardale bologna breath again?"

"Tuna fish on pumpernickel," Kelby beamed while anticipating being razzed.

"Pumperdinkle! What kind of queerhole sammich is that, Timmons?" Doing his best British upper-crust impression, Ollie joked: "I'll have mine on spiced pumpkin raisin toast."

"With nothing to drink due to impotent slugs," Kelby fired back. "I'd slug one of my mother's diet Tabs right now."

We both waited for Ollie to have the last word, but, uncharacteristically, he didn't say anything. Kelby's remark about the slugs had shut him up for a while. Actually, none of us said anything for a few minutes as we ate our sandwiches and chomped on the heavily seasoned chips.

"I'm going to pretend that I just heard the bell, so lunch period is over." Kelby once again assumed the leader role. "Let's get this corn inside those drainage pipes in Sunrise Gardens."

After gathering our stuff, we took off on our bikes to go about staging the shelled corn inside drainage pipes and beneath shrubbery in various locations around a particular subdivision. I didn't think any of us could have imagined that it would be our last time together at the fort.

It had been our meeting place and starting point for many juvenile adventures. As we searched the shadowy thickets for objects of interest, squiggly worm markings on tree bark looked like fossils of mysterious creatures, so we brought back samples of our find. A piece of glossy black boiler slag found on the overgrown broken foundation of an abandoned factory was thought to be obsidian from long extinct volcanoes when Illinois was near the equator. Plow scratches on stones might have been the alphabet of a lost tongue. As our imaginations ran wild, every time we returned home with the evidence, my dad quickly dismissed the stuff as being worthless, common material of no historical significance whatsoever. Spooky novelties that were found in abandoned barns that psychopathic killers once inhabited were also met with either tolerant smiles or derisive smirks by the grown ups. Our time would be more productively spent cleaning our rooms or finishing our homework they suggested.

It was hard to believe that we were even allowed to explore such places back then. What, with all the talk about inbred freaks who lived in derelict backwoods cabins that were spotted from time to time venturing into the outskirts of town where they sought to abduct unattended children. Even more so with the frightening reports by deer hunters of seven-foot-tall ape-like creatures with muddy, matted fur seen lumbering through heavily wooded areas.

We also heard some of the town's ghost lore – mostly phantom auto crashes with spectral dead lovers hitchhiking on lonely back roads. Being that we weren't teenagers who went on moonlit joy rides, the best that we could hope for was a visitation by Abraham Lincoln. According to stories I'd heard since I was a little tyke, an apparition of our 16th President sometimes appeared at the family dinner table when chicken fricassee and biscuits were served. Of course, he was a no-show the one time my mom attempted that dish – maybe because she didn't bake an apple pie, which was said to be Abe's favorite dessert.

The most enduring local legend – and the one that I most took to heart – was of a fabulous treasure hidden in the area. From accounts passed from generation to generation, it was believed to be in a walled-up limestone cave guarded by prairie rattlers. Others thought that it was in a specially constructed vault concealed by an artificial creek bed. And still others claimed that the only way to discover the horde was to cross seven decommissioned railroad bridges that were scattered on winding back roads, with the final one having to be entered at precisely the stroke of midnight. However, if the small concrete bridges and trestles weren't crossed in the correct sequence, instead of a portal of magnificent riches, the gates of hell would be opened.

Adding credence to some of the persistent rumors involving valuable ancient artifacts buried in the area was that our town was located in that part of southern Illinois known as "Little Egypt." As with other nearby towns with Egyptian names – such as Cairo, Thebes, Karnak and Dongola – it was believed that they were called so because of the land's resemblance to Egypt's Nile delta. Another explanation for the appellation was that the area was considered to be the state's breadbasket. More recently, it had been suggested that the nickname might be connected with legends of a colony established here by an ancient sea faring people thousands of years ago.

As the town's history teacher, my dad flat out rejected this notion to anyone who asked him about it. The whole idea of a trans-Atlantic voyage made in large Phoenician-style skiffs way back then was, in his words, "a bunch of poppycock."

Because of a series of strange occurrences over the years, many town folk who were convinced that there was some kind of untouched treasure trove, believed it to be a magnet for negativity.

Others felt that the very idea of an accursed treasure was complete nonsense. Any dark shadow cast over the town was the result of changes in traditional values. God was watching, they insisted.

Things were changing and had been for quite some time.

Bulldozers gouged the countryside as refugees from the concrete moved into 'white-flight' towns like ours. As ramshackle farmhouses, tottering grey barns, rusted grain silos and unvarying rows of crops gradually disappeared, I wondered when something hidden behind the monotonous tones might finally be exposed?

For the time being there were fish-fry raffles in the sun-dappled park and brass parades to show off the newest fire engine. If you needed a nail, you went to the hardware store. Weenie-Winks and Pizza Squares were served by lunch-ladies on sea-foam green trays in the school cafeteria. Pot-bellied hubbies drank chilled beer and grilled pork-butts on their smoky backyard Webers while listening to the ballgame on transistor radios. There were Mahjong luncheons and Tupperware parties. Children played whiffle ball on grass with fluffy dandelions as colorful laundry billowed on clotheslines.

All the while something continued to go unnoticed amid the humdrum. Those enjoying the bug-zapper patio culture of the endlessly blooming subdivisions were totally oblivious to this unseen otherness that I was somehow sensitive to. Until other town folk were able to perceive at least some aspects of its existence, I would keep quiet... would keep this to myself.

Although this presence (and absence) that I was keen to at times defied even partial definition, I was certain that it wasn't some inbred bogeyman that lived under a graffiti-coated railroad trestle. Nor was it a howling shaggy man-like beast crouched in the vast reaches of forest. It wasn't even a devil with cloven hoofs and a spiked tail that the fervently praying devout in their Sunday duds feared while giving thanks for Griddle Greats at the Perkins Pancake House. It was something far more terrifying ... and unthinkable. Not just to the Otis and Earlyne, Dermot and Jesslyn old timers who rode into town to scratch their heads at the new ice cream cone flavors or to see if a second traffic light had been erected, but for those newcomers who had rowdy poker parties in their carpeted basements and extramarital affairs with the swingers down the block.

❧

My mother hardly ever asked me what happened in class on any given school day, so there was no reason to tell her about making relief maps of China from salt dough and watercolors. Or, about how someone placed glossy paper cutouts of bugs in the light fixtures, thereby disrupting the teaching of a frantic Mrs. Rutledge until the janitor informed her that it was just a silly prank. Of course, I had other stuff at the ready if need be, but if not questioned about anything, I would save this for another time.

Mom did, however, ask if there was anything wrong after noticing my awkward seated position and continual shifting (to avoid seeing the fridge calendar) as I watched her prepare dinner in her daisy apron. She was fixing the dreaded Yakamish – a frying pan scramble of just about every food that I disliked, and certainly my least favorite dish in her limited repertoire. Being a bastardized version of a Japanese fried rice staple, the tsunami of soy sauce that it was drenched in was the only good part.

Thankfully, because it turned up on Addison's Day (coincidently?), I wouldn't be around to ride it out until the even more dreaded leftovers slot.

"Mom, can we get a cat?" I asked.

"A cat? I don't know, Addison. What kind of cat?" she asked while slicing and dicing.

"One with a mask and blue eyes like we had – I keep thinking that we had one before."

"Silly, we never had a cat," she smiled. "Those kind of cats – Siamese – are known to cause all kinds of mischief that would drive your father crazy. They're talkative…. needy… domineering. Real busybodies from what I've been told."

My dad entered the kitchen and removed a pair of gloves. He had been pulling crabgrass by hand out in the backyard – something that he was slightly obsessed with. Now it was time for his other late afternoon ritual of constructing a gin martini before fiddling with the flickering screen pattern on the Zenith in plenty of time for tonight's episode of *Daktari*.

"After not having breakfast, you're really hungry for Yakamish," he said with a taunting wink.

"Addison's not eating with us tonight. He's meeting his friends at the hot dog and root beer place," mom broke the news.

"King Coney," I said.

"Past the traffic light – King Coney? We have all that right here... for tomorrow. Hot dogs in the Frigidaire... and there's plenty of cans of soda in the basement –"

"It's not the same thing, dad. They've frosted mugs of creamy root beer," I explained, stressing the word, "creamy."

"Whoop-de-do," he scowled while pouring some Gilbeys.

"He's working on another school project. They've been converting the locker room of the gymnasium into a cardboard maze haunted house to raise money," my mom told him while adjusting the flame on the stove and brushing back her tinted bangs.

"I'm doing the cobwebby stuff," I added.

"That sounds really challenging – hanging threads." He rolled his eyes while opening a cloudy jar of olives. "What, were you the last to volunteer?"

Feeling somewhat better about things after the first couple of sips of the cocktail, he reached into the pocket of his baggy work pants and fumbled for some quarters.

"How much is that greasy crap gonna' cost me – with your poor mother slaving over a hot stove right here. Here's fifty cents. I'll give it to you this one time, but we're not the Rockefellers here. And let me tell you something, kiddo. Tomorrow night you're going to park your keaster at the dinner table and eat all your food with a healthy glass of milk."

"I heard that Abe Lincoln's mother died of milk sickness," I cringed.

"Yeah, well don't you worry, mister – those cows are feeling a lot better by now."

Stirring the martini with his finger, he gobbled down an olive and left the kitchen to go have at it with the snowy Zenith.

Mom struggled to open a box of Birds Eye frozen vegetables – the most ill conceived ingredients of the mixture, I'd long thought – which is why they most often wound up as half-chewed mush smuggled inside my napkin to the commode. She stabbed the varicolored block with a fork a few times before dropping it into a furiously boiling pan.

"When I stayed over at Kelby's last week – for dinner – his mom cooked these peas that were really fucking good."

Immediately, I realized what had slipped and braced for her shocked reaction.

Either because my using that word was so beyond the pale that it simply didn't register, or because she was so preoccupied with cooking, she just shrugged her shoulders and said, "Well, maybe they have them at the Tomboy?"

Maybe the unacceptable word hadn't sunk in yet? Unable to rule out the possibility of some kind of delayed reaction, I thought that I'd better hightail it. But then it hit me. How could I have forgotten about Addison's Day? The accidental word was blocked from penetrating her Yakamish-frazzled brain, and this action is permanent so long as I didn't glance at the calendar attached to a certain Coppertone appliance rattling for attention right next to where I was seated.

"Whoa, I'm going to be late."

I grabbed a ballpoint pen from the counter top, jumped off the stool and pulled out a sheet of paper with a typed note.

"Oh, can you sign this real quick? It's just you giving permission for me to work on the spook house tonight," I said with my knees bent like a track sprinter at the starting block.

"Here's the pen," I pressed.

"Okay, Addison, okay — just let me wipe off this bacon spatter."

I was in high-spirits while gliding into the entrance of the King Coney drive-in. All my ducks were in a row — as my dad liked to say. I was wearing black clothing for tonight's residential blitz. There were several cans of beer inside two sturdy Schnucks bags in my basket. Best of all, in my back pocket was a typed excuse for being absent from school that was signed by my mom. Plus, surprisingly, I wasn't experiencing any pre-corning jitters.

Next to a picnic table under the brightly lit canopy, Kelby's purple chopper and Ollie's snazzy Krate were on their kickstands. Glancing around the busy eatery, I saw that my friends were standing at a speakerphone in one of the few empty parking stalls. I slowly pedaled over to where their bikes were parked, and climbed off to take in the surroundings.

Pretty carhops in cheerleader outfits were carrying trays of chilidogs, onion rings and foamy glass mugs of root beer to the rows of cars parked by menu board speakerphones. The night air smelled of charred beef, drugstore Faberge and exhaust fumes. Beeping horns greeted newly arriving muscle cars as CCR's

"Suzie Q" blasted over steel-cone speakers. Insects swirled and batted softly against the restaurant's neon marquee, whose comical logo of a hot dog nestled in a bun beside a frothy mug of root beer blinked colorfully at twilight.

I watched Nestor approach in a King Coney uniform, but before I could say anything, Ollie's voice rang out under the corrugated metal awning.

"Hey, look, it's the Lord of the Fries at his night job – getting ready to do some serious swabbing."

"If I catch you unplugging the soda machine, you'll never set foot inside the Short Stop again," Nestor warned while reaching into his apron and flicking a limp French fry at Ollie's face.

Unfazed, Ollie picked up the fry from the unwiped table and dabbed it in a splotch of dried up ketchup before sticking it into his mouth.

"Never? – What, are you going to work there for the rest of your life? And what about when you're dead? I'm pretty sure I'll be able to come in then – "

Nestor slapped his palms together loudly. "Clap those erasers really good, tomorrow."

I was unable to suppress a smile in realizing how ridiculous the three of us looked dressed in similar black corduroy pants with black sweatshirts underneath black windbreakers.

"So, we got double-deckers with special sauce, a basket of onion rings and root beers. And we'll also get a megaphone to go… and my dad's paying for everything," Kelby told me.

I watched as Nestor jogged up to the sliding screen pickup window to grab something that he placed inside his apron before disappearing around the corner. I wanted to ask him about any calendars that might be visible inside, so I got up from the table to follow him.

"Don't let Ollie dump salt over everything," I told Kelby.

I hurried to the back of the building, but didn't see Nestor anywhere. Thinking it might be a good idea to relieve myself before drinking all that root beer, I opened the door to the men's room. Inside, Nestor glanced up at me with a sigh of relief while hunched over the toilet. With the seat lifted, he vigorously rubbed a hotdog bun all around the grimy, urine-speckled rim.

"Ollie?" I asked.

"It's for this guy out there that used to hock loogies at me and punched me in the face one time for wearing the wrong color socks. Plus, the toilet bowl could really use a good scouring don't you think? Don't say anything and I'll give you a free Stray Dog."

Nestor wasn't finished yet. From the depths of his throat he summoned a wad of phlegm and launched it onto the already filthy bread.

"One Lung Oyster Special coming right up," he announced.

Before returning to the table, I stopped at the pickup counter and asked for two large cups of shaved ice. Soon, we would have chilled cans of beer in the sturdy grocery bags.

The carhop had arrived with our tray of food when I rejoined my friends. She was a high school beauty with a light smattering of freckles on her cheeks and difficult looking textured braids of strawberry blonde hair. While smacking and popping her Wrigley's, she called us "Cute little Johnny Cashes." This was worth an extra few pennies tip.

After handing her a nickel, she pivoted gracefully, peering over her shoulder with a delighted smile. As she walked away, I could smell traces of her perfume on the waxpaper wrapper as I carefully inspected my sesame-seed bun. With flecks of relish in the yellowish special sauce, I was anticipating an even better burger experience than the one that I had for breakfast.

We listened to Herb Alpert and Otis Redding while pigging out on our towering burgers. When the novelty *Monster Mash* started playing, I heard the hard squeak of brakes and glanced up to see a rust bucket Apache pickup backing into a stall across from us. With its blemished patina, I recognized it to be Chooch's ride. Taking a final gulp of root beer, I put down the half-eaten Double-Decker and wandered over to the idling Chevy, figuring that if I thanked him for the beers again, we might be able to get more at another time.

"Hey, where's your mask, Zorro?" he asked.

"About time to hunt down a Stag," I said, mimicking the jingle on the beer commercials.

Noticing that he seemed to be confused, I winked.

"We just wanted to say thanks, Chooch."

His blotchy, pitted features looked even harsher in the glare of the flashing neon.

"I'm not Chooch. Just borrowing his truck while he's home picking mattress squirrels off his pubes from that scummy cornbilly stripper girlfriend of his. So, what's this about some Stags? Gimmie a can of that jackal piss. I know that you and your pop bubbler friends have some in those wowie-zowie bikes."

There was a loud rumbling as a "Spanish Red" Olds 442 Cutlass pulled up. With the engine revving high RPMs, the passenger rolled down the window and asked, "Chooch or Mooch?"

"You got a spare Kool in there?" Mooch asked.

The Cutlass peeled out with screeching tires and fishtailed onto the main drag.

While tasting burning rubber in my mouth, I saw Kelby frantically motioning for me to return to the table. I gave Chooch's identical twin brother a thumbs-up before heading back to my friends.

The carhop sweetie approached with a quart-sized waxpaper container of root beer (the chain's popular "megaphone") and set it down on the messy table. She then held up a shiny metal washer and dropped it amongst the empty glasses and plastic baskets.

"Whoever gave me this, we're no longer going steady," she said while making a funny sullen face.

"Nice going, Ollie," Kelby blushed.

As she walked over to sneak a drag from a customer's cigarette, I ran back over to Mooch and handed him one of the cans of Stag that Chooch had given us. I then hurried back to my friends who were already on their Schwinns. I climbed on my bike and waved goodbye to the carhop as the three of us pedaled across the raucous parking lot.

"What about your Stray Dog?" I heard Nestor shout.

With our bikes safely concealed near a drainage pipe, the three of us hunkered down behind some white birch trees a short distance from the backyard of our first subdivision target. Our pockets bulged and sagged from the weight of the kernels of field corn as we shared a can of Stag beer in nervous anticipation of what was about to come.

Although the pseudo-delinquent tradition was tolerated by most in these bedroom communities – responsible as it was for only a few shattered nerves and a scattered mess to sweep up the next day – there were those who didn't look upon the seasonal ritual as just a nuisance, but, rather, as an unlawful act of vandalism. As to these stick-in-the-mud types, at best you might get doused with water from an average Joe in a cardigan sweater who pops up from behind a bush with a garden hose. At worst it could be an unhinged Korean War vet charging from his front door while brandishing a M1 rifle with a bayonet. And in between these, there's the ironworker in a dingy wife-beater holding a baseball bat because he's pissed off that he has to get up for work in a few hours. Of course, the local police officers were another major concern. Indeed, when it came to creating a disturbance by showering the neighborhood with fists full of corn, there were many unforeseen dangers. Lack of streetlights and dark clothing made things a little easier, but you still had to be really on your game to not get caught.

After a final chug of liquid courage, we silently crept into the dark yard. There was only the chirping of crickets, and someone's grumbling stomach. "Are we having fun yet?" Kelby whispered – the signal to begin the sonic onslaught.

The clatter from the first volley against the aluminum siding caused a dachshund to start yapping, but it wasn't until we rattled a picture window with multiple handfuls that a bedroom light came on. After unloading another pocketful from an even closer range, we (inadvertently) trampled over some geraniums near the driveway while bombarding the neighbor's split-level. Once again, we directed most of our corn at the larger windowpanes, but a fistful or two clinking against the weatherboards was also an effective calling card.

Hearing fierce barks and scratching noises behind the front door of the next house, we tossed a small amount at the agitated snarls and dashed across the street. There, we continued to fire at windows, siding and gutters – anything that made noise. While darting between houses, we pelted patios, awnings and tin storage sheds. On it went until too many porch lights switched on, followed by cracked-opened front doors behind which deep-throated voices threatened to call the police.

Having trotted across a vacant lot to another block in Sunrise Gardens, Ollie was about to heave a handful at the white clapboards of a small house with an impeccably manicured yard when Kelby grabbed his arm. "Not the old fogey – mossback could have a heart attack. But, let's get Mister Nasty Crabapples," he said while pointing to the house with a crabapple tree in the side yard.

"Oh, Mister Nasty Crabapples that we all got sick from eating," Ollie taunted with his lips to the waxpaper megaphone that he had been carrying even though all the root beer had been drank. "Oh, Mister Wormy Crabapples – "

The lights from an approaching car appeared while slowly rounding a corner.

"Those look like police headlights," Ollie uttered; his voice amplified by the megaphone.

Even though the headlights of every car that we saw looked like 'distinctive' police car headlights to Ollie, we couldn't take any chances, and quickly took cover behind some nearby hedges. Moments later, a pastel blue Volkswagen bug putted by, possibly driven by an angry neighbor looking for those responsible for causing such a commotion.

Ollie had a novel (if not crazy) idea. Since we needed to reload our pockets, and seeing how the closest filled burlap sack had been placed inside a drainage pipe near his backyard, he suggested that we corn his own house. At first we thought that he was joking. But, seeing the thrilled look on his dorky face, we could tell that he was dead serious. Not having considered what was obvious to us, we told him that we didn't want any part of his foolish impulse, but that if he insisted on going through with it, we would wait for him from a safe distance. Maybe afterwards we could corn a half-built house, I kidded.

With that settled there was still the business of Mister Nasty Crabapples. A couple of years ago we had gotten bad stomachaches after stealing dozens of the tart bastards. So, it was now payback time. With all of the remaining corn that we had, we launched a full-scale attack. For nearly a minute the heavens opened wide and rained pitchforks and barn shovels. We even corned the dog house (and looked for a tree fort). The only thing that could have made things better, was if the owner had been home at the time.

Seeing the headlights of the Volkswagen again (my call), we headed to the next drainage pipe.

After re-filling our pockets to the brim and grabbing the remaining cans of Stag, we made the short walk to Ollie's parents' modern two-story house. Kelby and I positioned ourselves in a trench as Ollie slowly approached the darkened back patio in the crunch of fallen leaves. Just when we thought that he was going to chicken out and turn back, he began hurling handful after handful of corn at the large patio glass door.

When a hand pulled back the blinds after the light came on, Ollie stepped back with his arm cocked and ready to fire. When the heavy sliding door squeaked open, he made a final half-hearted toss before beating a quick retreat.

"Ollie, I see you, honey," his mother said with a smooth, untroubled voice. "Careful of my geraniums."

She stepped out onto the shadowy, corn-besprinkled patio with a paisley print silk caftan dress covering her trim form. Attractive facial features with a skillful application of makeup and a flicked up blonde bouffant made her look more like a glamorous magazine fashion model than a mom... or, at least, like the other kids' mothers.

While holding a glass of wine, she took a tentative step in her sandals, glancing down at the scattered corn kernels. "You're going to sweep up every piece — even if it takes an entire Saturday afternoon," she said with her not too convincing voice slightly raised. "Do you and your friends want to take a break? Come in for some spiced pumpkin raisin toast and orange Kool-Aid?" she asked as the crisp breeze rippled the shimmery caftan.

Without stopping to respond, Ollie kept on running until he jumped into the trench, crushing the waxpaper megaphone in the process.

"If I gotta clean up all that, she can look for her own ticks in the shower," Ollie said with his face flushed by anger.

"She just went back inside," Kelby said. "What's this about ticks in the shower?"

"When we got back from the Lake of the Ozarks she had me look for ticks in places that she couldn't see while taking a shower. I was hoping to burn the little sucker off her butt with a cigarette, but she said to use nail polish instead," Ollie said as he attempted to straighten the crumpled megaphone.

"You're both wearing bathing suits, though — right?" Kelby asked, no doubt conjuring up images of tiny dark critters being extracted from the hard to see naked contours of Ollie's pretty mother while taking a shower.

I could tell that Kelby wanted to further pursue this tick 'search and destroy' mission, but I thought the whole thing sounded weird and creepy (and probably never even happened). Instead of little parasitic bloodsuckers, we needed to get back to the task at hand, I thought while raising a fist full of corn. We were unruly hoodlum types dressed in black and causing the kind of ruckus that could land us in juvie hall. I wanted to leave the stinking ditch before Ollie's 'television' mom strolled up carrying a girl's tea party tray of refreshments. Was this kind hospitality on her part some kind of bonus Addison's Day effect, or were all of the Spitzers cuckoo clocks?

"Who cares about ticks and nail polish… remover, Ollie," I blurted out. "We've barely peeled the butternut." (As old lady Rutledge would say about anything she was teaching before giving us our lengthy homework assignment.) "Henrietta Rutledge's house is next. We might be rude and crude, but we are not uninformed about your address in Meadowbrook," I raised my voice to rally the troops.

After finishing our last can of "gusto" (most of which Ollie accused Kelby of secretively pouring out), we moved stealthily through the Meadowbrook subdivision on our way to Mrs. Rutledge's house. Once there, we planned to put forth our best effort, hoping that this would make up for our "abysmal" class grades (Kelby excluded).

While sneaking between houses, we were startled by a loud report that sounded like it could have been a gunshot echoing off aluminum siding. We paused and waited, but didn't hear anything else. "Probably just a car backfire," Kelby whispered. Not entirely satisfied with his conclusion, we continued across the lawn with a telling uneasiness.

Rounding the corner, we were about to pitch a handful of corn at the darkened windows when I noticed something curious in the driveway. At first I thought that someone dropped his or her laundry, but moving closer I could tell that it was a person lying motionless in a dark puddle. Hesitant to go any further, I managed to take a few tentative steps until I saw that it was a boy about our same age. The kid was dressed in dark clothing similar to ours and his hand was tightly grasping a brown sack of spilled corn kernels. What's wrong with the kid's hair, I kept thinking?

When I finally realized what I was looking at, there was an electric jolt in the palm of my hands, and my legs went rubbery.

From the back of the kid's split-open head, I could see bone fragments embedded in the spilled brain matter. Frozen in disbelief, I couldn't take my eyes off the wound. Rivulets of blood had trickled down the cement where there was more splattered tissue.

"Don't go over there," I heard Kelby's shaky voice. "Let's get back to our bikes."

Feeling so dizzy that the surroundings tilted, I buckled to my knees and almost heaved.

With blood pounding in my ears, I suddenly felt an enhanced state of alertness. We needed to leave before the same thing happened to us.

Just then, I heard a metallic rattling sound. Twin headlights from an approaching bicycle further illuminated the gruesome scene. Whooshing rubber wheels squealed on the paving. Everything seemed to be happening in slow motion as I turned around to see an older kid climbing off a radiant red Schwinn "Panther." I recognized him to be a high-school football player named Schramm. Wearing grey sweatpants and a *St. Louis Cardinals* jersey, he hurried over to the dead body and keeled down in the pool of blood. Reaching for the distorted head, he picked up part of the ragged gore and started laughing.

"Nice ballistic trauma, Koenig!" he shouted while looking up at the house.

Seeing the look of abject horror on our faces, he stood up and grabbed my shoulder.

"Easy man – it's a dummy. Did you think it was real? He pulled this same shit last year. Mr. Koenig, the art teacher."

"A dum-my?" I nearly choked as he broke out laughing again.

"Yeah. The brains are mostly just soggy bread, strawberry syrup and wadded up newspaper... Oh, and cauliflower. Here, check it out," he said while handing me a piece of the greyish-pink gelatinous matter to examine for myself.

"I knew that it was just a dummy," Ollie said. "Not even very realistic –"

"You're tick-tacking, right?" the jock asked. He reached into the bulging pocket of my windbreaker and grabbed a large handful of corn. "I don't know if he's home, but –"

Rearing back, he heaved a fistful that banged loudly against the glass.

"Whoa! That's primo Hubb's Stubs, isn't it? I remember that farmer's loud stuff."

The football player pulled us together in a huddle.

"The guy's a little light in his loafers. He's got a tiny bubble-top car with only three itsy-bitsy wheels – a Trident or something or other – with a fuzzy mirror warmer, the faggot. I mean, c'mon, what's with all the flowering dogwood trees?"

He picked up his bike and climbed on.

"Just over there, the whole block's been trashed. Not just by tick-tacking and ding-dong ditchers. There are corncobs shoved into tailpipes, shoe polish on windows and mailboxes blown up by silver salutes. Even slashed tires. If I were you guys, I'd avoid that scene. Maybe go to Willow View instead."

"Cool, do you want to come with us?" Ollie asked.

"Naw, I'm gonna get me some real action from a nasty paper shaker."

As the jock pedaled off, we headed towards the block that he was referring to. I was still a bit shaken by the sight of the dummy but didn't want my friends to know it.

"It looked pretty real at first," I said, "But how'd he know what it was made of?"

"He probably took the guy's class," Kelby replied. "Jocks like Schramm take easy things... like wood shop and small engine repair. Broken lawnmowers. They don't sign up for Algebra."

"You gotta be a real brainiac to study that green muck," Ollie chimed in.

We now had a tough decision to make. If the next couple of blocks had already been corned or worse, then we could be setting ourselves up to be ambushed by vigilant homeowners. Some might have even called the cops, in which case there would be a squad car patrolling the area. Ordinarily, we would just go to a different housing tract, such as Willow View, but Rutledge's house was right in the middle of the block that Schramm had pointed to, and the old biddy was our main target. Not only was it going to be tonight's grand finale, but, at our age, it would most likely be the last house that we ever corned. Weighing the pros and cons, we agreed that, under the circumstances, our best course of action would be to head over there in order to evaluate the situation first hand.

We didn't have to walk far to see for ourselves what Schramm was talking about. With all the activity from residents checking out their property damage, we quickly sought cover behind some bushes on the street corner.

Even from there, we could tell that those responsible for the destruction had taken what was supposed to be a seasonal celebration of mischief to the extreme. Instead of toilet paper-draped trees and the soaped and egged cars one might expect, we could discern porches with bashed in carved pumpkins and driveways with leaning vehicles whose tires were deflated. The victims of this damage appeared to be really teed off. No wonder parents had to inspect for tainted Halloween booty.

Suddenly, we heard a car speeding towards us from the end of the block. If Ollie had said they were police headlights, this time he would have been right. Slowing down to a crawl, a spotlight mounted on the cruiser swiveled into action, with its sharp beam of light sweeping across a lawn and moving along the facade of a house with a bright white halo.

We took off from the shrubbery and ran between the nearest houses. Stumbling over ruts on a narrow track between chain link fences, we picked up our pace as the ground sloped downward into a patch of tall weeds. There, we waited in silence as a spotlight switched on from the street behind us, causing us to lie flat on our bellies. The powerful beam arced back and forth across the knee-high grass until Johnny Law finally rumbled away.

Ollie's next idea was even more harebrained than his last one. Since Rutledge's block had been compromised, why not target the one person in town who deserved to be "tick-tacked" the most? He was referring to the oddball with the thriving mole whisker that I had encountered in the cemetery. As the subject of rumors and wild speculation, the old geezer had been ostracized by the town folk for questionable nocturnal activities when he was an undertaker. This even included outlandish claims of him later consuming those that were disinterred so as to supplement his diet of canned beef stew. Because of this gossip and suspicion, Molewhisker had become reclusive over the years and was rarely seen outside of his brooding Victorian near the railroad overpass.

Rejecting this back-fence talk, Kelby jokingly suggested that we corn Ollie's house again. Shaking his head, Ollie said that if he had to clean up that mess, he would put toothpaste in his mother's guiltless pleasure Oreos. That or stick a Black Cat squib inside one of her Virginia Slims.

Molewhisker's house was on the wrong side of the tracks, Kelby tried to rationalize with Ollie. By the time we got there and returned to our bikes we would be breaking curfew. To this Ollie countered that the weirdo's residence was actually not on the bad side of the tracks. It was located alongside the tracks close to where they ran under the small trestlework bridge that was one of the supposed Seven Gates to Hell. He then got my friend to admit that he was feeling a sense of defeat that we were unable to wreak havoc on the fuddy-duddy's composed world. When he pointed out that Molewhisker's was a trophy house, Kelby slowly relented and said that maybe it wasn't such a crazy idea after all. Not because of any local notoriety Molewhisker had as a depraved body snatcher, but simply because his house was in uncharted corning territory.

"Danger, Will Robinson," I said with a robotic voice. Knowing that to get to Molewhisker's place we would have to venture into the seedy part of town, I still wasn't too keen on the idea. Besides, whether he was a cannibal or not, the guy was definitely an unknown.

I asked Kelby about the "Old Fogey Rule", to which he responded that Molewhisker wasn't nearly as old as those fossils in their oversized cheap threads slouched motionless as statues on public benches, or like those drab wallpaper-in-motion haggard fusspots whose bedraggled grandchildren galloped on mottled hobby-horses. We might rattle his nerves, but we weren't going to stop his heart. "Let's get our treads over there," he said, looking for my nod of approval.

Somewhat reluctantly, I agreed to give it a shot, although with the stipulation that once we were near the railroad tracks we wouldn't mess with any other residences. I was vehement about this.

Walking as fast as we could, and even running part of the way, we got to the tracks in less than a half hour. The vibe there was different. It was an unsightly labyrinth that lacked subdivision symmetry. The low-income homeowners in their white boxes with pre-fab elements argued loudly and were more prone to violence. Wounds from accidental gunfire weren't that unusual in the nearby trailer park.

Many of the kids were bullies with broken teeth that hung out on the cluttered porches of dingy Queen Ann cottages and on the tin roofs of outbuildings that could use a fresh coat of paint. Even the whiffs from kitchen skillets smelled oddly unpleasant. Yes, it was a different vibe... and yet, however strange that it might seem, it was in these 'wrong side of the tracks' environs that I was able to most strongly perceive the faint impressions of some sort of... undershine.

Soon, we were walking down a lonely, semi-rural road with a real lack of streetlights. The stretch of gravel was called "ShadowCrest" and it offered access to the single-lane railroad overpass used mostly these days by drivers who were too impatient to wait at the crossing guard for passing freight trains. With no corrosive giant SweeTart to cram into his mouth, Ollie asked me for one of my mom's cocoa deathbricks. I handed him my last no-bake cookie, even though I didn't think that he wanted the thing for its gooey goodness. I was actually more concerned with the neighbors – hoping that my Addison's Day protective shield was still working. None of us were even sure what time it was, and Kelby once again mumbled to me how irritated he was that Ollie forgot to wear his Timex. "The fucktard," I concurred.

After passing a few old houses with television sets flickering behind drawn shades, we arrived at Molewhisker's residence. The foreboding Victorian with a steeply pitched slate roof and oversized windows on its gabled dormer was partly concealed from the road behind poplars and sycamores. The house was completely dark inside save for a dim glow that emanated from a corbel-supported oriel. Looking up at it, I couldn't help but wonder what was going on behind its curtained lead glass?

Parked in the gravel driveway in front of the adjacent garage, a vehicle with funny green cloisonné hubcaps was covered with a lichened canvas tarp. Ollie quietly lifted the metal lid of one of the garbage cans there. In doing so, a foul stench accosted our nostrils. Inside were dozens upon dozens of empty cans of beef stew – not the standard bearer, Dinte-Moore, of town rumors, but some generic 'Great Value' version. Ollie picked up one with a look of "I told you so", and dumped out some of the putrid broth. With shudders of disgust, Kelby and I watched as he licked some off his fingers.

After skulking around the garage, we crept over to the front of the house. The unattended lawn was covered with varicolored leaves – those that hadn't yet drifted onto the wraparound porch whose once-decorative touches were now in shambles. Together, we stepped onto the creaking planks of the veranda. Bathed in the pale brilliance of the moon, the peeling paint of the neglected support flaked off at the slightest touch.

It was now or never.

We each grabbed a handful of corn from our pockets. With our arms cocked and ready to pepper the dark windows, we heard the roar of a car approaching from the direction of the bridge. Turning to see if it was the police, we quickly hid behind the Doric columns. Just then, the female driver of a "Gold Mist" Buick Electra jammed on the brakes directly in front of the house. Windows squeaked down to reveal three high-school-aged girls who were all shouting incoherently.

With confused looks on our faces, we hurried over to see if they needed help.

The brunette driver was wearing a black Playboy Bunny ears headband along with the iconic tuxedo collar bowtie and a strapless black satin corset. The other two were blonde cuties dressed in high-school letter sweaters and tight bellbottom jeans. They all reeked of alcohol.

After they managed to calm down a bit, they lit cigarettes and pointed towards the bridge. From what I could gather, they had been tooling around in daddy's car, drinking Boone's Farm "Strawberry Hill" while trying to find the Seven Gates to Hell just for Halloween kicks.

When they stopped to relieve themselves under the popular teen hangout, they encountered what they took to be some kind of bizarre creature wading in a pool of brackish water. Whatever the thing was that frightened them, it carried a red shaded lantern and a pitchfork on which a frog was impaled. As they continued to talk about it, they once again became wildly agitated. Some of the words that I heard to describe its facial details were "wrinkled, distorted features hard to make out" and a "fuzzy, blurry domed head without a neck." The body was "darkly sheeny, almost like a rain slicker." Though lacking horns and hoofs, they believed that it was a demon that had emerged from some fiery portal beneath the sooty, graffiti-scarred bridge.

When their hysterics started again, the house porch light came on, drawing a flurry of moths. The front door opened slightly and I could make out a figure peering from behind the crack. Wrapped in a tatty bathrobe, the gaunt oddity with the long mole whisker stepped haltingly out onto the sagging porch. Without the fedora, his scanty ashen hair was combed back from the temples of his scowling mien.

As 'bunny ears' lowered the bottle of bum wine and shouted for us to get in her car, Kelby and Ollie flung their loaded handfuls at the house. With the corn's pebble-like consistency clinking against glass, Molewhisker glanced down at the scattered kernels with an expression of amused contempt. Ollie chucked the no-bake cookie, hitting the old coot square in the forehead, causing him to stumble backwards in his wool slippers.

My friends dove headlong into the back of the car as all three of the high school babes urged me to join them. With my gaze fixed on the Playboy costume worn by the girl they called "Trixie", a terrifying thought suddenly flashed into my brain. This was something that Kelby had told me during a recent sleepover, claiming that he had read it in the newspaper.

The story involved a guy who was hanging out at a Playboy club. While drinking cocktails and getting an eyeful of a couple of the gorgeous bunny waitresses, the lovely cottontails invited him to the apartment that they shared. Once there, after again gawking at their desirable attributes, the teasing bunnies drugged the guy by slipping pills into his drink. When he later woke up, he found himself naked as a jaybird while tied with rope to a chair. Much to his horror, one of the bunnies produced a pair of pliers from a toolbox. While making pleasurable moaning sounds, she used these to squeeze one of his testicles until it burst into a bloody, fleshy pulp. The other bunny then proceeded to do the same with his other hairy ball.

At the time of his telling me this, I found the story to be very disturbing. Even afterwards, I couldn't shake the nightmarish imagery from my mind. So upsetting was the mental picture, at that very instant, rather than climb into the Buick with the others, I decided to throw my corn at the house and escape through the backyard.

As the Electra peeled away, I quickly rounded the corner of the dilapidated Victorian, dodging assorted debris in Molewhisker's terribly overgrown lawn. I continued to run as fast as I could, hopping over tall grass matted with silken webs until I bounced off a barbed wire fence, cutting my lip on a rusty sharp point. Not sure where to go, I slipped through an opening in the fence and crouched down in a soybean field where dozens of small white spiders crawling in sheets of moonlit threads awaited nocturnal prey. (No, the irony was not lost on me.)

"Pretending to be dead, are you?" a gruff voice that I recognized to be Molewhisker's uttered in the darkness.

A flashlight clicked on with its weak beam directed right into my eyes.

"Playing possum like the other possums out here... or maybe you're a bean weasel up to no good. Was it you – dookie doo – who threw the rock at my face?" the rawboned figure standing over me in the threadbare bathrobe asked.

"It wasn't a rock. It was a no-bake cookie that my mom knows how to make," I said while looking up at the impassive mask watching me squirm.

Molewhisker kneeled down and directed the flashlight beam to where the cocoa deathbrick left an impression on the vertical furrows on his forehead.

"No bake? What does she use for Betty Crocker – a Boy Scout Handbook? Here I am in the middle of a no-peek casserole when – thank'ya much for the cornpocalypse. Yep, it's that time again hereabouts... though I'd much prefer to Glidden the porch with graveyard nettles."

"I'll clean all the corn up – if it's already past midnight," I offered.

The flickering bulb of the silver Rayovac went dark until he repeatedly banged on it in order to bring it back to some semblance of life. He then spewed a mouthful of tobacco juice so close to the side of my face that I got a whiff of its sickly molasses smell.

"Excuse my expectoration. A distasteful pattern, I'm sure most would say."

"Mister, I need to get home before curfew," I mumbled.

"You oughta gotten in with that cootersnatch – drunk from that shit boontrickle," he chortled while brushing back his thinning, brilliantined hair.

He wagged his index finger.

"*Schnickelfritz*... You're getting too big for your britches... *Schnickelfritz*..."

He pointed the flashlight beam at his nearly impassable backyard, contemplating the tall weeds with a strangely abstracted gaze.

"Grass sure is getting tall... Some innate desire, I suppose... to live as long as possible," he said with his scratchy twang.

He shined the light on my face again.

"That's a whole lot of wrong doing that you've been up to in less than twelve hours time, hot shot. Well, I've got my own tricks you'll learn soon enough. Now, go home, bean weasel, before they pluck you off the street.... And tomorrow, dontcha' pretend you got the holler tail..."

After this stern admonishment (for reasons unknown to me), Molewhisker hobbled towards his house.

Still scrunched down amid the soybean bushes, I got an unpleasant whiff of something that smelled faintly like burning cardboard. Along with the strange odor came this sudden feeling of uneasiness. It wasn't a sense of overwhelming dread, or anything like that, but more like an unshakable feeling of sorrow from some kind of tragic event that occurred there in the past.

Out of the corner of my eyes, I caught a glimpse of something swishing in the tall grass with a bristled dark tail curved like a question mark. Whatever this furry thing was, it hurried towards the backyard. After another breeze that carried a trace of the peculiar burnt odor (this time with a hint of moldy canned pumpkin pie filling), I rose to my feet. It was now way past my bedtime and I still needed to get back to my bike and pedal home without being nabbed by the police. I would then have to sneak into my room and climb into bed without being detected. Should I get caught, who knew the severity of my punishment? After all, it was no longer Addison's Day.

CHAPTER II
WILL O' THE WISP

Before my mother had a chance to tap on my bedroom door and say, "Wake up, sleepy head," I had gotten dressed for school. Even though I was still tired, I forced myself to be "bright-eyed and bushy-tailed", not wanting to leave any doubts about what time I sneaked in last night. After my parents' alarm buzzed, I hid my beer-soggy windbreaker and doctored the barbed wire cut on my lower lip with a rigorous scrubbing of "Lava" soap. If Lava helped fight against polio with the "Power of Pumice", it should work wonders against any potential tetanus.

With my early start in getting ready for school, I made the mistake of closing my eyes while sitting on the bed and must have dozed off again. Feeling even drowsier now, I stepped into the empty kitchen where, even though it wasn't Sunday, the air hung heavy with the smell of griddled pancakes. Hearing the sound of a newspaper rustling in the family room, I peeked around the corner, startled for a second by an imposing figure in a double-breasted frock coat that was sipping orange juice at the breakfast table. Unfortunately, even with the tall stovepipe hat, this wasn't a ghostly visitation by Abraham Lincoln.

Checking out my father's school Halloween costume, I saw that he had done a pretty good job of using makeup for a swarthy complexion. The clothes were also realistic, right down to the brass buttons. Dad was a stickler for detail – except when it came to 'Abe's' polished burgundy loafers.

"Jeez, I don't know about those loafers," I remarked.

With a smug grin, he raised one of them so that I could see the shiny penny stuck in it.

"Okay, yeah, I get it now – Penny loafers – because Lincoln's face is on one."

"His profile," the stickler made sure to correct me.

Putting his shoe back down on the carpet, he glared at the Band-Aid on my lip.

"Who would have ever guessed that hanging threads was so hazardous? And why are there cockleburs on your socks?"

"Because of these high-waters. I told you that high-water pants aren't happening."

I noticed that the pancakes on my plate were covered with a thick scarlet liquid. I also saw that candied corn had been spread all over the tablecloth, and hoped that there wasn't some hidden meaning behind these toothsome morsels.

"Whose stomach is growling for bloody pancakes?" my mother asked cheerfully as she entered the room wearing a quilted bathrobe. "It's really strawberry syrup… or is it?" She picked up my fork and stuck it in the stack of flapjacks. "My revenge has just begun! I spread it over centuries and time is on my side," she uttered, doing a terrible Count Dracula impersonation.

Seeing the Band-Aid, her smile went upside down.

"Oh, Addison – what happened?"

"It's nothing," I assured her while sitting down and poking my fork at the mushy pancakes.

My father tapped his finger on the newspaper.

"It says here that President Johnson has ordered a complete cessation of all air, navy and artillery bombardment of North Vietnam. Heck, you might not get drafted after all, and have to go fight those gorillas in the steamy jungle," he teased me for once being confused by the term 'guerrilla'.

"I know that they're not gorillas," I told him.

"Yeah, since when?"

"Since a while," I replied.

"Now that you are too old to trick-or-treat, it would be in someone's best interest to crack open the books right after dinner. It's time to buckle down, mister." He stood up from the table and adjusted the tall stovepipe hat before quoting part of one of Lincoln's speeches on education:

"A capacity, and taste, for reading, gives access to whatever has already been discovered by others. It is also the key, or one of the keys, to the already solved problems. And not only so. It gives a relish, and facility, for successfully pursuing the yet unsolved ones."

After a self-congratulatory smile, he stroked the fake beard and patted me on the back.

"Okay, put some of those pancakes in your gullet so that you can focus all your attention in school today..."

"I relish this relish," I told Kelby and Ollie over Marvin Gaye's "Ain't Nothing but the Real Thing" while carefully examining the special dressing on the seeded bun of my double-decker. "And this root beer is the best – isn't it?" King Coney was a mad house on this Halloween night as the crew of dainty carhops rushed to deliver trays of food to the boisterous patrons.

"Like piggies at a trough – back again… Oh, you poor thing! You want some Mercurochrome for that boo-boo?" the strawberry blonde server stopped at our table for a second before heading towards the annoying honking of an impatient customer.

Chooch's eyesore Chevy pulled into the parking stall right across from where we were seated at one of the brightly lit picnic tables. Seeing him salute me with a raised can of Stag through the neon-splashed windshield, I decided to go see what kind of trouble he was going to be up to tonight.

"What's crackin'?" I asked.

"Gutt waddin. The squad's a bit spazzed out tonight – too many tubbies to feed," he chuckled while deftly fishing out a Kool non-filter with his useable fingers.

"I gave your brother a brew last night."

"Mooch? I'll bet he had some kind things to say about Cherrie."

Taking a drag off the cigarette, he puffed out loops of smoke.

"Whoa! Circle the wagons", Chooch shouted out the window before ululating a savage war cry with his hand over his mouth.

Glancing to my left, I realized that this slight was directed at Nestor, a brown skinned, dark haired Bengali Indian who was wearing his convenience store shirt. Before I could ask him about this apparent mistake, he leaned into Chooch's driver side window, appearing to be slightly miffed by his stereotypical whooping – mainly because he wasn't a Native American Indian.

"I do not live in a tepee, bokachoda," Nestor said with a thick Bengali accent. "I have told you before that I am from West Bengal India."

"Oh, so that's just a mask – the whole red face thing?"

"Even John fucking Wayne really knew that settlers on the westward trail only circled the wagons so their cattle would be corralled at night," Nestor explained. "Maybe one of these was even a relation to the Hole-y cow, itself."

Judging by his downcast expression, whatever this "Hole-y cow" thing meant, it totally bummed out Chooch.

I tried to lighten the mood. "So, you're wearing your other work shirt."

"Yes, yes, and earlier today I wore my King Coney outfit to Short Stop. Ha ha ha! It is Hallofuckinweenie, man," he laughed.

My attention was diverted from Nestor's history lesson to the doltish machinist by the sight of a showy black hearse hot rod (1951 Packard Henney) cruising through the drive-in's lively parking lot. It was the same car that I saw at the cemetery yesterday, though up close I could see all its customized details. The funeral coach's matte black body had been given the full treatment – both chopped and lowered, with ornate lantern-shaped exterior lighting and its roof engirded with a strand of rusty barbed wire. The frame was tastefully pinstriped, and the side service doors were painted in a wildly cursive spectral green script that read: WILL O' THE WISP.

Moving slowly on whitewall tires, the green cloisonné hubcap medallions looked just like those on the vehicle that was partially covered by a tarp in Molewhisker's gravel driveway. Despite the souped-up motor behind fancy metalwork grille inserts, the car made no sound at all – gliding past spirited diners like a chrome-festooned phantasm.

I was dumbfounded that no one else seemed to be aware of the rolling apparition. The sheer peculiarity of it must have caught the attention of at least one of the customers. Even my friends appeared to be unaffected by its spooky nature while engaged in a contest of tossing French fries into an empty soda cup. With my eyes riveted on the bizarre street machine, while hesitantly taking a few steps closer, I could hear the ongoing sparring between Chooch and Nestor.

"How about a Squaw Dog? Can you bring me a Squaw Dog while you're in that injun costume?" Chooch further provoked Nestor.

"Yes, yes – Squaw Dog comes plain, man. But I can put special sauce on if you want? Thick and creamy – made by King Coney staff."

Through the open narrow window, I could see a furry green hand clutching a tall chrome stick shift whose knob was a stylized human skull. Seated behind the wheel was a vividly freakish creature that had an oversized greenish face with huge, bulging bloodshot eyes. The multihued grotesque mask turned towards me. From its exaggerated grimace, a croaky voice uttered, *"Schnickelfritz!"* This was followed by paroxysms of malicious laughter.

Just as the hot rod had seemingly appeared from out of nowhere, it suddenly vanished, leaving behind only the fading energetic imprint of its luminous taillights. When these winked out, I happened to glance up at the eatery's blinking neon marquee. The letters read:

CORPSE KING

This lasted only for a second before the letters blurred and reverted back to the chain's actual name:

KING CONEY

I turned towards Chooch and Nestor. "Where did that corpse car go?"

"It went othering," Chooch said flatly while ashing his Kool.

"Wake up and die right!" Mrs. Rutledge shouted while rapping my knuckles with a yardstick. My eyes sprang open as I jolted in my seat. Disoriented for a second, I glanced about a bright classroom that smelled like chalk dust and orange peel. I had fallen asleep at my desk and was having a weird dream about the King Coney drive-in before the sting of the ruler abruptly awakened me. I quickly adjusted my posture, not wanting to be struck again by the granny-heeled, Chantilly-spritzed troll for any frowned-upon slouching.

"Too bad studying isn't as contagious as the rhinovirus – especially with your deplorable grades," she scowled while tapping the yardstick against her palm. "Well, at least we know that you and your bedridden chums weren't among the miscreant hordes that invaded my block last night, causing outrage with their unceasing barbarity."

From the corner of her eye, she noticed a student chewing gum.

"Swallow that gum this instant, mister, or you will be emptying pencil-shavings in perpetuum."

She then returned her wrath back to yours truly.

"Before Addison here had the discourtesy of stealing forty winks, we were discussing the westward expansion of the American frontier by Lewis and Clark – the daring exploits of which we've barely peeled the butternut. Addison, in reading about Meriwether, what becomes quite apparent?"

Had I wanted to improve my status as a class clown, I would have said, "He was a little light in his loafers." Even though she had handed it to me on a silver platter, I wasn't in any condition to risk getting detention. Suddenly, I was feeling queasy from the undercooked pancakes expanding in my stomach. Whiffs of the

Pine-Sol mopped wooden floor didn't make matters any better. Gulping down salty bile, I was close to throwing up. It was only the humiliation of the janitor coming in and spreading minty sawdust on my vomit that kept me from doing so.

"I'll ask again. In examining Meriwether Lewis's character, what becomes most apparent?"

"That he was no coward... and it is therefore highly unlikely that he committed suicide – much less a botched suicide – because he was mentally depressed. Lewis was murdered because he was a liability. Maybe to a political rival... or to something else that wanted a certain giant discovery to be squashed-"

Her shriveled profile interrupted me with an irritating, empurpled smirk. "Let me pinch myself to make sure I am not dreaming."

After watching her make a pinching gesture to her liverish hand, I continued.

"Peeling this particular butternut might reveal certain truths that those in high places resorted to murdering a national hero to suppress. This might explain Lewis's missing journals and omissions from expedition diaries that have long vexed historians."

"Well, I must admit that someone's father is doing a sterling job. Although, where one comes up with such a wild notion is truly beyond me. Such a far-fetched theory, even for a high-school history course." Her teeth meshed tightly as she turned towards the scribbling on the blackboard.

For once the crotchety old bag was right. Even though I had no recollection of him ever doing so, I must have heard my dad say this at home so many times that it finally sank into my brain.

When it was finally time for recess, I couldn't wait to tell Kelby and Ollie about how the bridge fiend had given me a ride back to my bike. The thing that had so wigged out those girls turned out to be a really nice guy who was out frog gigging. He used a kerosene lamp to see the reflection in their bulbous eyes, and then impaled them with a three-pronged spear. What made them mistake him for some hellish creature was a fishing rubber chest wader and the mosquito mesh attached to his trekking hat. A guy who liked to sauté frog legs in garlic, butter and lemon – that was all there was to it.

Neither of them seemed too interested with this simple explanation for what caused everyone to over-react. Everything was about Trixie. Trixie said this. Trixie did that. They were almost calling dibs on her, which was quite amusing – like some popular high school girl would ever have anything to do with a couple of sixth grade dorks other than to toy with them while lazy eye wasted on sugary bottom shelf wine.

When Ollie went to take a squirt rather than have me chaffing him for running scared, Kelby asked me if I was going over to Ollie's house for dinner that night? When I said that I probably was, he told me that he hoped his mother would be dressed as "Barbarella." Who's Barbarella, I wondered?

Although I was still experiencing abdominal pain from the morning's gloppy pancakes, I made the effort to be at Ollie's house for a small Halloween party.

Since we were now too old to go trick-or-treating, Mrs. Spitzer tried her best to scare up some fun. For dinner she served "mummy sausage links" that were wrapped in flaky biscuit shrouds.

There were also glass jars of orange HI-C punch that had a fake dead fly inside one of the novelty plastic ice cubes that floated at the top.

To be polite, I bit off a portion of the sausage that contained the mummy's red pimento eyes, but that was all that I could manage with my stomach issues. I hoped that I would feel better later so that I could have a piece of her "Pumpkin Patch" Devil's Food cake, even if only some of the Brach's mellowcreme pumpkin candies that topped its swirls of chocolate frosting.

Ollie's bubbly mom appeared to be enjoying herself, sipping a glass of Chardonnay while handing out goodies to the early doorbell ringers. I didn't think that she was wearing a costume per se, though she donned the right color scheme with a bright orange shift dress and lunar white vinyl calf-length boots. Her blonde hair was cut shorter, and her long fingernails were lacquered glossy black.

When I had a chance, I asked Kelby about this "Barbarella" that he was all excited about?

"She's an astronavigatrix," he replied, having no trouble enunciating what sounded like a "Jeopardy" television show tongue twister.

"Huh?"

Kelby's eyes darted around the room.

"That's a strip teaser in outer space who goes all the way."

"Like a girly show?" I asked.

"Yeah, but the lady is in the galaxy and she does it with all the other people there."

"Why would Ollie's mom want to dress like a space floozy?"

Making sure that no one was approaching, Kelby pulled out a newspaper ad in *The Spectrum* for a newly released movie. After carefully unfolding it, I could see that Barbarella's flight suit included a see-through domed plastic brassiere and black leotards. Although I said, "Oh, cool," I was really trying to figure out if he seriously believed that Ollie's mother would be parading

66

around with breast windows at a kid's party? No, that wouldn't be embarrassing.

Kelby quickly re-folded the paper clipping and tucked it back into his pocket seconds before Ollie appeared, motioning for us to follow him. Whispering in our ears, he told us to check out how the ice cube with the fly inside that was floating in his mom's glass of wine was melting.

As soon as we entered the living room, she playfully whacked Ollie in the back of the head.

"You little snot. While I go dump this out, you guys can hand out the candy."

As she pretended to kick Ollie with her zipper-pull go-go boots, I needled Kelby by asking her if there had been any little Barbarellas yet?

"Oh, shoot," she snapped her fingers. "That would have been perfect."

It was now the peak time for trick-or-treaters as we watched the variegated droves going from house to house before approaching the flickering Jack-O-Lantern on the Spitzer's decorated porch. While dropping snack-sized Hershey bars into their opened bags, Ollie would close his eyes and make a snide remark about popular boxed costumes with cheap plastic masks:

"You're the tenth ugly witch, but the first one on roller skates."

"Spooktacular, it's only the fifth boxed Casper to float up here."

"Fangtastic, another vampire wearing P.F. Flyers."

After heckling the "craptacular" mish-mash of vampires, ghosts and witches, finally something unique showed up at the doorstep: a kid dressed up like an apple (either a "Red Delicious" or a "Jonagold") that had part of a large razor blade sticking out of its side. I had to applaud someone (most likely the boy's father) poking fun at all the unfounded reports involving twisted minds tampering with

Halloween treats. Even my own dad fell for these urban legend false claims years ago by carefully sorting through my bounty and eating half of the best stuff. Although I knew that Ollie appreciated the apple-razor motif, the jerk-ass couldn't help saying, "Alright, another apple with a razor blade hidden inside costume."

When a veiled "Jeannie" and her helmeted astronaut master left, the best costume of the night showed up. This was a junior Molewhisker who was accompanied by his mom. The little boy was wearing a scroungy bathrobe and his toes were sticking out of worn wool felt slippers. He had a child's fedora alpine hat and a really long black piece of thread glued to his chin.

Ollie's mom returned with a full glass of wine. She was dancing while singing some bubblegum pop hit when she caught sight of the mini-Molewhisker at the door.

"Look how adorable. And what are you supposed to be?" she asked.

"He's Molewhisker. Sheeze, how could you not know that?" Ollie frowned. "We just saw the real one at his house."

"Oh, honey, you and your friends should stay away from that rat-trap," the kid's mother strongly advised.

I noticed that she was holding an empty can of Dinty-Moore, which the kid must have got tired of carrying as part of the costume.

"My parents lived on ShadowCrest back in the early 1950s. When I was little, my sister and I used to watch these lights flit about in the field behind his house. Usually they were bluish shapes that hovered – at other times they drifted about. Sometimes the floating blobs appeared in what we called charming colors. When we tried to catch these, they always slipped away."

"Oh, how strange. What were they?" Ollie's mother asked.

"It was suggested that it was phosphorescent gas – from decomposing organic matter. Some thought rotting compost…"

She covered her son's ears with her hands.

"But, others called them corpse candles from the dead bodies that were said to be buried back there because the little cemetery he worked for was all filled up. Of course, the police dismissed it as moonlight reflected off of barn owls. Even stranger, though, was the bland-faced child who we would sometimes see roaming around the yard or on the porch. His indistinct features gave us the creeps. Of course, my daddy thought that we were just imagining things because Mr. Schaufler scared us... being that his job was an undertaker. Funny thing is, in German, the name means shovel. Anyway, when some of our toys went missing, we thought that the bland-faced kid took them, because we later found some of them on Maxx's property."

"Could he have been deformed or in an accident?" Ollie's mom asked.

"The ragamuffin? Um, maybe. This was a long time ago, so who knows, but it was more like he just wasn't solid in some ways. Being an artist, the best that I can describe it is like an accomplished sketch of a finished painting. Well, sorry if I freaked you out – but you kids shouldn't be messing around over there."

When she took her son's hand and walked away, Ollie was feeling more vindicated.

"I told these guys that he was a cannibal, but they didn't believe me, mom."

"Oh, Ollie, please. I think the lady was just telling you boys a scary ghost story."

I would have liked to stay longer to talk about these lights, but I was feeling weird about having to use the Spitzer's washroom again. I thought it would be better if I went home and climbed into bed where I could think about it without having to worry about becoming the target of endless ridicule from

Ollie (and the other kids in school) in the event of an embarrassing accident.

My intestinal cramps were so bad the next morning my mother took me to the doctor thinking that it might be an inflammation of my appendix. While pressing a specific area on the lower right side of my abdomen, the fellow asked me if I was experiencing a lot of pain? When I groaned that I was, he applied more pressure to the same spot and asked me to tell him if this caused a really REALLY lot of pain – because he didn't want to recommend an emergency appendectomy if one wasn't necessary. In accessing the amount of pain for the second time, I realized that it wasn't really REALLY that bad.

Eventually I was diagnosed as having Giardiasis, an infection in my digestive tract that was caused by the Giardia parasite. My first thought was the deflated pancakes. Of course, my dad was quick to blame unsanitary conditions at the King Coney drive-in. Believing that Nestor's toilet bowl seasoning was only payback for a particular customer, I still had to consider the questionable re-freeze patty at the convenience store, though I didn't dare tell the old man about that irradiated lump of grey goodness.

According to the doctor, the most likely source of my illness was contaminated water, possibly from a muddy creek, or even from a public swimming pool. After hearing this, I flashed back to the well water spigot in the middle of the cornfields. Could the purest, most refreshing water that I ever tasted really have harbored such a monstrous organism? Either way, I couldn't believe my bad luck.

I'd seen Ollie take a bite from a half-eaten Moon Pie that he pulled out of a bowling alley urinal on a dare. He could drink from a leper's spittoon bottle without any ill effects, but I get Giardia while practicing my backstroke in the sparkling water of the park's chlorinated pool.

I was told that it might take a few weeks for me to get better, and that there was nothing much as far as any treatment went other than time. Unable to eat anything for the first few days, I tried to sleep with the delirium of a fever or just gazed out the window at the depressing grey skies.

If I thought that missing school while I recuperated might be a good thing, I should have thought twice. So that I wouldn't fall behind in my studies, my dad arranged for a portable slate easel to be set up in my bedroom. A stick of chalk raced across the board with a high-pitched screech as he wrote down a list of daily lessons. It felt like scores of piranha were gnawing on the lining of my intestines, but I was still expected to keep my nose to the grindstone.

Kelby brought mimeographed class assignments to me. At the bottom of one day's math problems, Mrs. Rutledge had included a note that contained one of her favorite expressions: "You are rude, crude and uninformed." Under this she jotted: "I hope this makes you feel like you're here in class with us." As for this attempt to cheer me up, I doubted that it was her doing. It seemed more like something that Kelby would think to add as a way of letting me know that things on the 'outside' were still the same.

The days got shorter and shorter. Not that it really mattered, though, as there were rarely any breaks in the cloud cover for the sun to peek through. For both lunch and dinner, I slurped down a bowl of chicken soup made from bouillon cubes along with some dry toast. For dessert there was applesauce. Each night, I looked forward to a peppermint Lifesaver from the roll that my mom kept in her pocketbook.

After I was finished with my lessons, I would read some "Archie" comic books, attempt to build a "Revell" plastic model kit of a street rod, or sort through my collection of "Wacky Packies" punch-out trading cards.

This still left plenty of gloomy stretches to think about things that had long puzzled me. Much of this involved early childhood memories of people and events that both of my parents insisted never existed or happened. They assumed that these imaginary friends (that I interacted with on a seemingly regular basis) were just my way of flexing my mental muscles. They were the product of my expanding imagination, much like the secret pals that other children have been known to conjure up. But, unlike the figments of one's imagination that turned out to be a barn full of giraffes, most of the people that I could still recall with such vividness and clarity were actually quite ordinary. There was also coherence to the detailed accounts that I sometimes shared with others that memory distortion couldn't easily explain.

However, some of these childhood imaginings – if that's what they were – weren't at all typical, especially the series of episodes that involved a bizarre fellow who I called "Major Domo." The first time that I saw him he had emerged from a 'magic door.' This was a widening ellipse of lustrous black that had dilated from a barely visible vertical crack in the middle of the room. (Hanging oil spills and shiny tar pools I remember calling them). Standing at attention with his hands folded politely behind the back of a rectilinear mauve suit, his narrow albinistic visage, untouched with blemish, remained expressionless until the one time that the speckled topaz hues of his oddly slanted eyes stiffly winked at me.

When outside of the sheeny black openings, he often carried a peculiar looking tray with a glass of swirling greenish tints. This he delivered to a lantern-jawed figure with a slick dark combover who had been observing me with a careful eye. When Major Domo once brought him a bowl containing what looked like a miniature bedewed garden, afterwards the servant bent down in a strange way and dutifully handed me a morsel of some white chocolate delicacy. The pleasurable surges of aromatic sweetness continued long after its unfamiliar flavors penetrated my tongue.

On other occasions his disturbing golden-hazel eyes sang to me from a children's storybook. Although I can't recall what it was about, I think that it involved a sad armadillo. At the time, I was more fascinated by his pale countenance that contrasted with my own rosy healthiness. Some times he watched as I played hopscotch on a yellow-pebbled surface in a room with gorgeous cobalt-blue lighting. Oddly enough, there were two number sixes in the radiant chalk grid – an apparent error that his ever-watching master noticed. Fixing the servant with a threatening glare, he quickly erased one of the redundant squares before allowing me to continue playing.

When we were alone, Major Domo told me things that a child ought not have in their head. Some of this stuff that I later repeated stunned my parents, causing them to wonder how I might have inadvertently picked up such bizarre ideas? They much preferred that a make-believe polar bear lived in my bedroom closet.

One of the memories that frequently came to mind concerned "the star that is really two stars." I was in the backyard riding my red Murray pedal tractor. When my little piston-like legs finally got tired from all the scooting around, I stopped and gazed languidly at a bruised violet sunset. While sucking on the chalky mint flavor of a Viceroy candy cigarette, a few stars began to appear. As the sky began to fill with the sparkling points, Major Domo silently appeared in one of his expanding black voids and pointed to the constellation, *Ursa Major*. His golden slanted eyes told me to focus my gaze on a particular star in the Dipper's handle and asked me if I could see a second star there? What I was looking at was a naked eye double star, he sang. The brightest one was called Mizar, with its dimmer companion named Alcor. The ancient people used the star that is really two stars as a test, claiming that only those with sharp eyesight had the ability to perceive the separation.

For whatever reason, his pointing to that particular constellation drew a suspicious gaze from the more ordinary looking man with the greased dark hair who was grilling lamb shish kebabs on the trellised patio. When he set down the tongs and started to reprimand the fellow, the glossy black opening where Major Domo had been standing seemingly melted away against the indistinct background. That was the last time that I saw the curious egghead.

Thinking about it while lying in bed, the one thing that I couldn't figure out is why I was told that the double stars were a great riddle, and that only those with penetrating eyesight could see this? When I pointed out the stars in the asterism to Kelby and Ollie while camping out last summer, both wondered what the big deal was? It wasn't that hard to see the pair, so to use it as an eye test seemed "dumb."

Memories of occasions involving what I call "familiar strangers" were still so prevalent that I often wondered if I had been adopted? Were these grown ups that were so lifelike in my recollections my real biological parents? (Excluding Major Domo, of course.) Although I was assured numerous times that this was not the case – my parents appeared to be more exasperated than evasive – there were times when I still wasn't one hundred percent convinced, even after seeing my birth certificate.

After a few weeks of lying in bed with such concerns, physically I was now feeling much better. Although my appetite had returned to normal, I didn't want my mother to know this until after our Thanksgiving dinner. Ollie had recently told me about watching a turkey pecking the worms out of its own shit while visiting his grandparents' farm. He thought it was cool, but I couldn't stomach the thought of eating one, even though I knew the chances were low of that particular gobbler winding up on our table.

Going back to school wasn't as hard as I thought it would be. Even so, with the frigid temperatures, I hoped for a few midwestern "snow days." Pulling out the "Flexible Flyer" sled from the attic might not be worthwhile in these flat lands, but a snowball fight was always a fun winter activity – until someone like Ollie would sneak a rock inside theirs.

Being too old for toys, for Christmas I got new clothes, a lighted world globe of our aqueous gem in the cosmos, and a Sears wristwatch. In what was truly a miracle, instead of the traditional holiday bird (the filthy things!), my mom served "Taco Soup with Fritos chips." This was the best thing that she ever made – although I could tell that my dad was still hurting. When I asked her how she got the idea to make it, she told me that she found the recipe in an old *Boy Scout Handbook* that someone had donated to the library where she worked. To keep at least one tradition alive, my dad insisted we enjoy the "yuletide caprice" (a euphemism for "slap in the face") with a small crystal glass of his prized bottle of DeKuyper Crème de Menthe. Needless to say, this wasn't the most suitable accent, especially when there were grape sodas in the fridge.

Next was the birthday when I finally became a teenager. Adding to my suspicions that I might have been adopted at a very young age, my parents always celebrated the occasion at midnight (which was the time they said that I was born on January 17th). Only then would there be any blowing out the candles and cutting the cake. It was also at the Witching Hour that I was always given my presents. This year they surprised me with a solid black kitten. Because it had gotten into a lemon meringue pie and still had some of the whipped topping on its little black nose, when I was awakened by a series of meows close to twelve o'clock at night, my mom suggested that we name her "Midnight Meringue." This sounded better than dad's suggestion of "MyShadow."

After a couple more months of biting winds and snow flurries, one Saturday morning at the end of March I awakened to a dappled blaze of sunlight on my themed beige covers. For the first time in quite a while, I was optimistic about the future.

I probably should have waited with my whole positive outlook about the changing seasons thing. Spring might have been in bloom, but the one thing that wouldn't be growing any longer was my hair. My dad told me to go to "Jake's Barbershop." "Jake the Ripper", the kids called him. The shop was a two-man operation, but the chances were…

While waiting for my turn in the barbershop, I was playing around with a "Wooly Willy" game that clients could amuse themselves with until their name was called. The toy consisted of a generic human face that was printed on cardboard under a plastic bubble. The idea was to employ the provided magnetic wand to pick up tiny metal filings from a pile at the bottom that were used to add facial hair to 'Willy.' Instead of the usual mustache, beard, or eyebrows, I was making a long mole whisker. Before I was able to finish this, Jake motioned me to his chair.

"Hot lather razor shave?" he joked while fastening my cape and neck-strip. After adjusting the swivel chair, he patted me on the top of the head while puffing on a smelly cheap cigar.

"So, what would you like, sonny?"

Caught off guard by Jake giving me a choice, I glanced over at the wall chart with its 1950s cookie cutter haircut styles for boys.

"Just a little bit off... Not much on the sides or the back... And just a little off the front."

"Yeah, sure thing. So, then, just a trim – to clean it up a little. A haircut that doesn't look like you got a haircut, right?" he said while tapping off a lengthy ash from the battered stogie.

"Right," I said firmly.

Jake glanced over at the other barber and shook his head.

"These kids today – they're all a bunch of goddamn liars. His father called and said to give him a regular haircut. We're going to make his half-hippy ass look presentable for the school yearbook picture."

He held up the electric clipper and switched it on. With my gaze fixed on the dozens of combs suspended in a jar filled with a blue disinfectant solution, the "Ripper" went to work, puffing rigorously on the cigar as my shimmering locks fell to the floor.

My blue liquid reverie was broken by the sound of small bells ringing as Ollie opened the door and shouted, "How much do you charge to trim scroat fleece?" before hurrying away.

Jake shook his head woefully. "Yoosta be kids had respect for the pole."

Ten minutes later he was cleaning up the sides with a comb and pair of scissors. When he was finished, he turned the chair so that I could check out the completed result in the mirror.

"Now you don't look like a free spirit," he said.

"My mom's meeting me here and she'll pay you," I told Jake as he brushed away coils of light brown hair and clumps of grey cigar ash from the protective gown.

Feeling a bit down, I went back over to my chair to finish creating my version of Molewhisker. For whatever reason, Jake seemed interested to know what type of 'magnetic personality' I had made from the metal filings. Seeing the long mole whisker, he picked up the game to have a closer look.

"Is this supposed to be Maxx Schaufler with his long mole whisker?" he asked.

"Boy, I wanted to hack that thing off with a machete when he used to come in here back in the day... Yeah, I remember that slickback greaser with a dab of Brylcreem and that thunderbolt hearse of his – until he got caught with that corpsecicle – as some called the dead body."

"Did you ever see the lights behind his house?" I asked.

Before Jake had a chance to respond, one of his clients waiting for a trim raised his index finger. The pasty-faced fellow dressed in a cheap blue suit with the world's skinniest necktie was a charismatic local Pentecostal preacher named Roovert Purdy. Although there were only five people in the shop, he might as well have been standing at the pulpit in a Holy Roller revival tent.

"I saw the lights once but was not perplexed by them. Those who speak of barn owls and marsh gas – well, that's a bunch of hooey. The lights are undeniably the foolish fire of false treasure buried in the Devil's final stronghold."

He stood up with his Bible and began pacing about the unswept tile floor.

"I was taking some of the church's young-ums on a hayride at the time. Not yet filled with the Holy Spirit, they desired some ice cream from that new place with the high-falutin cones of rotating flavors. When I saw the foolish fire, I heard the boss man say, tackle temptation. Good old fashion Sealtest vanilla it shall be. We don't even need Neapolitan – let alone Burgundy Cheese Fudge Triple Ripple Dipple. Such amusements are one of Satan's new favorite weapons. Have you seen those wanton young girls in culottes – with their lust-of-eye legs in plain sight and their crowning glory sheared to short bobs – shamelessly moaning while licking a big bulbous licorice-black cone?"

He pulled out a handkerchief and wiped the perspiration from his forehead.

"Here's the straight dope, son. We're in a battle against the Devil. A resplendent spark like you shouldn't just sit there twiddling your thumbs. Put on the full armor of God and throw a tomato at that schmuck."

He clapped his hands, slowly at first but quickly picked up speed, hoping to whip up some Pentecostal church fervor.

"Mock. Rebuke. Fight. Mortally insult Mr. Devil with a strange tongue. You're the winklepicker to a cockroach in a corner. Get ready! Get ready to KO him! Get ready!"

"Don't go bouncing off the light fixtures, Roovert," Jake uttered while ashing the low-budget cigar, once again finding its cherry. "That's enough preaching for a Saturday. This is a barbershop. There aren't any snakes or tongues… just scissors and combs."

"I can't get no help?" Roovert looked around the nearly empty shop with his Bible held high. "You're right, Jake. I'm just a drenched in sweat, devil stomping, gibberish babbling, clogged bathroom shower drain anointed and appointed fire-baptized apostolic rebel. But just as you hope to find the cherry on that Dutch Masters – and you're battering my palette in doing so," he laughed – "I am looking for the fierce glow of the Holy Spirit. Now, can I get an Amen!"

"This pleasing aroma?" Jake pointed to the stogie while looking around for support.

Though I had only been to Sunday School a few times, I had never seen anyone quite like this character. All Mrs. Hazelbaker did was show us how to make craft projects. There were Popsicle stick "Jesus Crucifixes", Jesus as a "Fisher of Men" with Pepperidge Farm Cheddar Goldfish snacks glued to a paper plate that was colored with a blue Crayola and a toilet paper cardboard roll "Three Wise Men" template cut-out. Had this guy been the teacher, I might have wanted to go back a few more times.

The door's bells jangled again as a man wearing a black leather jacket and holding a motorcycle helmet entered. He looked to be in his mid-thirties, with attractive masculine features covered for the moment with heavy stubble. His combed back blonde hair made him look like one of those surfers that I'd seen in movies, but the penetrating gaze behind his horn-rimmed glasses made him appear more like a scholar. Add to this the biker helmet and I wasn't sure what to make of this stranger.

"Excuse me, what time does the library open?" he asked.

"My mom works there and will be here any minute," I said.

Just then she rushed in wearing her librarian turtleneck dress and Mary Jane straps. Looking a bit flustered about being late, she quickly pulled out some money from her pocketbook.

"Only a buck and a quarter and no more flower child," Jake mussed my hair again. "Cheer up, boy. It's not like I gave you a buzz flat enough for your pal to land a paper airplane on."

As Roovert headed to the barber chair, he looked back at me and once again raised his Bible.

"Remember, son, until God opens the next door, praise him from the hallway."

"Or in the storm cellar – this time of year in these parts," the stranger joked.

"Mom, this guy wants to use the library," I said.

"Follow us," she blushed.

As the three of us walked next door to the public library, the stranger commented on the bias towards red bricks on the main street, and how similar the ruddy building facades were to those in St. Louis. My mother then informed him that the predominately brick buildings in St. Louis were due to a massive fire in 1849 that burned down many wood structures, and because of the availability of the bricks from nearby clay deposits.

As my mom opened up the library, the stranger glanced around at the downtown exterior appearance and pointed out that, unlike the other red brick-laden buildings, the mortar that was used for the library bricks had an odd red glint, and that this 'invisible' effect was most likely achieved by mixing red brick dust in with the mortar. My mother and I looked around, and realized that the stranger was correct in his observation, although as to why this was done, he didn't offer an answer. What he did tell us was that he was doing research on a mystery surrounding the exploits of Lewis and Clark, and that there might be something in the town's library that could prove to be useful to his investigation.

Once inside, after turning on the lights, my mother wasted little time in providing library services by searching the card catalog for titles that dealt with the famous explorers.

"Brief Account of the Lewis and Clark Expedition from St. Louis... Tales of the Frontier... The Exploration of America... Nothing that you probably haven't already read, I'm afraid. There are some geographical maps if that helps? We're a little town with only one stop and go light. You've heard the jokes about a cultural latrine."

"Actually, I'm more interested in any microfiche from the town newspaper. Prohibition gangsters and underground railroads."

My mom closed the drawer with the card file.

"I can provide those services, although I'm not really sure what that has to do with Lewis and Clark?"

The stranger set his motorcycle helmet down on the desk.

"The project that I'm doing legwork on is for an Epigraphic Society. They are interested in certain things that Meriwether touched upon after encountering a strange tribe of light-skinned, blue-eyed natives. Recently, they came into possession of some of Meriwether's lost field notes – possibly even an authentic map to something that might explain what he was really doing during his mysterious absence for an extended period of time – actually, for nearly a year when he was thought to be recovering from a certain malady. Without going into detail, this newly-discovered map places him south of St. Louis, right smack dab in the middle of your little cultural latrine."

"White, blue-eyed Indians... Your friends – they're Pre-Diluvian theorists, I'm guessing."

"They're not your average pot hunters," the stranger replied.

"Well, we've scads of those here," my mom said.

"Pot hunters?" the stranger asked.

"Yes, those... as well as offbeat history enthusiasts looking to shake things up with the whole Columbus wasn't the first bit."

She pointed to me and smiled.

"The kind of thing that really gets your father's dander up."

"Bush-league – he would say," I added.

Seeing the stranger's puzzled look, my mom tried to clarify things.

"He's a history teacher at the high school. The myopic opposition."

"I'm aware that there are two camps with divergent opinions. You've the isolationist viewpoint and that of the diffusionists. You could call us radical diffusionists, but before you make any snap judgments, unlike some other heretics – those at odds with the prevailing version of things – our methodology is sound. Without sufficient proof… some physical provenance that will measure up to the vanadium steel yardstick of mainstream academia, I assure you that we won't be looking to make any changes to your husband's text books."

"I'm sure he'll sleep better knowing that," my mom said with a faint smile.

"Something tells me that this discovery by Meriwether was not merely a threat to the sovereignty of the country, but will have a profound impact on consensus reality. What exactly it was that drove him to the brink of madness – if, indeed, he did go off the deep end – is what I'm trying to unriddle. I just need to keep digging to see what might be found behind the conventional scenery. And, I like to keep my claws sharp. Oh, yeah, one other thing for the underdogs: Preserved in the folklore of this tribe that Lewis had encountered is the story of the big canoe of their semi-divine ancestors – those Sea Kings who they referred to as the sun-filled ones. Of course, myths and legends aren't exactly history, are they?"

My mother greeted a couple of elderly locals who came in regularly to read magazines, and then turned her attention back to the stranger.

"Well, it all sounds very imaginative. Advanced civilizations without a developmental phase and the equally sensationalistic catastrophic decline of such elevated civilizations. Has all the makings for a paperback best seller, especially if traces of these antediluvian patriarchs were to turn up among the Midwest cornfields."

"In Little Egypt," the stranger added. "We'll noodle it out," he winked.

My mother turned on the microfiche reader.

"Where should we start: Prohibition-era speakeasies? The runaway slave network? Or, artifacts of sunken Atlantis? I believe there was a liberty station in Cairo... Illinois..."

"Mom, can I please have fifteen cents to get some packs of Wackies at the bakery? And what about lunch? I could get a Longhorn Torpedo from the filling station if you want."

"Talk about an advanced culture," my mom said while smiling at the stranger. "A gas station hoagie."

"Infrared toasters – Ah, the catastrophic decline," the stranger joked back.

"Only if you empty the trash afterwards," my mom said while opening her change purse.

At the bakery on the other side of the barbershop, I bought three packs of Topp's Wacky Packies die-cut cards (from a 1967 box) and peeled open the wrappers to see if any contained the one card out of the 44-card series that I needed to complete the set.

No such luck, I quickly realized, frustrated at getting three of the same "Jolly Mean Giant" cards in the same pack. I now had nearly a dozen of these, but still no elusive "Gadzooka Gum" Wacky. Both Kelby and Ollie had doubles of this card, but neither would trade one to me.

When I returned to the library to do my chores, I saw that the stranger was engrossed with something that he was reading on microfiche.

"Any good ones of the silly things?" my mother asked me while picking at a split end.

"No, I got gypped with three more Jolly Mean Giants," I said while showing her the parody of the popular consumer product whose green giant mascot was shown stomping on terrified little peas, with a spoof label that read: "He Loves to Split Peas."

"That's pea-brained, alright," she shook her head. "Hey, but that reminds me of something that I've been meaning to talk to you about for a while."

I felt a lump in my throat in thinking that she had recently recalled my using the F-word back on Addison's Day. Was I finally going to be punished, I wondered?

"Darn it... What the heck was it? Oh, drat, it will come to me eventually."

Hoping to derail her train of thought, I showed her the funny "Kook-Aid" Wacky.

"Kook-Aid. Sounds like what I've been doing today," she said while gesturing to the stranger.

"Did you ever find out anything about those weird lights I asked you about?" I reminded her.

"Yes, I did," she replied.

"The faint scintillations of light is called a will o'the wisp. It's like a candle-flame that has been observed flickering over marshlands. Some believe that the glow comes from spirits of the dead who were not allowed to enter heaven or hell, but are doomed to wander the earth for eternity because of some bad deed they did while alive. The funny thing is that when approached, the light moves away, but if a person turns away from it, the light follows them —"

"Like Midnight Meringue does sometimes," I said.

"Others think that the lights mark the exact location of a buried treasure, but this might just be a ploy to lure foolish people astray. So, do you understand? It's a warning to be careful of who you follow... and not to be foolish and led astray. This would be good subject matter if we were toasting marshmallows around a campfire, wouldn't it?"

"That's a really good idea you have. Why don't we make some tonight."

"Well, if the Weber will suffice as a campfire, maybe we can. But, don't get all worked up about the lights. Modern science thinks they're just rising gases from organic decay. Gosh, maybe we'll see some floating around in your messy room."

Not only were we toasting marshmallows on the patio grill (using slim tree branches for skewers as I insisted), my mother surprised me (and my dad) with another great recipe from the *Boy Scout Handbook*. This time it was "Wormy Apples", with the 'worms' being sausage links that were placed inside cored apples. After being wrapped in foil, they were tossed on the coals.

While licking a gooey brown marshmallow with my scorched tongue, I told my mom to tell my dad about the stranger. Picking off the black crust of her charred one, she told him that his name was "Zerrill" and that he was visiting from California. She said that she had an odd feeling about his story. He seemed to be more interested in the bookshelves than the books themselves, inspecting them as if looking for hidden compartments. From the corner of her eye, she even saw him checking out some wood block book dummies that he possibly thought might trigger a movie cliché revolving bookcase passage.

Listening to her talk about him, I unthinkingly picked up my father's can of Stag beer and was about to take a drink when, seeing him glaring at me in disbelief, I set it back down and raised my hands in a gesture of compliance.

"He's looking for some kind of treasure," my mom said.

"What treasure?" My dad threw up his hands to express his irk.

"I believe in the treasure," I said.

"You believe that jungle gorillas are launching rockets at our military helicopters" he responded, still annoyed about the persistent rumors of ancient artifacts buried in the surrounding area.

When my mom mentioned to my dad about the white-skinned, blue-eyed natives that Zerrill was researching (pushing his buttons?), he grumbled something about paradigm-shifting nonsense of laypersons that lacked any analytical discipline. "Sounds very bush-league," he uttered before grabbing his beer and going inside to watch television.

While he was gone, I asked my mom if she had found out anything about Mister Schaufler (Molewhisker) in the microfiche archives?

She told me that she had found an article from the early 1950s in the local paper that she would paraphrase for me. It had to do with a regional Hot Rod club that Mister Schaufler had been the leader of. They had meetings at private garages and local hangouts – even at the library where she now worked. When they weren't racing on back roads late at night, they performed charitable deeds, raising money from car washes and dances. They also helped out stranded motorists.

One night while cruising through the local drive-in in an old hearse that had been converted into a hot rod, Mister Schaufler was pulled over for having burned out taillights. When the police checked the decorative coffin in the back that was part of the car's theme, they discovered that it contained a dead human body. Being the local undertaker, Schaufler explained that the corpse was a recently deceased buddy of his that was also affiliated with the club. His desire had been that – in the event of his death, before he was buried – he wanted to be placed inside the coffin car, and cruise around town for one last time. Mister Schaufler even showed the authorities a signed statement from the deceased that attested to this request. Because of this, and the club's community service, he wasn't arrested.

"That's all that I could find in The Spectrum. This is probably the origin of all the nasty innuendos about his... ghoulish activities... when, in reality, he was just being loyal to his friend in respecting his last wish. I couldn't figure out why you wanted to know about this, until I read the name of the Hot Rod club. 'Will O' The Wisp.' Okay? Now, you should probably get a head start on your weekend homework. But first wash those hands after handling all those dirty twigs. Oh, have you got any more ideas about getting a part-time summer job?"

"Uh-huh, but only if I can take the Jake."

CHAPTER III
AURICHALCUM

I was beginning to think this might not be such a great idea after all. Ollie had already backed out, saying that he had lacerated his tongue on the pull-top lid of a can of tapioca pudding (even though the talking horse in the television commercial had warned kids not to play with it). Bwak-bwak-bwak! It was the hottest day of the year, and here I was pushing my dad's Jacobsen lawnmower (complete with the grass catcher) along the bumpy sidewalk while digesting a fluffernutter in the nauseating fumes of a heated tanker truck spraying tar on the road up ahead. Cutting Molewhisker's jungle still beat an early morning paper route, I kept telling myself, so I tightened up on "Jake's" coke bottle grips and continued on to ShadowCrest.

When I finally reached the old Victorian with its craggy gables and rotting shutters, the severely overgrown lawn looked exactly the same as it did the last time that I saw it. Walking up onto the creaking veranda, I noticed that the kernels of hard corn were still scattered about, but didn't see any trace of the cocoa death-brick that Ollie had thrown at the oddball during the corning

89

incident. I felt a lump in my throat as I pounded on the door, half hoping that the grumpy old bumpkin wouldn't answer.

Moments later the door cracked open and the disheveled figure with the long-tailed mole appeared. Wearing the same dirty ashen bathrobe as before, he gave me the once-over with a puzzled look in his unnerving blue eyes.

"Hello, Mister Schaufler. My name is Addison and I was kind of hoping I could mow your lawn… and then if it looks okay, you could pay me what you think my job is worth."

He opened the door further and stepped outside to check out the push mower's rusted cast-deck.

"Gotchawitcha," he said in his croaky twang.

"Uh-huh, it's my dad's Jake," I replied, not exactly brimming with confidence, but much more at ease now that he was at least reacting to my offer without his usual mean-spirited demeanor.

"Mowjob, huh? Two-stroke Jacobsen rotary pull-start. Humph. My Briggs is more broken – with a dingblasted carburetor, but I got extra gasoline in a can somewhere about. Well, tell you what… Without spilling ink, you've got a deal young feller. Gotta watch out for a litter of kittens or colony of baby rabbits that might still be nesting in the thatch. With that sharp turbocone blade, that would be gosh-awful. Might be some other tidbits in there, too."

"Cool," I said while looking over the knee-high grass that was probably the habitat of robust crawling things as well. I certainly had my work cut out for me. Getting right down to business, I removed the grass catcher bag for the first go-around and cranked up the Jake on the second pull. When I pushed the mower forward, however, the rumbling, smoky engine sputtered as the heavy blade bogged down in the thick grass.

Still on the sagging porch, Molewhisker watched with a thin-lipped grin. When I fired the Jake back up and pushed the lever to full throttle, he expelled a mouthful of chew and shuffled back inside.

Assessing the situation, I decided to take a more gradual approach. Pushing down on the handlebar, I lifted the front end up and laid the rattling mower gently down so as to cut the grass to half of its current height. Once a large patch of this was done, I continued to scalp what remained. With this more manageable plan to conquer the monster, things went a bit smoother.

With the sun jabbing my eyes, I continued with my overlapping passes, watching through the mirage-like ripples of heat distortion as bluebirds flickered from the tree branches in a repetitive loop that was, once again, not unlike the low-budget background animation in a *Flintstones* cartoon. It was Looney Tunes all right, but why was I the only one who noticed these weird things?

Just when I was beginning to make good progress, I heard a loud thump that stalled the engine. Uh-oh, I had walloped something that was hidden in the wilderness. Seeing what looked like shredded white fur, I suddenly remembered Molewhisker's warning to watch out for a litter of kittens. Thinking that I might have just mutilated one, I felt a sickening sensation coursing through my body. Much to my relief, however, when I examined a length of the fur, it appeared to be some kind of cotton stuffing. Several yards away, I found the hacked up head of a snowy white little lamb with a rayon plush coat. I picked up the child's toy along with pieces of a ribbon collar that had tiny bells attached to it and tossed it all towards the sun-blistered vinyl patio furniture.

I was sweating like a dog and itching like crazy, so I took the opportunity to turn on the outside water faucet. Hoping to taste the same invigorating water that had revitalized me last autumn in the cornfields, when I knelt down to take a gulp, instead of a cold refreshing stream flowing into my mouth, a frail daddy-long-legs spider that I had disturbed dropped down. As I jumped back, there was a tap on my shoulder. Looking up, I saw Mole-whisker standing there.

"There's green drink in the frost-proof if you want?"

Before I had a chance to reply, he doddered away in his shab-by robe.

What happened to the champion crabapple, I wondered? Was the yammering ass-crack really a pushover?

Pulling vigorously on the starter rope, Jake fired right back up. I continued with my mowing pattern, striving for an even, uniform cut in a maze of invented geometry. While gliding along, the hypnotic drone of the engine must have eventually put me into a peculiar semi-conscious state. The more grass that I cut the more remained unmowed, as if the yard – including the crappiest sections that I would have sworn that I already cut– was somehow expanding in length. This illusion was beyond strange, but I soon came out of the monotonous tone-induced trance when another piece of debris killed the engine. This time the object was an old wooden "Winky Blinky" toy fire engine from the '50s that was missing one of its wooden yellow wheels. Seeing the goofy face with rolling eyes on the front, I picked it up and heaved it closer to the house.

Though I hadn't reached the checkered flag, the mower's fuel tank was about empty (and I had already used what was left in Molewhisker's can). I was also plenty tuckered out, so I walked towards the house to tell Mister Schaufler that I would have to finish the job the next day.

There was no sign of Molewhisker in the messy kitchen, so I looked for a clean glass in the cabinets near the flyblown sink.

Unable to find one, I convinced myself that I wasn't thirsty anyway. Even so, out of curiosity, I opened the refrigerator to check
out the green colored drink that he had mentioned. The Tupperware container appeared to be half-filled with lime Kool-Aid
that, oddly enough, had thin strips of what looked like bologna
floating inside. Thinking that the stringy pinkish stuff could be
anything, I gagged for a second and shut the door.

Wandering into the dining room with its mildewed wallpaper, the sun filtered through drawn curtains to reveal an antique
lacquered buffet that was embellished with a few gaudy enameled mementoes. Hanging above was a European 16th-centu-
ry fowling piece that was draped in cobwebs. The only other
piece of furniture was a table with a faux-wood grain laminate
upon which was set a smudged bowl of dusty bruised fruit. Sadly
enough, there weren't any chairs.

Calling his name, I entered a drape-dimmed living room
that was also musty with neglect. The water-stained oak flooring
was littered with crumpled plaster from the ceiling that, like the
antique muzzleloader, was swathed in tangles of dirty old spider
webs. A chronic halitosis pervaded the drab and cheerless interi-
or. Calling Mister Schaufler again, I sat down in an upholstered
chartreuse recliner that was placed in front of a rabbit-eared television console with a scarred mahogany veneer.

The titles were rolling on the screen for a black and white
movie that was going to have some kind of sunken treasure
theme, I guessed, because the opening sequence showed scuba
divers floating around an ancient shipwreck whose wooden hull
was thickly encrusted with sea growth. The next scenes were
grainy close-ups of the stumps of mastheads and the quarterdeck
rotting in the depths. As the titles ended, an enormous fish suddenly dwarfed the wreck that lay undisturbed in its coral grave.

The camera gradually widened to reveal that the sunken vessel was actually a miniature model that was used as an ornamental piece for a small saltwater aquarium. The scuba divers were toy figures as well, with the fish being an ordinary sized Golden Mini Grouper that made several loops around the decorative wreck before swallowing some tiny brine shrimp. This was followed by an establishing shot of a port-holed dockside bar, with a caption that read: FOURNI ISLAND, GREEK ARCHIPELAGO.

The taverna's interior was crammed full of nautical props, including a ship's teak steering wheel with a brass hub and handles, an old copper deep-sea diving helmet, navigation instruments, marine specimens, and walls covered with oceanographic charts, lateen sails, mooring rope, anchor chains and a monkey's fist paracord.

Although the sailor's haunt was closed at this late hour, several people were gathered around an oak table drinking Navy grogs while examining the co-ordinates on the map of a shipwreck graveyard. The volume on the television set was barely audible, but I heard one of the figures mention something about a cache of early Spanish doubloons and ancient Greek drachma. There were close-ups of the faces of each principle character cast in a wan light: The savvy treasure hunter and his beautiful young daughter, a ship's captain sucking on a pipe in his battered yacht hat, and the debonair European partner of the private entrepreneur whose eyes were more on the pretty girl than the treasure map.

The sunken treasure subject matter of the movie excited my curiosity, but I called again for Molewhisker, wanting him to know that I would return in the morning with more gas. There was still no sign of him, so I continued to watch as an abrupt jump cut took us outside the harbor bar.

In an under-lit, claustrophobic studio exterior shot, the charming European fellow and the treasure seeker's lovely daughter strolled along a mulberry tree-lined promenade under a glistening silver 'studio' moon. In the painted shadows, they were talking about "the possibility of a Jonah being among them" until the scene was diffused by an optically created mist.

Another ragged jump cut showed the team aboard a yacht anchored off a coastline in an expansive sun-flecked sea with great pinnacles of rock. The caption read: EAST AEGEAN SEA. The skipper continued to puff away as the European suited up in scuba diving gear. After adjusting his mask, he tumbled backwards from the deck near a buoy that was bobbing in the cream-capped waves. As he submerged, the buxom blonde girl looked on with concern; her sun-bronzed sculpted body clad in a high-wasted bikini bottom and a matching top.

Below the water, the diver swam through a stony labyrinth filled with agitated crustaceans emerging from sea anemones. Like many movies that I had seen on the "Bijou Theater" (especially the late night "Creature Feature"), the production values were poor, and the substrate invertebrates in the stock footage were shown in a sepia tone. Soon, the diver was inspecting the ghostly, barnacled wreck of an ancient Phoenician galley (a Quadrireme) whose painted eye was still visible on its deteriorated prow. Scattered on the murky seabed were piles of encrusted Greek amphorae.

As the scuba diver picked up one of the ancient clay jars, there was a swishing sound that didn't come from the movie soundtrack, but, rather, from the staircase in the house. It was the scrunchy polyester lining of a cheap navy blue plaid leisure suit worn by Molewhisker as he entered the front room. From the bubbly shoulder lines hung an adult cloth bib in which the embroidered motto read:

"MOBILIS IN MOBILI."

The picture on the television screen wavered to snow and static.

"You ain't dithering, are you?" he asked.

"We're out of gas and I was just waiting here to tell you that I'll have to finish tomorrow."

He spat some green-tinted tobacco juice into a dulled pewter jug by the recliner.

"Pardon, but I'm not especially fond of seaweed tobacco. I was just having lunch with Prince Dakkar... or Captain Nemo, if you'd prefer, and I'm not particularly fond of what comes out of the galley on that pizzazzy tube as well. Dolphins' livers and pickled Zoophytes. Connoisseur, my puckered brown eye. I've got my Mayrose eats in the Westinghouse... Did you see? Bologna chunks in the green drink —"

"You were reading the story by Jules Verne?" I asked.

"I was on board the Nautilus as a guest," he said with a penetrating tone.

"How'd you do that?" I humored the crazy old fart, although I did notice that his fancy napkin appeared to be freshly stained with something, which he glanced down at with a look of disgust.

"Anemone preserves. Now, I've got to affect perichoresis again to return this. Well, I didn't get there from the frigate U.S.S. Abraham Lincoln, that's for sure. I entered the book – a vividly kinetic experience, not to participate in the adventure, but to ask him for the umpteenth time to catch me an ornery fish that can live in my tank. A carnivorous one – that will jump up and eat these consarned biting horseflies. Though, I've about exhausted my patience with the aquatic prince."

He pointed to a dirty fish tank on a stand in the corner of the room that I hadn't noticed before. Inside the cloudy, yellowish-brown water, a single fish – a grouper similar in appearance to the one in the movie – floated in the algae. Even crazier, though, there was a miniature ancient shipwreck decoration of hand-painted resin among the dried coral skeletons on the murky gravel floor.

Outside, I heard the music box jingle of an ice-cream truck announcing its presence. A rainbow bomb pop sounded dang good, and I thought I had enough change in my pocket to buy one.

As promised, I returned the next morning with a full can of gas and some gardening tools, including a weed whacker and rake for the grass cuttings. I had gotten a ride from my dad in his backfiring Pearl White VW Microbus. Although I thought that he would be curious to check out the town's clodhopper Mephisto (and his unkempt yard), he just told me not to do "what some people called a half-ass job" before handing me a metal scoop and taking off.

The pull-started Jacobsen surged until it warmed up as I pushed it into the backyard. While cutting the tall grass, I focused all of my attention on the parallel lanes, not wanting to experience any trance effect shenanigans from the engine's hypnotic drone. Even so, after about 30 minutes, the mental tomfoolery began. There was a scraping noise under the heavy blade as I mowed what appeared to be the exact same area that I had already cut short yesterday. This was total bullshit! It was as if the grass blades in this section had somehow grown back to their previous length over night. But, not only that. The cotton stuffing that was blown out of the discharge chute turned out to be another snowy white plush little lamb toy with a torn soft plastic vinyl face and black hooves. Was the yard chock-full of these dipshit things? With Jake still idling, when I went to check and see, there was no evidence of the other 'lamb chops' by the patio furniture, although I did see the "Winky Blinky" wooden fire truck with its big painted eyes rolling at me. All I could do was to continue mowing, but this time I took on the mind-blowing illusion while singing a little improvised ditty: "Liddle lamzydivey, kidzedyvy too… but Molewhisker can lick my gassy yawner."

When I had finished to my satisfaction, I let myself in the back door to hopefully get paid. In the dining room, I thought about helping myself to a piece of fruit, but whiffle-whaffled (as my mom liked to say) due to its yucky appearance. The spotted overripe bananas were squishy, and the oranges were discolored with white specks of mold. The lone apple looked crunchy, but when I tapped its skin, I knew that it would be mushy brown inside.

While leaning on the table and staring at the bowl something remarkable happened. More spell casting stuff, I thought, or, more likely, evidence of some obscure neural affliction that caused bizarre visions. For a split second, the rotting fruit transformed itself into the aromatic, unblemished pickings of some wondrous grove whose rinds of vibrant exotic hues and intricately cored flesh were unlike anything that I had ever seen in any grocery store. The peeled moist treasures included seafoam-green cubes, segmented wisteria and cerulean pomace in magenta and gamboge husks, pellucid citrine wedges and flame-orange chunks.

Clusters of berries cascaded from the glistening shapes. Placed next to the chilled platter was a metallic utensil whose gleaming complexity reflected the dewed faerie hues until the luscious pieces of fruit wavered back into the original mealy produce that one could find in the Tomboy's dusty wicker baskets.

Trying my best not to think about what had just happened, I called for Mister Schaufler as I headed into the living room. Glancing over at the television set, I couldn't believe that the terrible 'sunken treasure' movie with the poor continuity and cheesy dialogue was being shown again. Waiting for some response, I once again plopped myself into the recliner to watch the stinker.

Two scuba divers were entangled in a dramatic knife fight near an underwater reef. As they violently slashed at one another, a menacing looking shark that was obscured by marine life came into frame. Distracted by the sight of this man-eater, one of the divers let their guard down long enough to be stabbed by the other in the chest. The resulting cloud of blood attracted more sharks. The victorious diver attempted to retrieve a leather purse from the seabed, but was unable to do so because of all the frenzied creatures. With a spear gun at the ready (where was it earlier?), the diver eluded the circling predators while being rapidly propelled to the surface by kicking rubber fins.

An exploded yacht pitched and tossed in the swollen waves while engulfed in flames. As the sun set on the cloudy horizon, dead passengers scattered among the splintered floating debris could be seen through the plumes of dark smoke. When the surviving diver popped up from the sea and removed the rubber mask, we realize that the treasure hunter's beautiful daughter had squeezed into the wetsuit. As she looked around for her father in the shark-infested water, a shock close up of his lifeless expression brushed against her frantic screams.

Suddenly, her face was bathed in a brilliant irradiation that issued from an electric contrivance on the bristling metallic hull of a strange ancient submarine that emerged from the waterline in green, steely blue and amber tints. Seeing the elongated cylinder of the fictional Nautilus, the girl fainted and sank beneath the heavy swells.

Another sloppy jump cut took us back to the interior of the dockside taverna that was shown in the opening sequence. Again, it was late at night and the place was closed to the public. The blond babe (once again scantily-clad in her bikini) was sitting alone at the bar, drearily sipping on a Navy grog. Noticing the Golden Mini Grouper swimming near the miniature ancient shipwreck ornament in the aquarium, we can tell that a thought had just occurred to her. She got up from the stool and slowly walked over to the tank to have a closer look at its decor. Reaching inside, she picked up the painted model of the vessel and removed it from the water. Feeling inside a manufactured rotting wood hole in the starboard side, she pulled out a leather purse and untied it. Inside, she discovered a handful of priceless ancient Greek drachma coins. With a close up that showed that the obverse was stamped with a depiction of a Quadriga (a four horse drawn chariot), she closed her eyes and smiled, knowing that the treasure had been placed there by...

"Captain fucking Nemo," I said. "How retarded is that."

As the music swelled and the closing titles rolled, there was still no sign of Molewhisker. I walked over to his little fish tank, noticing that it still needed to be cleaned. Funny, his shipwreck piece, too, had a rotting wood hole in its starboard side (a hideaway for fish). This all seemed a bit strange – enough so that I wondered if he might be messing with me? Why?

To test me? But, how could he have known that I would hang around to watch part of the movie? Yet everything seemed to fit together – including the stuff about Captain Nemo.

Calling him with a much louder voice this time, I gazed down at the tank decoration as the grouper swam in circles around it. This was so similar to the movie that I just had to check.

I reached into the murky water and lifted out the hand-painted shipwreck. I stuck my finger into the 'hideaway' hole, but didn't feel anything inside. However, when I turned the ornament over, something fell onto the floor without making a sound. Bending down to pick it up, I saw that this was a disc of some kind with a strange reddish copper color. Examining it more closely, I saw that the object was blank on both sides – kind of like one of Ollie's slugs. Whatever it was, it was extremely light to the touch – almost having no weight at all. Looking around, I stuck the thing into my soiled denim pocket… mainly just to show Ollie. But, if grandpa pants wanted to play games…

Where was Molewhisker? Taking a nap like a small child? On the growler with his dangling elderberries waiting for a nugget splashdown? Or maybe he walked into some Tom Sawyer book in his library to ask Huckleberry Finn to catch him a fish that eats horseflies since Captain Nemo wouldn't do it! I nervously waited for another half hour, but he never came downstairs. Ticked off, I went back outside to gather the garden tools and the empty gas can, which I stacked on the Jake before pushing the clunky thing home.

When I showed Ollie the disc, he said that it was way too light to fool the mechanism of any vending machine, and therefore it was worthless as a slug. It was probably just an old bingo token, he guessed, or a new Tiddlywink squidger. Even though the doohickey, as I now called it, was lighter than Styrofoam ("frozen smoke" is how I would describe its weight), it was made of some really tough material that would instantly spring back to its original shape when bent. After demonstrating its uncanny flexibility to Ollie, he just shrugged and said that it still wasn't worth trading for his "Gadzooka Gum" Wacky double.

I actually didn't want to trade it for the Wacky. Nor did I want to use it as a slug for a single bottle of soda. I had more fun playing with it, and was curious as to what it might be if not some piece of newfangled plastic that Molewhisker kept inside a treasure galleon in his fish aquarium.

Though I kept a close eye on it, a couple of days later I almost did lose it. I was at the local bowling alley playing a few games of pinball with Kelby when I went to get a drink from the vending machine. I'm not sure how it happened but I must have accidently stuck the disc into the coin slot. After this, several odd things occurred. First of all, the machine was stocked only with some new chocolate beverage that I had no choice but to accept. And even though the bottle had been dispensed, the machine returned my 'coin.' At first I couldn't feel anything in the return slot, and when I peered into the opening I swear that didn't see anything either. But, after sliding my finger around, I felt the doohickey. It had come back to me like a puppy to its owner. Realizing my mistake, I carefully placed it back into my other pocket.

As I was about to take a sip of the "Yoo-hoo" like drink, a hand grabbed the chilled bottle. Turning around, I saw that it was the funny-talking preacher who was at Jake's barbershop.

"Are you daringly different, my friend?" he asked in his charismatic manner. "That's what the advertisement says – New Devil Shake – for people who are daringly different."

"I just want the bottle deposit money," I replied.

"Without divine assistance, son, God and his mighty concourse – not to mention yours truly in these white tasseled loafers

– don't see how you can finagle that? Not when you're putting more money into the machine… unless you've got some kind of mysterious doodad?"

A smile cracked on his pallid face as he suddenly recognized me from Jake's.

"You're the kid who was interested in Bubba Ho-Tep's house."

He read the soft drink's mod bright pink and orange label for everyone in the place to hear. For the most part he was drowned out by the cacophony of balls rumbling down the lanes and crashing into wooden pins.

"Shake-N-Enjoy!"

Glancing about at the customers, Roovert raised his voice to be heard over a blaring jukebox and the dinging bells of a few arcade games.

"Until that perfect day… when many on the earth will shake… but few will enjoy. There are many doors – routes to God, but none to be found amongst this demonic razzmatazz. Here, we have a glitzy new drink… Satan's pretty doggone glitzy, don't you think? Personally, I would rather drink spunk-water from a rotten stump than the brown swill of any company that's hobnobbing with the devil. Can I get an Amen!"

"We just came to play some pinball. The hayride farmer's game over there," I said while discretely trying to get Kelby's attention in case there were going to be any gospel aerobatics or freakish tongues like Jake the barber had mentioned.

"Just playing a farmer's hayride pinball game. Don't fall for Satan's new plan, friends. The next phase is called subliminal MAN-nipulation. Did you read what it says on that farmer's hay-ride game? Frenzied ball action with rubber rings. E-Z latches… for thumper bumpers… No sir, they're not just paddling the pink canoe, these days."

The Pentecostal preacher waved his Bible towards a hippy couple dressed in tie-dyed tees and flared jeans that were standing against a painted mural near the bowling alley's snack bar.

"Though I expect those types aren't concerned with wearing any rubbers while belittling the boss man with their trips to a counterfeit heaven."

We climbed out of the Army surplus tent that we had pitched in Ollie's backyard for the sleepover and stood under the glint of stars. Before stepping out onto the empty street, Kelby said that he thought that he had seen the silhouette of Ollie's mom watching us from behind the drapes. Ollie insisted that this was just a lampshade, and that his mom was sound asleep at this late hour. Thinking that he was probably right, we took one final hard look before leaving the yard on our latest after-curfew adventure.

We were sneaking over to Molewhisker's house to look for any will o' the wisps that might be floating around in the soybean fields behind his backyard. Since the walk was over thirty minutes, Ollie brought along a can of Vienna Sausages in case we got hungry. That's what he said, but I knew that he had planned to use the smelly baby franks as a peace offering should Molewhisker catch us.

While keeping an eye out for Bosworth's patrol car, Kelby was telling us about a new paperback that he was reading. It was about this guy with psychic powers named Edgar Cayce. While in a trance, he prophesized that part of Atlantis would rise again after having been destroyed by some terrible event many thousands of years ago. This would occur sometime this year and it would be discovered under the slime of ages. He also said that before it sank beneath the waves, Atlantis once shone with the red flashes of a special metal called Orichalcum, but that today no one was sure what this sacred alloy really was.

When we arrived at the right place without having to risk taking ShadowCrest, I was completely dumbfounded while glancing around at the darkened surroundings. Where were the rest of the soybean fields? And what happened to the barbed wire fence that caused me to have to dab my cut open lip with monkey's blood for a couple of weeks?

There was a dulcet buzzing sound in my head that lasted for only a second. This was followed by a smell that I could only describe as aseptic vanilla ice cream. Looking down at where the sanitary tropical fragrance was coming from, I was amazed to see that all of the stains on my faded jeans and sweatshirt had vanished. The crud on my sneakers had also disappeared so that the 69ers now appeared straight out of the box. Glancing over at my friends to see if what they were wearing had also been (somehow) laundered spotless, I quickly saw that this was not the case. Not only were their clothes and shoes darkly soiled from trudging through the fields, seeing Kelby and Ollie standing next to me at that moment was like looking at them through a dirty window or cloudy lens. Even stranger were the vapory images left behind when they moved.

Not sure what to make of all of this, I took a couple of tentative steps forward in my hygienic aura until, incredibly, the throbbing brilliance of another world appeared within an invisible framework. Instead of standing in the monotonous crops, stretching before my disbelieving gaze was a spacious expanse of the most aesthetically pleasing manicured grounds that any master landscaper could ever have imagined.

Under the infinity of stars, Molewhisker's backyard (and much of the field) had been transformed into a carpet of intricate scrollwork in a curious harlequinade of greenish shades. Multiple tiers of ingeniously sculptured foliage extended in equidistant rows to the back of his house, making the ramshackle Victorian look like it belonged in a different reality. Along with the abstract topiaries of some futuristic agronomy, a series of vertical trellises of leafy mosaics ornately framed pedestalled luminous vivaria that were teeming with a bedizening array of marine wonders. Beneath these luxuriant orb-aquariums, miniature forests of lavish exuberance were engirded by limpid pools that reflected the boughs' riotous majesty.

As I moved closer, a walkway of luminous paving squares unexpectedly appeared near abstract flowering delights trained in all matter of unfolding variegated patterns. Stepping into the viridian rhapsody, euphoric surges of vegetative perfumes saturated the path edging. Awestruck by the kaleidoscope of delicate tints in Lilliputian lagoons, a shadow darkened the shifting dreamworld. I found myself standing beneath the hexagonal silver undercarriage of a sleek recliner that was anchored in the scented breeze. The floating lounge emitted a pleasing low frequency resonance while suspended above the red-bronze luster of a tiny crystal-topped obelisk.

The enriched ventilation that I breathed was now pulsating through my body. All of my senses became more refined as I seemed to be coexisting in two different worlds that bumped together in a peculiar manner.

"So, you didn't get paid anything for this? It ought to be worth something at least," Kelby said in a hushed voice as he pulled out a small compass.

"What? You could sell tickets to see this…" I was lost for words.

"Jeez, Addison," Ollie snickered. "Yeah, right that would ever happen, but it's still not bad for your first try. Sell tickets to see a stupid mowed lawn. Now, that's a good one."

"Hey, my compass is going crazy," Kelby uttered excitedly.

"Are you kidding me?" I was flabbergasted – "This is unlike anything…"

I quickly realized that my friends weren't seeing what I was. What I perceived was either a rare glimpse of the 'innershine' that I've had a faint penciling of in the past, or the full-blown hallucination of some mental abnormality that was getting much worse. That, or Molewhisker was someone who was willing to spare no expense for a good practical joke. If my first thought was correct, then I was the only one amongst us that was *othering* (to use the term that came to me in a dream – although I can't remember who said it). And if I had shifted, how long would it last? Of course, I wondered the same thing about an abrupt episode of mental illness? But how could that explain my now immaculate clothes?

Suddenly, a black ellipse appeared like a magic door and rapidly expanded perpendicular to the palpable intensity of the sheeny verdure. Within the opening, I saw what looked like an intricate geometric tree. From one of the self-luminous beige fabric appendages of the elaborate configuration, a Siamese cat jumped to the ground with what resembled a lively fishing lure in its mouth. With a bristled 'question mark' tail, the cat released the wriggling thing when it saw me standing on the swirling patterns of the ornamental paving.

The humped cat hissed at me before pouncing on the realistic-looking decoy. Batting at its head with its dark furry paw, the energetic tiny beak of whatever it had captured began clicking, squeaking and whistling. This caused me to step off the (vanishing) square and bend over to get a better look at what the glistening fixity of the cat's dilated sapphires were focused on. I was open-mouth shocked to discover that what I thought to be some rubbery piece of fish bait was actually a 'living ' miniscule dolphin that was no longer than an inch in length. While toying with its grayish-white skin, the minute creature escaped the cat's clutches. It then surged vertically backwards and began tail walking across the matchless green.

Spinning around into a crouched position, the cat watched the dolphin's peppy gymnastics with irritated flicks of its puffy tail. As it inched closer, I heard Ollie utter:

"Leave the damn thing alone, Addison, or we'll get caught. It's just a cat messing with a bug."

With his crippled perceptual filter, my friend didn't see how the tiny dolphin next sprouted little iridescent wings and began playfully twirling over the moon-dappled paradise.

Out of thin air, another liquid black aperture dilated with a lightning-fast motion. From this glossy opening, a mysterious figure with unpigmented skin and an expressionless physiognomy floated out while seated on a cushion of intricate azure webbing. With a pair of bongos between his knees, the man's mercurial shirt depicted the picturesque scenery of a sunset lagoon that was accompanied by the sounds of an ecstatic calypso rhythm. A gesture with his pale tapered finger caused a multihued dot to instantaneously appear on the cat's fawn coat. As if reacting to some electrified poke, the feline beat a hasty retreat back onto one of its artificial tree branches. With little effort, the freaky, shaved-headed albino caught the tiny dolphin while it was still engaged in a ballet of airborne revolutions. Cradled in the palm of his hand, he tossed the quivering thing into the strikingly blue 'water' of the lagoon that was interacting on his strange garment. Making a 'wetless' splash on the shirt's dynamic material, the tiny creature did not surface from the expanding series of frothy ripples.

As the 'sunset lagoon' portal slowly rotated, the narrow visage of the figure scanned the yard's virid spectacle. Feeling a strange giddiness at the nearly synthetic neutrality of his rigid facial anatomy, I watched as his peculiar slanted golden-hazel eyes now peered in my direction. They reminded me of the imaginary childhood friend that I called Major Domo, although the face didn't appear to be exactly the same. Still, I had to wonder?

With his unexpressive manner, the seated figure pointed something at me. A jeweled flash with a resplendent vapor caused me to blink. After the dazzling glare lifted, the magnificent perspective that had seemed realer than real was seamlessly replaced by an ordinary darkened backyard that for the most part looked the same as it did when I mowed it last Sunday afternoon.

I heard the rustle of Kelby and Ollie take off towards the front of the house as Molewhicker pointed the barrel of an old "Buck Rogers Sonic Ray Gun" that emitted a piercing buzzing noise along with a series of bright red flashes.

"Get off my lawn before I disintegrate all of you with this ray shooter!"

The futuristic toy pistol's side-fin lit up brilliant red again.

"Damn you guttersnipe running amok on my freshly mowed grass!"

When I hurried to join my friends, the headlights of my dad's idling Volkswagen Microbus were illuminating the flaking gingerbread trim on the Victorian's sagging wraparound. We stopped in our tracks as the driver's window quickly squeaked down. My dad stuck his head out to see what was going on with the red flashes coming from the hand of an elderly figure in a mangy bathrobe.

"Hi, Dad," I said as casually as if he'd just come home from a day's work.

"Yeah, hi there, Addison," he replied just as calmly. "You boys want to get into the van. Ollie's mother called me. She was very upset after watching you leave the yard."

"That skuzz bucket shouldn't have done that – pretending to be a lampshade with her face all smeared with Noxema," Ollie gritted his teeth, indignant that it was his mother who called.

"I was just trying to get paid," I said while pointing to the yard.

My father stuck his head further out of the window.

"I apologize, Mister Schaufler. "You know, boys will be boys," he waved at the toy ray gun-brandishing old coot while anxious to leave the unwelcoming house's gloomy ornate elements.

"I thought that we had an arrangement?" Molewhisker glared at me as I climbed into the back of the Volkswagen.

Before getting in, Ollie offered him the can of Vienna Sausages.

"You want some baby dicks?"

"Aren't you the boy that tossed that Hershey bullet at me?"

"Sorry again for any trouble, sir," my dad peered into the rearview mirror before backing out onto the street with a series of backfires.

"Dad, you should have seen his backyard. It's better than the park or anything."

"Oh yeah, were there any roasted pigs wandering around with carving knifes stuck in their backs… handing out iced bottles of Budweiser along with that award-winning Cockaigne cheese falling from the stars?"

"No… But there was a tiny flying dolphin," I mumbled.

"Hey, look, this street is paved with pastry, boys."

I could tell that my dad was getting angrier by the minute, and wondered what my punishment was going to be?

"Open this pack of Wackies for me, okay?" I asked Zerrill while he was seated at the microfiche reader in the public library, still searching for something of interest in one of the archived local newspapers.

"I shall gladly oblige you, sir," he replied while peeling open the wax paper wrapper of the pack of trading die-cuts that I handed him. Once done, he spread out the five punch-outs that were inside, along with a thin pink slab of bubblegum. Disappointed, I saw that there was no "Gadzooka Gum" Wacky among them.

"Still jinxed," I shook my head.

He showed me the card called "Cover Ghoul", which was a parody of a "Cover Girl" makeup bottle that comically depicted a chubby, ugly female face that was covered in acne and sores.

"I think that I might have seen the model for this one last night at the Town Lounge," Zerrill winced. "Quite similar maquillage, that's for sure."

"Flirting with the ladies nippin' at the juice." My mother seemed mildly amused.

"I only go there for the toasted ravioli and a schooner – oops – I mean a fishbowl of Busch."

"Addison is here to do some research for his essay on Christopher Columbus." My mom's eyes widened as she waited for Zerrill's reaction.

"Yeah, I heard that you unzipped the old fart sack to engage in some mischief making the other night. Oh, the mishaps of our youth. Christopher alias Columbus, huh. How about I give you a hand with this painful undertaking?"

"Oh brother!" my mom blurted out. When she stopped laughing, she tapped her pencil on the desk as she and Zerrill shared a mischievous smile. "You know, why not? Even though we're supposed to be teaching Addison a lesson... and not his father."

"I just want to put right a few things that might still be muddled in school textbook history."

While seated at the table in the family room, before the remains of frozen sausage pizzas were tossed in the trash, my father began to read to my mother and I the copious notes that he had made from the graded copy of 'my' typed punishment essay.

"Columbus did not discover the Americas – either by accident or otherwise. He was not a Genoese mariner, and he didn't come from humble beginnings. His name is, itself, an alias. He was a Knights Templar pirate, which is why the red cross pattée was emblazoned on the sails of his three caravels. The same Templar emblem that is now stamped onto... Oreo cookies... as a parody of Communion wafer – which also explains why no priests were brought on the voyages. Columbus was in possession of maps, documents and diaries of those who had made repeated landings in the – placed in quotes – New World long before 1492. Clues of these much earlier journeys are carved into dated ancient European stonework that depicts corn, aloe and coconuts."

He placed the essay on the table for a second and looked up at both of us.

"And here's where I really think that we should heat some Jiffy Pop to properly enjoy this fabulous theater of the make-believe."

He picked up the paper, cleared his throat, and continued to read:

"This nautical and cartographic data – which represents part of the secret wisdom of an antediluvian civilization – was smuggled out of Paris by the fugitive Templars in an ox-drawn hay wain and taken to their fleet of ships harbored at port. The Templars discovered this treasure under the ruins of the Temple of Solomon, to whom it was entrusted by the high priests of the Zadokite dynasty, who, themselves, received it from those mysterious personages who became simply known as the Watchers. Rather than being the rebellious angels of Biblical propaganda, these cultural exemplars were the surviving inhabitants of a sunken landmass – the same unknown superior race that Enoch alluded to in rejected ancient texts. The Columbus subterfuge is part of the secret objective of a certain organization to create... or, rather, to re-create the utopian society of our ancestors that once inhabited the Mid-Atlantic ridge ... which is why species of eels and turtles still migrate to the Sargasso Sea to breed in its floating seaweed. By the way, Columbus did, however, invent the game of beach volleyball while in the Bahamas with his salty dogs from the Pinta."

He placed the papers back on the table and glared at me.

"Obviously, you didn't write this nonsense. So, who did? Well, let's see. Who sits on their keaster at the library all day — when not punching his beer cards at the Town Lounge trying to impress the small town floozies with his degree in crackpotology from Berkeley in California? Could his name be Zerrill?"

"Oh, c'mon, Ray. It's just a joke. Why even punish Addison by having him write an essay instead of just telling him that he can't watch Flipper for a month… or taking away his allowance for a while?"

"Because, he needs to plant his feet firmly in reality. I'm aware that he has an overactive imagination, but these crazy ideas – let's not fuel the fire. Oreo cookies with a Templar symbol…. and turtles that keep on truckin' back to Atlantis. I have some major concerns that I'm trying to address, Deedra, and I would appreciate you not undermining my efforts."

"So, there's no popcorn or anything?" I asked.

"Hey, if you're such a Columbus naysayer, then maybe you should go sit in the classroom on his holiday instead of celebrating it here," my dad snapped his fingers.

"There's no such thing as the Easter bunny, but it's still a school holiday for you," I reminded him.

"Well, why did the pirates fly the Jolly Rogers?" my mom asked. "With the skull and crossbones of Masonic symbolism. Some of Zerrill's seemingly radical ideas are intriguing. Maybe it's time to revise some history – "

"Sure, maybe I should teach that Columbus brought back syphilis with his coconuts. Deedra, don't swallow this hogwash. You could lose a good paying job."

My mom got up from the table.

"I wonder why the only book that Columbus authored – *La aventure de America* – has never been published, but still remains hidden in the secret archives of the Vatican?"

It seemed like half of the town had shown up at the park this evening for the Mayfest. In the dusty gold light, Kelby, Ollie and I looked for familiar faces in the maze of motion as we walked over flattened popcorn boxes, sawdust and deflated rubber balloons. Under the rumbling of cranked up generators, there was an anxious excitement in the shuffling lines of the carnival attractions, along with the joyous screams of those already strapped in on the dazzling spinning rides. Inhaling the aroma of batter-coated corndogs, grease lubricants and the caramelized sugar of the floss candy cart, our faces reflected the buzzing neon in the diesel fumes of screeking machinery. Passing the bright vivid colors of the gypsy fortune telling booth, we stopped at a food stand with a garish veneer on a towable trailer.

Nestor appeared at the counter and quickly flipped us double birds. Seeing the string bean with the oily complexion in his Salvation Army cloths, Ollie closed his eyes and opened his big mouth.

"Three Dixie cups of soda... jerk. So, who's holding down the Short Stop and King Coney and other cafeteria pearl diving jobs that you might have?"

"Hey, go unplug that machine anytime, Shit-spitter, cuz I got canned just for alerting customers about the horseflesh in those infrared patties."

"I was going to get one now," I said. "What are they made of here?"

"The world's smallest horse's flesh," Nestor deadpanned. "No, not really. Probably earthworms and a little sawdust. After puking from riding the Tea Cups, you might be better off getting a greasy empanada at the next booth, anyway."

"Empa...fuckin' what?"

I glanced around at the other vending trailers to see what he was talking about.

"My friends and I are starting a house painting business. When I save up enough, I'm going to have my own store... in an Airstream or something. Gonna call it "NESTORE" with an 'e' on the end. Get it? Any of you chumps interested in being preppers? How about you, Not-so-Bright? You could probably be a scrapper."

"But, until then – it's Nestor the carney," Ollie outstretched his hands. "Let's go see if Chooch or someone will get us a quarter silver bucket of beer."

"Would that be a red quarter, Spitzer?" Nestor asked, alluding to one of Ollie's slugs.

When we walked away, the gypsy woman in a sequined headpiece who was seated in the fortune telling booth motioned to me with a slender beringed finger. In the coruscant reflections, the indigo tracery of the tattooed dark skin above her richly costumed breasts added to her already exotic appearance. When she gestured to me again, I pretended that I didn't see her and turned away.

As the three of us headed down a straw walkway illuminated by flickering rainbow bulbs, sordid barkers in excessively bright clothing shouted for our attention. With the tooting of a calliope's steam whistles, we passed the shooting galleries with their clinking knock em' down punks and shelves of cheap chalkware prizes. The guessing booth had the usual plush rabbits and the booby prize for any winners of the rigged "Milk Bottle" game was a plastic monkey on a stick. Ignoring the grease painted clown who was mugging for the ragtag hordes waiting to climb into bumper cars, we continued past the noisy activities of these florescent booths, hoping to find Chooch reveling at the Mayfest's more adult activities.

When we were close to the beer stands, I heard my mother calling me from the pavilion where people were seated at picnic tables for a charity fish fry that was sponsored by the local Masonic Lodge. Telling Kelby and Ollie to wait for just a second, I hurried over to where my parents were eating.

"I heard that dad got dunked in the water tank," I laughed.

"Are you and your friends having fun while staying out of trouble?" my mom asked.

Before I could reply, Zerrill walked up to say hello.

My dad quickly stood up to shake his hand.

"Hey, I just figured out the stuff that Freemasons don't want anyone to know. It's about escaping from their nagging wives by plotting god-awful fish fries and chili cook offs with their cronies. That's their great secret," my father laughed before taking a gulp of his foamless beer.

Zerrill nodded his head in agreement.

"There are no women in the Lodge, Wilma. Yeah, I've also heard that the only great secret of speculative Freemasonry is that there is no great secret."

His eyes widened behind his glasses.

"Or, could it be that the true secret isn't readily digestible to the rank-and-file brethren busy with their pancake breakfasts... even in good fellowship to the members of the convivial society."

"Well, why don't you join us for some over-cooked catfish and beer that's lost its head. I'm anxious to hear the latest paleobabble."

My mom placed both hands on the top of her head and gave an embarrassed smile.

"We're going to ride the Octopus or something," I said.

"Okay, but don't get home late," she reminded me for the umpteenth time.

Moments later, I joined my friends near the ticket booth for beverages containing alcohol. From there, we proceeded to the gravel stretch where the local tavern regulars were having their Octoberfest-style silver buckets re-filled with Budweiser from foamy spigots. At this hour, there was no "vanilla mayhem" – not even from guys with names like Alva Skidmore and Jay Zoltman, who were dressed in barbecue sauce-stained tank tops. Before too long, though, a haymaker would land on at least one of the town toughs in their choice color of flannel shirts. In the coppery blotch of faces, I made eye contact with Chooch as he took a drag from his Kool.

"Hey, freaky-deaky," he said while approaching with his head bobbing to his own rhythm. "How'd you make out the other night when you said you were going to camp out? Just checking because my friend's drink that you took a gulp from might have been a little electric... You know, shake and enjoy... and I heard something about some green McDazzle shit going down."

"Mac-what?" I said with a confused look.

"We were hoping to get a prairie cocktail before checking out that mermaid thing," I chortled.

"You don't know jack squat about her!" Chooch erupted. "Do you really need to gawk at that, dude? Why don't you go try to win a fucking ceramic duck?"

He flicked the cigarette into the yellowish gleam of the beer garden and strutted over to the table with a spinning prize wheel. Still visibly agitated, he reached into his pocket and slammed some change down on a couple of squares.

I wasn't sure what had just gotten into Chooch – it was "like exploding pudding", Ollie commented – but seeing his intense anger, we quickly left the beer stands. Both Kelby and Ollie wanted to see the Freak Show exhibits, so that's where we went next.

Not far from the dazzled eyes of children revolving on gaily-painted wooden horses with faux-jeweled saddles, an enormous banner on a fairground truck contained garish illustrations of the sideshow curiosities. The disturbing tableau included the "Alligator Boy", "Devil Baby", "Human Pretzel", and the star attraction, "Mermaid of Poseidia." Outside, the pitchman described these freaks, as well as what could be viewed behind the black partitions for some extra money.

"Step right up! Human oddities. Right here, folks! Grotesqueries. Monstrosities. Anatomical curiosities! See a beautiful woman with a fish patootie. Arcane marvels in the dime museum to the left. Dancing girls backstage… for gentlemen only, folks."

"The curtained-off area – that's the Striporama," Kelby whispered.

"What's in the dime museum?" I asked.

"The world's largest Stuckey's pecan log… Shoot, I don't know," Ollie spat out a wad of chewed Fruit Stripe gum.

Having paid for our tickets, we were ushered inside a poorly lit space along with the other customers. There, we were introduced to the distinguished Professor Otto Dekelspiel, who was going to be the lecturer for the mermaid exhibit. He was an elderly, bearded fellow in a grey flannel suit who was carrying a leather satchel. He wore a monocle that was attached to a wire and puffed on a pipe from which plumes of sweet tobacco smoke further obscured our vision.

"Professor Dekelspiel at your service while you witness one of the earth's greatest mysteries."

Behind chicken wire a large cylindrical tank was filled with vivid bluish liquid. Floating in this solution was something that made my hair stand on end. It appeared to be a woman's face in a tangle of scintillating white hair. Her upper body was seam-lessly attached to a scaly fishtail. It was hard to take it all in with the pushing, but the tail looked like it matched the marvelous complexity of her sparkling metallic swathing, right down to its myriads of tinted reflections.

The professor continued to go through his repartee with charismatic persuasiveness.

"How about that, folks – the Mermaid of Poseidia. Pickled and preserved in the electric blue of energetic Atlantean wa-terways in hermetically sealed cylindrical glass. A creature of the dark-side of nature or the glowing testament of a maritime mystery? Imagine if you can – her being propelled by vibratory forces through orichalcum columns constructed by levitational methods we simply can't fathom."

I tried to make out the details of the mermaid's elongated face while peering into the tank. Although it was terribly dis-torted in places – almost to a Picasso-esque degree – the most haunting feature in the disturbing artistry of the albinistic tones was her oddly slanted golden-hazel eyes. Even when glazed in death, these were truly the fabled eyes of a masterwork of nature. That, and the great serenity of the delicate lineaments made her look like an abstract porcelain doll that was still radiating an otherworldly mysterious beauty.

Barely perceptible in the watery substance was a shriveled up tiny iridescent dolphin that appeared to be fused to her left ear. I wouldn't have recognized this strange feature had I not recently seen the same thing in Molewhisker's 'other' backyard. What was it doing there and what was it doing here? I made a mental note to check the library to see if such things even existed?

"Notice the necklace of forgotten jewels. Mighty fire crystals. Watch out for the current, folks. Mighty fire crystals. Don't let it irradiate that ten-cent frankfurter, my good sir. You won't get your money back."

❧

The glittering Octopus juddered overhead as I sat in the grass breathing the dense fumes belched from the whirling ride's noisy motor. I was talking to the high-school footfall player, Schramm, as he and his date – a lip-glossed cutie in a halter-top and bell-bottom jeans – shared a small bucket of cold beer.

"So, what's up with the mermaid in the freak show?" I asked him.

"Seeing that thing last year, I can tell you that it's authentic. Genuine rubber and authentic modeling putty. And what about that Professor Dinkelfink with his stupid owl lens? Did you notice that he was also hawking tickets for the guess how many M&M's booth? I don't know why Chooch flipped his lid, but it probably had to do with that bulldog eating mayonnaise that Mooch calls Chooch's girlfriend Cherrie's... rather delicate part of her anatomy."

"Oh, wow – that's really sick," his date said while laughing.

"Hell, she's probably one of the cootchie girls back there," the jock added.

Just then a man with a dirty perspiring face crawled out from behind the loud generator. Wearing a greasy industrial shirt, his protruding stomach overhung the belt line of patched trousers. With a large wrench in one hand and a paper sack half pint in the other, I guessed that the fellow with the grim expression was either the Octopus's operator or mechanic... or both.

"You're talking about Chooch and that mermaid gaff? He was the one who sold the damn thing to us... many years ago...when he worked as a roustabout. He said that he found it in a soybean patch, but we figured that he just stitched some junk together. Whatever he did, with that scaly flapper and queer noggin, it was good enough for the rubes in two-bit towns like this. Now days, add all that LSD-laced shit and it's even better… With all the fried chicken legs, pork clouds and taffy apples, the little whippersnapper was in nickel heaven. But, now, it's time to re-roof the barn, if you catch my drift."

The carney dropped the wrench and pulled out a pack of Chesterfield Kings. He snapped open a Zippo and tried repeatedly to get it to spark in the night breeze.

"By the way, have you ever seen him and his twin brother, Mooch, together at the same time?"

It was hard to believe that Nestor's first painting job was at Molewhisker's deteriorating abode, but there I was on a Saturday afternoon scrapping away the timeworn patina on the porch columns. The yard needed to be mowed again, but I didn't want to deal with that craziness.

Peeling paint was much easier, and, besides, my dad probably wouldn't let me use the Jake considering all the damage that the junk in the tall grass had caused to its blade the first time.

With all the prepping that was needed before the wood could be primed, I only hoped that Nestor had charged enough so that he wouldn't quit before getting paid. While working on the house, I also would have a chance to return the doohickey to the resin shipwreck model inside the dull fish tank.

That chance came sooner than later, I thought – because the winds were picking up and I heard the patter of rain on the house. In the sweet, pungent smell of ozone, it felt like a storm was brewing. Nestor rounded the corner in his King Coney uniform and told me to keep working on the veranda as he went to get more supplies. He was also going to grab some lunch and said that he would bring me back a free Stray Dog.

As soon as he pulled out in his crappy Nova, I went inside the house under the pretense that I was going to get a drink of water. After checking to see if Molewhisker was downstairs, I pulled out the doohickey and walked over to the dirty aquarium. Sticking my hand into the cloudy water, a speckled black butterfly fish with fins like the wings of a bird went right for my fingers. Rather than let it bite one, I quickly pulled my hand out of the tank.

"What are you doing?" I heard Nestor ask while standing in the doorway.

With streaks of lightning and claps of thunder outside, he had decided to return. Water was still dripping from my hand when he saw me holding the metal object.

"I was just feeding the fish," I replied.

"What's that in your hand?"

"Just one of Ollie's slugs," I said.

"Can I see it?" he asked.

When I handed the thing to Nestor, one side became covered with a splotch of eggshell primer that was still wet on his fingers. Catching a glimpse of the strange reaction that the doohickey had to this, I grabbed it and acted like I was scraping the paint off with the tool's metal blade. In doing so, I scratched the surface of the object. As part of the doohickey's self-healing properties (that I had witnessed before), the marks on the metal instantly vanished. With no trace of the primer either, I acted like the scraper was responsible for cleaning it and stuck the object back inside my pocket before the lanky dweeb could ask to have another look at it. From the puzzled look on his face, I think that he might have already seen too much, although he didn't ask any more questions about the thing. Instead, he asked me if I had seen what was happening to the skies?

Hurrying out onto the steps of the veranda, I looked up to see a frightening wall of bunched up clouds that were tinged an eerie shade of yellowish green.

"The will o' the wisp," I muttered.

Rattling hailstones popped off the ground and whipped around in circles as the glaucous cloud wall grew darker. My ears popped during a sudden change in the air pressure. The wind shifted direction, and then died down. Suddenly, everything became very still.

Just as I was about to say that the storm had passed, the outdoor public "air-raid" siren sounded.

As it wailed in the distance, Nestor started to get concerned.

"We better take cover in the basement in case a tornado touches down... and sweeps all my painting money away. Where's Schaufler? He needs to take cover, too" Nestor shouted.

Taking one last glance at the ominous green sky, I hurried back inside and ran up the stairs to tell Molewhisker that the tornado warning had sounded. When I reached the hallway, I heard the clicking of an old manual typewriter. Heading to where the sound was coming from, I found the old gritter sitting at a desk in his small library, calmly typing something while listening to the strains of some weird music on an antique Philco floor model console tube radio (that, surprisingly, sounded better than my parents' new Hi-Fi). As he continued to peck away in his tatty bathrobe, I warned him to stay away from the window. Just then, a strong gust of wind that smelled like freshly mowed grass whistled through the opened window and blew a couple of sheets of typed paper behind an old Kelvinator chest freezer. Amid all that was going on, I couldn't help but to wonder why he… why anyone… would have a horizontal meat freezer humming in their upstairs den?

CHAPTER IV
IMPALANADA

I emerged from the cellar hatchway carrying a can of gasoline and walked over to where Molewhisker was pacing about in his scruffy bathrobe. It had been two years since I was last in his damp basement, having taken cover during a tornado warning. Although a couple of small twisters were reported to have touched down in a nearby county, the only damage caused by the storm in our small town on that day was from some fallen tree branches.

The dirty canvas tarp had been removed from the old Packard Henney Hearse hot rod that was parked in the gravel driveway. Wearing his black leather jacket over a "Blue Cheer" *Vincebus Eruptum* tee that was tucked into light brown corduroy jeans, Zerrill walked around the street machine, stroking his facial scruff while examining the customized metalwork. As I poured some gas into the tank, I could smell the wet reek of chewing tobacco over my shoulder.

Molewhisker's rheumy eyes widened. "I hear it guggling."

"I dig the lettering – like hot licks," Zerrill remarked while gesturing to the flamboyant spectral green script that read, "Will O' The Wisp" on the hearse's streamlined matte black frame.

"The original motor was a Thunderbolt L-head eight cylinder that did 180 horses – the one for 51 – but this has a bit more giddy up. Runs like a scalded dog, boy. Still has the selective silent slushbox, though," Molewhisker pointed to the chrome skull stick shift knob.

"Enough rumpity-rump to get three speeding tickets in one night and still cross the Seventh Gate of Hell at midnight," Zerrill laughed, repeating something from an article that he had read in the local newspaper that was archived on microfiche.

Molewhisker spat some tobacco juice near one of the white-walled tires.

"Well, that's what the paper said – parts at least – a bunch of hobble-gosh… Just like when they call Johnny Marzetti mostaccioli on the school cafeteria lunch menu."

Zerrill peered into the narrow window to check out the wooden coffin that had been placed in the back of the hearse for decorative purposes.

"The Nu-3-Way side service feature – back in the day, when she was still stock – that must have made it a lot easier to load and unload caskets. Eliminated the need for several pallbearers… if you didn't mind some dirty fingernails, that is." Zerrill gave Mister Schaufler a cryptic glance and waited for his reaction, as if his ambiguous last statement had some hidden meaning.

Either Molewhisker wasn't in the mood for any perplexing brevity or he simply didn't have a ghost of a notion as to what Zerrill was referring to. Either way, whatever he meant (if anything?) about "dirty fingernails" was totally ignored.

"It also had a regular back door," Molewhisker said as he struggled to climb inside the hot rod. When he turned the key to the left of the steering wheel, the rumble of the engine idle put a smile on his angular face as he gnawed on his raisiny chew.

"It ain't no turnkey hot rod", he shouted over the exhaust gargle. "And, like I said, feller, she ain't for sale neither."

Zerrill had recently returned from California "to do some more noodling," but also promised a friend that was interested in old hot rods that he would check out Schaufler's "Body Buggy." The funny thing was that he only found out about the coffin car from me a day ago, and at the time he didn't seem particularly interested. But then he read about Maxx racing through the back road passageways back in the 1950s. According to the paper, during his mad dash in the funeral coach, he had received three speeding tickets. Molewhisker said that this "whopper of a tale" was right up there with some others written about him over the years, but he didn't elaborate any further.

When we left the house, I heard Zerrill mumble, "Yeah, something isn't quite right."

"Do you mean his really long mole whisker?" I asked.

"What long mole whisker?" he replied. "Oh, you mean that horrid dark thing sprouting from the mole on his chin – I half expected a spider to be dangling from that sucker."

We both laughed at this joke for a second, but then my mind swirled with darker thoughts.

I didn't tell Zerrill about any of the other stuff that had happened to me at Molewhisker's house, mainly because I didn't want him to tell my mom. If I had mentioned anything about these things – such as the *othering* – my parents would certainly consider this to be the product of a very disturbed mind and would take me to see a shrink. If the doctor diagnosed these things as psychotic episodes, they might stick me in the loony bin and throw away the key. Besides, I hadn't had any of these weird experiences in a couple of years and felt like I was completely free of being pulled down by the undertow of some mental disorder that had tormented me in the past.

Maybe this was because I hadn't seen Molewhisker in all that time? Even though the idea of him having a horizontal freezer in his little upstairs den bothered me, I still didn't think that he was some kind of bone-jacker that cannibalized dead bodies by slicing them into thin strips that he drank in his lime Kook-aid. I had stopped trying to figure out his twisted inner workings a long time ago, even though I knew – as did Zerrill – that something wasn't quite right about the scraggy hunched figure with the meat wagon speedster.

The thing that bugged me the most was the image of the tiny dolphin that I had seen in his (other) backyard. This was mainly because of the identical looking one that appeared to be fused to the earlobe of the pickled mermaid in the carnival's freak show exhibit.

I had gone back to see the so-called "Mermaid of Poseidia" twice again, and each time – despite all the naysayers – I stood there mesmerized by the shriveled body floating in a blue colored solution. I gazed intently at her "exotic physiognomy" as the professor rolled on with his strange people spiel. While checking out her distinctive features, a host of disturbing possibilities invaded my mind. But, even with her jumble of hair that was whiter than snow, and those silky white lashes that contrasted with her sunken golden eyes, I always found myself drawn to the dolphin. The closer I looked, the more it took me back to that night when I saw one that was seemingly alive. I needed to stop coming back to see the exhibit. It was the one thing that stood in the way of any imagined normalcy.

I guess that I had finally learned to apply myself – something that my father had urged me to do ever since I can remember

– because my grades improved dramatically in Junior High, so much so that I made the honor roll. All of the subjects came easy to me except for history, ironically enough. The higher the marks that I got, the more hair I got to keep. That was the agreement that I had with my parents, although there was nothing in the handshake about wandering around town in a soiled tie-dye tee and faded tattered jeans.

As Ollie continued with his old tricks – the latest being replacing stop signs with green "GO" signs – and Kelby remained fascinated with his paperbacks about mythical places, I was secretly ripping off vending machine products with my trusty doohickey. After taking a chance and inserting it into a unit at a local snack shop (mainly out of curiosity), when my selection dispensed and I also got the doohickey back in the change return, I never looked back. I had now used the super slug hundreds of times and always came out a winner, no matter how much the products cost. Mainly I used it on cigarette machines in order to sell the free packs to people at a slightly lower price.

The "king coin" had become even more baffling to me over the past couple of years. I could not damage its super-flexible material. When bent or scratched, it repaired itself, mimicking the blood-clotting process of biological systems, only much faster. If I forgot to hide the thing, it became so dark that it couldn't be seen – with all visible light somehow being absorbed into the material. I probably should have shown it to my father, or someone, but I was making good money. Plus, I could use the packs of smokes as bargaining chips in High School to avoid getting pummeled in bombardment, or when at the mercy of the upper class dicks in the hallways. Not to mention being tortured while required to do minute-long "dead cockroaches" in my gym shorts under a lit cigarette.

Even though I was making bank, I never spent a nickel on a pack of Wackies. All of the boxes from 1967-1968 were long gone, and I no longer cared about the "Gadzooka" bubblegum die-cut that I was planning to paste onto Mrs. Rutledge's rear car bumper ("Annoy your teacher. Chew gum in class".) What I once thought was funny, now seemed idiotic. About a year ago I placed all of the cards into a shoebox and stuck it inside my bedroom closet.

I was holding on tight while bouncing on the back seat of a yellow Yamaha Enduro dirt bike that Zerrill was driving on a rugged trail. Passing disemboweled autos with deflated tires in the back-yard disarray of a row of begrimed houses, we were headed towards the strip mine to negotiate its steep climbs and other challenging terrain. After hitting a bone-jarring dip that nearly threw both of us off the bike, the crazy bastard regained control and revved the throttle to get us up the muddy incline. Minutes later, we were zigzagging through the woods until he downshifted to slow down while pointing to a large abandoned brick building in the middle of a large field that could be seen through the trees.

"Let's take a gander," he shouted.

He veered off the trail and headed across the field towards the derelict structure whose rectangular façade had been painted with graffiti under a series of horizontal broken windows.

"This used to be a poor farm – a dumping ground for social outcasts," Zerrill explained.

"Orphans, epileptics, vagrants... and piss-smelling alkies. Even the severally mentally retarded that were chained to their beds. Pretty medieval, huh?"

Tucked away in a grove of trees were the remnants of a brick shed.

"That's what's left of the bug house where the clothes of new residents were boiled. Somewhere out there is a potter's field where paupers' corpses were buried in unmarked graves. Kind of like what an Order associated with the Black Penitents did centuries ago in Europe – providing burial services for the poor who were found dead. This abandoned rural almshouse is indicated on another map that the Epigraphic Society I belong to recently acquired."

While Zerrill continued to check out the structure, I pointed to an elderly woman a short distance away from us who was dressed in 1950s farm overalls and had her face shielded by a wide-brimmed straw hat. The lady had just placed a rusted old red gas canister in the middle of the field that contained numerous shallow pits.

"What's she doing?" I nudged Zerrill.

He raised his eyes.

"Yeah, I wonder?"

He pulled out a copy of a crudely drawn map and slid his index finger to a particular spot.

"Just getting rid of some junk, I guess."

"What's up with all those holes?" I asked.

"Lots of digging for something. Could be people looking for mason jars filled with gold dollars that were buried by someone who never had the chance to spend them... or maybe the person only hid one jar but forgot where. That, or rabbits burrowing," he said while lowering his voice in case someone else was listening.

Soon, we were back on the dirt trail heading to a strip mine that was once owned by "The Egyptian Coal and Mining Company." Before we got there, I asked Zerrill to make a quick stop at an old house that Nestor had recently inherited after his grand-mother died. Similar to the other rural decay along the trail, its dull chipped paint was crawling with ivy and the windows were shaded with dingy fabric. The broken rain gutters above the rot-ted sills contained pieces of the rusted mast of a rooftop antenna.

Parked in the weed-choked backyard behind a rickety fence were several off-road bikes, including a Rupp Roadster, a Honda Mini-Trail 50 and a shiny purple Taco. Individual stick-on mar-quee letters above the basement's outdoor bulkhead read:

NESTORE

As we were about to head down the cinder block steps, a cou-ple of teenage dirt bike enthusiasts emerged from the cellar entrance. The bigger of the two finger-flicked his friend in the Adam's apple while warning him that if he ever left him alone down there again with that creepy zit-farm, instead of zapping him, he would punch his lights out.

"Do you know this guy?" Zerrill asked me with a funny, taut expression.

"Yeah, he's cool," I said.

As we entered the makeshift store, a couple of kids were sift-ing through a cardboard box of candy bars that were dimly-lit by a couple of naked bulbs hanging from bulges in the ceiling's mildewed paint. The cramped space had a musty smell that was made worse by swipes of putrid mop water on the concrete floor.

"Floor's slippery when it's wetted." I recognized Nestor's voice coming from behind a sump pump. "Did you see that spe-cial on sodie?"

Zerrill was having trouble trying to muzzle a laugh as he checked out the meager stock. There was a Coleman ice chest with assorted cans of soft drinks floating in the slushy water. On the wooden shelf above this I saw the cartoon hillbilly on the familiar label of bags of Ozark BBQ potato chips. Near an antique brass cash register were a few sundry items, including hard candy in Nestor's dead grandmother's bowls of Christmas-themed Spoad china, old Bazooka bubble gum, and individual cigarettes priced at a penny each. There were even a few Stray Dogs in their King Coney foil wrappers placed next to a cloudy jar of Vlasic gherkins.

Nestor appeared in a clean white uniform that had his "Short Stop" nametag pinned to it.

"Hey, it's Addison… our one millionth customer," the gangly dweeb uttered. "You guys are riding on the trail, huh? So, how do you like my latest enterprise? Still got a long way to go, but I'm getting there. Plenty of room to expand."

"This is a great way to make king coin from all the dirt bikers going to the strip mine." I patted him on the back. "Maybe get some linoleum and mouse traps going —"

"Location. Location. Location," he grinned like the cat that ate the canary.

He set the mop down and motioned for us to follow him to a rusted old "Sno-Master" shaved ice machine.

"This is the schnitz," he beamed. "Makes rainbow icees… and a soft swirl machine will be coming soon. Sheeeit!"

Seeing that Zerrill was about to lose it, I grabbed a can of root beer from the cooler and placed it near the bulky register.

"Isn't King Coney suds, but a lot better price." He scratched his acne while ringing it up. "And seeing how you're the one millionth customer, have a couple of Oreos on the house."

I didn't say anything to Zerrill, but the real reason that I wanted to check out the place was to see if I could strike up a deal with Nestor by selling him goods for a reduced price (that

I could obtain for free by using the doohickey in vending machines). There could be a hefty profit for both of us, but I would have to wait until we were alone to hit him up with my proposition. Of course, I wouldn't tell him anything about the super slug – just that I knew a way to get discounted stuff.

A few days later I had a chance to talk to Nestor during a short break from his shift at King Coney. I told him about my idea of providing him with some tasty stuff for his little business at great prices. He wondered how I thought that I could find cheaper prices on things than he had while scrounging around town, but then remembered Ollie's pocketful of slugs. Would I be getting these products for free he asked? I told him not to worry about it. After thinking it over for a minute, he agreed to give it a try, but winked that he didn't have any knowledge about merchandise illegally taken from vending machines. Before I left (without a handshake), he asked me about the guy who was with me the other day.

I said that his name was Zerrill Sand, and that he was once again visiting from California. He was in town looking for stuff that's not supposed to be here. Out-of-place artifacts he called these things, and they might be the reason that the area is called Little Egypt. I further explained that the people who he was involved with have maps that they are using to search for traces of an advanced culture that arrived in the Americas long before Columbus. Meriwether Lewis might have known about this, and it could be the reason that our own government murdered him. Recently, he had told me that these "sun-filled ones" might have originated in the last place that anyone would ever have guessed.

Just then the manager approached and handed Nestor a mop.

"Out-of-place artifacts," Nestor said as he played with his complexion. "Do you mean stuff that should be in a museum, and worth a lot of money?"

"Zerrill thinks that a notable museum would pay big time just to keep them hidden. But, hell yeah, we're talking king coin."

"Verrrry interesting," Nestor replied, doing a pretty good job of impersonating the catchphrase of Arte Johnson's Nazi soldier character on *Rowan and Martin's Laugh-In*.

ᔕᕼ

I quietly laid my bike down behind some thin white birches and slowly approached a junkyard school bus that had been deteriorating for decades on an overgrown lot near the abandoned dairy processing plant. I had run into Chooch earlier in the day and he had asked me to deliver a few packs of Kools to the old hulk tonight. He told me to come by myself, and further instructed me to tap on the rear with three sets of three knocks.

Taking a couple of steps closer, I thought that I heard muffled voices within, but since all of the windows were blocked out, I couldn't see anything. The rusty relic that had been put out to pasture not far from ShadowCrest now looked even more foreboding with its gray coat of paint illuminated by a gibbous moon in the cloud-mottled sky. After summoning up the courage, I gave the password knocks and waited by one of its flat tires in the tall weeds to see what would happen. Moments later, the door squeaked open and I was greeted by a lady who looked like a beautiful witch.

"Welcome on board the Notilus," she said with a slight huskiness in her voice.

"I'm Trixie."

Draped in a dark black bohemian-style dress with lace crochet and bell trumpet sleeves, she seemed to float back up the colorfully painted steps, leaving a lingering scent of patchouli, black currant and vetiver.

"Hi. Addison," I said with a nervous laugh. "Here with some smokes for Chooch."

"He's in the salon with Topo Gigo – getting supherbly high on a nodge of charas."

Sensing my unease, she gave me the once over with the faintest trace of a smile. I then followed the sound of her clunky wooden clogs through a beaded curtain.

"Well, it's not the Good Ship Lollypop… but it's a sweet trip anyway."

On the other side of the rattling beads, I could see that the rows of seats had been removed so that the bus could be converted into a plush stoner's pad. In the luminous haze, the centerpiece was a brass hookah set on a low Moroccan coffee table with decorative carvings that was placed on a hand-tufted oriental rug. Above this, a celestial inspired tapestry was attached to the ceiling. The walls were hung with posters whose ornate rubbery lettering and black light-responsive phosphorescent imagery were glowing vibrantly (I didn't hear a generator). The soft glimmer of churning lava lamps were reflected on embroidered cushions in turquoise, crimson, amethyst and tangerine. The more I looked, the more psychedelic iconography accosted my eyes: trippy rainbows, black stars and stealie logos in richly saturated colors.

Chooch was inhaling the pungent drifts of a chunk of hashish that had been placed on the tip of a bent safety pin under a glass. In the sputtering flames of candles dripping wax onto Pepsi bottles, he flashed his dingy teeth at me through the ghostly arabesques of smoke. Against the spectral colors of entopic-like blobs on the posters, he stood up and offered me a turn with the earthy vapors trapped under the glass.

"As you can see, the motto of our Notilus is Mobilis In Immobilis, and not just because of all the flat tires," Trixie winked.

Chooch coughed harshly after exhaling some fumes and gestured to the guy sitting next to him.

"Hey man, this is Topo Gigo, guitar player with Silver Cirkus. We call him that cuz he kind of looks like the Italian mouse on Ed Sullivan... at least when I'm high. He just brought back this dynamite Nepalese charas straight from Freak Street in Kath-fucking-mandu."

"Wow, polysyllabic cursing," Trixie giggled as she sat down on a black damask pouffe.

"I was hoping to score some Mad Honey, but it eluded me again," Topo said with a fatalistic tone.

With long, dark frizzy hair and John Lennon-inspired colored glasses, Topo was dressed the part of a rural town rocker. Under a sequined vest, he wore a tight black silk shirt with white amoeba-like designs, and his faded blue Levi's were emblazoned with counterculture patches.

"So... what do you think of the Notilus?" Chooch asked with a gruff voice. "It's a 39 International Harvester just like the Merry Pranksters have... but instead of a washing machine drum viewing thing, this baby's got a periscope taken from a Nazi midget submarine."

He walked towards the front of the bus and peered into the sight on a long steel tube that was wrapped in multicolored chiffon.

"We use this sucker to watch out for any bacon cruisers that might be lurking about. When it retracts, the old air conditioning unit that is mounted on the top disguises the scope. Too bad that Captain Nemo won't be joining us tonight in his leisure pad... once again," Chooch said while flicking a toggle switch before returning back to the hashish.

"Of course, the Pranksters' bus actually ran," Trixie teased Chooch while nibbling on a Triscuit cracker that was smeared with creamy peanut butter.

"Want some hash?" Chooch asked me.

"Cool, but I really can't hang long tonight," I replied. "I just wanted to make sure that you got your smokes." I reached into the pocket of my windbreaker and pulled out three packs of Kools.

"Are you sure?" Chooch frowned. "There's some gusto in the galley." He reached inside an ice chest and fished out a can of Stag. "We're going to hit SIU later for some killer pizza empanadas. Going to take my Impalanada and groove to some Quicksilver on the Philips. There will be flocks of college chicks milling about, and we can get some zigzags for giggle smoke at Mindwarp."

"And a proper chillum," Trixie added.

I chewed my knuckle while trying to decide what to do. If I went with them, I would definitely get home late and there would be a lot of explaining to do to my parents. Plus, who knows what might happen with a stoned two-fingered Chooch behind the wheel of a vehicle that hauled ass. On the other hand, if I went along for the ride, it would be a great opportunity to hang with some of the older crowd, including Trixie. I stole a glance at the alluring face that was watching me with an unwavering gaze while leaning against a florescent tapestry.

Thinking it over, I kept my eyes fixed on the swirling rainbow globules of the paraffin and oil mixture in the glass vessel's incandescent glow.

"Give me some of that jackal piss," Trixie's voice broke my thoughts. "I need something to wash down this cruddy Peter Pan."

"If you ever go again, let me know," I said while handing Chooch the cigarettes.

"We're going again tomorrow night," he burst out laughing. "See you manana for some empanadas in the Impalanada."

Before leaving, I paused to check out a painted bookshelf that contained a dozen or more copies of street comix. Quickly sifting through them, I saw titles that included, *ZAP, THE FABULOUS FURRY FREAK BROTHERS, YARROWSTALKS* and *JEET.*

Trixie looked up at me as I grabbed issue #1 of *JEET.*

"The Notilus's ever expanding library of mind expanding underground comix. That's Jeet, the anthropomorphic antics of the ribald Panzerschwein. Take it with you, but don't let it get over due or you'll have to pay me the fine," she said, doing a pretty good priggish librarian stereotype.

After handing me the cheap publication, she placed in my mouth a half-eaten peanut butter-laden Triscuit that she had just bitten into. I gulped dryly as her green eyes sparkled naughtily in the candlelight. Without saying a word, I followed in her wake of perfume as she passed through the bead curtain and opened the bus's back door. With the saliva-wet cracker still in my mouth, I stepped off the Notilus.

The atmosphere at night on "The Strip" near the campus of SIU in Carbondale was electrifying. It was my first time in a college town, and I eagerly took in the sights while riding in the back of Chooch's jacked up Tuxedo Black 1964 Chevy Impala.

Mobs of people had gathered around hip boutiques and sidewalk cafes. I saw a vegetarian restaurant called "Lettuce Inn" and a bar & grill named the "Purple Moose." Between these was a brightly lit "Mister Donut" whose logo was an orange mustachioed chap. Vibrant psychedelic graphics were posted to telephone poles, including Frank Zappa and Procol Harum concert posters along with the Grateful Dead's "Kaleidoscope." Political activists with megaphones competed for attention with the various street performers. As spirals of smoke rose from a popping joint of Michoacan that Chooch had rolled in strawberry flavored paper, passersby of student hangouts gave the thumbs-up to the Impala's rumbling engine.

Chooch's dirty waist-length hair hung from a puffed train engineer cap that bobbed up and down as he looked for a parking spot. Sitting next to him was Topo, with the Inca Silver Fender Telecaster that he had been strumming on his lap. With me in the back was Trixie, wearing a black cowl neck sweater and patchwork jeans. Even with her sparing use of makeup, she still looked like an erotic vamp with her beaded headband and other feminine touches. I could smell faint traces of violet leaf coming from her silken alabaster skin, especially during those sharp left turns that were becoming routine for the gung ho driver of the Impalanada.

The plan was to find a clay pipe for Topo's temple ball joss, and then to grab some empanadas.

"What's up with the dog head?" I asked, gesturing to all the people with a black dog head graphic on their maroon tee shirts.

Trixie would be attending SIU in the fall, so she was quick to provide the answer.

"It's a Saluki. The royal dog of ancient Egyptian nobility and the mascot of the University's athletic teams, the Salukis. I just read about this in the student paper, *The Daily Egyptian*."

Earlier during the drive, I had mentioned to Trixie that I was the kid at the house that night years ago who didn't jump into her car when she and her friends were scared to death by the creature under the bridge. With a big shit-eating grin on my face, I asked her if she knew what the thing really was?

"It was Ogilvie," she calmly replied.

Turns out that Ogilvie was the last name of a neighbor of hers who regularly went frog gigging by the railroad tracks under the bridge. She said that she just wanted to "scare the bejesus out of the girls" by pretending that the man in the ridiculous looking outfit was a hellish demon.

It was just a little Halloween prank of hers – a trick – like her namesake, she said with a mischievous grin, adding that she had probably done the girls' parents a big favor by validating the as-inine dogma that they had been spoon-feeding them from birth. The Playboy bunny getup was also a deliberate act – her way of scoffing at their sexual hang ups and the eternal damnation that they both feared after balling the quarterback (in the missionary position, of course). She said that she could only imagine the hell-bound ticket that they thought would be issued by their God if they had engaged in some of the "Zodiac Positions" with Biff, or whoever it was that caused them to cream their jeans.

Her last statement had caused Topo to turn around to add his stoner version of "Family Life and Sex Education."

"The more dirty the sex... the more guilt... and the more desire to try it. But, it's no big deal. Just do what Cleopatra did and shove crocodile poop into the fun tunnel so that you don't get pregnant. That or use the loophole... or, hell, blame it on a public toilet seat."

"Stick with your hashterbation, Topo," Trixie had playfully smacked him on the back. "When it comes to the ways of the quivering quim, we don't need any more wisdom from masters of the obvious."

"Did you guys know that Cleopatra lived closer in time to the moon landing than to the building of the pyramids?" I blurted out, hoping to change the subject.

"Bullshit! Really?" Chooch was totally blown away. "I'm gonna use that in a money bet. Cleopatra lived closer to the moon than to the pyramids," he repeated to himself before recovering his earlier train of thought. "I hate it when Mooch says things like bloody axe wound when talking about Cherrie's vadge."

"I've never seen Cherrie," I said to Chooch.

"None of us have," Topo laughed.

"That's because she's busy working. When she's not dancing – she operates a road grader. A fucking Caterpillar, dude." Chooch emphasized this last line as if hoping to put an end to any further speculation about the tangibility of his girlfriend.

"Zodiac Positions?" I mumbled, confused as to what astrology had to do with the conversation?

Trixie cracked up when I blushed upon seeing the twelve different Kama Sutra-like methods of sexual union depicted on the "Zodiac Positions" poster. Its colorful phosphor inks popped from the buzzing tubes in the head shop's black light room, as did numerous other black-flocked prints in the tubular ultraviolet glow that was also eerily fluorescing on us. The room smelled of sandalwood and strong body odor. Not wanting Trixie to think that I was the culprit of this funk, I snuck away from the vibrant phantasmagoria only to find myself stepping into another section whose psychedelic décor was even more visually stimulating.

Pulsing apparitions of acid chimeras appeared in rapidly blinking strobe lights along with loops of trippy montages that were projected onto a wall. These were accompanied by wah-wah petal distortions combined with the monotonous drone of an Indian sitar. Swirls, zigzags and spirals were flashing everywhere as "Mindwarp" pushed the velvet envelope.

Feeling dizzy, I made my way from the luminous phosphene splotches into a partitioned area where a couple of bookcases were filled with street comix of the underground revolution along with cheap newsprint pamphlets that were also designed for a hippie audience. The socio-political themes included comical graphics of taboo sexual fantasies and the hedonistic lifestyles in skeevy drug-infested Haight-Ashbury. There were also a couple of issues of *JEET*, with a roll of outrageous armadillos on the cover. In the middle of all this cultural upheaval was a thin little novel onto which someone had stuck a paper label that read: DON'T READ THIS.

The book was entitled *In Watermelon Sugar* and from what I could gather the story took place in a post-apocalyptic commune where the sun was a different color everyday. Thinking that I might impress Trixie, I took it up to the counter and fumbled for a quarter.

An aged hippie-looking dude with a sprawling smoky gray beard picked up the book and examined the cover through funky tortoiseshell glasses.

"What's that strange-looking thing in your pocket? It looks like something that I've never seen before," the thin figure in the poncho said.

"What do you mean?" I asked while glancing down and feeling the outer part of my pocket to make sure that the doohickey wasn't doing something unusual.

"It's something that Fred dug up at the Forgotten Works," he added.

"Who's Fred?" I asked, thinking that the old freak was high on dope.

"It's from the book," he replied while adjusting his spectacles. He then leaned towards me with a mock psychotic grin and whispered, "I don't care about watermelon bricks made from black soundless sugar, but I wish that we had singing tigers that would eat my parents."

I ignored the non-mutated beatnik and grabbed the novel, taking it into a room where I thought that the others might be. A Red Krayola tune was blasting over the JBLs. Bobbing to the beat was Chooch in his locomotive hat. In the scented glimmer of pillar candles, he and the others were looking for a chillum among the drug-related paraphernalia in a long glass case that included prismatic bongs, metal pipes, stash containers, roach clips, and flavored rolling papers.

Just as I walked up, Topo found the clay pipe.

I presented Trixie with *In Watermelon Sugar,* but warned her not to read it.

Chooch had been laughing uncontrollably at everything that he saw along the way when we brought the empanadas back to his car. However, he was now completely silent while seated behind the wheel, holding up the crescent-shaped pie to the dome light while staring with intense fascination at the darker perforations along one edge. As he continued to do so, I glanced over at Trixie for an explanation for this rather strange behavior.

"He dropped some Sunshine," she glowered while picking out tiny chunks of sausage from the flaky turnover's cheese and pizza sauce filling.

"He's grokking on the crust patterns," Topo added.

"Have you guys ever checked out the patterns on an Oreo?" I asked.

Taking a bite from my empanada, I glanced out the window at the students ambling along the sidewalks until I nearly choked on the stuffing. I had to do a double take, but there was no doubt about it. My mother was across the street, sitting at a table on the patio of the Purple Moose bar. She was alone, but there were two glasses of wine on the tablecloth, with one being placed at the seat across from her. Even more surprising was what she was wearing: a psychedelic orange mandarin collar mini dress with sheer black pantyhose. She also had her hair down and was wearing more makeup than I'd ever seen her put on before.

I quickly slouched down in the seat so that she wouldn't see me hanging with this group, especially Chooch whose dilated pupils remained transfixed on the pouch of fried dough.

"I'm totally freaking out – it's my mother – in the orange dress," I uttered to Trixie.

She peered out the window and quickly saw the woman that I was referring to.

"Whoa, momma's letting it all hang down. Shake loose that hair, lady. Looking like the hot librarian... Queen of the Dewy-Decimal system. Good for her –"

"Shush," I cringed.

"Shush – that's her line," Trixie laughed.

My dad's latest thing was grilling lamb shish kabobs in his special marinade on the backyard Weber, something that he now insisted on doing every Friday evening. This all began when my mom brought up the idea of using the "rolling campfire" to make something called "Armadillo Eggs" from a recipe that was in the *Boy Scout Handbook*. It was little things like this – his blocking her "left-field" dinner whims– that first made me wonder if my parents were having marital problems. There were no loud arguments or even the constant bickering that I had heard at some of my friends' houses, but I still sensed some distance between them. The main bone of contention seemed to be academic freedom. The more she needled him about his unbending stance on traditionally accepted accounts of American history – as opposed to Zerrill's more controversial views (including sweeping rewrites of what he believed to be textbook lies) – the more he retreated to his open flames on the patio grill, squirting lighter fluid as if he had some deep atavistic drive for fire. This wasn't only on Fridays, but now on Wednesdays as well, with brats and sauerkraut. Watching these silly games was funny at first, but, now, having seen my mother at a bar with someone else, I was really worried that things were going south.

As the briquettes erupted into big licking flames, my mom was at the kitchen sink trying to scrub a smeared ink club stamp off of her wrist.

"Is this damn thing not water soluble?" she uttered while getting more frustrated.

"What's that?" I asked.

"Oh, an ink stamp from this place I was at last night. It was anti-poetry night. College students reading the ingredients listed on boxes of cereal, if you can believe that. I guess if you smoke enough of that jazz cabbage – as Zerrill calls it – anything seems artistic."

"What?"

"I got roped into going to this seminar with Zerrill. It wasn't by the epigraphic organization that he belongs to, but some Midwestern Society of Antiquities. Since the topic was out-of-place artifacts, your father wasn't interested."

"Oh… so he saw you then," I said, a bit relieved.

"What do you mean?" She gave me a confused look.

"Nothing." I was suddenly mindful that I wasn't supposed to have seen her there.

Maybe I was reading more into this than there really was. Mom was just good naturedly teasing dad's skeptical nature when it came to these fanciful beliefs of Zerrill's. And, for his part, the guy in the canary-colored bowling shirt just preferred charring his favorite foods over flames rather than pretending to enjoy his wife's fun camping ideas with goofy names that were designed for Boy Scout troops.

"What was the show about?"

"Anachronistic artifacts. Or so they believe. Relics discovered that are too advanced for the time period of a certain culture… such as an electric light bulb in ancient Egypt… or this pre-Columbian Viking coin dated from the eleventh century that was allegedly unearthed from a Native American Indian settlement. To his credit, even Zerrill dismissed most of the stuff. Except for this map… What was it? Oh, yeah, Piri Reis it's called – that apparently shows the coastline of Antarctica in pre-historic times before it was covered with ice. That's what he wanted to see. Afterwards, we had a glass of wine and – well, now – I'm permanently marked unless I can foil this thing with nail polish remover. Do you think you can bring me some? And a cotton pad… before old charcoal nails back there incinerates that retched lamb."

She sniffed the air and wrinkled her nose has if she smelled something rotten.

"What's his seasoning? Digitaria sanguinalis?"

Seeing my puzzled look, she pointed towards the backyard.

"Crab grass," she mock-scowled while playfully elbowing me in the side.

"Next week let's have those Armadillo Eggs," I said, wanting to show her that I wasn't picking sides in this curious tiff.

"Well, I was planning on making Yakamish," she said while scratching her head. "Just kidding."

It took several years for brand-name acid to trickle into our sleepy little town, but once the psychedelic revolution arrived from Babylon by the Bay and the Midwest dullsville was transformed into a prairie wonderland, there was no shortage of those paying the two dollars for the aluminum foil-wrapped tabs. As those who were bored out of their gourds explored the 'beyonds' of sanity, the "Oh, golly gee" folk were unsure what to make of the recent reports in the local paper's Police Blotter:

An Honor Roll student was hauled off to jail after speaking incoherently while seemingly entranced by the swirling moth trails around a streetlight. A freckled face Junior High girl was questioned and released to her parents after attempting to create an avant-garde work of art on a public playground by spreading glistening Smucker's jam onto the monkey bars. And a couple of hicks were arrested for pre-dawn trespassing while duck hunting in the garage of the town's gas station. Making a crazy situation even crazier, they were found making mallard grunt calls and aiming shotguns while seated in an aluminum fishing boat that they had placed on the oil-encrusted concrete.

Worst of all, though, were several high-school field trip mishaps that occurred when over fifty per cent of those on the bus with signed permission slips dropped acid. With no planetariums to trip out on, the first outing was the Amish experience. As the class petted animals and looked at crude tools, a group of Amish youth asked some of the bad seed types if they had a spare joint that they could sell them for when they got a chance to take a break from their chores. Instead of firing up a doobie, one of the heads handed them (for free) several hits of "White Lightning" LSD, explaining that it would be a far better way to enjoy the panorama of patchwork fields and geometric quilt patterns. The kid then said that he expected them to write reports "by the feeble glow of propane lamps" on the Owsley experience. Smiling appreciatively, the group of bearded bowl cuts returned to their much-publicized traditional family values at the roadside stands. Later that afternoon, after a sample of shoofly pie, telltale signs of tripping balls Amish youth style were evident by all the out of control horse and buggies on the backcountry roads. Because these ungrateful doofs fessed up over their cornmeal mush breakfast that the "urbanites" had tricked them into eating the devil's candy, no classes from our school were ever invited back to the tucked away idyllic village where God hates rubber.

The second field trip where things didn't go exactly as planned was at the Meramec caverns in the Missouri Ozarks. Once the doses of Orange Sunshine started to take effect, a dozen or so kids flipped out after straying from the well-lighted walkways in the system of limestone passageways. They were looking for Jesse James' hidden gold (to some it was Tom Sawyer and Huckleberry Finn's lost hoard), and scores of rangers had to be called in to locate these miserably babbling souls who were terrified by the insectoid faces under the olive green Smoky Bear caps. The bus arrived back at the school six hours late – minus three bummers that had to be hospitalized – and all future requests to the "melting and churning" tourist attraction were politely declined.

I wasn't at the third outing where things really got out of control, but since this took place at Abe Lincoln's home in Springfield, Illinois, my father was. Kelby was also there, and he provided me with the details. This time Pink Owsley and cheap vodka were involved. When some of the more wacked out students found out that the president with humble beginnings (and obscure past) wasn't born in Illinois, they went into a rage and proceeded to trash the place. They destroyed antique chairs, clocks and a sewing basket. When the unruly few were escorted back to the bus, they witnessed the elderly driver helping himself to the drumsticks in the Kentucky Fried Chicken buckets.

Being that it was in Kentucky that Lincoln was said to have been born, in their highly enlightened state, they sprayed the old fellow with "Halt" dog repellent and yanked the toupée from his head. Then they began to hurl pieces of "Colonel Cluck" at the tour guides who were gathering up the splintered mahogany. Needless to say, that was the last time that any class from our school got to set foot inside the National Historic Site with the quaint green shutters.

Back in town, word got out that that Bosworth gave his small police force orders to arrest any kids that appeared to be mystified by the emboss on popular chocolate cookies with creamy fillings. The paranoia among the acidheads increased when other rumors like this spread, including the belief that common electrical junction boxes were actually police cameras being used to document the town's drug-induced madness. After the kids destroyed some of these units, people went without power for days.

At the height of the LSD panic, the parents of one teen called to inform the cops that their son was calmly interacting with the cartoon menagerie on a cardboard box of ice cream cones. This was yet another typical (and hilarious) article chronicled in the paper.

After reading another one of his paperbacks dealing with the supernatural, Kelby told me that he felt that all the negative happenings in our town were due to its close proximity to the leftover advanced technology of Atlantis. He compared it to the "Devil's Triangle" phenomenon in the Atlantic Ocean where numerous ships and planes had disappeared over the years as a result of some mysterious influence. The same unexplainable forces were at work here, he figured, and the 'nothing seems right' impressions that people were experiencing was the reason behind their sudden desire for altered states of consciousness.

I didn't tell Kelby that I had taken acid several times, mainly because each time it had no effect on me except for a little fuzziness in my head. Chooch was amazed at my tolerance to the stuff, and insisted on watching me swallow a whole tablet of "Black Owsley" in order to prove my immunity. After a couple of hours passed, I wasn't giggling at the shifting visages of leprechauns wearing propeller beanies in the moss on tree bark (like he was), and never experienced any "stained-glass torrents" or "curtains of delirium." I really didn't care either way. I had no problem with something that turned fried empanada dough into the canvas of a Hieronymus Bosch painting, but if the acid didn't work, so be it; I'd already had my fair share of vivid hallucinations in my non-partying state of mind.

Or maybe I had a completely different reaction to it? Over the past couple of weeks I had become increasingly agitated. However, this time it didn't seem like I was having the same kind of *othering* psychotic breakdowns. Instead, I felt very lethargic, like something was draining my battery. I was also very forgetful. Many restless nights were spent worrying about the holes in my memory. (Even those vivid recollections of my imaginary playmates were slipping away.) Granted, for the most part, these were little things of no real consequence, such as the whole ancient eye-test thing, which I couldn't remember if it involved distinguishing one flying bird from a pair? A more recent example of these blank spots involved the park rangers who were looking for those students who had blundered off the walkway while on Sunshine. Were they wearing olive green Smoky Bear caps, or miner-style hard hats? None of these things were important, but it still bothered me. It was as if pieces of my mind had been removed.

As a way of releasing tension before going to bed one night, I was sitting at the desk in my bedroom, spinning the doohickey coin by flicking it vertically with the tip of my index finger.

When the last rotation fell off the edge of the desk and rolled across the carpeted floor, my black cat, Midnight Meringue, pounced on it. Instead of toying with it further, though, she hissed and quickly backed away with a bushy tail. Rising from the chair, I noticed that the flattened surface of the thing had suddenly taken on a strange luminosity.

Getting down on my knees, I picked up the doohickey, expecting to see the reflection of the lone streetlight on our block. Instead, like one of those visual perception puzzle illusions, my brain struggled to process the confusing mishmash of shapes, colors and sizes until it finally registered that what I had been looking at in sharp relief the whole time was an extraordinary specimen of the feminine physique. With my perception now adjusted to this oddity, I quickly recognized the startling features of the woman as that of the "Mermaid of Poseidia" – only, now, in the vividly realistic display of the object, her gorgeously sirenic presence was very much alive.

Reclined in glaucous webbing, her strikingly pale white skin was clothed with swirling violet wisps that adhered to parts of her body (where need be) like miniature cloudlets. Instead of her upper torso being fused with a scaly fishtail, a pair of flawless, shapely legs adjusted position. Snow-white wavy tresses changed colors with subtle distinctions in a curious spectrum while the mysterious pigmentation of her almost inhuman countenance was contrasted by eyeshades that suddenly rolled back like jeweled tidewater to reveal an extreme close-up of her bright golden-hazel iris.

Over this richly glistening eye, unrecognizable blueprint typography appeared along with a flurry of slightly darker golden symbols that morphed into even more complex graphic puzzles. After this enchanted gaze winked at 'me', I heard a pleasant humming sound as her earlobe could be seen with a tiny dolphin performing playful aerial tricks in a spiral around the delicate white flesh.

The doohickey's perplexing outer layers re-appeared for a second, with a series of smaller diameter discs encircling the larger central one displaying scenes of the captivating figure engaged in numerous unfathomable activities. (Things that my mind was unwilling to accept?)

As if responding to my not-so-pure thoughts, after the meager 'cloud-suit' dissipated back into a violet container, the woman's ghostly pale naked curves pirouetted through coalescing swatches of resplendent material until she was fitted in an intricately appliqued greenish-silver metallic swathing. With her fingers alone, she peeled back a layer of 'air' in the closet as if it were a glossy page in a magazine, or as if the dazzling fabrics in her wardrobe were but a vibrant mirage.

Inexplicably, she was now standing in another area, facing a replica of herself that duplicated even the slightest bodily motion. If this 'other her' was some kind of mirror, oddly enough, the reflection wasn't reversed. After considering her new eye embellishments, she stuck her slender fingers into an achromic opening in a luminous cobalt-blue mosaic and selected from the row of tubes an ultra-thin prismatic rod. As she casually inserted this into an almost invisible orifice in the middle of her elongated forehead, a shiny black slit suddenly appeared on the 'vanity-twin' that rapidly expanded into a vibrantly realistic display that focused sharply on something that caused the woman to take notice.

What she was gazing at with intense interest was something in the soybean field behind Molewhisker's house. It was an early winter's morning, and a light frost covered the ploughed earth. In the hazy greyness of wood smoke, a small child dressed in a cowboy outfit was curled in the fetal position on a piece of torn cardboard. His arm was wrapped around an antique rifle.

As the woman swiped the bleak imagery on the screen blank, a freaky albino gentleman with an inscrutable visage appeared. In the suffused glow of cobalt blue lighting, the uninspired figure was impeccably dressed in the boxy abstraction of a black formal tailcoat. In his rigid stance he was balancing a tray with a thin crystalline thermos of orange juice and a tray of iced cinnamon rolls. I had seen this stodgy butler figure with the upturned nose before, only, this time, with his jacket and starched vest; he wasn't on vacation in the tropics. He bowed before backing up with the loaded tray, but while doing so his image became distorted, with the frozen layers of the chromatic aberration resembling a wild piece of modern art.

My heart fluttered as I suddenly felt an abundance of electricity surge through my body. This must have been something that I accidently triggered with the doohickey, I guessed, because instead of peering at the stunning visual aesthetics of the interference pattern on its surface, I was now experiencing the surroundings as if I was actually there in person. I could distinctly hear the chirping of a few birds, and smell the furrowed dirt in the frosty patches of the soybean field. As I inhaled this hoary scenery, I could also perceive everything that was going on in my bedroom. I was coexisting in two places at the same time, and couldn't tell if one was more real than the other. Before I had time to panic at the thought that I might be trapped in this split reality, several things happened in rapid succession.

From the corner of my eye, I saw something moving that was almost beyond description. Floating like a gleaming soap bubble in total silence just above the ground was a single person capsule-like transport. Seated upon the padded recliner inside the object's contoured translucent metallic casing was the lady with the slanted golden-hazel eyes and wavy snow-white hair. She had a quizzical look on her alabastrine face that I could discern through viewing panels that pulsed with minute luminous graphics.

Hurrying along behind this extraordinary conveyance was the butler-figure with the wooden expression. He appeared to be carrying a flexible mask that he waved for the woman to see.

Startled by the sheer strangeness of bio-morphic protrusions that unfolded like shimmering wings on the mercurial envelope

bounding the form of the woman, the child who had been sleeping in his cowboy getup leaped to his feet. While doing so, he
grabbed the antique firearm that was placed next to the cardboard mat. Getting a better look at the kid's facial features, he
looked like a young Chooch (or was it Mooch?).

In the same instant that the metallic sheathing took on the
appearance of the dreary brown surroundings, there was a loud
pop from the rifle barrel. For an instant, a blinding white flash
turned the dismal overcast morning into a bright sunny day.
Having cloaked itself for only a split second, the capsule's translucent metallic skin erupted with an intolerable brightness in a
strangely silent manner. With a whirling storm of brilliant silver
filaments, the object quickly re-assembled itself, but the lady inside had either been blown out or ejected from her protective
shell. I saw part of her body cartwheeling across the field as she
managed to hold onto a malfunctioning shiny handlebar device.
A section of the capsule's forward viewing panes must have instantaneously transformed itself into a personal crash 'helmet',
because her head was now encased in a transparent globe that
was crowned with a radiant gloriole. When I turned back to the
interior of the object, I was horrified to see that her pale slender
legs were still pressed tightly against the lustrous curve in the
narrow housing. At the sight of the ragged limbs that remained
after the whoosh of evaporated blood, I nearly retched the metallic bile in my throat.

With a confused look, the boy in the singed cowboy hat took a
tentative step towards what remained of the woman. He paused
and stuck his hand out, trying to touch a series of unintelligible
heliotrope-colored symbols that were bouncing about erratical-
ly above her motionless body. When the faint coloration of the
nimbus encircling her head further dimmed into fuzzy shades of

grey before flickering out completely, the child took off running across the field, holding tightly onto the antique Winchester.

What at first appeared to be the seething chaos of an iridescent anthill, I soon realized was the mysterious self-healing process of a piece of debris. Next to this nacreous complexity, I saw the doohickey lying in a patch of burnt grass. It wriggled for a second before lifting itself up, and then began rolling unsteadily towards the dead body. The leaden sky returned and the unearthly hush was broken by the warble of birds.

The ruffling breeze smelled funny, as if the aroma of the cinnamon buns and the stench of the mildewed cardboard had somehow been greatly magnified. I flashed back to the phantom odors of sickening pumpkin pie filling and burnt cardboard from years ago. How could this strange miasma have lingered for so long, I wondered? Just then, one of the miniature noisy dolphins tail-walked across the blackened yard towards the butler who was standing at attention with his usual unemotional profile. The features of the mask that he was holding looked exactly like the woman's supremely beautiful pale complexion, except that it had protective deep blue-tinted eye shields and was coated with a semi-gloss sheen like a glistening lotion of some kind.

Before I had a chance to observe the terrible scene any further, I heard my mother walking down the hallway. With the sound of her footsteps, my confusing bilocation perception dissolved. I quickly pushed the blank doohickey under the bed as she tapped on my door and said, "Sweet dreams."

When the initial shock wore off, I decided that I should probably show the thing to my parents. I strongly doubted that what I had experienced was some kind of delayed effect from the few tablets of Owsley that I had recently taken – the so-called acid flashbacks. Psychological factors still had to be considered, although I had never heard of a mental disorder that manifested technological wonders that included sentient earrings and synthetic albino butlers. Once my dad had seen some of the mind-boggling stuff that the artifact was capable of doing, how could he call it a crock of shit? My biggest fear was that when it came time to demonstrate these things, the doohickey would play possum. I would be babbling about how it might be some kind of personal satellite, and it would just lie there like a piece of junk. On the other hand, if it decided to be responsive, it would certainly be a tremendous jolt to his belief system. Would he be able to handle such a radically different way of viewing the world? Be willing to expose what many would consider to be the proof of a past advanced civilization? If I just showed it to my mom, the second she saw anything strange, she would take it right to my dad. Plus, the woman wore fewer clothes than Barbarella. Who knows what kind of embarrassing activities the device captured? Even if I didn't tell my parents about it at this time, I no longer felt that such a marvelous, historically important item should be used as a vending machine slug – even if it was always returned in the change slot.

For over a week, I flicked, dropped, rolled, tapped and pressed the surface of the doohickey – all to no avail. Now seemingly dormant, I stuck it inside a balled up pair of clean socks and placed them in my lower dresser drawer.

It took a lot of afternoons of searching through the microfiche at the public library, but I finally managed to find the birth announcement of Russell Pitts, which was Chooch's real name. As

I had suspected would be the case, there was no mention of him having an identical twin.

I also found out from talking to some old timers that Chooch had an abusive alcoholic father who locked the little boy out of their trailer for the entire night when he misbehaved. He once stabbed him in the hand with a knife while reaching for a piece of stale bread at the dinner table, and made him chew and swallow an entire box of crayons after finding colored streaks on the wall.

The craziest story that I heard about his father sounded like an urban legend, although I was assured that it really happened. For thirty years, Mr. Russell worked on the kill floor at the stockyard where it was his job to use the stunner device on the cows that passed through a chute.

For his final cow, instead of using the stunbolt, he decided to put a bullet through its brain by using his prized 1895 Winchester Saddle Ring Carbine. While aiming at the animal from the catwalk above, he slipped and dropped the rifle. It discharged and the bullet struck him right between the eyes. He was killed instantly in the same manner that he had killed thousands of cows. In the only instance where a cow was taken back through the stockyard's one-way Blue Door, "Holy-e Cow" as the workers later named it, was trucked to a rich velvety pasture where it spent the rest of its life grazing.

This explained why little Russell had been sleeping in the soybean field and also where the antique firearm came from. It also made me feel saner as to certain things witnessed at Molewhisker's house and reaffirmed my belief that the doohickey had captured true events. I was curious to know if Chooch had, in fact, confabulated an identical twin brother, but needed to be careful not to cross any personal boundaries. I devised a plan to make sure, but it would require Chooch rendering himself unconscious. That was the easy part. The hard part would be – if he did indeed create Mooch – finding a tactful way to confront him about this.

A week later I returned to the Notilus bus where I finally remembered to ask the others about the sunken treasure movie that I had watched at Molewhisker's. When I found out that none of them had ever heard of it, I was further convinced that the enigmatic geezer had, for whatever reason, meant for me to 'find' the doohickey.

Later that night, Chooch, Topo and I drove to Carbondale to meet up with Trixie at a Rathskeller where "Three Stooges" shorts were projected onto the wall. After "scooping the loop", as the students called meandering up and down the streets where their hangouts were, we were going to grab some empanadas. Things didn't go as planned, though, due to campus unrest. Anti-war protesters caused street takeovers by the rowdy students who had already congregated on the sidewalks.

Trixie told us that things started to get out of hand during the "Pigs versus Freaks" softball game when hundreds of drunken spectators began publically urinating after realizing that no porta-potties had been provided for the event. From there things got worse when a few of the more radical demonstrators threatened to napalm a Saluki dog. Those 'peaceniks' that weren't protesting with a candlelight parade, were throwing bottles, rocks and cherry bombs. As the confrontations continued and the police presence increased, we decided to get out of Dodge, but not before Chooch and Topo smoked some Afghan hash out of a bazooka barrel hookah that some scruffy Vietnam vet had set up in a tightly packed parking lot.

Back at the Notilus, after Topo had passed out from "sucking the devil's dick" (taking a bong hit), Chooch crashed on a bean-bag thanks to a couple of Quaaludes that he washed down with some Harvey Wall Bangers. Once he was completely out, I was able to mark the flesh behind his left elbow with a tiny green dot from the felt tip marker that I had placed in my back pocket.

The next day, I told Chooch that I needed to meet with Mooch at the King Coney so that I could give him the few packs of Kools that I owed him. Sure enough, the burn out showed up pretending to be Mooch, which I found out with certainty after seeing the telltale mark.

I didn't get a chance to call Chooch out until we made another junket to SIU during the Christmas break when most students had left the campus. Out of the handful that chose to remain, some had requested Chooch's "Holidaze Santa Claus Blotter" acid, not wanting to take any chances that someone would spike the fruit brandies. Having glued on a bad fake white beard, the dealer wasn't about to play the Grinch, especially since the empanada stand had remained open.

Later that night, while the The Grateful Dead was blasting on the Philips, "Casey Jones was driving that train high on cocaine." Singing along, Chooch doffed his engineer's cap and trounced the accelerator of the Impala, using only his little finger to guide the heavily shaking steering wheel through the light snow flurries on the narrow roads. While joking for his "Rudolpho" with its well-polished Crager rims to go airborne, he was truly getting into the holiday spirit by shoveling cocaine up his nose and chugging peppermint schnapps.

As he snorted the Peruvian flake and downed the sugary liqueur, I took my chance and asked him if he thought that Mooch had gone to the drastic length of maiming his own fingers so as to remain identical twins? Instead of replying with some psycho-babble about not wanting to individuate himself, he looked over at me and said, "Do you want to hear some really crazy shit?"

"Okay," I replied, taking a sip of the syrupy stuff.

"There is no Mooch. I pretended to be him because I thought that I needed to," he mumbled.

"So you could get stuff for free?" I asked.

"It's way crazier than that, dude."

"Why, then?" I handed him back the pint bottle.

He pulled the noisy Impala in front of a suburban yard whose bare trees were strung with colorful flashing bulbs. The lawn was also crowded with illuminated blow mold holiday figurines, including a large plastic angel.

While sniffling with his 'coke' nose, he looked me directly in the eye.

"Because I fucking killed an angel... Shot her with a rifle ... accidently... and busted her flashing halo. I'm not shitting you, man – it really happened – when I was a little tyke. She was just trying to bring me some hot cocoa... and I killed this fucking angel..."

He slammed his fist into his uneaten empanada, causing the pizza sauce filling to splatter all over the windshield. As it poured down the glass and dripped like blood from the sun visor, he started sobbing.

"Was this angel the same thing as the freak show mermaid?" I asked. "I heard from a worker that you sold her to the carnival."

"Yeah, when I ran away from home they gave me a job as a gazoonie."

There was pained look on his face as he took another pull from the bottle.

"I didn't mean to do it. Who would want to kill a fucking angel? That's why I made up the whole Mooch thing. If the cops came after me for murder, I could blame it on my identical twin brother, who was always saying bad things about women... just like my dick father did with my mom."

He gestured to the house with the elaborate holiday decorations in the yard.

"I'll bet they have satin bulbs in there. Cotton snow, silver tinsel and a fucking bottle of Rhine wine. My mom always wanted some satin bulbs, even if we didn't have a tree."

"Bad things – like he says about Cherrie." I nodded.

"Yeah... but there's no Cherrie either. These are the kind of things you have to come up with when you accidently kill an angel... and sell the rotting body... to a rinky-dink carnival..."

"Chooch, listen, I know that it was just an accident... and not at all your fault... Just like I know that it was orange juice that she was bringing you, and not cocoa."

"How?" he looked at me while drying his eyes.

"Because I saw it happen."

"What are you on and where can I get some?" he managed a faint laugh while poking the smashed empanada and licking the pizza filling off one of his good fingers.

On the way back to the Notilus, we drove over the small trestle bridge and made a right turn onto ShadowCrest. Chooch slowed down in front of Molewhisker's house to move around a maroon Ford van that was parked across the street. Instead of passing it, he stopped to take a look at something placed in the front yard. The unusual shape turned out to be a snowman. In the bright moonlight we could make out its details. It was crudely formed from three spheres of mostly exhaust-stained snow. It had branches for arms, but instead of the customary stovepipe hat, it wore a black fedora. It had dark button eyes, a carrot nose and a mouth that was formed from pieces of coal that curled into a frown. What caught my attention the most, however, was a strand of shoestring licorice that protruded from its chin… like a long whisker. A shovel that leaned against the snow sculpture brought to mind the meat holes that Schaufler once dug, thus completing a wintery caricature of the man that someone had probably intended as a cruel joke.

"Hey, Frosty, you've got nothing on this snowman," Chooch laughed while snorting a line of cocaine from his wrist. "Should we snag that fucking candy strand?" he asked.

Giving the Impala some gas, we slowly passed alongside of the van. I saw that there was a person in the driver's seat that was bundled up in a blue Arctic parka with a snorkeled hood ringed with fur trim. This was just like the one that I recently saw Zerrill wearing. Actually, lots of people in town were wearing these now that the deep freeze was on.

Whoever this person was, he was training a camera on Molewhisker's sagging porch. Suddenly a flashcube popped, illuminating the surroundings for an instant. A second flash from the camera quickly followed this.

"Whoa!" Chooch uttered. "Déjà vu! That same icicle fell twice. I saw it hit the porch… go boom… and when I looked up, I saw it fall again… and go boom. Déjà vu!"

"You're tripping," I said as we pulled away.

"That was trippy, man," he laughed. "You didn't see that?"

CHAPTER V
PANZERSCHWEIN

On the last field trip of my freshman year we visited an institution for severely developmentally disabled children. No one expected any of the usual shenanigans this time around because the school board had decided that the worst past offenders could no longer take part in these class outings. Bummer for them because afterwards for lunch – as a reward for our good behavior – there would be a buffet at "Shakey's Pizza Parlor." Ollie was allowed to go with us, but he had to sit with the teacher on the way so that she could keep a close eye on him.

Before entering the building, we were instructed by our teacher (once again) to be courteous and not to laugh or make fun of the patients regardless of what happened. If someone found things too disturbing, they were to return to the school bus.

Once inside, I felt queasy. In the minimalist clinical atmosphere, an overly smiling psychiatric nurse greeted us. She told us not to be frightened by any of the patients' actions and to just show good manners. I put on my most serious face as we were escorted into one of the wards. In an attempt to make the place more cheerful, rainbows had been painted on the walls. Glancing around, I thought that even the distraction of puppies sucking on lollipops decor wouldn't keep the place from being coldly detached.

Right away, an epileptic patient with a drooping head and soaked pajama bottoms began to puke after squeezing a tube of Pepsodent toothpaste into his mouth. Crawling around him, some of the more brain-damaged kids were making unintelligible noises while using their fingers to create crude designs with the slick chunky vomit. Others were screeching and giggling while slumped in wheelchairs. A little girl with her lip pressed against her nose was seated alone in a corner, rattling a shrill tambourine into one of her ears.

While moving in single file with my classmates, I noticed a boy who was seated in a chair with a stack of white paper in his lap. With rapid motions, he masterfully folded several sheets into perfectly formed paper airplanes. After writing something on these with a pencil, he sailed them across the room so that they landed near other patients.

He became extremely agitated the instant that he laid eyes on me. I didn't know why he singled me out, but he was soon frantically pointing his finger while repeatedly shouting the word, "Dummy." Hearing this, some of the kids in my class couldn't help but laugh. They nodded their heads in agreement, saying, "You're right – he is a dummy." When I smiled at him, this only exacerbated the situation. With a look of sheer terror on his face, he kicked up the production of paper planes, cranking them out with lightning-fast speed. After drawing something on the wings, soon dozens were bouncing off the rainbow-splashed walls. He was folding and tossing them so quickly, several staff members had to be called to constrain him. As they attempted to administer a sedative, he continued to scream, "Dummy."

I was still a bit unnerved by the kid's strange reaction to me as the class filed into the spacious office of one of the institution's top doctors. Before being allowed to enter, we had been instructed to wash our hands thoroughly, something that I didn't understand until I saw all the antiques in the well-decorated room.

Seated behind a large executive desk with elegant scrolled details was an elderly man dressed in an immaculate white suit. The glow from an ornate porcelain table lamp gave a ruddy appearance to his shaven pate and otherwise ashen complexion. As he continued to scrutinize us, the steely glint in his gray-blue eyes made me feel slightly on edge. Hunched on his lap was a miniature dachshund with a black patch over one eye. The narrow snout of the dog resting on the desk's cherry finish was comical, but the expression on the doctor's face was austere to the extreme. He spoke with a slight German accent, but, to my surprise, in a friendly, gentle manner.

"Good morning class, my name is Doctor Hubertus Wegener. I am a pediatric endocrinologist… and this little fellow with the manly eye patch is my assistant, Strudel. First off, thank you for your courtesy and attentiveness. Now… I understand that you will be served lunch later at Ye Public House of Shakey's. Well, be sure to sample the Mojos. These are little flattened potatoes like crispy fritters… or your tator tots… and they are quite tasteful little fellows as you shall soon find out. Sometimes smaller is better — like little Strudel here — who is just as happy as any larger German shepherd. So, although, as you have seen – our challenged brood here – in this institution – are well cared and provided for, it is still my wish that in the very near future similarly disabled children will no longer need to be placed in hospitals when they surely would be more comfortable with their legal guardians in a loving home environment."

At that moment an attractive young woman with braided blond hair hurried into the office carrying a porcelain cup of tea that she nervously set down on the desk doily.

"Ah, my tea finally arrives. Thank you, Miss Mrugowsky. Perhaps with an éclair next time for little Strudel's sweet tooth, eh", he said while winking at his pretty secretary.

As the doctor was about to lift the cup, he noticed a tiny chip on the rim. As he examined it closer, this seemed to darken his mood.

"*Abgebrochen?* This cup – it is chipped... You didn't notice? *Teetasse wird gesplittet,*" he barked to her in German, causing the dachshund to growl. She leaned over to examine the chip for herself, acting as if she didn't see any damage. Visibly perturbed, the doctor gestured for her to leave the room. "*Abgebrochen!*" The dachshund yapped as she obsequiously backed away.

When she had shut the door, he returned his attention to the class.

"So... to make this dream of ours happen – to make things more efficient – I am involved with a little experiment, all very ethical you will agree, involving a procedure called growth-attenuation therapy. This is accomplished by medically stunting the child's growth between the ages of three to six to that of a four-year-old child. At that permanent height, the child is much more manageable to the parents in all its diverse needs. The child will be a happy little munchkin... just like in the Wizard of Oz... that I trust you all have seen. Nice, friendly little munchkins that are easy to place in the stroller for as long as they live... like little ragdolls, you see..."

As he spoke, he seemed to be still acutely aware of the tiny chip in the cup. He kept looking at it with his flushed face – unable to let it go – scowling while rubbing the rim with his fingertip.

"The treatment involves using high doses of estrogen and closing the epiphyseal growth plates. Yes, just a little of the hyaline cartilage plate that's located at each end of the long bones. Femurs, tibias... fibulas. Now, are there any questions so far?"

Ollie closed his eyes and raised his hand.

"Yes," the doctor said.

"Uh, that lampshade on your desk is really cool. Where did it originally come from?"

"I really couldn't say. Famous Barr in Saint Louis, if I had to hazard a guess... but, do you have any questions about growth-attenuation therapy?"

Managing to keep a straight face, Ollie asked:

"Do you consider this treatment to be the final solution?"

I was still upset about being called a "dummy" by the kid, but the rumpus at the pizza parlor had me feeling a little better. As we sat at long picnic tables, scarfing down as many slices of pizza that we wanted, a mustached fellow wearing a striped red vest and straw-boater hat was pounding out some great ragtime on the piano while another guy dressed in the same costume picked a banjo. The only downer was that my soda was flat. Checking for any change in my pockets to use in the vending machine outside, I pulled out the doohickey. I didn't remember bringing it, but what the heck – one more time couldn't hurt. (I only had three pennies anyway.)

When I went outside to use the machine, the doohickey worked just fine. However, I didn't realize that Ollie had followed me and saw what went down.

"You still got that thing? Damn, it's the king of slugs! I should have traded you for my double Gadzooka whacky. Hey, check this out. I snagged a couple of that loony's paper planes."

He unfolded part of the paper that contained a pencil sketch of what was clearly my likeness – right down to the shirt that I was wearing. Beneath the crude portrait, he had scrawled the words,

"FAKE SKIN"

"Fake skin," Ollie laughed. "The poor imbecile doesn't know the difference between clothes and human skin."

I couldn't stop thinking about why the paper airplane kid had drawn pencil renderings of me with the words "Fake Skin" scrawled beneath them. Was he some kind of idiot savant that could read my thoughts? How else could he know that at times I felt so different from the average person that I questioned whether I was, in fact, the genuine article? (And I'm sure that I had worn thin the patience of my friends over the years with excessive questions about their mental and physical state to use as a form of comparison.)

During the winter months, I had been so consumed by these thoughts that I spent most of my time lying around watching the television. Along with the uncertainty about my true nature (I realized how weird that sounded, but doubts about my very essence were part of whatever neurological condition that I suffered from), at times I would suddenly lose my sense of touch and experience other unusual physical sensations. This absence of feeling was similar to the numbness from having one's circulation cut off; only it wasn't always confined to a specific appendage.

As I seemed to float about like a human will o' the wisp in my 'fake skin', even my dad referred to me as a "walking corpse." He was constantly telling me to go hang out with my friends. Better yet, he said, I might want to think about getting a part time job. The local Tomboy market was currently looking for a stock person. With summer coming, he suggested that I go apply. Because I was also experiencing mental blocks (as if my nearly sixteen-year-old brain were already filled to capacity), I wondered if I could even handle such a job? Especially with the added clutter of having to remember where the canned goods aisle was located?

On the few occasions that I ventured outside, I realized that Chooch was trying to ignore me. When I finally managed to corner him in a stall at the King Coney, he seemed a bit stand-offish at first, but then smiled with his yellow teeth in the blinking neon and told me that he really had me going with the whole 'killing an angel' joke. While puffing on the fattest joint that I had ever seen, he recanted everything that he had admitted to on that night and warned me not to repeat any crazy shit that I might have heard him mumble while he was crashed out. He also told me not to worry about Mooch because he had recently purchased a one-way Trailways ticket to Peoria where he got a job working in the Union Stockyards. He was going to be slaughtering hogs, which he (Mooch) referred to as "the squealing pink." When I asked him if he recalled ever seeing an albino butler-like person in the past, he gave me a puzzled look and said, "You mean Captain Nemo? When did you see him on the Notilus, dude?"

Later that night, I tried to put together some pieces of the puzzle. First there was the doohickey test. Next came the Notilus bus, which Chooch said belonged to the albino oddity. Had Molewhisker also wanted me to find something there – as part of some other test that his disturbed mind conceived? The only connection that I could make between the two was Trixie. I had met her on the Notilus after missing my chance years ago in front of Molewhisker's house on the night of the "Cornpocalypse" (as he called it).

After trumpeting a gleaming new fire apparatus in the annual parade that heralded the beginning of summer, it didn't take long for what many old timers considered to be a curse rearing its ugly head. In this case, the devil appeared in the guise of a decorated Vietnam War vet. In what the newspaper caption dubbed as "The Apple Shot", an ex-Marine sharpshooter had forced his daughter's prom date to balance a shiny "Red Delicious" on the top of his head as he warned him not to do anything "dishonorable" with the girl. To further hammer home the point, the hard-nosed sniper took aim at Tomboy's finest with his bolt-action M40 and made applesauce with a single loud bang. The battle fatigued 'William Tell' didn't get any jail time, (and poor Beallah didn't receive many suitors afterward), but he was required to pay for the cleaning of the kid's rental tux. Many considered this incident to be the town's crowning folly, but it was actually only the beginning of even zanier headlines yet to come.

The local heads had started calling Chooch "The Fryer" as he cruised around town in his rumbling Impala, peddling hits of purple microdot for parties that often featured lawn darts played late at night. Although none of the injured had died as a result of the oversized, sharply-pointed metal things missing the bulls-eye, a couple had pierced the skulls of those looking up into the night sky for the rapidly falling missiles. The solution was to douse the tips with kerosene and ooh and ahh at the fiery trails, but the first flaming "Jarts" contest ended when a neighbor's house caught on fire. There were several deaths, however, from those who preferred to inhale furniture varnish prior to playing around with their parents' guns during similar gatherings.

One case involved a kid who had accidently grazed one of his close friends in the face with a bullet the week before killing him with another unintentional shot. "At least he was already embalmed," his friends joked at his funeral.

For those who didn't have access to guns, "Chicken Tracks" became the popular antidote for boredom. The game involved stopping one's car directly on the railroad tracks as a horn-blaring freight train approached. The driver then removed the key from the ignition and dropped it onto the floor mat, feeling around and pretending that he couldn't find it until the very last minute. He then quickly reinserted it and started the engine before screeching away. Since most of these cars were old clunkers that didn't fire up right away, the object was both to scare the passengers and receive a tallboy beer trophy for the daring deed.

Zerrill told me he thought all the shit going down was caused by Schaufler after his hot rod hearse had barreled through the seventh gate in the wrong sequence and thus had inadvertently opened the Gate to Hell. He further added that most of the negativity was occurring in a close proximity to where his haunted Victorian was located. Around the same time that he jokingly proposed these theories, Chooch told me that he thought that Zerrill (last name being, Sand) was a king pin LSD manufacturer in the area. Although I didn't believe this, it did make me think twice about how he was always searching for abandoned buildings or speakeasy-like hidden chambers in large brick structures.

As the weather grew warmer, a stranger arrived on the scene. He was a black guy in his mid-twenties whose name was Dovie. I wasn't sure if it was because he was the only negro in town, or if it was his shiny white loafers and purple velvet beret, but all of the local freaks wanted to hang out with him. He drove a 1959 white Rambler Ambassador Super, but if you wanted to ride with Dovie you would have to sit in a Sears & Roebuck webbed aluminum lawn chair identical to the one behind the steering wheel. With his familiar greeting of "What's the riff, silly," Dovie offered to buy under-aged kids six-packs of beer, but always kept two cans per sixer for himself. If anyone wanted change back, after giving a sly grin he would calmly explain that the rest of the money "fell down the toilet."

Dovie was in the habit of driving on the freshly mowed grass in the middle of the park. One day, while sucking on a quart of Schlitz malt liquor and toking on a flaming fat roach, he crushed the legs of the police chief's young son by pinning him against a concrete wall in the pavilion where he was walking a yo-yo. Getting up from the collapsed lawn chair, Dovie claimed that he had accidently lost control of the car when he was repeatedly stung by yellow jackets while eating a tartar sauce-laden trash fish sandwich. With all of the capsules of chocolate mescaline spilled onto the floorboards, the cops carted him off to the pokey, convinced that he was in the process of trying to sell his "Doors of Deception" to young children.

Later it was widely repeated in the local taverns that if Dovie was released from his jail cell, the police chief bragged that he would bury him alive up to his neck as the final stake on his backyard croquet court. For some recreation after a Sunday church, with a mint julep in one hand and his favorite ivory mallet in the other, he would peg out by whacking a boxwood ball through the last wicket and "crack the coon's head open with a blow right between his bug-eyed stare."

My mom opened the back door while I was in the backyard playing with the cat.

"Hey, if you didn't like your Deviled Ham, don't leave half of the sandwich on your plate and put it in the sink," she shouted.

"I don't know what you're talking about – I ate the whole thing," I replied. "But, you're right, I didn't like it."

"You left half of your soda in the glass, too. Too busy torturing the cat to pour it out first before leaving it with the dirty dishes?"

Seeing my blank expression, she shut the door. A second later, she opened it again.

"Hey, when did Ollie get his driver's license? I didn't think that he even had his learner's permit."

"He doesn't," I said while motioning for Midnight Meringue to go inside.

"That's funny. When I left to go shopping I saw him parked across from the Johnson's in his mom's car. The pretty green one."

"The XJ6... Mrs. Spitzer's Jag? That's crazy."

"You mean you didn't see him?" My mom seemed a bit confused.

When the phone rang and she went to answer it, I followed the scurrying cat inside.

"Addison, it's Kelby." She handed me the receiver before going back to putting away the groceries.

As I stood there listening to Kelby, he told me that Ollie had just been to his house. He said that he had told him that he put sleeping pills in his mom's grapefruit juice and stole her car after she passed out. He was planning to drive the Jaguar to Las Vegas and wanted to know if he wanted to go with him? She was probably still conked out from all the Seconal, Kelby said, and wondered what he should do? An anonymous call for an ambulance to the Spitzer's house might be the best thing, I suggested.

After hanging up, I recalled that Ollie used to talk about running off to Las Vegas to play the slot machines with his best slugs. Knowing that he had been parked in front of our house an hour ago, and that the front door was never locked, I had a bad feeling. I hurried to my bedroom and opened the bottom dresser drawer where I kept my clean socks. Seeing that some were no longer wadded up, I reached inside to see if I could feel any thing. When I couldn't, I frantically searched through the balled up ones. Still no luck. Unable to find my prized possession anywhere among my stuff, I went into the living room and opened the front door. Lying on the front step was a crumpled SweeTart wrapper that I picked up and held close to my nose. There was an artificial grape smell. I couldn't believe this. That fucker Ollie had stolen the doohickey while I was in the backyard trying to teach my cat to fetch. Of all the stupid things!

At dinner that night, I thought about asking my parents if they had found a "funny bingo token" in my room, but decided to wait a little longer. I hadn't heard any more news about Ollie, so he probably didn't get caught yet. Still, I figured his mom would call to ask me what I knew once she had awakened from her barbiturate nap.

Even though I was pretty sure that the doohickey was gone, I continued to search my bedroom that night. Why couldn't Ollie have just used piano wire or coat hangers? I also couldn't help but wonder how the object's sacred alloys would react to a one-armed bandit? I imaged Spitzer the millionaire in his Jaguar, but then thought about him getting caught while trying to hustle the mob. They'd mangle his fingers worse than Chooch's and the doohickey would disappear inside some cabinet along with the other slugs and devices used by cheaters. Why did it allow itself to be taken in the first place? As I continued to search every inch of the room, I found hidden under a shoebox the copy of the underground comic entitled *JEET* that I had borrowed from the Notilus's library (and was now long overdue). In order to take my mind off of the doohickey, I opened it and began to check out its comical graphics and accompanying speech bubbles.

On the first page of issue number one (written by "NO NAME WILL DO"), an introductory monologue was expressed in a rectangular caption box:

"According to zoologists, nine-banded armadillos always give birth to four genetically identical young who are developed from the same egg. As the only known mammal to reproduce in this manner, the quadruplets even share the same placenta.

Recently this recurrence in nature happened again – but with one visible difference: The leathery carapace of one of the quads contained only seven stripes. (It also had its eyes closed at birth.) His name was "Darbilius", but later shortened to "Darby." Darby's parents expressed their disdain of this shameful abnormality, and often encouraged him (in a certain and explicit way) to attempt to cross the nearby roads without the slightest fear or hesitation to any approaching conveyances. All he had to do was jump straight into the air just prior to impact and his indestructible scales would protect him while colliding with metal fenders.

Darby took their advice for a while, but after each vehicle managed to dodge him, he abandoned this pursuit to shuffle about on his home range where he became a prolific digger of insects. Unfortunately, his holes provoked the ire of a farmer who considered all "armored pigs" to be marauding pests. Hence, the sodbuster and the armadillos became sworn enemies.

When they weren't snoozing 19 hours a day, Darby and his three brothers foraged for grubs and listened to the Beatles (having poor eyesight, after all). Even though his siblings with the nine bands constantly made fun of Darby (with his seven), treating him as something other than a brother, he nevertheless shared with them their parents' heartfelt advice to cross any nearby roads without the slightest fear of any oncoming traffic. All they had to do was jump."

Following the narration on the establishing page, a panel showed the solitary Darby rooting among the dozens of holes dug into the ground near the farmhouse.

The next tier contained a sequence of events featuring the other three armadillos – all of which were depicted with human characteristics. Unlike Darby, they were stoner types who wore hippie bandanas and tinted sunglasses. Even their leathery carapaces had counter-culture patches on them. In these frames we were given our first taste of the low comedy antics of these anthropomorphic 'dillo freaks – a cross between the laid back mischief of "Cheech and Chong" and the destructive mayhem of "The Three Stooges." Cloud-like speech balloons with pointed arrows provided the 1960s lingo as each of the three brothers took turns poking fun at Darby:

"Pyoo-wee, what's that smell? Oh, it's just Darby catchin' some rays. Oo-wooh, that fart would have made a nice blue flamer to toast my lawn grubs, Darb."

179

"Remember the time he painted two black stripes on his scutes to pretend that he was born with nine? Oh, wait – those were tire tracks from that old Mercury that's always bookin' around. Nice try, Darby!"

"If I get the munchies later, I might have to slurp up that gibberish-speaking long-legs spider hanging under the eave that he's always harshing my mellow with."

With a patch on his armored shell that read, "I AM AN AGITATOR", this was by far the most antagonistic armadillo of the three brothers. After having a good laugh at Darby's expense, the gags turned to marijuana smoking.

"Gimmie that roach you were bogarting," the most aggressive 'dillo demanded.

The accused armadillo stuck out a long sticky tongue that was covered with bits and pieces of a half chewed up cockroach that was frantically attempting to re-attach its scattered insect parts.

"It's stuck on my tongue, man."

"Not that roach, dude. The stub of leafy treasure that you were toking on with smoke pouring out of your snout like a locomotive chimney."

The third armadillo stuck out its tongue to show his brother the unlit marijuana stub.

"Where's that Cricket lighter?" the hostile 'dillo asked while thrusting his snout to the ground.

Using his forepaws, he quickly snatched a cricket from the grass and squeezed its abdomen until the insect belched a stream of fire from its mouth that set his brother's entire tongue ablaze.

In the next panel, the third armadillo was distracted by the sight of a sexy female armadillo whose lacy white slip was showing beneath her armor shell as she shuffled about in a patch of leaf litter.

"Whowee! It's snowing down south, Miss Darlina. I wouldn't mind swapping spit with that. Hey, you don't need no armadildo tonight chickabiddy – cuz it's not just my carapace that's hard.

If I say padiddle and you say padunkle, then we're good to get it on in my log. I might need a crowbar, though – to pry off that four-teated armor brassiere."

In a small box placed next to this, a bunch of crows were seated at a seedy bar on the top of a telephone pole. While brooding over a martini, one of the blackbirds asked another, "Did he just say crow bar? I don't want those blind galoots knocking over drinks in here."

In the next frame, the antagonistic 'dillo had a speech bubble with a tail pointing to him that read:

"Quit your lip flappin' and pass that roach. A snorkwhomper like you aint never gonna make it with that stuck up scute. But with a magnificent shine, I might," he said while rubbing "Armor All" car care protectant over his leathery carapace.

In a panel on the next page, an angry farmer (depicted with a blurry outline due to the armadillos' poor eyesight) was standing by his opened screen door. He was wearing denim bib overalls and brandishing a rifle in retaliation for all the holes dug in his grass. A smaller box within the frame warned us that this blurred figure was named, "Flattop Emmett." Unlike the other speech balloons, the one with a tail pointing to him had an unfriendly jagged design.

"Scat! Panzerschwein! Scram! You've dug a heckuvah hole in my grass – so I'm gonna put a heckuva hole in your ass. Then I'll turn that shell of yours into a proper git-fiddle and play you like a beaner's charango. It's gonna be Armageddon, cuz Armageddon rid of youz."

In a segment of action, he fired the rifle at one armadillo. The bullet ricocheted off its hard scales, which, in turn, bounced off the armor shell of his brother before once again ricocheting off the third armadillo, only to strike the farmer in his stomach. With blood spurting out of the farmer's wound, the tail of the speech bubble was pointing to the off-frame third armadillo.

"Oops. Better drop a pipper-plop into a glass of swamp water."

The farmer replied with an even more unfriendly speech balloon:

"I'll have a seltzer right after I have my possum on the half shell! I've heard tell that you goddamn speed bumps taste just like pork."

The next panel showed the familiar seven stars of the Big Dipper twinkling above the farmhouse.

Darby was watching a daddy long-legs spider that was dangling from a tangled web attached to an eave on the farmhouse. A caption in a separate box informed us that this was: "Mister Dangles – the wisest pholcid on the prairie." Indeed, Mister Dangles' peanut-shaped body had an ecclesiastical aura about it, with a long beard, rimless glasses and a kippah-like skullcap on the back of a tiny head with seven braids of hair.

Darby greeted him with: "Hello Mister Dangles. Jeet?"

The fragile pholcid that was hanging upside-down replied:

"A few tasty morsels of decayed matter. A nickel a schtickle. Not exactly a blintz... but the night is young."

"Why is it that you only come out at night?" Darby asked.

"Well, as much as I admire the tinted flashes of sunlit dew on our glorious emerald table, I'm especially attracted to the splendid lamps of this asterism that hangs in the celestial tapestry. Call it what you want; the heavenly Wagon, Plough, or Big Dipper – as it dances to an endless circumpolar freylech. Plus, Darby, no offence, but your brothers – well, let's just say that I have encountered glyptodonts close to our time that were more cultured

than those unfinished goilems. Such a shame really. Those klum-
niks... nudniks... Ekl, what do you call brainless lunks?"

"What is so special about those seven stars?"

"Stars?" Mister Dangles adjusted his glasses. "Oh, yes, the
stars. Tell me, Darby, do you notice anything unusual about the
sixth star from the Dipper's handle?"

"We armadillos all have poor eyesight," Darby replied.

Well, even with my six eyes... or is it eight?.. feh!.. My vision is
not what it once was. I have heard from those who are able to read
the starry script – the sons of Zadoq the priest, namely – that the
sixth star from the handle, Mizar, is a naked eye double star whose
faint companion is called Alcor. It was once a test of one's vision by
the ancients, but that doesn't necessarily mean an eye exam for
those fatal images of nature. The penetrating vision here is in one's
keppalah. So, perhaps, we need to gas up the old Merkavah! Darby,
you are a digging machine. At least that's what I read in the caption
inside the rectangular establishing box of this underground comix."

Darby made a sad face and said:

"I'm often afraid of falling into the holes, though."

"Afraid? You are about to fall into the schmaltz pot! The seven
stars up there have an analogue with the seven gates below. As
above, so below.

These, in stages, can lead one to receive a vision of the other
world. With a little chutzpah, you can make the inward journey – a
voyage of discovery – where revealed are the secrets behind secrets on the paths of night."

"You've lived a long time haven't you, Mister Dangles?"

"Well, I sometimes think that there has been a great number
of the exact same Mister Dangles hatched over the eons. And, yet,
we still can't manage to construct a decent web. Ekl! Look at this
shmatte. It's a wonder that there's anything to nosh. But, getting

back to what I have told you, are you still afraid of falling into the hole, even if it leads to PaRDes?"

In the next frame, the aggressive 'dillo was eavesdropping (literally in this case, as the caption in a smaller box said) when he accidently knocked over a garbage can while digging for some scraps of food. In a poor attempt to cover his tracks, he faked a sneeze.

"Gesundheit," Mister Dangles uttered as his web vibrated as if shaken by a strong gust of wind. "Now please move along you nosy schlub. You are crowding my personal space."

In the next tier, the clumsy armadillo skittered away to a narrow burrow where his other two brothers were passed out (as expressed by a series of large "Z's" in their vibrating speech bubbles). Excited, the armadillo woke them up – with a speech balloon that read:

"Wake up dudes. I was out clucking with tail-wagging Darlina when I heard that Darby is going to a pot party in that rumbling Mercury. He doesn't know it yet, but we're going, too."

As I was about to turn the page, my dad knocked on the door and stuck his head into my room. Seeing him, I quickly closed the freak comic.

"Would you mind telling me why you only finished half of your math final? Mister Zugglesby was scratching his head when he told me about it in the teacher's lounge. He couldn't figure out why you stopped after correctly solving all of the problems on the first page? If you weren't feeling well, he'll allow you to take it again, as a favor, unless you'd prefer summer school to make up the credit?"

"You're kidding? Dad, I did every problem. Summer school?"

"That's right, buddy-boy. It's time to quit giggling at the funnies and get serious with your life. Speaking of which, that bag boy job is still open."

Intrigued by the mention of the naked eye double stars in the underground comic, the next evening I pedaled over to the Notilus to return the borrowed copy and to see if there were any other issues of *JEET* on its painted shelf.

Cutting through the abandoned old dairy processing plant that was now used as long-term storage units for classic cars (and where Chooch usually parked the Impalanada without permission while hanging out on the psychedelic bus), I noticed a car pulling out with a large antenna, black rims and a spotlight – the telltale signs of an unmarked police vehicle. What caused me do a double take was that the driver's front passenger was a black man who looked like Dovie without his trademark purple velvet beret. Before it turned onto the darkened street, I took note that the car was a light green Plymouth.

When I tapped on the back door of the Notilus with the correct sequence of knocks, the frizzy-haired Topo Gigo opened the squeaky thing with his guitar strapped on. Pointing the Telecaster's headstock down at my feet, he burst out laughing.

"Where's your other shoe?"

At first I had no idea of what he was talking about, but once I realized that I was only wearing one sneaker, I quickly made up something.

"Yeah, it fell off and some tractor flattened it like a pancake," I laughed. "Hey, guess what, I just saw a narc car maybe – a Plymouth Valiant – leave the old Prairie Farms with some guy on the passenger side that looked kind of like Dovie without the hat. But, I know that he's still in jail."

"You didn't hear about the police station mescapades?" Topo said as we climbed up the steps. "Yeah, all the Hershey-cut doses disappeared from the evidence room. Dovie got released with just a traffic ticket because of those bees that he said stung him. He probably sleeps with that beret, but I'll get Chooch to periscope up if the Valiant comes back."

"Yeah, he probably should take a peep if he's still frying brains? Anyway, the reason I dropped by was to see if I could check out another one of these?"

I showed him the copy of *JEET* that I was returning as I walked towards the cluttered bookshelf.

"That's some funny shit," Topo laughed. "I loved the part when the armadillo is digging inside the tunnel – using a pickling jar full of fireflies to see – and later gives the chthonic worm gatekeeper a rusted 7Up bottle cap in exchange for a token with gibberish written on it that's the password for the second gate."

He started to laugh even harder.

"Here's my required schlock for a token of your gibberish."

This confused me because I had just finished reading the comic last night, but didn't remember anything about Darby being inside a tunnel.

"Are you sure that was in the first issue?" I asked.

"Yeah, man. You didn't get that far? He trades junk for gibberish."

"Oh, yeah – now I remember," I said just so he wouldn't think that I was an idiot. I then started sifting through the various street comix on the shelf until I found the only other copy of *JEET*. Seeing that this was issue # 3, Topo seemed a bit freaked out. His voice took on a serious tone as he looked at the cover.

"You're lucky this is still here. I still don't know why it didn't burn... the flimsy cheap paper. We were torching one of Dovie's fat joints when it got dropped on it. I guess some butane... lighter fluid got spilled on the cover... I saw the flames start to spread, but they quickly went out… by themselves… and there was no trace of burn marks. It was really freaky, man."

Thinking that this fire resistant paper story was just another one of those incidents that stoners think happened when they're tripping balls, I changed the subject.

"Hey, has Captain Nemo been on the bus lately?"

"Nemo? You mean Captain No-Man… No, man, I've never seen Nemo."

"How about Trixie?" I asked.

"She's been hanging with some bald-headed freakazoid who looks like the drummer in the band, Spirit. It sounds like she's getting into some heavy shit. As we scooped the loop at SIU, she kept going on about this British author who practiced occult things."

"Wow."

As soon as I got back home that night, I plopped myself down on the bed and began to read the third issue. On the first page, the three freak armadillos were gathered inside their hollow log abode at night where they were puffing away on a grey marijuana pipe that had nine bony rings around it. When the bowl was cashed, one of them tried to re-light the ashes by using its long claws to squeeze the abdomen of a live cricket that belched a tiny flame from its mouth.

"Time to re-fill the old cricket with hot sauce," one of them said in a speech balloon.

"Where'd you score this crazy pipe, dude?" the other brother asked in another speech bubble.

The antagonistic armadillo with the "I AM AN AGITATOR" counterculture patch on its leathery carapace had a speech balloon that read:

"I ripped it off – off of your body when you were crashed out. It's your tail, man… with a few ingenious alterations."

"Ouch! Why'd you do that, man?"

"Because the other pipe – your brother's tail – was totally clogged."

The aggressive armadillo then showed his two brothers a sling-shot and a perfectly round 'dirt-clod' that had traces of blood on it.

"I'm going to use this to knock Mister Dangles out of his tangles. We'll interrogate the fragile little pholcid until he tells us how to crash Darby's private pot parties."

"How did that dirt clod get blood on it?" the more recently tail-less 'dillo asked.

"Oh, that. Sorry, dude, but when you were passed out I also removed one of your testicles."

In the next frame, the word, "OUCH!" was boldly capped in a large speech bubble.

Peeking out of the hollow log, the hostile armadillo saw Darby out in a field attempting to catch fireflies so he could put them inside a pickling jar. As he did so, the female armadillo, Darlina, was wagging her tail as she shuffled about. She had a thought balloon that read:

"Is that a dill pickle for me?"

The antagonistic armadillo was leering at her as she pretended to forage for insects.

"Look at that little scute, Darlina, with that tight body of hers in that pleated panoply."

"Yeah, dude, but how many times do you want to be kicked in the nuts by her hind legs?" his brother asked.

"A few more," the drooling 'dillo replied. "There's Darby out there gathering golden phantoms for his lantern. He wouldn't know stacked tin cans if all four fell on him."

Oblivious to Darlina's advances, in the next panel, Darby was standing under the eave of the farmhouse, waiting for Mister Dangles to appear. With patches of clouds in the night sky, he had an idea. Unscrewing the lid on the pickling jar, he released seven fireflies. As they ascended into the air, each of the seven blinked at the same time while forming a pattern that resembled the Big Dipper. A second latter, the daddy long-legs appeared – hanging upside down in his messy web.

Darby greeted him: "There you are, Mister Dangles! Jeet?"

"Just a light snack – of decomposing nibbles. A nickel a schtickle, but thanks for asking, Darby. How goes the search for PaRDeS? You know, the otherworld."

"I haven't found it yet, but I'm still looking."

"From my vantage point up here, I just espied another dirt encrusted 7Up bottle cap. Another piece of schlock – this one for the third gatekeeper. Tell him that it's your yarmulke. Fortunately, chthonic worms aren't that picky."

At that point, I must have fallen asleep with my mother later having turned off the light. When I awoke as Midnight Meringue jumped onto the edge of the bed, I was disoriented at first to be looking at the glowing bright white text in the copy of *JEET*. I couldn't see any of the illustrations – only the words themselves, but the clarity of the text in the darkness was uncanny. Somehow, radiant white ink must have been mixed with the black ink to create some printing effect that I'd never seen before… or even imagined.

The dialogue in the speech balloon was that of the angry farmer (I assumed).

"Scat! Panzerschwein! Scram! This ain't no passion pit for giving birth to more glorified roly-polies. For turning my grasslands into Swiss cheese – if I don't find you dead on a spur – I'll pepper the whole place with stinky mothballs! And leave my gibberish speakin' pholcid alone… with his ambiguous symbols and such, the purpose of which is to baffle and lead into error everyone except those which God loves and provides for."

"To lead into error... to lead one astray," I said to myself in a low voice. "Just like the will o' the wisp does. Molewhisker – he's still trying to pull my strings."

The more I thought about it, the more it seemed that Molewhisker was behind this. There had to be a connection. Maybe it wasn't Trixie that he wanted me to meet. What if it were the copies of *JEET* that I was supposed to read after being planted on the Notilus by the albino, Captain Nemo?

The next morning, I heard that Ollie had been pulled over somewhere in Texas without a driver's license and a dead armadillo (of all things!) on the windshield. Talking to him on the phone, he didn't think that the juvenile court would go that hard on him because he had been promised the Jag when he turned sixteen and he took it the day after his birthday. It would probably only be six months of probation, which would give him plenty of time to clean off the armored road kill after its mid-air collision.

More important to me was getting the doohickey back. When I asked Spitzer to come clean, he swore up and down that he didn't kipe it. He had come over to the house to see if I wanted to go for a ride, but when no one answered the door, he didn't walk in. He said that he checked the backyard and saw the cat but no sign of me. I wasn't sure what to think. How could he have known that Midnight Meringue was out there at the time?

As Ollie continued to deny having anything to do with the disappearance of my super slug, over breakfast one morning, I heard my mom tell my dad about an advertisement in the "For Sale" section of *The Spectrum*. The ad was for ancient Egyptian artifacts that the seller was claiming had been unearthed right here in southern Illinois. My dad's response was a typical dismissive smile, but as he continued to sip his coffee, I quickly grabbed the paper, curious to know if someone had found the doohickey. It was a long shot, but certainly worth a phone call.

When I called the number, I recognized the voice on the other end to be Nestor's. He told me that he had found the items in the basement of what used to be his grandmother's house. There were several boxes filled with these things and although he didn't know much about them, they appeared to be very old looking black stones that were etched with mysterious symbols and such. After hanging up, I managed to convince my dad into taking a look at them by telling him that he could save a lot of suckers from wasting their hard-earned money if they were fakes.

Days later, when we walked down into the Nestore to have a look at his findings, it was obvious from the start that they weren't just pioneer curios or scratchings on flat rocks from farmers' ploughs. To the astonishment of both of us, there were hundreds of these artifacts.

Sorting through cigar boxes that were filled with dark grey ovals, my dad thought that most were argillite that had metamorphosed into shale or slate. Other tablets looked to be fragments of limestone or white marble. Most of the pieces were emblazoned with crude illustrations that would certainly be considered Egyptianesque, while others were carved with the motifs of a bewildering variety of ancient cultures that included the Greeks, Carthaginians and Minoans. The peculiar mixture of art forms and other hybridization on the same artifact was a dead giveaway of a recent forgery to my dad, but we nevertheless continued to examine the strange pictographs.

The most interesting carvings depicted what appeared to be millennia-old contact between Egyptians with an extinct culture of native Indians (the enigmatic mound builders or, possibly, the Illiniwek or Yuchi tribes) on the banks of the Mississippi River system. Some even showed trans-oceanic scenes of ancient ships with massive sails that were navigated by bearded figures with Egyptian-style headgear using celestial star maps such as the circumpolar constellation, Ursa Major (shown by the asterism of the "Big Dipper"). Other discoidal stones contained hieroglyphics whose highly polished black surfaces were engraved with jackal-headed deities, sunbursts, scarabs and lotus flower ornamentation.

When we were done checking out the collection, my dad politely told Nestor that they were almost certainly modern fakes. Because of the jumble of different styles and epochs found together, along with the apparent use of man-made components with the raw material (my dad found black smudges of shoe polish on his hand while handling one of the more brittle pieces), the hodge-podge of striations were most likely fashioned by using contemporary tools and copied from published works by someone with an amateur's knowledge of ancient history. What he didn't know was whether or not the curiosities had been fabricated as part of some hoax to fool the gullible, or if the garbled workmanship was just someone's quirky hobby?

The whole thing might have ended there, but it didn't. My dad was only a small town high-school history teacher, and not an expert of antiquities, so Nestor invited others with more credentials to get involved. In the meantime, he sold as many of the things as he could and even changed his story (twice) as to where the 'treasure' was originally discovered. The first location involved what he referred to as an ancient Egyptian tunnel city. This wonderful labyrinthine was soon downgraded to pockmarked depressions on an isolated farmstead, whose whereabouts he would not divulge. Fearful of such things, the property owners – who had known of their existence for centuries – were more than happy to get rid of them.

With all the local hoopla, people with a scholarly interest in archaeological esoterica were traveling from all over the country to view the peculiar artifacts and to add their own opinions. Who would have guessed that one article in the paper would finally put our little town on the map? Those with various academic backgrounds debated the authenticity of the items, evaluating everything from the stones' geological composition to the anomalies in a series of lozenges when subjected to microscopic analysis. There was much talk of fine-grained siltstone, diorite and nummulitic limestone. Some even suggested that a modern stylus was taken to crystalline marble chunks of desecrated old tombstones.

There was as much discussion between the university-trained experts as to the mish-mash of images and scripts as there was to corrosion patterns and induced patination. Could all of the garbled iconography be some kind of a hidden code of "gibberish with meaning" employed by a secret society with their own agenda for producing the confusing markings?

Or, were the historical oddities on the objects faithfully reproduced by some ancient seafarers who had lost touch of their own history over the centuries? If this were the case, could the local Indian traditions of white-skinned foreigners visiting the Americas long before Columbus be true? There were committees and conferences. As the Epigraphical Societies cried data-suppression and the historical groups called for proper testing methods (hoping to discredit what they knew couldn't be genuine historical records), one magnetic Pentecostal preacher had the answer to all the controversy.

Roovert Purdy and his minions had parked the church's hay-wagon sideways across a major street in order to have their say. The pasty-faced preacher held up a portable calculator and shouted into a King Coney megaphone:

"Since Genesis and this Pocketronic tell us that the universe is less than 6,000 years old, the stones must have been put here by the Devil to deceive us. Just like the dinosaur bones were, unless old Stegosaurus was a pet of Cleopatra's. Personally, I'd rather buy a thrift shop photograph of Jesus than some stupid rock with primitive stick figures planted by a scalawag. Don't believe all this hogwash about a bunch of bongo-Congo kings floating over here on large tree branches. The same academic pissants would have you believe that your own kin were limb-hopping monkeys. Trust me, friends, you don't want to make the boss man mad. What does the Bible say: Now His head and His hairs are white like wool, white as snow; and His eyes are like a lamp of fire... Eyes like a torch of fire! And he's gonna return again to establish his kingdom, so I hope you like your grape juice unfermented. Amen!"

Despite Roovert's stern warning, a treasure hunting mania took hold of the town for well over a month. High-school dropouts suddenly had an interest in ancient Egyptology. Weathering patterns on medallions with Hebrew characters were discussed in the Tomboy. Eye of Horus iced cookies became the favorite at the local bakery. The hardware store quickly ran out of shovels, as did those in neighboring towns. Hundreds of people took to digging in patches of woods hell-bent on unearthing the next cache of valuable objects. As they sunk spades into the hollows, drunken conversations among construction workers in the smoky taverns centered around a process of reverse alchemy. It was suggested that gold artifacts had been coated in soft dark clay and then baked hard in ovens before being deposited as ordinary-looking rocks in streambeds for safekeeping. (This idea became especially popular once the rumors started to spread of state legislation by both the politicians in Springfield and the federal authorities for antiquities protection). Many locals also didn't forget the old tales of the fabulous treasure associated with the seven back road bridges. When some of them began racing about in the countryside, I got a phone call from Ollie asking if I wanted to help him paint a 'Road Runner' tunnel on a concrete wall that was near the supposed sixth trestle.

When Zerrill learned that Nestor had once asked a landowner if he could take samples of mudstones from his property, he questioned a local geologist and lapidary to see if moist black clay or poorly lithified ooze could be artificially hardened into argillite and vice versa, if hardened argillite could be artificially softened? When he told me about this possibility to explain how the perpetrator of the hoax could create so many specimens, though I believed that Nestor had the means for cooking the stones, I doubted that he would have any clue as to what to engrave on them. For this, he would definitely need help, and I soon had a thought as to who his partner might be. Who did we both know that had an interest in ancient cultures along with numerous paperbacks filled with illustrations of these bygone civilizations? Who would be smart enough and willing to go along with such a creatively deceptive enterprise? I could only think of one person. Kelby.

Once the town people heard through the grapevine that Zerrill's highly specialized organization possessed a "Lewis" map, many surmised that this pertained to the treasure of Meriwether

Lewis that was rumored to have been buried in southern Illinois after the "Corps of Discovery" returned and Lewis became a Master Mason of the St. Louis Lodge. I remembered Zerrill pulling out a crude hand held map after I pointed to the shallow pits in the abandoned field near the dirt bike trail, but, at the time, he shrugged off the evenly spaced holes as common animal burrows.

As the treasure hunting mania reached a fever pitch, Zerrill got an earful from the locals about this so-called "Lewis map." Sensing the 'torch and pitchfork mob', he finally agreed that he would produce the map and that there would be a public dig – in an organized fashion – with the discovery of anything of value benefitting the entire town.

Hundreds of the town folk had gathered in a large field on a Saturday afternoon to watch the digging. The atmosphere was festive – like a large picnic – or even a Fourth of July celebration. With blankets, lawn chairs and ice-chests, those waiting for the idling backhoe to be positioned near the 'X marks the spot' according to the coordinates on Zerrill's tattered map were already doing their own digging into baskets of fried chicken, egg salad and ham sandwiches.

As members of the Historical Society adjusted their cameras outside a cordoned off area where men wearing hardhats marked a grid, locals exchanged pleasantries in anxious anticipation of what might be unearthed. Children with sugar highs were running around in circles laughing while guzzling Mountain Dew as whiffs of skunkweed wafted from the direction where some of older kids were pitching horseshoes. Over the discordant crowd,

the tinny 'music boxes' of several ice cream vans simultaneously repeating the *Pop Goes The Weasel* melody out of sync rattled
some nerves, as did the occasional bang of leftover fireworks.

After Zerrill gave the okay sign to the pudgy operator of the
backhoe, its hydraulic pistons went to work.

When the digging bucket gouged the field, old timers dressed
in baggy hayseed clothes thumbed open bottles of beer with
skeptical grins on their large pink pumpkin heads. Toddlers im-
itated the powerful mechanized arm by putting handfuls of dirt
with stiff robotic motions into steel-pressed industrial orange
Tonka trucks. The diesel engine of the old Ford wheezed "like a
rented mule", someone said, as the steel boom, stick and bucket
continued to move with great force until a worker shouted to the
operator that the clanking scoop had struck something.

Using a hand-held shovel, he cleared away the loose soil
to reveal a human skull. Further digging revealed that it was
still attached to the rest of the skeleton that was somehow buried in a vertical position. Feeding on the excitement, dozens
more volunteers with shovels continued to dig until sections of
green enameled metal along with traces of yellow paint could
be seen around the human remains. A comically macabre picture began to take shape – one that had the workers scratching
their heads. It was a perfectly intact skeleton sitting erect on the
pan seat of an old (1941) John Deere tractor that appeared to
have been buried decades ago.

Children whose faces were smeared with the chocolate of
frozen novelties stared in horrified fascination at the odd spectacle as their equally aghast parents tried to comprehend the
shocking sight.

As several police officers approached the skeleton strad-
dling the antique tractor in the burial pit, Zerrill appeared to be

dumbstruck while consulting the treasure map. All the while, the volunteers continued to dig, revealing more of the John Deere's frame, and even its big rubber tires. The condition of the tractor was uncanny – almost perfectly preserved, as were the bones of its skeleton driver.

The voice of one of the old timers broke the silence.

"It's Lewis Scruggs, I reckon, on his forty-two GM Row-Crop."

"No parts wasteland for Lewis," another said. "My tractor will never be red either."

"Check out that old fashioned grill. He must have bought that beauty from a Blacksmith shop," a younger farmer joked.

"I reckon its got a conversion kit that made it run on gasoline," the oldest one mumbled.

An elderly woman dressed in rustic clothes and wearing a wide-brimmed hat made her way through the crowd. I recalled seeing her at the exact site of the burial pit before it had been disturbed. At the time, she placed a canister of gas in the same area where today's digging had started.

"All you ought to be ashamed. Coming here lookin' to find oodles of gold and messing up my daddy's final resting place. Pa loved that tractor so much that he arranged to have her buried here with him behind the wheel when his time came. Crops... corn, that's the real gold treasure in these parts. Not King Tut. You city-slicker societies ought to be ashamed."

Just when it seemed that things couldn't get more farcical, the old women broke through the orange tape and clambered down into the large hole.

"What's you doing, Gert?" an old timer asked.

"To make amends for this desecration, I thought I ought to at least change the spark plugs while the hole's open. Pa wouldn't want no rough idles or misfires while he's tractor-ing. Pa always used to say fouling is a sure way to burn down the barn."

The backhoe operator checked out the spark plugs that she was holding.

"Well, darlin', if you're really serious about carbon fouling, then I'd suggest you go with Autolite plugs. 3116's. I wouldn't put those damn things in my dinky weed eater."

As the town folk began packing up their stuff, I watched as teary-eyed children tried to figure out their parents' awkward explanations (those who weren't tongue-tied). At the same time, I listened as those involved in the digging tried to console the sheepish Zerrill by acknowledging his good intentions. It wasn't the first failed attempt to find buried treasure, they said, citing Montezuma, Blackbeard and Mosby as examples. Plus, the mistake was understandable. Who would have ever guessed that a farmer named "Lewis" had stated in his Will that he wanted to be interred astride his beloved tractor? But, why hadn't any of these people asked why the other members of Zerrill's special organization didn't bother showing up to the site, I wondered?

A decision had been made to re-fill the trench with things left exactly as they were. (There was also some discussion about adding a grave marker with the appropriate color scheme, of course.)

Before the front-loader part of the tractor began scooping up the piles of dirt, I couldn't help but notice Zerrill's seeming interest in the farmer's exposed skull. There was something about it – something unnoticed by the others – that caused him to take a closer look. I couldn't determine exactly what this was from where I was standing, but judging by the look on his face, it must have been something important.

The whole thing seemed fishy to me.

Though he had appeared to be perplexed by that which had been unearthed, something told me that Zerrill knew all along that the name "Lewis" scrawled in the bottom corner of the little map had nothing to do with the explorer Meriwether. First of all, he was way too careless about the map – even if its treasure was of a historical nature – almost as if he wanted lots of people to know that it was in his possession. It seemed more likely to have been an ingenious ploy on his part to deflate all the treasure hunting fervor (that he had helped to perpetuate). Not only was it designed to quash the town's enthusiasm of all that glitters, it was intended to serve another purpose – that of a smokescreen to divert attention away from something else.

Whatever the reason, the town eagerly took the bait. Now that its believers had been thoroughly humiliated by articles in the bemused local press – as well as in the larger newspapers such as the *Saint Louis Post Dispatch,* who had a field day with one little town's foolish obsession with a historical identity – Zerrill was free to pursue his own agenda without having to constantly look over his shoulders. I honestly wasn't sure what he was up to – what caused him to leave us with egg on our face and our tail between our legs, but I was pretty sure that it had something to do with the ghoulish enterprises of the former undertaker, Molewhisker.

Even though Zerrill had voiced his skepticism of Nestor's artifacts – calling them childish nonsense and a practical joke – I had recently seen him purchase one that in my opinion looked different from the others, having on its polished surface a symbol that seemed more modern. Actually, timeless might be a better way of describing it. I might have been imaging things, but the design resembled one that I had seen on the doohickey while it was displaying moving images.

Nestor was telling some of his angry customers that he had indisputable proof that his artifacts were genuine, and that one day soon he would produce this evidence. When I called Kelby to ask about his possible involvement in the matter, he told me not to say anything to anyone, but the truth was that he knew exactly where Nestor's artifacts had been buried, because in a past life he had worked on a trash barge in pre-dynastic Egypt, and that back in those days of ancient sunlight they had used what is now southern Illinois as a garbage dump. Once his labors were finished and the rubbish had been disposed of, he had been walled inside the cave – according to tradition while still alive – so as not to reveal its secret location. As he awaited death, he could only hope that his next incarnation was better. Ha! That was Kelby for you. Was he also chagrined by the whole thing, but cleverer in disassociating himself from the madness?

Although my dad had been the skunk at the tea party, he was now vindicated for his stance on both the phony artifacts and the treasure map incident. My mother, on the other hand, still appeared to be embarrassed.

With a startled gasp after almost running over me in the hallway, once she regained her composure and said that she was sorry that she didn't see me, she told me that she was feeling a little guilty for inventing the arcane symbolism in the ornamental pattern on the Oreo cookies when Zerrill and her were playing a little joke on my dad with my silly punishment essay. (To me, the strange thing was that it was the third time that day that someone had ran into me with a surprised scream, only to apologize and claim that they didn't see me.) I told her that it wasn't anything to worry about and that it was actually kind of funny.

The funniest thing of all, though, was that once the town people had enough of the "Little Egypt" moniker, even the wowzers in the park that dropped tabs of acid stopped meditating on the Oreo emboss, saying that they were "over" searching for any hidden meaning. From that point on, the cookies, if not dunked into a glass of milk, were just crunchy chocolate wafers that people often unscrewed to lick the creamy filling.

Towards the end of July, rumors began circulating around town about something really big that was about to occur. The first hint of this was only the word, "MORE" which was passed along in hushed tones to a certain crowd so that the wrong people wouldn't get wind of it. As speculation grew about this major happening, the rumors continued to be spread by word of mouth. The occasion was not to be publicized and nothing was to be discussed verbally that might arouse suspicion from the authorities. Whatever this event was, I was assured that it was going to shake things up.

CHAPTER VI
INITIATRIXIE

The hushed whispers turned out to be a person's last name. "More" was Troy Moore, a local college kid whose parents owned a large farm on the outskirts of town. On the appropriate date of August 15, with his folks away, he hosted an event that was dubbed "MOORESTOCK." For the pint-sized imitation of the famous rock festival that occurred a few years ago, a flatbed trailer parked on the spacious lawn had been converted into a makeshift stage that was crammed with musical gear and lit by a handful of Fresnels. The word of mouth plan had been a great success, as hundreds of people from nearby towns converged on the site for the celebration, bringing with them chairs, blankets, coolers, tents and lots of dope.

When I arrived just before dusk, "Silver Cirkus" was performing to a cheering crowd that was glistening with perspiration. As some guzzled Ripple from leather Bota bags and others smoked joints, Topo was warning the audience over the P.A. system about the nasty side effects of the "Devil's Cherries" – a Belladonna concoction that had already caused numerous girls to experience partial blindness. Though the Nightshade was 'brown acided', no one seemed to be having a bum trip from the Windowpane that was sold openly in capsules of leftover Mr. Wiggle candy corn orange gelatin. Ditto with the newly discovered DOM (or STP), whose intense hallucinogenic effects included "fantastic prisms of light" according to what I heard while making my way through the crowd.

While inching closer to the stage, I felt someone grab my arm. Wheeling around, I saw a swarthy complexioned woman with dark ringlets of hair tumbling from a Bohemian headscarf. The opening in her flaxen blouse revealed indigo cleavage tattoos that I quickly lifted my gaze from when she introduced herself as "Talia without the H." Raising her voice to be heard over the music, she told me that she had tried to get my attention once before when she had a gig as a fortuneteller at the Mayfest. She had taken the job to earn some quick cash, she admitted, and even though the crystal ball was just a glass prop, she truly was a medium.

Wrist bracelets jangled as she spoke in a highly animated manner about things that I didn't have an inkling of. 'Age of Aquarius' type shit. She said that at the time of the spring carnival my atmosphere had fascinated her – the desirable shifting colors of vital magnetism that were of an extremely unusual character. She further explained that when I hurried away after she waved to me with excited interest, she didn't want to intrude, though she could have followed the radiant particles that sloughed off my subtle anatomy in a similar manner to the scent that a bloodhound trails. But now the colorful emanations were quite different. She was getting bad vibes and could feel dark holes in my auric radiations. To her psychic sight, the vividly luminous streaks from the hubs of my ethereal wheels were now being cast off as a sickly-colored exhaust. Whatever it was that I was struggling with required magnetic healing – so that once again my subtle body would be strongly charged.

When I smiled and asked her if she had partaken of any Windowpane, she made a sad expression and simply said that I was a sputtering candle. Deep inside, I knew that she had perceived something about my energy level, and for this I was a bit unnerved. In truth, I wasn't merely a guttering candle. As for any radiant gyrations of rainbow dynamism or whatever it was that she was rambling about, lately I had been so listless and unable to think clearly that it didn't come as a surprise that someone gifted (or cursed) in these matters would describe the layers of my aura as a curlicue of smoke from a snuffed out black match head.

As I was about to ask Talia without the H where I could find this mystical oriental medicine (even though I was more concerned about peculiar body sensations than I was about auric out-sparkings), someone bumped into me from behind so hard that it nearly caused me to lose my balance. While bracing myself against the person drinking from a wineskin in front of me, I heard a startled shriek. Turning around in time to grab hold of the fluttering bell sleeve on a black chiffon blouse that kept this woman from falling, I managed not to tear the material. Looking up, I saw Trixie standing there. At first she seemed pretty weirded out, but quickly composed herself.

"Addison Albright, why did I not see you?" she said while adjusting the sheer blouse.

"I don't know – it's getting darker," I offered lamely while staring at the pretty oval face that was framed by straight long dark hair that nearly reached her faded fringed jeans.

She gestured towards the band. "Good timing for the song."
"Huh?"

"Treatises On Ludicrously Faked Sunsets. It's the song that Topo wrote. He played parts of it for us in the Notilus. The band's doing it now."

"Is that Maja?" the psychic asked.

"Well, sort of," Trixie replied. "It's not the stuff in the Rexall... not Myrurgia – it's my own version – but it does have a similar vibe."

The perfume brought back memories of cruising in the backseat of Chooch's Impala. (Speaking of which, the Fryer was completely wasted on something, clicking his grody teeth while moving about unsteadily near the stage.)

At that moment, I noticed the flashing red beacon of a police car down by the farm's long gravel entrance. Then more light bars began to appear, with the red and blue strobes reflecting off the numerous cars and vans parked on both sides of the road. There must have been dozens of them from the various counties, all converging on the peaceful gathering.

"Hey, look at 'em all," I uttered while pointing to the approaching line of flashing lights. "It's a bust! You want to split?" I asked Trixie.

As "Silver Cirkus" continued to perform their opus, I grabbed Trixie's hand and told her to follow me. We pushed our way through the oblivious crowd, quickening our pace while nearly choking on the haze of Michoacan. Looking over my shoulder at the multitude of flickering cop lights, I pointed to a field that was surrounded by darkening golden-orange woods.

Breaking into a run, we found ourselves amid the colorful plumage of a dozen or so free-ranging peafowl. With shrill cries, they scattered away from bits of cabbage placed near some wooden roosts. Though I was planning on just ducking behind some trees, when I saw a narrow path that wound into the forest, we followed it until I felt that we were far enough away from the massive police raid.

"It's a good thing I didn't wear my clogs," Trixie said while catching her breath.

"Man, they are at the trough. It's gonna be carnage," I said excitedly. "I remember this Moore guy being a 4-H bumpkin. He never hung with the stoners. I'm guessing he's a narc who helped the cops toss a net over the whole lot. I'll bet Dovie is involved, too. I don't want to be thrown into a paddy wagon and hauled to jail. I'm planning on grabbing a King Coney dog after this."

"Fuck, you're making my mouth water," Trixie said while jabbing me in the stomach.

She pulled out a small flashlight and shined it further down the well-defined trail.

"Wow, check it out."

I could see what looked like a series of tree forts and crude wooden huts that blended in with the natural landscape. As Trixie moved the beam about, I thought that the small dwellings might have comprised some kind of hippie commune. But what were they doing on the Moore's property? When we cautiously entered the largest rustic structure, not only was it uninhabited, there wasn't any sign that someone ever lived there. Not a single piece of trash anywhere. In the pristine setting, a shallow creek was flowing right in the middle of what might have been the cabin's living room.

Trixie's eyes widened as she paced about with a faintly bewildered look.

"So... if neither one of us are holding... or even high... and we haven't been drinking..."

I sat down on a carved log bench by the gurgling water and placed my hands on my forehead.

"Yeah, why'd we beat feet without any stash?" I said while shaking my head. "When I was little, my friends and I would follow the mosquito-fogging truck on our bikes. We'd be right inside the cloud of pesticide, licking our frosty Popsicles and inhaling the toxic fumes while pedaling up and down the streets. And there were lots of dirt clod battles. I got hit in the head many times. Did you ever eat that white gunk – Elmer's paste – when you were young? Yesterday, my dad asked me why I only mowed half of the lawn? Because I can't think clearly – untested bug spray and snowball fights with rocks inside – that's why, dad..."

"We chased the insecticide-spraying truck, too. Only we licked Banana Fudgesicles... if that makes any difference?" Trixie was unable to repress a smile as I tightened the grip on my forehead. Changing the subject, she asked me about Talia without the H.

"Who was that woman that looked like a gypsy?"

"She sounded like the lyrics to that Aquarius song. She said that there are holes in my aura. Probably because I used to chew on my pencils and eat the erasers."

"Well, now what?" she asked while playfully shining the light onto my face.

"I know you're dying for some charred flesh," I teased the vegetarian.

"I can honestly say that I'd rather chomp right through a number two pencil."

"What's that mystical gleam?" I joked, gesturing to her necklace pendant.

Unsure what to say at first, after a short pause, she lifted the Egyptian amulet so that I could have a better look. In the faint light, the strange creature depicted in the vermillion gleam of the faience had a canine or jackal-like head, with long erect ears and a curved snout. I noticed that the beast also had cloven hooves and a stiff forked tail.

"It looks kind of like that Saluki dog," I said.

"It's the totemic animal of Setekh – the ancient Egyptian god of the foreign lands beyond the desert. Not much is known about the creature itself – it's unrecognizable – but because of Setekh's association with the serpent, another Nightside zootype, its cult has been repressed and demonized by the alarmed peasantry. The magical revival that I'm part of identifies the deity as the giver of the Black Flame – the teacher responsible for our questioning intellect. Do you want to know more?"

"Does he bite?" I asked with a half smile.

"Is he dangerous? Well, I think that depends on where one's head is at. The ancient Egyptians believed that Setekh helped the dead ascend on the ladder of the seven imperishable stars to their thrones among the gods in the celestial vault. Now, what most people fail to realize is that the dead who are spoken of here weren't physically dead. They weren't deceased. Being dead was an allegory for those living corpses who were uninitiated into certain esoteric teachings."

Unsure if she should continue, she glanced down at the reddish luster of the glazed ceramic.

"So, let me guess. If you told me, you'd have to kill me," I kidded. When she didn't answer right away, I asked her what she hoped to gain out of all this?

"The object of my desire – a Magical Child," she said almost inaudibly.

She then began to speak a little more as to some of the hazards facing practitioners of left-hand path ritual magic.

"In theory, with a focused projection of consciousness, the magician gains access to the pathways hidden behind nature's veils... on the shadowside of the qabalistic Tree of Life. Lying in wait, though... as the final obstruction to those who aim to attain mastery of this Arte is the Dweller on the Threshold — that which separates and divides. With the disintegration of one's ego, the mental processes that activate the Nightside gates and underlying tunnels to the uncharted regions of the psyche mustn't be undertaken lightly. "

"You haven't changed much," I said with obvious sarcasm.

Confident that we could find our way back into town without having to return to the Moore's farm (both of us had gotten rides there in separate vans), we followed the twisting path to the other side of the woods. We then skirted a few cornfields until I recognized the forest up ahead from my youth. It was the same sloping woody terrain that Kelby, Ollie and I had often explored for anything of interest. Along the way, Trixie answered some more questions that I had concerning her interest in these occult matters.

I was surprised that she had not sworn an oath of allegiance when it came to divulging the Order's rituals. There were no membership dues or secret passwords. The initiatory grades and degree ceremonies also differed from that of other quasi-Masonic lodges, she explained.

All that was required was innovation, with the prime focus being the exploration of the alternate dimensions of consciousness and to map this arcane topography with signposts for fellow travelers. Although the exclusive keys to the magical system were communicated in a coded twilight language, she had no qualms about attempting to elucidate some of the more nebulous concepts of magic (not to be confused with stage illusions à la Houdini and others). But first I needed to wipe the slate clean. This included the purposeful fabrications propagated by the Church and influential Hollywood misconceptions – those occult clichés that we all grew up with from watching the late night movies.

She said that she was currently receiving qualified guidance on the techniques used for the mastery of her mental and physical functions. This included meditative postures, breathing exercises, magical chastity and banishing rites. The curriculum that led to expanding the boundaries of one's mind was extremely demanding, although it didn't necessarily involve an austere lifestyle, let alone self-inflicted razor slashes for any shortcomings.

As to why she subjected herself to such rigorous training, she told me that she didn't want to flounder in mediocrity. To spend her life as just another herd animal. Most organized religions were mud-clotted gems – pearls cast before swine – meaning their lackadaisical followers. She would rather go to the hells of all the world's religions than cower before some perverse God who was created in man's image and whereby humanity's worst traits were projected onto the divine.

She was willing to surrender all in order to realize the untapped potential that slumbers inside us. As a practitioner of left-hand path magic – whose mysterious operations were performed with surgical precision in one's laboratory-temple – the ritual procedures were based on working in polarity in order to cultivate sexual energy whose 'positive' ecstasies were used to raise potent forces. With regard to the subtle power-zones of our occult anatomy that generate valuable essences, she stressed the importance of the rapport between partners whose charged co-mingled substances could be channeled and siphoned off to be utilized by the magician for various purposes. The focused Will required for fulfilling one's desire – for birthing and nurturing magical offspring – in order to be successful demanded extreme concentration. Intruding thoughts could introduce something unwanted into the operation. Besides the possibility of a deep-seated psychosis, lingering tangential phenomena could also occur after the completion of the ritual, despite all of the safeguards.

When I asked what she meant by success, she replied that it was to break the mind locks placed on us. Nightside workings were designed to whittle away our illusory nature… to tear asunder the tangled web of deception… the flimsy mirages of daytime 'reality.' With clarity of thought came true sovereignty, she emphasized. And to that end, she was making significant headway.

While passing yet another cornfield under the moon's narrow sickle, Trixie continued to talk about the malleability of reality and the glamours of the phenomenal world. Knee deep in weeds now, we found ourselves standing before the rickety wooden fence that confined the private cemetery where I had first encountered Molewhisker several years ago.

Rather than walk around it, we decided to enter the unkempt grounds through a gap in its rotting barrier. Moving slowly through a maze of timeworn headstones and lichen-covered statuary, Trixie trained the sweep of her flashlight beam on some of the mysterious epitaphs and ambiguous symbols etched in the weathered marble. She seemed particularly interested by a moss-shrouded bronze plaque whose Latin inscription read:

NON OMNIS MORIAR

Even more intriguing than the cryptic funerary graffiti were the grave markers that had two different death dates incised for the same person. With her flashlight tracing several other anomalies engraved into the faded stone, I noticed that the conflicting death years all began on January 17, which just so happened to be my birthday. Weird, I thought. Next to these defaced head-stones was an askew slab whose carved motifs had been daubed with painted green flames that encircled scrawls proclaiming:

MAXX HELL FOR THE WILL O' THE WISPS

As we proceeded along the meandering narrow path, I felt a tug on my sleeve. In the stillness, there was the faint clinking of a pick. Kneeling in the soft earth behind the crumbling stone edging of a tombstone, we could make out in the distance a canvas lean-to where two indistinct forms were digging near an eroded obelisk-shaped marble grave marker that was dimly illuminated by a shaded lantern. With strangely synchronized motions the identically dressed figures were re-opening a grave as was made evident by a pile of dirt in front of the shielding blanket. After hearing the cracking of wood, we watched as the men quickly extracted a corpse that was im-peccably dressed in a mauve-colored suit. The exhumed body was placed on a tarp with its head rolling on its shoulders and its arms dangling to the ground. To one side of the lean-to, I perceived Molewhisker's old hot rod hearse parked near a shed with a galvanized roof.

While leaning forward to look for the man himself, we were both startled by a strident cackle. I could feel the blood standing still in my body as I turned to see a pair of polished Oxfords in the grass next to the sickly raisiny expel of chewing tobacco. Glancing up, there he was – Molewhisker – sour-visaged as al-ways. With his gnarled venous hand clutching the walking stick's regal flourishes, he was dressed exactly as he had been the first time that I had laid eyes on him, wearing a tailored black suit with a grey cravat, mauve hanky and a black fedora hat.

Tense with expectation, Trixie rose before the gaunt figure with the twisted angular face and rheumy dark blue eyes. I could tell from her expression that the long mole whisker that coiled from his chin some three inches long repulsively fascinated her.

Noticing the scarlet glint of the majolica amulet that depicted the totemic animal of Setekh on her necklace, his indignant gaze turned to one of cynical amusement. Looking me straight in the eye, he gestured towards the despoiled burial plot. With irritation that bordered on resentment he uttered, "I do this only for the third mind."

When he shambled away, we hastened down the winding path, Trixie unable to keep from looking back with her mouth agape.

When we made our way back into town, we headed straight to the Notilus where Trixie was planning to spend the night. However, when we arrived at the overgrown lot, we were both surprised to see that the derelict psychedelic bus was no longer there. At first we weren't sure what had happened, but it soon dawned on us that our sanctuary with flat tires had most likely been towed as part of the police crackdown. Maybe it would serve as a drug awareness display in the town square next to all the brick taverns. With nowhere else to go, I walked Trixie to her parents' house. The entire way, she grumbled about their tertiary pastime of Sunday Mass with its liturgical diarrhea followed by their blobby neighbors hooting and hollering at a Red Birds' kegger party. Which reminded me, the King Coney was about to close.

The police raid on the Moore farm was the talk of town for a couple of weeks. The local paper reported on the numerous arrests for narcotics, which prompted further action from the town officials to completely eradicate the problem before chromosomal aberrations led to "mutants with eyes in their knees." The elbow-benders in "The Cracked Hoof" joked about measures taken to keep tripping teenage sitters from mistakenly placing babies in ovens and pizzas in bassinets. While downing shots of "Lord Calvert", the shit kickers were particularly bemused by the interview in *The Spectrum* with a Pentecostal firebrand (Roovert Purdy), who wondered why anyone would want to storm some counterfeit paradise when the world's original hippie freak welcomed them with open arms to the real McCoy once baptized in the Holy Spirit? In the Blue Double Dome of heaven there would be plenty of Orange Sunshine!

The arrest of Chooch for what was found in his Murine bottle would almost certainly result in a lengthy prison sentence. (I chuckled to myself that he might want to send his fictitious bother, Mooch, a Trailways ticket back home in case an identical twin was needed for any jailhouse chicanery.) Without the "Fryer" making his rounds in the Impalanda, the mischief in the sunny park and nightly revelry inside the kaleidoscopic hulk, the vibe in town had changed. But that's not all that changed. For whatever reason, my health began to improve…dramatically. I was no longer extremely fatigued or clinically depressed. People weren't accidently bumping into me, and my parents were relieved that I didn't only change half of the litter box.

As the summer ended, my thoughts turned to the "Scientific Illuminism" that Trixie had attempted to explain – even if in the sketchiest manner – before she returned to college for the fall semester. Taking into consideration what my mother had once said about the will o' the wisp leading people astray, I didn't feel that Trixie had been ensnared by the tentacles of some malignant brilliancy. Her ideas about magic had little to do with the brooding abstraction of black-cloaked adepts with jeweled daggers and sacrificial virgins that one could read about in lurid bus stop novels or that were graphically depicted in nocturnal spectacles on scratchy celluloid strips flickering at the midnight marquee. Setian magic didn't involve making diabolical pacts with motley devils from spirit catalogues to obtain banal advantages. It wasn't about earthly pleasures or worldly gain. It was about adjusting the perceptual filters in one's grayish curds, and the trans-human potential of a physiological nexus. The erotic mechanisms of tantra mainly concerned the occult (i.e. hidden) hyperchemistry of human anatomy − psychosexual fluids with mysterious qualities that stimulated stagnant minds and activated long dormant neural circuitry. It was inner alchemy.

Trixie once told me that she wanted to venture with her subtle body into dimensions that were strange beyond all imagining. *Strange beyond all imagining!* I had stubbed my toe in such otherworldly realms. How many times had I stepped off the canvas of consensus reality to glimpse what existed behind the scenery? For many years I had gnawing doubts about my mental state, but now Trixie had me wondering if I had already somehow plumbed uncharted depths? The question was: without any ceremonial hocus-pocus (and mystical exultation!), how did I have the ability to breach the seamless stitching of the commonplace phenomenal world into the otherness − shifting between that which separates and divides? Was I born fully integrated into this magical environment that she spoke so eloquently of? Receiving faint impressions of the next evolutionary step... or were these quasi-human forms just phantasms of an imagination gone berserk? Speaking of mind-stuff, what did "the third mind" that

Molewhisker claimed to be the reason for his body snatching have to do with it all?

The sun finally glinted on the fall pigments as I drove towards one of the brooding trestles that were supposed to make up the Seven Gates to Hell located on these winding back roads. With a little over a month to go before I took my driver's test, I was grinding the gears of my dad's old VW Microbus in the rain-slicked countryside with my learner's permit stuffed in my back pocket.

Zerrill was seated next to me as the van's pearl white frame passed under the graffiti-covered passageway and continued to swish through the twisting amber-orange woodlands.

"Add engine misfire to the loose fan and holey muffler, but at least the wiper blades on this shame train work", he grinned while counting off the numerous mechanical issues the "Vee-Dub" had before bracing himself against the metal dashboard as I pumped the brakes and skidded into a gravel turnoff.

"Sticky brake caliper," Zerrill touched his pinky finger. "So, when the time comes, what are you going to use to fill this box up?"

"Well, I was thinking about getting a job pumping gas at the Clark station," I frowned.

"Just make sure to call yourself a Petroleum Transfer Engineer when you're trying to score points with the ladies," he winked.

"When you once said that Molewhisker had accidently opened the gates of hell, you were just kidding, right?" I asked.

"It's not Santa Barbara, but it's not hell either. We're not seeing whitewashed steeples and root beer saloons while floating in a lake of boiling hot magma. It's not the skirl of demons that you hear – it's a squeaky distributor shaft. Of course I was joking. Okay, so you said you had something that you wanted to tell me, but that you wanted to ask me something first. Was that it?"

"How come you let the people here think that the little map belonged to Meriwether Lewis when I'll bet you knew all along that it had to do with that dumb farmer named Lewis?"

"That's what you think? Wow, that's pretty good, Addison. You're right. But, I couldn't just start digging up the field on my own. I convinced the locals to help – which they were more than happy to do. I got what I wanted when I saw that someone had taken a can opener to that dumb farmer's skull in precisely the correct location for something to have been removed after some pretty handy trepanation work. I didn't come here looking for the evidence of some mysterious tribe of white-skinned natives. What I'm really looking for is evidence of a particular family. The last of their kind, perhaps. They were said to be pale-skinned… like albinos… only their eyes aren't pale blue. They have eyes that are golden. The sun-filled ones. The family of a bygone age. The people of myths and legends."

"Is Mister Schaufler part of this family?" I asked.

"Well, he's not what he appears to be, that's for sure. But that doesn't necessarily mean –"

"So why did you buy that one rock from Nestor when you called the others fakes?" I changed the subject.

"Because the symbol carved on it is unlike anything that was known in ancient Egypt. The moment I saw it, I was attracted like a magnet. And it continues to exert its influence on me. I think it serves as a protective shield. It creates a barrier of protection against something… but it also brings negative energy to the surface so that it can be properly dealt with."

"Like a curse," I said.

"Like a very effective curse," he emphasized. "But, then again – it might act as an antenna that picks up signals from spiritual dimensions."

"But it's so simple looking."

"Don't be fooled by its simplicity. It has exceptional properties."

"So, if I have a friend that reads a lot about this stuff, could he have seen it in a book?"

"It's very doubtful. Impossible really. It remains virtually unknown to modern scholars. What I can't figure out is how your friend, of all people, copied it onto one of his bogus artifacts. It's not like the gangly grocer gained access to the akashic records. He must have seen it somewhere. But, he's not talking. I've practically bought the entire inventory from that little cellar shithole and he still has nothing to say."

"Why is it so important that you find this family?"

"That they might be the last of their kind – that's not enough? How about to overturn old conceptions about our past civilizations? Which reminds me, I'd appreciate it if you don't say anything about this to your father. Even though he'd just call it balderdash, or what is it that he says?"

"Bush League. So, I know someone who might be able to help you. Other than her necklace looks like the logo on cans of Deviled Ham, she's pretty hip when it comes to weird Egyptian stuff. She's a Setianist."

"Setekh? Well there goes the neighborhood. A Setianist among the sodbusters."

"Have you ever seen the Mermaid of Poseidia that's on display at the Mayfest freak show?" I asked.

"Nope. I can't say that I have. What's that like – the Wild Man of Borneo? A freak show attraction? I'm starting to think that this hasn't been a fair exchange so far, Addison."

"Forget about the bogus fishtail, but look really closely at her face."

"Now what are you trading – dog shit for diamonds?"

"Look really close at her face!"

"Okay, the next time something wicked this way comes, I'll pull a shiny quarter out of my pocket."

He placed his hand on the gearshift knob and drummed his fingers.

"We're currently at bridge number six – which is considered to be a twin to the bridge just around the bend. For some reason both are believed to only count as one gate. Who knows why that is... but let's get this window licker back home before the Hounds of Hell come a calling should we have a blown engine. Setianism amongst the fluttering cornstalks... and a carnival mermaid from Poseidia." He rolled his eyes and shook his head.

In the gloaming on a crisp Halloween night, I was exiting the Tomboy market with a box of Domino sugar when I noticed a woman with a long grey ponytail that looked vaguely familiar. As she checked out the postings on a bulletin board, it soon occurred to me that she was the lady whose young child was dressed as Molewhisker while trick-or-treating in Ollie's neighborhood. When the subject of the old Victorian came up, she told us that she had lived next door to Mister Schaufler while growing up in the 1950s. She said that she had witnessed the will o' the wisps in the soybean fields behind the house and also mentioned a disturbing bland-faced kid that she referred to as a ragamuffin. At the time of the telling, I had wanted to hear more about these strange occurrences, but her son was anxious to move on to the next treats. Since that night, our paths had never crossed. I remembered that she said that she was an artist, and since there were splotches of paint on her Adidas, I figured that it must be her.

"Excuse me, miss. Did you use to live on ShadowCrest in the nineteen fifties?" I asked.

"Yes, that's right," she replied with a puzzled look. "Why do you ask?"

"When I was younger you were taking your son trick-or-treating and you told my friends and I some great stories. Since then, I wanted to hear some more. I used to do odd jobs at Mister Schaufler's house, and saw some pretty crazy stuff there myself."

At the mention of Schaufler's name, her expression darkened.

"Oh... I don't know. Um... Well, I'm going next door to Hattie's for some coffee. If you want to join me, I guess we can have a little chat about some things. What's your name again?"

"Addison Albright."

"I'm Cassidy."

"Yeah... There's just a couple of things if that's okay?"

Hattie's was the newest shop in the little plaza next to the Tomboy. It sold sandwiches, pies and non-alcohol beverages. I hadn't been there yet, but when I stepped inside, I felt like I was in a grandmother's kitchen. The décor was old-fashioned country, with lots of muted shades of primary colors. Among the kitchen kitsch were figurines of porcelain roosters, rustic linen prints, antique butter churns and glazed Hummel plates that depicted apple trees. We sat down on wooden stools at a small table with a checkered cloth that was aglow from a ceramic ivory hurricane glass candleholder (even though the interior was brightly lit). Instead of the daily specials printed on the chalkboard easel,

Hattie's sermon for the All Hallows' Eve tradition read: DON'T LET YOUR CHILD WORSHIP THE DEVIL EVEN ON ONE DAY A YEAR.

As squirrely blonde high-school sisters Shandi and Shiloh (or was it Sawyer?) took orders from the few elderly customers, Cassidy decided to have a piece of cornbread with her coffee, while I chose a brownie and an orange "soft drink" that was served in a quaint mason jar.

"Do you know Russell Pitts?" I asked. "His nickname is Chooch."

"Oh yes. I always knew he'd wind up in trouble. Of course, with that father of his, who could blame him? His twin brother – I forget his name – used to ask me for table scraps. He said they were for his dog. I'd give him a peanut butter or cotto salami sandwich. He'd then ask for licorice – again for his dog. Pretty soon the little whippersnapper was asking for cigarettes."

"For the dog I'll bet," I smiled.

"Oh, no – for him. Oh, you were joking," she blushed.

"Could Russell have been the bland-faced kid that you used to see hanging around Mister Schaufler's lawn?"

"Russell? Oh, no – not at all. The ragamuffin had just a white orb for a face with some fuzzy details. Like an artist's sketch."

As she said this, I could tell that she was discreetly examining my own facial features.

"Besides the floating lights, did you ever see anything else out of the ordinary?"

"Well… Yeah, but you might not want to hear about these things."

"No, really I do," I said.

"Um, okay then, I guess. The strangest thing… it's hard to explain, really… because I'm still not quite sure what it was really. This happened before I saw the bland-faced child. When the lace curtains were open, I watched through the window. At first I thought that he had that fancy funeral coach parked inside his house… and was working on the engine with tools. But then I saw a woman's body that was lying on a narrow black couch… or a bier… unclothed. She had the skin of a dead person… like bleached wax with a faint pink tinge. Maxx was darkly robed… or wearing a mechanic's overalls. He was much younger then… and had this presence. For whatever reason, he kept passing the palm of his hand over different parts of her body – without ever actually touching it. I've never been able to forget the intensity of his manner, though. I couldn't stop watching him and, actually, I could see things with an increasingly clear focus."

"This was happening in one of his rooms?" I asked.

"In an octagonal room that was painted jet black, with bizarre symbols that were unintelligible. There was a circle of dark bluish flame… like sterno… or some jellied alcohol around the dark parquetry. There was a strange mirror of obsidian…pretty orchids… and a pinned butterfly. There were more hand strokes slightly above the stiff body… and, again, that deep penetration of his eyes…"

As she spoke, Cassidy stared into the glass candleholder. At the same time, without looking down, she stuck her fork onto the piece of cornbread and began slicing into it – breaking it up into smaller fragments. When I looked up at her face, there was blank numbness, as if the wavering flame had somehow hypnotized her.

"Metal discs were placed over her body in certain locations… Strange gleams like funny little hubcaps. A gadget covered her genitals – a marked plaque of some sort? And then I thought that I saw what looked like one of her fingers moving. Oh, my lord

– was she alive? Her eyelashes fluttered convulsively in the mask-like rigidity of her face. Could she be having an epileptic seizure? Her quivering caused more strange gestures from the palm of his hand – the motions never touching her nakedness. If the woman was alive, she was being used as some kind of battery. At least, that was the impression that I had."

As Cassidy continued to describe what she saw, her eyes remained transfixed on the candle flame. It appeared to me that she was becoming more deeply entranced – something that had me a bit unnerved – although the things that she was now whispering were truly fascinating. (Of course, being that it was Halloween, part of me was wondering if she was just pulling my leg?)

"As the gyrations continued… her body was now bathed in perspiration… and I mean drenched… until it seemed like her flesh was covered with a glittering foam. And then, suddenly, from a state of rigidity, she – this thing – sat bolt upright."

All the while she kept pushing the fork deeper into the corn-bread. Soon, instead of the hunk of baked batter there was just a large pile of crumbs on her plate. I don't think that she was consciously aware of what she was doing, but the giggling of the sisters who had been watching her doing this from the counter broke the spell.

"I screamed and ran to tell my father," she said with a more normal voice.

Hearing the girls' laughter, she looked down at her plate, embarrassed by the collapsed mess.

"That's a bad batch. The oil's turned… and the coffee isn't that fresh either," she mumbled while trying to save face.

"So, what happened after you told your dad?" I asked.

"About the mummy unwrapping? Um, my daddy had a talk with Mister Schaufler. Afterwards he told me that Maxx was quite a character. Instead of having a dinner party game like Charades to entertain his friends at the funeral parlor, he and his wife had decided to host a mummy unrolling party like those that were once popular in London… when Egyptomania was the craze. Of course, the mummy itself was a fake… but with a realistic anguished face. As part of the decorations, there were hieroglyphic panels and a variegated catafalque. Alabaster jars filled with sherry served as props to enhance the experience as the bandages were slowly removed. Mister Schaufler apologized if this had freaked out the children peering though the window… and that was pretty much the end of it. Now, I really should be going."

As she got up to leave, she took one last look at my face.

"You know, Addison – what features the ragamuffin had – they kind of resembled yours."

"So, that's what it was – a dinner party game?"

"I know what I saw," she replied with a cryptic smile.

I was sitting at the small desk in my bedroom, trying to make sense of some stuff in the third issue of the underground comic *JEET* when my mom leaned in to tell me that I had a phone call from a woman named Patricia Madigan. Not knowing who this was, when I picked up the receiver, I was surprised to hear Trixie's voice. After exchanging a few pleasantries, she told me that she had recently taken some charcoal rubbings of the peculiar grave markers in the private cemetery where Molewhisker had confronted us after the "MooreStock" gathering last summer. She had also found out some interesting things about my birthday of January 17th. Would I like to ride down to "C'dale" in her new Alfa Romeo on Saturday to check out what she had discovered? Topo's band was playing in some club on the Strip that night, and after the show I could catch a ride back in their equipment van.

"Sure," I said without hesitation (even though I was supposed to be working that night). Before hanging up, she told me that she knew of a squalid hotdog shack in Moo town in case I wanted to masticate on one? Ketchup was strictly banned, but they had several other toppings, she said, knowing about my predilection for chili. When I got off of the phone, I had a shit-eating grin on my face. I couldn't wait to see my parents' reaction to some gorgeous college girl picking me up in her sports car – especially knowing about SIU's reputation as a premiere party school.

Rather than share a dorm with other girls, Trixie had rented a small upstairs room in a house near the campus. She had her own attached bathroom and use of the downstairs kitchen. In addition, she paid extra money to use the attic, with the under-standing that no one else was allowed to enter it as long as she lived there. The reason for this (she told me) was that she had converted the space into her private magical temple. It would be solely her dominion – the place where she prepared the Vessel for ceremonial workings.

When I asked her more about it, she said that it was pretty basic. A magical circle painted on the black floor, with a High Altar and a handcrafted closet for her robes and ritual imple-ments. Standing there in her faded bellbottom jeans and a maroon "Saluki" sweatshirt, I tried to picture her as a "Sister of the Mysteries" gowned in silky iridescent brocades.

As for her bedroom, it was tightly furnished with a mattress with lavender bedding, a small table, a dresser with a bohemian lamp, a wooden trunk, a mini-refrigerator and a Marantz stereo receiver. There was also a bookcase that contained occult titles stamped with gilt mystical designs. On top of this were carefully arranged *objets d'art* – mostly Egyptian turquoise-blue funerary ushabti figures and Tibetan metalwork butter lamps filled with ghee. One entire wall was covered with a richly embroidered silk tapestry that Trixie referred to as a tantra-inspired thangka scroll. The room was redolent with incense – one of her lunar blends, she informed me. Surprisingly, there was no plush "Snoopy" from her childhood, although who knows what was inside the storage chest that several violet candles were dripping wax onto at the end of her bed.

From the mini-fridge she pulled out a bottle and poured some of the greenish liqueur into two teacups. When I winced and choked after gulping mine, she laughed and tossed me an open box of Triscuits.

"Remember when we were talking about this creepy Mole-whisker fellow being a grave robber?" she said while taking a bite out of one of the stale crackers.

"You told me that many thought he was a cannibal, but I said he might be a corpse-molester. Well, I read about this eccentric German scientist that was also believed to have been involved with necromancy. In the nineteen-thirties he had fallen in love with this young Cuban beauty who died shortly later from tuberculosis. Instead of leaving her body in peace, one night he entered the mausoleum and carted her off to his secret laboratory. Many years later he was accused of co-habitating with the decaying corpse – little more than a wax dummy, or Plaster of Paris likeness at this point – but after his arrest he claimed that he had been successful in his attempts to bring her back to life by using advanced medical procedures."

With the gulps of Chartreuse burning a hole in my stomach, I continued to listen as Trixie described some of the 'medical' appliances that were used in this lunacy. They included circulating pumps for life-renewing chemicals, magneto shocking coils, brass rods, glass electrodes of violet-ray wands and a battery of electrical devices to produce cure-all energy fields.

"A real nut job, right?" she smiled while pouring more of the god-awful green stuff.

"Well, I never saw any evidence of gadgets like that in Mole-whisker's house – "

"Exactly," Trixie interrupted me, "And I wonder if this reclusive scientist had any either?"

"But, I've been told some things that sound similar – the Plaster of Paris appearance of the body for one thing," I said.

"This might be a stretch, but what if the story involving the medical experiments used in his defense contained allegorical codes for an occult operation that was enhanced by erotico-mystical techniques? Maybe the quackery of sparking apparatuses was just a disguise for something even stranger? It's the same with your Molewhisker's unsavory undertakings. What if he's not a necrophiliaic, but a practitioner of ritual magic with tantric elements? He might even be attempting to produce a homunculus. A Magical Child. Remember what he said to us that night: I only do this for the third mind... meaning... a third consciousness."

She then proceeded to show me some of the charcoal rubbings of the tomb inscriptions that were spread out on her table.

"Here are some of the rubbings that I took from markers in the cemetery. Most of them came from marble tombstones that were badly tarnished. Non Omnis Moriar. It means: I shall not completely die... or, not all of me dies. Suppose that this Mole-whisker takes something from those who are buried there? Some lingering energy from the shades of the dead or biological residue from the moldering corpses that he uses –"

I covered my mouth with my hand.

Trixie's eyes widened. "You're not squeamish, are you?"

"Nuh-uh," I replied and then softly burped.

"This green stuff stings a little."

"The vegetal elixir does?" she said while licking her lips.

"So... maybe that's why Zerrill was so interested in the hole in that farmer's skull, even though he said it was to release his spirit or something –"

"Whoa, who's Zerrill?"

"He's this guy that I know who is looking for evidence of the last family of a vanished civilization. Like Atlantis, or something. He was the guy with my mother that night."

"Family of a vanished civilization? Here... in twentieth-century southern Illinois?"

"In Little Egypt," I reminded her.

"Where are they supposed to be living – amongst the tallest corn stalks?"

"Yeah, or maybe by a soybean field," I said.

"Sure, or inside an earth mound," she joked while rolling her eyes.

"So, look again at these grave markings. All have the same date of January 17. I think this must be a password or coded message for someone. Maybe used by a secret fraternity. Here's the reason why I say that. That date often surfaces with those who are involved with the pursuit of arcane wisdom. Such as Nicolas Flamel, who both achieved an alchemical transmutation and was inwardly transformed on January 17, 1382. With the help of his wife, I should add. And get this: after he was laid to rest, when grave robbers broke into his casket... no body was found. Also inspired by a vision of a book was the Elizabethan Magus, John Dee, who famously communicated with angels. On January 17, 1585, he was shown a bone-inlaid ancient tome in a dream that contained writing that at first appeared to be gobbledygook – but which later turned out to be alchemical fragments. Going much further back in time, January 17 is the feast day of St. Anthony of Egypt. He's the patron saint of lost things and was also called the sainted alchemist. The list goes on."

"And it's my birthday," I said. "That's so weird."

She walked over to her dresser and without giving any notice quickly pulled the sweatshirt over her head and changed into a purple moiré halter-top. I should have figured that a girl who talked openly about performing erotico-mystical rituals wouldn't have any reservations about switching tops in front of me, but it still took me by surprise. She then brushed the long dark hair that framed her face, falling even to her waist, and straightened her perfectly trimmed bangs.

"Maybe that French green stuff isn't so bad after all," I said while holding my teacup out for a refill. "It matches the color of your eyes."

"Uh-huh," she said with an exaggerated husky voice while taking a couple of steps towards me. Standing inches away, she put two slender fingers on my chest. Before I had a chance to react, she slowly glided them higher and gave me a mock Three Stooges eye-poke.

"It's time to hit the Strip," she said while grabbing a black leather jacket.

As we crawled along Illinois Avenue in the Alfa, hundreds of students were 'scooping the loop'. I didn't know if it was due to the frigid weather, but the nightlife on the north end of the Strip had mellowed considerably since the last time I was there. No one was throwing rocks or bottles or cherry bombs. There were no burning mattresses. No evidence whatsoever of any of the diverse elements taking over the streets. I only saw one protester – a bearded dude perched atop a flagpole who was shouting at the top of his lungs about the evils of something called "disco."

When we turned down an alley, a Mexican guy who was dipping his fingers into a can of Vienna Sausages offered to sell me some "panty droppers" for my "chica sucia."

I glanced over at Trixie. "I didn't know that baby franks worked like Spanish fly."

"Spanish fly? I think he's talking about a heart shaped box," she deadpanned. It's Quaaludes, you numbskull." She took her hand off the wheel while giving me a Stooges' head conk.

Another person wanted to know if I wanted to "cause Ma Bell some grief?" When Trixie appeared to be at a loss, I told her that he was selling a Cap 'N Crunch toy whistle with a 2600 hertz tone that you could blow to make free long distance phone calls. I knew this because I had seen Ollie use one of the cereal box prizes to make prank phone calls to the White House years ago. For whatever reason, instead of applauding me for being streetwise, more Stooges' slapstick ensued with my hot chauffeur giving me a playful nose-honk.

As I checked out the Bavarian touches in the basement of the "Rathskeller", Trixie grabbed one of the candlelit booths along the wall. No one had bothered to check my ID, which I assumed was because they couldn't imagine that a girl with Trixie's looks would go out with some under-aged dweeb. In front of the Three Stooges clips projected onto white painted bricks, an attractive blind woman was playing an upright piano while singing dirty limericks. Between the X-rated rhymes, she would stand on her head while rapidly chugging a mug of draft beer to the fist pumps of the boisterous frat boys that cheered her on.

When the limerick lady took a break, I pulled out of my jacket pocket the copy of issue number three of *JEET* and placed it in front of Trixie.

"Don't give me a conk on the head or anything, but I'll bet that PaRDes isn't really a pot party. There's something more going on with this thing. Look at all the mentions to the number seven and the Big Dipper stuff you talked about… Plus, what's up with the babbling daddy longlegs?"

Trixie thumbed through the pages of the freak comic, running her finger along certain lines of dialogue in the various speech bubbles with a puzzled look on her face. A couple of times she turned back to re-read previous pages. Finally, she looked up at me and nodded in agreement.

"You know – you might be on to something here, Addison. I always thought that this was just another hippy-dippy acid-trippy rag, but maybe there's more to it than the funny hijinks of animals trying to acquire cannabis? I don't know what PaRDes means, or why its spelled like that, but the word gibberish is derived from the eighth-century Persian alchemist, Jabir, due to his habit of writing incomprehensible text. Actually, the texts weren't gibberish at all, but were coded in such a way that only fellow alchemists could decipher them. Most of his experiments revolved around the creation of a golem or homunculus that was subject to the control of its creator. It was called a takwin… I'm pretty sure that's the name... which is a magical offspring... just like we've been talking about."

"Wait, slow down. Okay, tell me once again about alchemy? I know it's not about turning lead into gold – "

"It concerns the transformation of the alchemist... by accelerating certain processes of nature. It's the fluorescence of potential. Remember what I told you – the chemical reactions and profound changes observed in the alchemist's bubbling apparatuses mirror the elaborate processes that occur within the corresponding subtle zones of our human anatomy once generated by tantric-inspired magical operations. For left-hand path workings – just to simplify things – think of alchemy, sex-magic and tantra as one and the same. They're all interconnected."

"Okay, that's that, but are you sure that these copies of Jeet aren't just a game that leads to the finding of a prize?"

"I think, because of the puzzling nature of the tunnels and chthonic gatekeepers – that this pertains to the Nightside of the qabalistic Tree of Life. The seven stars of the Big Dipper here represent the seven hot points or power zones of our subtle anatomy. Someone in the know is attempting to communicate something of a highly esoteric nature by using... But, why use these silly critters? Who in the world did this?"

"Someone who can also do this."

I picked up the limp street comic and held it over the lit candle inside a glass on the table.

Trixie looked at me like I was crazy.

"Hey!" She tried to grab it from my hand.

"Don't worry, it won't catch on fire." I smiled fiendishly while trying my best to ignite it.

To Trixie's utter amazement, not only did the flimsy paper resist burning, there was absolutely no indication of it being placed over the dancing flame for nearly a minute.

Suddenly, there was a commotion as a frosted blonde chick dashed across the floor while completely naked and quickly ran up the winding staircase.

"Whoa, there's something you don't see every day," I laughed.

"Around here you do — once swallowing goldfish became passé," Trixie sighed. "Just another campus streaker — Hi-balls included."

Once again, part of Trixie's magic was getting me into clubs without being asked to show my ID. After walking through a tunnel-like hallway that was completely covered with thick orange shag carpet, we entered the main stage area of the "Magician's Monocle." It was too early to experience the electric aura that was associated with the bar. Way too early, as the only other person in the place was our friend Topo, who was on the stage setting up his gear for the night's show. Seeing us approaching, he stopped what he was doing.

"So, I heard that the Vee-Dub is sick in Das Autohaus," he chuckled.

"Yeah, the old man said that it was in tip-top shape before I started driving it."

"That door-prize," he laughed.

"Topo, where's the best place around here to get freak comix?" Trixie asked.

"I guess it would be Mindwarp… now that the Notilus is MIA."

"Hopefully, we'll be back before you start. There's some freaky goings-on that I'll tell you about later," she said before dragging me towards the exit.

"Right on, Trix. Grab number seven," Topo shouted while brushing back his corkscrew stands and playing a chunky barre chord on the Telecaster.

Mindwarp was still pulsating with a hippie vibe, or at least as a haven for those in need of head supplies. Lava lamps churned colorfully atop glass displays for drug paraphernalia as Fillmore concert posters glowed vibrantly in the ultraviolet lights that also exposed human residue on the paisley couches. A couple of bare-foot girls in tie-dyed dresses were sorting through a casket filled with trinkets of counterculture ideals as we made our way over to where a few bookcases were located. These contained but a handful of dusty underground comix, and there was only one copy of *JEET*. Fortunately for us, it was one that we didn't have, being issue number six.

At the checkout counter, I recognized the same elderly beat-nik-type that rang me up before. As I handed him the copy of *JEET*, he peered suspiciously over his tortoiseshell glasses and stroked a long grey beard that cascaded with unkempt wisps onto a stained hand-knit poncho.

"Z'up?" I nodded.

"Same old thing. Still imprisoned in a mental labyrinth of my own devising," the oddball replied while adjusting the drug-rug.

"You're running low on weird 'zines," Trixie said. "Has issue seven of Jeet been published?"

"Number seven is very scarce. Rare as rocking-horse shit that I've yet to step in. If it weren't for some curiosity of nature, even this one wouldn't be here," he nodded.

"What's that mean?" I asked.

"Some pale white gent with weird eyes walked in last night. He had the dull despondent look of a degenerated species. Those with a predisposition for darkness... Those who cele-brate the starry nights. An albino. He introduced himself as No Name... as in No Name Will Do... the anonymous cartoonist of this self-published work. But, he only had this one copy that he wanted to sell. I certainly didn't find that rather strange," he laughed inwardly.

I suddenly thought about the albino figure that I had seen when *othering* at Molewhisker's house. Whoever he was – Major Domo, Captain Nemo – could someone have sent him here with a copy of *JEET* that was filled with elusive riddles and such for me to find? But how could he have known that I'd come looking for it? I tried to dismiss the idea as being crazy, but what wasn't crazy about all this stuff?

"That albino seemed to be troubled by ultraviolet wavelengths, but ultraviolet wavelengths are nothing compared to... I'm just glad that he's far enough away from Africa. Do you know what they do to albinos on the Dark Continent?" the aged dissenter asked while ringing up our purchase.

"What?" I asked.

"Albinos are considered to be evil spirits. They are hunted down by tribes and mutilated for their body parts. These trophies are then sold to witchdoctors who create charms and magic potions from them. These are believed to bring good luck because albino bones are thought to be filled with gold."

There was still enough time before Topo's band started playing for Trixie to skim through parts of issue number six while we were seated in her car outside of the club.

"Okay... so... Darby's getting closer to finding PaRDes – the far out pot party that his brother dillos think that he's been invited to – once he passes freely through the seventh gate. However... there seems to be some kind of trick or illusion that's associated with the sixth gate. There are two chthonic worm gatekeepers. One is blue and the other is yellow. One of them leads to a false tunnel. It's going to be a real peccadillo – I love it – for Darby to decide on the correct one... Mister Dangles tells

Darby that when the stars are correctly aligned – okay, so there's an astronomical code involved… without any shlock left… that he must take a leap of faith… and just jump blindly… across something to reach the paradise on the other side… Man, there's a lot here to take in," she said while flipping through the pages. "Like… what is PaRDes… and why is it spelled like that?"

Working the night shift at the filling station really sucked. While standing under the lit canopy in the spring drizzle, I was dreading the next customer who, besides wanting a fill up, asked for my advice about valve clatter or how to seal a gas cap? When a pair of headlights glared, I was thinking about walking away until I saw that it was Trixie's black Alfa Romeo that screeched to a stop in front of one of the pumps. She rolled down the window and held up the copy of the *JEET* comic. There was excitement in her voice.

"PaRDes is an acronym for… first, the surface meaning… second… hints of the allegoric or hidden meaning. Next is to seek further… and, finally… you get the esoteric meaning. To obtain the key that unlocks the true meaning, one has to eat… Hence the title, *JEET*, which is slang for did you eat?.. In order to absorb the revelation."

"Is there anything else?" I asked.

After a pause, she said, "Yeah, can you check my oil? Get in here. What do you think I came here for – a free car wash?" she said while holding her palm out in the light sprinkle.

"No, I mean that we need to light it with matches or something to see if it will burn," I said.

"Um, okay, but not until we figure out some things."

When I climbed inside, she continued to tell me what she had figured out over the past few weeks.

"Armadillos – they're diggers. Just like Molewhisker, who's digging for special substances –"

She was interrupted by a horn beeping repeatedly. I quickly realized that the obnoxious honking was coming from my mother's new white Dodge Colt sedan as she braked with a jerky motion at the next pump.

"Fill'er up, fellow!" a voice shouted rudely. "I'm a member of the family!"

Although she was just kidding – proud that I had a real job – I could tell that Trixie was confused by her antics. With no attendant in sight, she climbed out of the car and looked around until she spotted me waving at her from inside the Alfa. With a contorted expression she walked over to us a bit unsteadily.

"What are you two up to in there?" she asked while leaning into the opened window.

"We're just talking. Why are you so dressed up?" I asked, seeing that her hair was curled and that she was wearing a new printed jumpsuit.

"Wow, look at that necklace of yours," my mom said. "What is that? Oh, I know. It's a Saluki dog."

Trixie and I both tried to hold back a smile.

"Yeah, mom – it's the SIU mascot," I joked.

"Oh, you must be Patricia. I'm Deedra, Addison's mom – although he sometimes doesn't believe it."

"Mom, have you been drinking? You're acting a little goofy. Can I get you something to eat? Jeet?" I turned and smiled at Trixie.

"Oh gross. Not another one of those Eighteen Truckers' sandwiches... Or that Rawhide Submarine thing."

"Eighteen Wheeler and Longhorn Torpedo," I corrected her.

"I was with my friend Zerrill," she burped. "He took me to a repertory theater to see a play –"

"Not on the back of that death-trap rice burner, I hope?"

"It was Akhnaton... Egghead-naton," she giggled. Ray didn't want to go. He'd rather sit at home and grade papers. Afterwards, we went to that new Hardees and then we had a couple of glasses of wine back at Zerrill's nice place."

"Zerrill, isn't he that guy who has one foot in Atlantis?" Trixie asked me.

"Yeah, he's a digger, too," I mumbled.

"He's fascinated by red bricks and old speakeasies... and with YOU, mister," she said while mussing my longish hair. "Whatcha reading?" she asked after noticing the copy of *JEET* that was open on Trixie's lap. "Darby the Dilla!" she uttered song-like. "But... oh my gosh – what has someone done to that sweet armadillo? Turned a wonderful children's book into raunchy doper trash."

"Darby is also in a children's book?" I asked after noticing Trixie's furrowed brows. (The mentioning of this brought back memories of having it read to me as a child by the 'imaginary' "Major Domo", who I was beginning to realize shared many traits with the *othering* lady's inscrutable albino manservant.)

"For as long as I can remember, he was. The story is about being okay with yourself. Even if you're different... and you're made fun of... kind of like Addison, here," she joked. "Did he tell you that he likes these special peas that are really –" she mimed the word, "fucking" so that Trixie could read her lip movement... "good."

"Geez, Louise." Trixie feigned being shocked by my use of such profanity.

"And that he lost his dad's prized Joseph's Coat Swirl?"

"Oh, no! No, he didn't. We're really just good friends," Trixie said. "Not in a relationship that's deep enough to share such dark secrets."

Somehow I knew that my mother hadn't forgotten about that sixth grade cuss word blunder of mine, but I had no clue that she was also aware of the marble that I had lost to Kelby in a game of keepsies. Obviously she hadn't told my dad about this, and was probably holding it as a bargaining chip for just the right occasion.

"Oh, shoot. I left my good jacket at Zerrill's place," my mom grimaced. Her expression then changed to one of concern. "That's not a Saluki. That's quite the little devil there," she said sternly while wagging her finger.

"Just go drink a cup of coffee," I said. "I'll pick up the jacket and bring it home."

"Okay, I will do that… But, not until I get my new Dodge Colt filled up by a qualified professional petroleum transfer engineer named Addison Albright."

"Strong fucking (I mimed the word) coffee, mother."

With no answer after knocking on the door and ringing the bell several times, I took the liberty of letting Trixie and myself into Zerrill's modern townhouse apartment. Trixie had come out of curiosity, even though I told her that I had been to the place several times before and there wasn't anything out of the ordinary or of special significance in his bachelor's pad during my previous visits.

Seeing my mother's jacket hanging on the back of a chair at the dining room table, I walked over to get it, calling Zerrill's name at the same time. On the table a couple of binders were opened with some of the contents spread out on the dusty oak finish. They appeared to be architectural or engineering drawings complete with grid structures and color-coding schemes.

I would have ignored them if something hadn't caught my eye. Written at the top of one of the pages were the words:

SCHAUFLER'S VICTORIAN ON SHADOWCREST

Beneath this were a series of photographic images that showed detailed close-ups of a jutting corbel supporting an oriel window projecting from the upper story of Molewhisker's house.

According to the hand-written note beneath this, the ornamental feature had inexplicably shifted position by a foot over the course of a day without causing any structural damage or even cosmetic blemishes.

Even stranger, so the remarks below claimed, in a couple of shots that were zoomed in on the glass, the reflections shown were indistinguishable, even though they had been shot from precisely the same angle at different times of the day... several years apart!

Intrigued, Trixie and I continued to examine the papers, realizing that they contained the results of some kind of photographic superimposition scheme. Other examples of peculiarities showed camera images of the branches and leaves on a sycamore near the wraparound porch. Incredibly, all the leaves appeared to be frozen in the exact same position even though they were snapped during different days, months and years (during the same season). There was even a reference to some footage of birds whose flight pattern contours while flitting from branch to branch were shown to be happening in an identical repeating loop – something that was contrary to nature. There were more examples: A beetle on the wall with a quivering antennae that hadn't moved an inch in over a year and a fireplace chimney that repeated identical smoke patterns. Again, the notes indicated that the images were taken at various times and were matched by the same background features.

This brought back memories of how I used to notice that the activities of birds in neighboring yards mimicked one another to such a degree that it reminded me of the cost-cutting measures of repeating the exact background scenery in certain cartoons, such as the *Flintstones*.

In addition to the technical details that were used as evidence of the high strangeness associated with Molewhisker's house and property, there were also several stone rubbings of some grave markings. Some of these were on low-opacity bond paper that contained the same inscriptions featuring the January 17 date that Trixie had taken.

Attached by a paper clip to one of these sheets was a single photo of me. Scrawled beneath it were the words:

JANUARY 17 BIRTHDAY

Seeing this, Trixie edged closer to me.

"The plot thickens," she said.

I awakened to the sound of clanging metal bowls coming from the kitchen as "Owl Jolson" crooned about "The moon-a and the June-a" in a Merrie Melodies cartoon on the television. In my mustard-stained fingers I was clutching the remaining few inches of a messy foot-long gas station chilidog that also left dried bits of onion and shriveled beans stuck to my arm.

I must have fallen asleep on the couch in the family room before I could finish the cello-wrapped behemoth. While ditching the smelly remains into a plastic mini wastebasket, I disturbed Midnight Meringue as she stretched her sleek black frame at the end of the couch.

Seeing that her whiskers were encrusted with a brown sauce, I couldn't help but smile as the jazzy owl sang "Just a little song that makes a black cat lucky." Spotting an empty can of Stag beer on the carpet, I quickly pushed it under the sofa before one of my parents tripped over it.

Something wasn't right in the Albright residence. Here it was a Sunday morning and the entire house wasn't permeated with the greasy aroma of pancake batter ladled onto the griddle. Stepping into the kitchen, I was alarmed by a bottle of soy sauce on the counter, but quickly breathed a sigh of relief after seeing that the mixture of ingredients in a bowl included a couple of tablespoons of Worcestershire. This was the "special touch" in my dad's grilling marinade.

My mother shuffled in wearing her quilted bathrobe.

"Addison, can you please find me a reputable spike removal service in the Yellow Pages for the one that's currently stuck in my brain?" she grimaced.

My dad was right behind her, wearing a wrinkled *St. Louis Cardinals* jersey over his boxers.

"Someone doesn't feel good this morning and we both know why," he needled her.

"Please, Ray, please." She pressed both hands against her temples.

"I brought your jacket home. So what did you think of those papers on Zerrill's table?" I was probing to see if she might have any involvement in this Molewhisker strangeness.

"What papers, Addison?"

"Oh, just about bricks." I shrugged the question off, seeing that she didn't appear to be interested.

"Yeah, he still thinks there is something of historical value under the library."

"So, what play did you go to again?"

"Akhnaton. He was an Egyptian pharaoh. Maybe you've seen photos of the sculptures of his oddly shaped head and such? His ideas about adoring the sun instead of the gods were contro-versial – so much so that after his death, he was erased from the official list of kings."

"Was he an albino?" I asked.

"A wino?" my dad chuckled. "You mean like your mother here?"

"An albino." I pronounced the word slowly so not to be misunderstood.

"That would be news to me," my father grinned. "But, he might have been the first example of a scientific mind... realiz-ing that the sun was more important to man's existence than a bunch of animal-headed gods."

"What caused his death?" I asked him.

"Archaeologists aren't exactly sure. The identity of the mummy thought to be him has long been disputed. But if it was the remains of Akhenaten, it didn't show any signs that he had suffered from a physical affliction – like an endocrine disorder... or any genetic anomaly – like that depicted in temple carvings. Of course, I'm sure that the resident expert on these things – Zerrill – has other ideas about this puzzle. Unfinished play that Akhenaten is."

"If he does, he didn't say anything," my mom said. "There was just the usual stuff about a cultural heritage... A civilization without a previous development... that seems to have appeared overnight."

"Why would anyone make himself look deformed if they really weren't?" I asked.

"Maybe he wasn't venerating the sun's rays, but was trying to tell us that they were detrimental to him... or were responsible for the demise of an entire race? Perhaps he was invoking protection against the harmful energies... which is why his strange appearance was highlighted in the contradictory new art form... When it comes to the heliocentric theory, I think your scholars have barely peeled the butternut. Maybe they should consider the possibly of a cataclysmic celestial event, with the blazing spheroid representing either the close passing of an asteroid or even a cometary impact which caused wholesale destruction that left only the remnants of a lost civilization. Fire-hail... Fire from heaven."

"Where the hell did that come from?" my dad asked.

"I don't know. Maybe Kelby told me."

In truth I had no idea as to the meaning of the words that had just abruptly sprung from my mouth. I had uttered them after feeling a strange impulse to do so. It was as if they were the words of another person speaking through me – something that happened occasionally – and which I was always quick to ignore, being yet another example of the weirdness that plagued my existence.

"More sensationalistic drivel from a rotating paperback stand," my dad scowled.

"I'll buy that explanation," my mother said, "if it comes with a couple of aspirins and a glass of orange juice. One thing's for sure, though – you gotta love our breakfast conversations," she added while picking up the receiver of the phone on the first ring.

"Really, Addison, who might have told you such things?" my dad asked again, seeming to be more concerned than impressed. "Are you sure it was Kelby?"

"It's Zerrill for you Addison," my mom said while handing me the receiver.

"You're saying that Molewhisker's house is haunted?"

"No, that's not what I said," Zerrill replied while re-organizing a folder that contained some of the photographic evidence of the anomalous features that he had discovered while investigating Schaufler's Victorian.

"It's more like the reverse of a haunted house or, even better, of a Potemkin facade – based in part on what you've confided in me through that little eye-dropper of yours. The real house – or whatever it is – seems to be encased by some kind of protective barrier – a bubble that gives the appearance of a regular home. This enables it to blend in with the rest of the neighborhood. To co-exist with our perceived norms. But, as realistic as this effect is, there are certain imperfections that one can see in the photographs and such. These problems attracted my attention. Same with Schaufler and that exaggerated mole whisker that makes him unusual. Who knows what the old coot really looks like?"

"I get what you're saying, but that's some crazy shit, dude," I whistled.

"I don't know if the barrier is some kind of mental construct – induced by a hypnotic suggestion, or if it's created by some unknown technology that distorts the structure's true appearance."

"Hypnotic suggestion?"

This was something that I hadn't yet considered. Could all of the unusual phenomena that I had experienced over the years simply have been the product of some hypnotic induction? Hypnosis could even explain the onslaught of phantasmagoric imagery brought on by the doohickey. But, if this was the case, again, I had to ask myself why? Why would anyone want to tamper with my mind?

"As an explanatory hypothesis, we can't completely rule out that your othering experiences weren't the result of some kind of powerful hypnotic-type suggestive state. Maybe we've both been victim to some stimulus, although I don't see how any hypnotic chicanery could affect the camera mechanisms? That would be quite a trick. The ability that you say that you have to somehow at least partially perceive these things – it must have something to do with your relationship with Schaufler, wouldn't you agree, Addison?"

"Yeah, I guess."

"How else do you explain how you were able to do this?"

"I already told you that don't know," I shrugged.

"So, let's talk about the man. If I'm correct, Schaufler might be the last lineal descendent of an advanced civilization of immense antiquity – one that's now firmly in the realm of myth. Call it what you want. Atlantis. Lemuria. Poseidia. I refer to it as civilization X. That's quite a statement to make, I realize, but I'm not the only one who believes this might be the case. Let's be clear on one thing. The inhabitants of civilization X weren't supernatural.

They were intellectually and technically superior humans compared to those far less developed people that they later encountered. After the cataclysmic events that changed things, the handful of survivors traversed the globe… as seeming gods… to bequeath civilization to others… getting them off to a running start… right up to what it is today… as sad as that might be."

"You sound just like a friend of mine —"

"They left lots of clues behind. Telltale fingerprints of their advanced culture in stone monuments and traces of their presence in the enigmatic verses of ancient writings. These can be found in the so-called apocryphal and pseudepigraphic texts, as well as in accounts from the Old Testament. They were the mighty men… the men of renown, otherwise known as the Watchers or wakeful ones who instructed mankind in scientific matters. For their transgressions of teaching man forbidden knowledge, their priest-magicians became the bad guys in those fantastic events that played out on Biblical terrain. We even have consistent descriptions of these serpentine people. Their oddly-shaped heads, white hair and spectacular golden eyes – "

But Molewhisker's eyes aren't –"

"As one of their off-spring, Schaufler undoubtedly retains some of this knowledge – which he hides behind in his disguises. From what my source has told me, I'm pretty sure that he has preserved for posterity his story – his unique heritage – in a diary of sorts. And that's exactly what I'm hoping to find."

"And you think that this is hidden under our town library?"

"I do because of the signal that we've been given."

"What's that?" I asked.

"Minute traces of a particular metal in the brick mortar."

"Oh yeah, that stuff."

"Have you ever given any thought to trying some more of this othering, Addison? Putting both Timothy Leary and Evel Knievel to shame. From what you've told me, there doesn't seem to be any specific method that you use to initiate the experience. But if you could somehow gain access to this other realm and bring something back in your pockets, we'd certainly know more. Any concrete object would help rule out thought-stuff from hypnotic susceptibility on your part. Unless the tangibility factor of the hypnotic suggestion is extremely powerful."

"Yeah, it usually just happens," I said.

"Usually?" he raised his brows.

I wasn't quite ready to tell him about the *othering* type of experience that once happened after I touched the activated doohickey.

The difference in that instance was that the events that I stepped into had occurred sometime in the past. They were like bizarre home movies that had been taken using a method that made watching them seem like I had actually been there in person while the incidents were occurring. However, since I no longer had the doohickey, its 'open sesame' abilities didn't really matter. The only value of knowing about it that I could think of might be the fact that I had taken the object from Molewhisker's house after having been coaxed into doing so while watching a treasure hunting movie that didn't seem to exist outside of his own television cabinet.

Although Zerrill had been more forthcoming as of late, I hadn't completely ruled him out from my short list of suspects that stole it. After all, he was aware of one of the mysterious symbols associated with it. True, it appeared that he had found the design on one of the fake artifacts that Nestor was peddling. But how could I be sure that he hadn't used some sleight-of-hand trickery to make it appear that way? Plus, I still harbored suspicions as to his true motives in all of this. He now claimed that he was interested in finding some diary of Schaufler's.

Which made me think – though it sounded strange – could the doohickey be this book? It seemed to contain certain things that had to do with him, or at least with those who were involved in his life.

For the time being, I would keep the doohickey type of *othering* to myself – just like I'm sure that Zerrill wasn't telling me everything that he knew.

CHAPTER VII
ZOTHYRIANTICS

"I've never seen so many pairs that only have holes in one of the socks, but I guess that's what happens when you don't wear both of them at the same time like some people with two feet have been known to do," my mom chided me while putting away some freshly-laundered socks in the lower drawer.

"If you got them all the same color then it wouldn't be a big deal," I said while doing some homework at my desk. Frustrated, I closed the book. "How does this prepare me for the real world? And… aren't I already living in the real world?"

"It looks like you've got quite a bit of the real world on those smelly sneakers. Better hand them over. I remember that pair that you used to have in grade school that never had a speck of dirt on them. Too bad your feet grew."

Before closing the drawer, she noticed something.

"What's this doing in there? Looks like one of those metal things that made Ollie clatter like a shaken piggy bank. It feels kind of funny, huh? Almost like nothing."

"Hey, give me that!"

Realizing that it was the doohickey that she was talking about, I got up from the desk and grabbed it out of her hand. I couldn't believe that she had just found it in my sock drawer. What was going on here? Had the person who took it returned it, or had it been in there the whole time? Did I only search half of the drawer? Whatever the case, my excited reaction to my mom casually checking it out had now made her suspicious.

"It's just an old Tiddlywinks squidger," I said while stuffing it in my blue jean's pocket. "They called it frozen smoke, I think."

"If you say so," she said while giving me dubious look.

After having it my possession again, I tried everything I could think of to activate the thing. I spent hours at a time shaking it in a Yahtzee dice cup before rolling it across the green shag carpet. When this didn't work, I set it on the vibrating metal field of an old electric football game and watched it rattle while going around in circles just like the "tru-action" plastic players used to do. When my parents were gone, I placed it inside a hand-held eggbeater and vigorously cranked the metal handle. I even stuck it in the kitchen blender until I burned out the motor. For all my effort, all I got were the occasional warped gleams. Just as I was about to give up on trying to reactivate it, something unexpected happened one night while I was playing a predatory game with Midnight Meringue in the backyard.

The cat was batting the doohickey on the lawn while I encouraged her prey drive. When she flipped it back towards me with her hooked paws during a frenzied volley, a pulsating mosaic suddenly appeared on its surface. Flaring with a fantastic vividity in the grass, I hesitantly bent over to pick it up. Placing it in my palm, I tried to make sense of the sequence of events occurring in the smaller diameter circles that orbited along its edge with a curious fluidity.

Once again I was unable to comprehend the strange drama taking place within these brilliant displays, even though the puzzling imagery affected my eyesight in such a way that it enabled me to perceive with startling clarity details that should have been too minute to distinguish.

The perplexing miniature theatrics along its circumference were only part of its visually absorbing aesthetics. Within a golden iris that radiated at the center of the disc (the albino woman's slanted eye), data swirled like the twinkling flurries in a shaken glass snow dome. As complex graphics morphed into infinite variations, the glistening speckles of the iris intensified. Losing myself to panic, I tried to pull way from their magnetic force. Fearful of experiencing the same abrupt transition as before, I tossed the thing back into the grass. Even then, the golden flecks continued to beckon me with the dulcet tonality of a seraphic tongue.

While backing away from the lilting repetitions, I felt my body detaching from the familiar surroundings. Before I had a chance to react, the backyard fragmented into a delirium of colors that quickly coalesced into a different reality.

With a glossy sterility tingling my face, I knew that I was stuck in one of those freaky home movies that mysteriously unfolded from the object. As before, I was seamlessly co-existing in two distinct settings. Although I was still in my backyard (and could see Midnight Meringue poking at the luminous doohickey), I was simultaneously in a place where something of a shocking nature was occurring. The shifting of my perception between the two actualities was the most unnerving aspect of this kind of *othering* experience. Still disoriented, I wobbled on the lawn with a nauseating vertigo until I managed to steady the distracting fluctuations and focus solely on the disturbing spectacle.

Within the misty fluorescence of an octagonal temple, two figures with alabastrine skin were engaged in a tantric ritual. While conjoined on a pliable black cube that rotated inside a circle whose complex variegated diagrams radiated under a cupola of stars, flame patterns danced on their naked flesh. Framed by stark white plaits that were fantastically dressed, their mysterious profiles exchanged sidelong glances. Locked in a contorted embrace, eyes like golden gem-fire darted about in a bizarre synchronized manner. Unable to look away from the sorcery of their tongues, I observed the hyper-erotic display through the haze of burning perfumes.

The woman's breathing pattern changed as the male began the elaborate process of turning her body into a complex circuit by using subtle formulas of a magical engine in the form of peculiar auric stokes.

I recognized the female from my last *othering* experience and as the dead freak show exhibit known as the "Mermaid of Poseidia." As for her male partner, who shared the same strange features, there was something about him that seemed familiar – a vague sense of recognition from the earliest memories of my childhood (whether real or not). Despite the disturbing albinistic traits, I sensed that he might have been the authority figure with the pomade in his dark cowlick that always seemed to be watching me. Unlikely as it seemed, I was starting to think that he and Molewhisker were one and the same, which meant that at a younger age Mister Schaufler had disguised himself as a 50's greaser. Likewise, I thought that the oddly behaving albino servant who kept an equally close eye on me (after popping out of openings that literally appeared out of nowhere) might have been a younger version of the stodgy butler that I had encountered at Molewhisker's house while *othering* in more recent times.

With his palms facing down, the magician continued to make mesmeric passes with specific mudras over the female's invisible anatomy. The intricate system of hand gestures never actually touched the erogenous zones, but glided over her ivory bareness with a mechanized precision that caused her to react with spasms of pleasure.

Although the ritualized sex was genuinely mystifying, had Trixie not explained some of these tantric procedures, I would have been absolutely dumbstruck by what I was now witnessing. Still, even though it wasn't my idea to be there, I couldn't help feeling like some kind of creepy peeping Tom while glued to the snakelike squirming of their glistening bodies inside the night-canopied temple.

After a slight readjustment of my shifting perception, I was better able to discern the temple furniture through drifts of glowing aromatics in filigreed thuribles. What caught my attention the most was an obsidian speculum that was slanted to the glittering heavens on the High Altar. At times, swirls from the pungent braziers shrouded its polished black surface. When not obscured by these ghostly tendrils, a faint sprinkling of star clusters was visible.

While the male figure magnetized certain astro-sexual plexuses, subtle radiations generated by his ballet of lightning-fast fingers congealed into a shimmering coating that resembled a prismatic varnish on the priestess's quivering flesh. As his strangely fluid movements continued to cause convulsions in her pelvic region, her ecstatic sighs turned into a disturbing phlegmy gargling. As her body shuddered violently, amethyst-lidded eyes remained transfixed on the dark mirror.

Along with the strange utterances that issued from her mouth, I could now discern offbeat rhythms and an oblique insect shrill that was followed by sparkling gusts of astral effluvia. As the tribal syncopations and tantric glossolalia grew louder, I noticed that the surface of the looking glass had started to become encrusted with deposits of iridescent flecks. As these flashes of starfire accumulated on the telesma of the magical mirror, the deep indigo flames of lamps that were arranged around the periphery of the protective circle spiked in intensity and took on a vivid mauve color.

As the milked secretions further crystallized on her pallid flesh, the glittering flurries that had settled upon the mirror in exquisite patterns suddenly scattered. Once completely stripped away, they were replaced by the familiar asterism of the Big Dipper that was somehow reflected with a powerful magnification. (The metal amalgam that coated its surface?)

The star pattern then multiplied into four separate Big Dippers, with each one marking its position in the celestial quadrants. With my gaze fixed on these stellar displays, the Dippers' radiant handles aligned themselves to form a magnificent new constellation that resembled a stylized swastika. As the effulgent symbol began to rotate counter-clockwise around the Pole Star, the flickers of light were soon spinning at an incredible speed. Once the blazing alignment became blurred, the incandescent whorl burst into intensely brilliant star trails that faded in the mirror's blackness. In their absence, wondrous new space-marks soon appeared in the twinkling cosmos.

As the ritual neared a climax, numerous star pricks brightened in the depths of the mirror to form what appeared to be an ensilvered face that had the quizzical expression of a child. I was stunned to realize that the features of the dazzling sculpture bore a vague resemblance to my own as recalled from my earliest memories. Whoever the face depicted, the luminous portrait was now the focus of the magician's intense concentration as the priestess remained in a profound trance.

Rising from the obedient cushion in the magic circle, the naked seer approached the looking glass and daubed upon the stellar eidolon an etheric substance that looked like liquid rainbows.

In doing so, a butterfly with wings like fire-delighted jewels alighted from the drooping petals of a mauve orchid that had also been placed amid the ritual furnishings. While he continued to smear the image of the childlike face with the tantric essence that he had collected from a graven plaque that was positioned under the genital outlet of the priestess, the boyish outline in the angled mirror suddenly assumed a different form.

At the same time that the facial outline changed, my parents rounded the corner of the house, having just returned from their duty as prom chaperones. As if nothing out of the ordinary were occurring – much less a Triple X drive-in movie screen in the middle of their little backyard – they calmly walked right up to me. Needless to say, were they able to perceive the vividly realistic octagonal temple, the deviant nature of the rites would have shocked them to their core.

"So, turns out this wasn't needed for any guys caught fooling around at the afterglow," my dad laughed while squirting me with a stream of water from the plastic boutonniere on his checkered polyester suit.

At this point, I was having some difficulty with the bi-location elements and desperately hoped that the doohickey would shut off its bizarre imagery. Instead, I noticed that the ritual participants ensphered in the temple were watching with intense interest the candescent visage that now enveloped the fantastic mirror. The inscrutable countenance had slanted topaz eyes that peered back at them as their tapered white fingers curiously traced the sparkling features that were in stark contrast to the child's. With its peculiar physiognomy and distant expression, the refulgent image was almost certainly that of the blasé servant that I referred to as Major Domo.

My mom removed the corsage from her yellow flare chiffon dress and attached it to Midnight Meringue's pink collar.

"Who's gonna take this little cutie to the Top of the Riverfront for a candlelight din-din? Better than Friskies for our finicky feline."

In that instant, both the doohickey and its projected imagery went blank.

"Whatcha got there, girl? Is that Addison's thingamajig?"

I stumbled backwards against a tree as a stream of someone else's thoughts raced through my brain. From these mental impressions, I got the distinct feeling that something had gone terribly wrong during the final phase of the couple's magical operation. The psychosexual dynamics had inadvertently triggered something unwanted and the undesirable outcome had entered into their world via the outpourings from the occult center between the eyebrows of the priestess. This was caused by a magical glyph whose improper use – or lack thereof when the stars were right – could have fatal consequences.

That I had been able to perceive imagery in the mirror that actually occurred in the deeper levels of the magicians' consciousness (which I had learned from conversations with Trixie about erotic esotericism) was in itself strange. But, that I also received impressions of something unexpected that had happened as a result of an interpenetration of dimensions at the culmination of the rite made me wonder if I was in some way plugged into one or both of their minds? Or was this awareness just another incredible feature of the doohickey?

258

Feeling an even stronger sense of the repercussions from this magical side effect, I glanced over at my parents. After taking several heavy breaths, I picked up the doohickey and took off running as fast as I could. To where, I didn't know. To anywhere, I suppose, just to get away from there.

I was finally ready to tell Zerrill about the doohickey and my recent experience with it. When I pulled up to his townhouse the next day, I saw Trixie's Alfa Romeo parked in the driveway. What was she doing there, I wondered? I had phoned her a couple of times in the past week but when she didn't pick up, I figured that she was busy doing college stuff. That, or engaged in her darker extracurricular activities.

I thought about leaving but decided instead to see what they were doing. When I knocked on the door, there was no answer. Knocking again, I cracked it open and stepped inside after hearing faint voices. Announcing my presence, I continued into the dining room where they were sipping Heinekens at the table.

"I thought that I heard someone at the door," Zerrill said. "And turns out it's better than your average Jehovah's Witnesses."

"Addison?" Trixie seemed surprised. "I didn't know that you were dropping by."

She looked amazing (for my scholarly older friend who seemed to have a way with the ladies?), wearing a black halter neck sheath dress with her dark hair hanging from a raven wing bowler hat. Brushing back the glossy tresses with her hand, the reddish faience of the Egyptian amulet of Setekh glinted in the diffused sunlight. As I drew closer, I could smell the jasmine undertones of her oriental perfume.

"Me neither," Zerrill said. "What brings you here – besides that I just bought a case of imported beer? Have you ever tried a bottle of Heineken?"

"Growing up in these parts, I'll bet that he'd prefer a warm Busch to a cold Heinie," Trixie joked.

Zerrill couldn't help point out that this caused me to blush.

"Would you call that beet red, or a slightly different shade?"

"I was driving by and saw her car so I thought I'd say hi," I said while turning away.

"Your friend and I have been discussing hyper-eroticism and I must say that I'm quite impressed by her knowledge of invisible anatomy."

"Zerrill won't tell me how he became initiated, which he obviously is," Trixie said.

For some time I had wondered if the Epigraphic Society that Zerrill claimed to be a member of was in reality an occult fraternity based in California. Now, I had my answer.

"Well, there's probably more people into it in California than here," I suggested.

Noticing both of their half-smiles, I realized how lame that sounded.

"That may be so, but your resident Magus, Maxx Schaufler, makes those adepts in San Francisco and elsewhere look like hacks. The moralistic hodgepodge they study and practice in their elitist pursuits is wholly insufficient to produce what he has succeeded in doing... from a tailbone. Make no mistake – he is the genuine article. Just imagine it – a surviving repository of the most powerful magic ever known. Should his knowledge fall in to the wrong hands... well, even the most qualified occultists would be mercifully protected by their own ineptitude."

"He's talking about Molewhisker," I reminded Trixie.

"He is also quite the jester, your Molewhisker," Zerrill added. "But according to the Great Sayings of the Upanishads, The Knower of Truth should go about the world outwardly stupid like a child, a madman or a devil."

"Whatever. The hypno-toad can still make mistakes," I mumbled.

"Oh really? Does he have demon servitors that aren't house-broken? The boy is holding out again. Speaking of which, what happened to your Mayfest exhibit? Did the mermaid get an up-grade to the more lucrative waters of Barnum and Bailey?"

"The guy selling tickets didn't know what happened to her, and Professor Dekelspiel wasn't there either. I'm just saying that certain things that he's done have... well, not backfired, but –"

"Ricocheted," Trixie said. "It sounds like you're talking about tangential tantrums."

"No. He just isn't perfect... Like you said, he's a jokester."

"We'll noodle it out later," Zerrill gave me a cryptic wink.

"So, this is what I came to show you," Trixie said while re-moving several charcoal rubbings of the peculiar grave markers from a leather satchel. "Addison has already seen these."

After examining the tracings for only a few seconds, Zerrill pushed the rubbings back to Trixie.

"I see you've been trespassing in his little private cemetery. Non Omnis Moriar. Translation: Not All Of Me Dies. Some-thing a thanatologist – an expert on death like Schaufler – knows quite well. Earlier, we were talking about the opacities of alchemical literature – the torturously abstract riddles by the masters of obfuscation. You've established that their metals were living substances that have analogues with the hormonal-rich excretions distilled in specific zones along the cerebrospinal axis and, more importantly, with their subtle counterparts —"

"The profound reactions that unfold within the glass alembic mirrored mysterious biological processes that occurred within the hidden recesses of the alchemists themselves," Trixie said.

"Correct. The co-mingled secretions correspond nicely with the chemical marriages and regal copulations mentioned in the moldering tomes, but what are we to make of all the spectral entombments and glorious rebirths that are also mentioned in the same vernacular? To save you agonizing years to decode this nebulous subterfuge, there is a part of a cadaver that survives necrobois... putrefaction ... decay. It is a post-mortem residue of activity in the Mauve Zone, which is the source of one's imagination. I trust you're familiar with the alchemical maxim: Visit the interior of the earth and by rectifying you shall find the hidden stone, the true medicine. This pertains to the death-borne elixir... the treasure of treasures in the burial chest.

"With an ante mortem agreement from the members of his convivial society, Schaufler extracts this substance — often the mother lode — and uses it to nourish his magical offspring... so that it doesn't deanimate."

Trixie shook her head in disbelief.

"He asks for written permission to body-snatch?"

"Yes, he does. A written instrument legally executed by which a person makes disposition of his/her estate to take effect after their death. The estate here being one's own corpse. Just like he did with his farmer friend, with the only difference being that the fellow preferred to be buried in the fields that he toiled rather than the cemetery of the Masonic federation Schaufler presided over. Compare the absorption of this facet of the Mauve Zone

– the Glitter of the Sleepers, which is also the Dream of the Dreamless – with the freshly liberated spirit of necromancy."

For the first time that I could remember, Trixie appeared to be flummoxed.

"Where did all of this come from?"

"The confession of a resurrectionist with misgivings. He was a member of the Confraternity of the Black Penitents whose illicit practices a certain Cardinal Falconieri left in the archives at the Vatican. In the south of France, the Arch-confraternity of the Misericordia assisted criminals that were condemned to death and also provided burial services for the poor... after, that is, performing gruesome experiments that involved a dangerous species of Atlantean magic. It was said to be the greatest secret in Schaufler's Grand Arcanum until, without any explanation, he shut the doors to his Inner Circle – the Den of Thieves as he called it. With this action, any forbidden knowledge from those with dirty fingernails was silenced."

Trixie pulled out issue number 6 of *JEET* from her satchel and handed the underground comic to Zerrill. As he thumbed through it, she waited for his reaction.

"It's masquerading as a freak comic – amateurish even at that, but it's certainly something more," Trixie suggested.

"Well, yes. The two chthonic worms, one blue and the other yellow – when blended together they become green, as in the langue-verte or green tongue. The slang used by those wanting to convey something to fellow players without having their message understood by outsiders."

"Like the gibberish of the alchemist, Geber," Trixie nodded.

"Precisely," Zerrill agreed. "To cast a mist."

"The double stars in the Dipper's handle are also blue and yellow," I thought I should add, wondering if I should also tell Zerrill about the comix's fire-resistant properties?

"The seven stars are, of course, externalized as the seven etheric vortices or chakras whose swastika-like whorls perfume the tantrika with subtle essences… the divine efflux. May I borrow this? It's not what I've been chasing after, but it's definitely a message for someone."

There were a couple of things Zerrill said that really stuck out with regards to my own situation. Enough so, once again, I decided not to divulge anything about the doohickey. In particular, I was intrigued (and, to be honest, somewhat depressed) by his saying that Schaufler used this unique substance – the death-borne elixir he called it – to nourish his magical offspring… so that it didn't deanimate. Who, or what was his magical offspring? Although I wasn't sure that I really wanted to know, I had to find out if my suspicions were correct.

After thinking about it for over a week, I decided that my best course of action would be to sneak the doohickey back into the resin treasure galleon in Molewhisker's murky fish tank before confronting him about this homunculus or whatever it was that Zerrill claimed he had created.

Under the pretense that I was just checking to see how he was doing, I drove the Vee-Dub over to the old Victorian. When I knocked on the door there was no answer. Figuring that Molewhisker was probably upstairs, I walked inside while repeatedly calling his name. Looking around at the peeling wallpaper and crumbling plasterwork, I pinched my nostrils at the pungent odor of mothballs and the lingering stench of spit tobacco.

The place hadn't changed much since the last time that I was there, except that the little aquarium was gone. Now, I would have to think of another way to return the doohickey, unless he had moved the tank. Hearing the sound of music above me, I crept up the staircase, careful not to break the loose baluster spindles of the rattling handrail. With the warped floor creaking from my footfalls, I entered the room where the strains of music were coming from.

There was no sign of Molewhisker sitting at his desk. Glancing at the old Philco radio, I was surprised by the high-fidelity sound and total lack of static coming from it, especially with the greenish patina on the shellacked woodwork, the warm orange-scarlet glow of the tubes and musty smell of its tattered grill cloth. The music itself was equally strange. Although I was familiar with the spooky classical pipe organ notes that were used as the horror theme for the television Bijou Theater "Fright Night" B-movies, whoever was playing the dark flourishes kept stopping and changing certain parts as if they were currently in the process of composing the piece. During these brief interludes, two high-pitched voices were conversing in what sounded like the German language.

While they continued to talk more excitedly, the old Kelvinator chest freezer started shaking loudly. Curious as to what was inside, I lifted the lid wide enough to get a glimpse of a bunch of frozen skinned albino squirrels. In checking out the motor's death rattle, I noticed a couple of sheets of typing paper stuck behind the thing. I recalled the pages being blown under the appliance many years ago during a spring storm that I thought was going to spawn a tornado. Picking them up, I shook off the dust.

As I started to read the first sentence, it seemed as if the type had played a trick on me; the words instantaneously changing so as to be better suited to my reading ability, even though, in many instances, the adjustments still exceeded my level of comprehension. Perhaps Molewhisker had originally typed this in a different language and it was somehow translating itself right before my eyes? However, when I quickly glanced down to the bottom of the page to see if this was the case, I didn't see any foreign words, everything appeared to be in English. Not sure what was going on with this perceived rephrasing of the text that I had experienced when I first started reading, I began again from the top of the page:

Although I still maintain considerable control over the Third Mind, with each passing day it grows more independent, a salute to the efficacy of the working, even though certain mischievous tendencies were not anticipated in its adumbration. Solidity remains strong – is hardly distinguishable – and the subject even experiences oneiric activity that I have captured. So, the question becomes: Will this egregore make for a suitable Terma, or should I abandon my design? At this stage of its development – having been well-nourished with the bricolage – receiving generous gifts of the Vapor of the Bone, etc. – discontinuation would seem tantamount to magical murder! (I am not looking for any dispensations in this case.)

Conspicuously, the oneiric-records mentioned feature the emigrant of an unanticipated perichoresis (believed to be incalculably old – archaic junk – as categorized in Nightside probabilities). I am now convinced that this intrusion was not the result of any miscalculations involving siderealisation, such as disputed alignments of the Pole-Lords. Nor was it the result of errant choreography with the mudras (mudra of Daath), or the tainted deliquescence of specific resonances. Rather, its transition was a mistake of linear exactitude associated with the appropriate sigillum. This alone enabled it to seep through the cracks – to enter from the outside – via the anti-sephira.

I flinched as the voices speaking in German (?) paused and the swelling church organ chords resumed on the radio. This was followed by a waft of a most agreeable scent that quickly masked the room's distinctive halitosis. At the same time, I noticed that the hallway was now suffused with a gorgeous blue tinge that appeared to be emanating from the adjacent room. Curious, I set the papers next to the manual typewriter on the rickety desk and went to investigate.

The moment that I peeked into the room, I knew that I was *othering*. In the semicircular expanse with cymophanous walls glowing cobalt blue, a figure was reclined on a throne-like seat whose rounded edges consisted of a quietly fluctuating pearlescent cushion. I was unable to recognize the person's face as a spread open newspaper that was held by pallid tapered fingers concealed it.

The shimmering golden fabric of a gently palpating blanket covered the rest of the person's body. Beneath its multiple effearaging 'hands', the white brilliance of the throne was seamlessly molded into a conical base that curved into the floor. Through a series of slanted vertical transparent panes, soft multicolored beams shed their energies on what appeared to be some kind of wondrous distilling apparatus. Moving closer into the fragrant aroma of elevated herbals, I strained to see aqueous solutions circulating through a series of delicate coils. Beneath this synchronized process, metallic oils were separating and recombining in tiny bubbling globes before the opalescent trickles of the spagyric preparations wetted an enclosed miniature garden at the bottom that was burgeoning with a fantastic proliferation of shapes.

Shifting my gaze from the virid splendor and vivifying rays, the lustrous throne quickly dissolved. In the feeble glow of a naked bulb, a scrawny figure was reading a paper while seated on the stained porcelain of a white tank toilet with reddish-brown corroded fixtures.

While backing away from the bathroom, I heard the rustling of the newspaper followed by Molewhisker's gruffly twang.

"What in blazes are you doing snoopin' round while a man goes about his business?"

"You should shut the door when you're on the growler. I just stopped by to see how you were doing – heard the radio – and then I find you sitting on this thing with rainbows shooting out of your butt."

As I headed back to the den, the old coot was fastening his tatty bathrobe right behind me. Turning around, I saw that the mole whisker had grown considerably since I last saw him.

"Snoopin' with your second sight are you, dookie-doo," he mumbled.

"Look, I'm getting sick of you dicking around – playing games with this hypnosis stuff... making me think that I'm losing my marbles," I shouted over the repeating organ passages. "This isn't really an old typewriter – this Model T – is it? It's some other kind of a machine," I banged the keys on the manual typewriter. "And what's the deal with this freaky-ass radio?"

"The radio-player? It's Bach tinkering with his famous Prelude in D minor – composed while he was testing a new organ with his eldest brother. Thing's not calibrated correctly – not the organ – but those sound waves captured at the time sure takes all the guesswork out of it," Molewhisker grinned. "Care to reckon how old J.S. was?"

"I really don't give a shit. Just like I didn't give a shit when you said that Captain Nemo served you dolphins' livers for lunch."

Hearing the funny voices conversing in German again, I started to come unglued.

"And you don't fucking control me. Not my thoughts or my memories, so leave me alone before people think I'm skitzo… when it's really you that's got a great big fucking screw loose."

Glancing down, I noticed that what my mother referred to as "indelible grass stains" on my white sneakers were now laundered spotless. Maybe I could dirty them up by rubbing them against some grass rather than try to explain what happened.

"I've got real parents!"

"You're the busy body pokin' your nose into others' business – disturbing me while I'm reading the paper."

He paused for a second, and then cast a wary eye at me.

"Do you remember that hero black fella years ago who got stung terribly by all those hornets, my gosh, while he was helping the police chief's young boy after he flung his yo-yo into their nest?" Molewhisker chuckled.

"I don't know – maybe?" I replied after giving the question some thought. Something didn't seem quite right. It was almost as if I was being set up for some kind of trap. I didn't know what kind of game he was playing, though, because I did remember when Dovie saved the kid from the swarm of hornets in the park that afternoon.

"You're talking about Dovie?" I asked.

"Yep, that's the name. Well, today's paper said that he's now the newest member of the police force."

"Now you're trying to distract me. Messing with my head again. Good for Dovie. I don't know what's crazier – you or this house? But, I'm getting out of here for good. Oh, there's a beetle on one of the walls outside that's hardly moved in… maybe five years or so. Yeah, my friend Zerrill – he's on to you. Knows all about your odd habits – the tomb stuff and this bogus house. He speaks with a green tongue."

"Green tongue, you say? Sounds like this fella wants to adopt someone… for what's locked away… the mind secrets. Let's hope he knows his stuff – how to revitalize one's garment – when it comes time for me to go," Molewhisker said in a grave tone as he sat down behind his desk.

"Yeah, where's the mole whisker going?" I laughed at my deliberate rudeness.

"To land's end. Finisterrae," he calmly replied.

Zerrill called a meeting with Trixie and I to further discuss the 'gibberish' in the freak comix. On a humid summer's night we were seated around his dining room table listening as he attempted to elucidate the occult word play of the comical pholcid known as "Mister Dangles."

"In a pseudepigraphic work, the Shamir is said to be a miraculous stonecutting device, but it is actually an endogenous mystification. With its uncanny penetrating glance, the worm-like organism feasts… burns away a certain membrane – a protective shell in the human anatomy, thus creating a traversable micro-wormhole. The membrane in question is the so-called qabalistic false sephira known as Daath – the transliminal portal to everything imaginable in the Mauve Zone. The hidden path on the shadow-side that leads to this region, however, is dichotomous. At the sixth gate there is a trick or illusion – as the creator of this underground publication informs us – one that's quite a peccadillo, to use his clever pun."

"We're talking about the awakening of the Third Eye chakra, Ajna, that's also associated with the door of knowledge in Tantric belief," Trixie added.

"The Opener of the Way enables a person to experience the Grand Dreaming of a Treasured Eye… Something better than any of your best daydreams, Addison," Zerrill kidded. "But, with the lifting of the veil, there could be a steep price to pay. These aren't parlor games. With the magnitude of the energies encountered on the Nightside, an unwelcome intrusion is possible. To breach the Mauve Zone gives this interloper – something that exists beyond the human domain – the ability to enter the terrestrial sphere via the same etheric doorway."

"Meaning that in the Tunnels of Setekh, a confrontation with one's hidden self is likely." Trixie interjected. "Something not to be banished, but… integrated."

"At first this emigrant might not be deemed threatening enough to be banished. Perhaps it will even appear to be entrancingly desirable, not unlike the seductive glimmer of a will o' the wisp.

But, think about Plato's warning in his narrative concerning the sinking of Atlantis that coincided when the divine portion in man began to fade away. To an occultist of Schaufler's standing, there's a genuine mystery concerning this change in the nature of humankind that will eventually end the species, as we know it. Consider the deeper meaning of this – which was Plato's intent to convey. Whether it's a magical operation performed in a sanctified temple or a little esoteric cannibalism per an engagement in a private cemetery, I'm sure that the secret of activating the shamir is all but openly revealed in Maxx's terma… or diary. Which made me realize that someone meant for me to gain possession of this little gift… just to make things easier."

Noticing my incredulous expression, he pointed to the copy of *JEET* that was lying on the table.

"Questions, Addison?"

"Yeah, where's one of those skunk-funk beers?"

"Okay, but afterwards I'm going to need to borrow your mother's library key."

"Who breaks into a small town library in the middle of the night?" I said with a hushed tone while parting a window blind to keep an eye out for any police cars that might be patrolling the area. Maybe even Dovie, although I had yet to see him in a uniform.

"What small town library has orichalcum mixed in its brick mortar?" Zerrill replied while training a flashlight beam on a row of index cards that he was searching through in a file cabinet in the darkened room.

Trixie was also watching out for the cops while peering through the slats covering a window that faced a different street.

"Here we go," Zerrill said with a sigh of relief while pulling one of the cards from the file. "Keep watching while I go check the shelf."

With the card in his hand, he rounded a corner of tall bookcases. A few minutes later, I heard a dull thud coming from the direction where he had gone.

"What was that?" I whispered to Trixie.

"Don't know," she whispered back while letting go of the blinds.

After several minutes had gone by without hearing from Zerrill, we went looking for him in the shadowy aisles. There was no response to our repeated calls and no sign of him anywhere. The only thing we found was a book lying on the floor in the children's section. Trixie bent over to pick up the thin volume and saw that the title on its colorful dust jacket was "DARBY THE DILLA" by "ANONYMOUS."

"That's sure interesting," Trixie said with a puzzled expression.

We continued to search for Zerrill without any luck. He wasn't in the bathrooms, the small office, the back storage room or the broom closet. He had simply vanished. After waiting another half an hour, we had no choice but to leave (with the children's book), making sure to lock the door.

Hurrying to Trixie's Alfa Romeo, we saw that Zerrill's motorcycle was still on its kickstand.

Where the hell was he, we wondered?

Both Trixie and I were freaked out by Zerrill's vanishing act. We went to his townhouse several times but on each occasion everything was exactly as it had been the night we left to sneak into the library. As for the children's book, there was nothing in it we could find that might offer a clue. Unlike the freak comix, it was pretty straightforward with its moral about how it's wrong to treat people (in this case, anthropomorphized armadillos) unkindly just because they appear to be different.

After nearly three weeks had passed, we noticed that Zerrill's motorcycle had finally been moved from Main Street. Even though there was no mention of it in the blotter, we figured that it was most likely impounded by the police. Were they concerned about him having gone missing, we wondered?

Because the library was the last place that we had seen him, I discreetly asked my mother how things were going at work? When she replied that everything was pretty much the same as always, a few days later, I asked her if she had ever experienced anything out of ordinary there? After giving my admittedly 'left field' question some thought, she told me she had once seen a floating black circle near a bookcase. This was an enlarging blind spot that only lasted for a few seconds. Although it was similar to those "floaters" when she had a migraine, this time its shape wasn't irregular. Plus she didn't have a headache, she told me, while shrugging her shoulders.

If it wasn't a migraine that affected her eye, could it have possibly been one of those crazy *othering* doors that she glimpsed? Thinking about this some more, I decided to sneak back into Molewhisker's house to have a look around while he was napping (telling him that I left my filling station keys there should I get caught).

As he snored, I searched several rooms but didn't see anything that indicated Zerrill had somehow ended up there (What this evidence might have been, I wasn't sure?)

However, I did find something that led me to believe that Zerrill's ongoing quest to obtain Schaufler's "diary" might have been anticipated by its enigmatic author. This was something that was written on the second page of those old typed papers that I found earlier under the rattling freezer. Both copies were still on the desk, so, after reading the parts that I didn't get to the first time, I copied them on my own notepaper to show Trixie. (After 'sneaking up' on the dusty page to see if I could detect any automatic changes in the text by some mysterious manner like I was pretty sure happened the first time.) Although I didn't see this 'trick' happen again, certain passages as they appeared were quite alarming:

While I continue to ponder the situation, it appears that I have attracted someone who considers himself to be the pre-destined terton, or, at the very least, a person with mutual interests in exotic phenomena: the physio-chemicals of quantum biology and geometric correlates in the holomovement.

Although this person who shuns the prevailing mechanistic dogmas in favor of theoretical abstractions thought by most to be metaphysical fantasies, he nevertheless comes uninvited to fulfill his mission, being ill suited for the task. Speaking of which, what about my Zothyrian blunder? Being something more than an average thought-entity, even with prolonged concentration, is it even possible to dissolve?

Back to the problem of that which desperately seeks an autonomous existence with its objective consistency: Rather than dissipate, there is an alternative to consider. That is of incorporating the functioning energy manifestation with another. Halves of wholes! Such an undertaking would require exceptional measures beyond polarized erotic energies and the Vapor of the Bone (were it still available). With similar behavioral traits, as is to be expected by the law of association; I shudder to think of the mental interaction of such an amalgamation!

Near the end of summer I arranged to get together with Kelby and Ollie, both of whom I hadn't seen much of over the past few years. We planned to meet at the new McDonalds that was built where the old King Coney used to be, figuring that the lines wouldn't be too long by those who came to marvel at the famous Golden Arches if we got there an hour before they closed.

While catching up on things in a brightly lit booth, I joked that the employees preparing the food were probably as fake as the plastic shrubbery that was used to landscape the place. Pointing out their robotic movements, I suggested that they might be illusory creations performing to the founder's high standards. The mechanized fucks were tricking people, just like Ollie's slugs used to do to vending machines. Ollie laughed at the idea of "dangling burger puppets" while watching the assembly line, but after sucking his shake dry he told us that he needed to head back home. His mom was going to buy him a new Corvette Stingray in a few days and although he had decided on Mille Miglia red as the color, he still wasn't sure what options he wanted to select from the dealership brochure. Custom interior trim was definitely on the list, though.

After Ollie left (but not before complaining to one of the sanitary employees that he had to pick dozens of brown pickles off his burger), Kelby leaned in and told me that the idea of mental puppets was more real than I probably thought.

He had recently read a book entitled *Magic and Mystery in Tibet*, whose author was an intrepid explorer in forbidden Tibet in the early 1900s. During her many extraordinary adventures, she had gained the confidence of isolated mystics who instructed her in their secret lore. This included psychic phenomena in which human thoughts could be externalized. Such mental constructs were called tulpas. Tulpas could be inanimate objects or living things – even human beings could be imagined into existence after the prescribed concentration.

After spending years studying in remote lamaseries and locked in deep meditation while isolated in anchorite caves, the book's author began to experiment with the idea of animating her own mindform. The blue print on the blank canvas of her mind was that of a jovial monk-like figure.

Eventually, the mental impression took form outside of her head, becoming her constant companion, with the illusion persisting to such an extent that it quickly became an independent reality that could be perceived by others. But, as time passed, the tulpa escaped her control – becoming increasingly troublesome – so much so that its creator was eventually forced to reabsorb it back into her mind.

While many critics thought this rebellious manifestation was merely the product of a deluded mind – one taken to flights of fancy in the solitudes of the Himalayas – or that the author was inventing colorful tales to aggrandize spiritual traditions that were virtually unknown to westerners – Kelby believed that the stories were true.

With my eyes on the burger 'conveyer-belt', I confided in Kelby that, far from being skeptical of thought-forms or the evidence of occult activity, I could show him proof that such things were happening right here in our little town.

On a sunny afternoon, Kelby and I were parked in front of Molewhisker's house. While seated in my Microbus I told him to keep an eye out for a certain cardinal that was about to appear, and to pay close attention to its flight path. After observing it, we would return the next day at the same time so he could witness the property's *Flintstones*-like repeating background scenery. Sure enough, at the precise time that I told him it would alight on a certain tree branch, the bird did so, only to take flight once again exactly like I said it would before landing on another limb.

The next day, at the same time, the same cardinal flew from branch to branch in the exactly the same manner. After witnessing this inexplicable occurrence, I let him read part of Molewhisker's papers in which he suggested that he was engaged in creating a "Third Mind." I told him that I had a friend who referred to these mental entities as either being homunculi or magical offspring.

I should have known that Kelby couldn't keep such a mind-blowing thing to himself. His first mentioning of the possibility that thought-forms were amongst us occurred after he heard about an experiment conducted by "The Society of Psychical Research" on a late night radio program. The aim of the Canadian group was to attempt to produce a collective hallucination. Once its members penciled a sketch and agreed on Philip's (their fictional character's name) basic personality traits, in weekly sessions they endeavored to turn their mental picture into a physical realization. After changing the parameters a bit, they claimed to be successful with their undertaking. They not only conjured Philip into a tangible appearance, but they even managed to get him to answer certain questions that were in the biography that was created for him. It wasn't long, however, before the apparition tried its damnedest to free itself from the makers' control. Shortly later, Philip faded away, not wishing to answer certain questions that were posed to him by the members of the group.

That's when Kelby took the ball and ran. The local rumor mill did the rest. It started innocently enough. Almost as a joke – like the one that I made about the lockstep McDonald's crew. The word "tulpa" was used as a derisive term to describe anyone that was deemed, to be charitable, as slow. Like the new bartender at the "Cracked Hoof" when he seemed mystified by having to use a bottle opener to pry the cap off of a bottle of imported beer. On the wall of the bowling alley a sign hung on the billboard about hiring a new pin-jockey. Tulpas were encouraged to apply, someone had written at the bottom. Tulpas were those laborers that wore orange vests while staring into holes in the asphalt during road repairs. Because I pumped gas at the filling station, I was probably seen as a tulpa with greasy fingers. On and on the kidding went.

Admittedly, I was relieved that Kelby had interpreted Molewhisker's scheme to animate a mindform in the plural, meaning that there could potentially be numerous tulpas amongst us.

Once again, the larger papers in the area had a field day with the town's latest obsession. A few articles suggested (sarcastically?) that it was an attempt to promote tourism. Visitors would soon be flocking to the boonies of Mfkzt (pronounced Moof-kooz-tee) to snap photos of ordinary folk that were proclaimed by the hucksters on the town council as "a gaggle of hapless illusions created by some grand mental experiment." The funniest column ended by stating "And, yet, they still have to pay taxes."

After *The Spectrum* mentioned the strange disappearance of Zerrill, suddenly the notion of thought-forms was no laughing matter. Some of the more fearful town folk took to pricking their fingers to draw blood while others held them over a stove flame as if to prove their own realness.

With his basement store on the dirt bike trail having not lived up to expectations, Nestor went door to door (wearing a clean white lab coat, no less) to promote his latest enterprise. Using special photographic techniques that he described as "bioelectrographic", he claimed to be able to capture a person's coronal discharge, thus determining who was real and who wasn't. He even printed up slick brochures that featured the high-tech equipment that was used for aura detection in his "underground laboratory."

Even with the high-frequency power supply, electrodes and metal conducting plates, I was pretty sure that Nestor's aura vibrations were bullshit. Still, I took Talia without the H over to his workplace one night to see what she thought. The ex-fortune teller may have been anxious to see what she referred to as the "Kirlian effect", but I just wanted to have a look around. Examining the colorful glowing haze that 'emanated' from the various subjects on the contact prints, she told Nestor that she wasn't particularly impressed by the overexposed photomontages. While the two argued whether or not some trickery was involved, I wandered around in what remained of the cut-rate bodega until I found a couple of old Polaroids next to the cobwebbed Sno-Master shaved ice machine. These clearly showed the symbol that Zerrill had been so interested in. Although this led me to believe that Nestor was most likely the person that stole the doohickey, rather than accuse him of this, I slipped one of the photos into my pocket.

It wasn't until Kelby mentioned Molewhisher's bonkers house that the shit really hit the fan. Had the grim beeper inadvertently opened the gates of hell after passing under the seventh country road bridge in the incorrect order, they wondered? If so, was he now a black master residing in some fright dome where his warped mind was busy creating masses of obedient underlings? Believing this to be the case, someone tried to burn down the decrepit Victorian. When it wouldn't catch fire after repeated attempts, those who toyed with the idea that he might be some kind of black magician became even more alarmed.

In the weekly gatherings that he held in the pavilion in the park, Kelby urged his captivated audience not to engage in arson. He reminded them that if something should happen to the "tulpamancer" that scores of his human marionettes might simply vanish... just like his mindform named Zerrill did. Who knows, he confided to some, with Molewhisker's death, the entire town could dissipate into utter nothingness. To those who got too caught up in all this, this didn't seem outlandish.

After Kelby's mesmerizing speeches, a surprising number of town folk quit their jobs and rarely left their houses.

In thinking about the futility of their soulless existence, they relied more and more on the bottle. Before the "lemmings jumped off the cliff", someone needed to take action, the majority concurred.

Those who found the whole thing to be utterly ridiculous didn't want to be embarrassed all over again by some outrageous nonsense spewed by a high-school kid who, to quote my dad, "had spun one too many drug store paperback racks."

Little did they know that things were about to take a turn for the worse. Kelby had spent the past few weeks posting notices on bulletin boards in neighboring towns about some shocking revelation concerning Jesus that he planned to announce in the pavilion on Christmas Eve.

When the day arrived, droves of hippie-looking Jesus freaks gathered in our small park to hear what he had to say. Sitting on blankets inside the pavilion, they sang their religious cliché songs and asked locals for "love offerings." Scattered on a carpet of hay in front of them were the illuminated figures of an outdoor nativity scene that Kelby had assembled as a backdrop for his "stunning announcement." Along with blow mold sheep and camels, the richly garbed Three Wise Men were gathered around Joseph,

the Virgin Mary and the baby Jesus. Above the cardboard sta-
ble a large plastic "Star of Bethlehem" was glowing. As Kelby
began speaking through a battery-operated megaphone, the
counter-culture Christians put their acoustic guitars down.

"Might Jesus have been a mindform?" he began. "Was that
why the Magi – from which the word magic is derived – had come
to witness this Virgin Birth? And what about the so-called Star of
Bethlehem? Why couldn't King Herod see this celestial beacon
that the three Wise Men had followed? Let me share with you a
little known astronomical... fact. In five phase cycles – that is –
over an eight-year period, Venus, on its clockwork course, traces
an enormous pentagram in the zodiac. That's right – that persistent irritant to the church – a little irregular, perhaps – but still a
fully formed pentagram. The points are defined during an inferi-
or conjunction, meaning when Venus – the bright morning and
evening star that Jesus identified with – is hidden... or occulted
by the sun as observed from the earth. That's why King Herod
couldn't see the Christmas star. He wasn't initiated into the invisible college that the Magi were. Wasn't privy to the secrets and
symbols of the advanced science that they preserved."

Before the crowd had a chance to react, he held up a copy of
the Bible.

"I have a witness – someone that I have known since childhood – who will swear that he has seen those with hair as white as
snow and with eyes like lamps of fire right here in our little town.
That's right – just like the description of the Watchers... and by
those who encountered Jesus. What if the Atlantean sorcerers
dusted off their earlier creation? Or, created... all over again...
this venerated thought-form with its mystical shimmer – "

"What time does the man with the net get here?" Roovert
Purdy interrupted Kelby while speaking over his own mega-

phone. "Don't listen to this young man with his Age of Aquarius babble. If you want to believe in Atlantis, you better find yourself a hat for those flying horses that poop. Angels shacking up with Bubba Hotep! Fallen angels, maybe. I've never heard such a hotch-potch of bogus hocus-pocus lose your focus be plagued by locusts like the prophets told us would croak us bunch of malarkey. That's rubber wall stuff! As for these hibiscus tea drinking Jesus hippies with their new thought hooey: they are not truly Pentecostal. Standing here with my J.C. Penny clip-on tie, I can tell you that the only thing that counter-culture Christians know about the Second Coming is that it lasted longer than the first squirt. Don't pick the Devil's red boogers, folks. Join my flock and keep an eye on the clock. Now, can I get an Amen?"

As the tension in the pavilion increased, Kelby smiled and put his lips to the megaphone.

"Roovert wants his Amen. Will someone please ask the pastor why he is always invoking the name of the powerful Egyptian god, Amen – who was said to be Mysterious of Form?"

There were lots of confused expressions among the Jesus freaks. Even the fiery Pentecostal preacher appeared to be taken back.

A couple of days later, I was talking to Trixie on the phone. When I asked her opinion about this whole Jesus being a mind-form idea of Kelby's, she thought that it was quite a stretch. However, when it came to Jesus being a magician – this elicited a very different response:

"So, I take it that the Bible thumpers were a little discombobulated," she laughed on the other end. "Actually, the notion that Jesus was a magician doesn't faze me at all. Even one initiated into the left-hand path of sexual gnosis by his erotic consort. The so-called sinner. With all that's been glossed over and blotted out by the censors, there are still plenty of hints in the standard scriptural accounts that the whole Christ mythos typified those wonder-workers that were prevalent in Egypt in those days. It seems that the things Jesus as Magus did just stuck. Was riding into town on a jackass supposed to be symbolic of a follower of Setekt? And what about the Eucharist-like practice of eating Christ's flesh? Is this the same magically efficacious black meal that Schaufler partook of in the cemetery? The raising of HIS Lazaruses from the dead. But, good luck convincing the goody two-shoes that their savior – if he even existed – flaunted all the credentials of one initiated into the dark arts. I once asked my parents how they would feel if Jesus wasn't what they thought he was? Was, more likely, a contradiction of everything they believed? They told me to go straight to my room and pray for forgiveness about having thoughts that would, at best, send me to purgatory. Yep, God's crowded waiting room."

Even though Trixie relished in pissing off mainstream Christians – most likely as a way of rebelling against her strict Catholic upbringing – was the idea that Jesus had practiced tantric-inspired magic really that far-fetched? Like Trixie, Jesus went against the grain. He mocked the established religion of his time. He spoke in esoteric parables and engaged in wish giving. There were banishings of demons and magical illusions. His secret initiation was meant for only a select few? Was changing water into wine allegorical for turning ignorance into knowledge? And most important of all – were his personal tribulations and glorious resurrection symbolic of the transformation from average awareness into divine consciousness? Jesus certainly talked the talk and walked the walk of a left-hand path magician. And to the Romans, in those days, practicing magic was a criminal offence that was punishable by being nailed to a cross.

I didn't know what Kelby's motivation was to do these gatherings. Especially when public opinion began to sway against him after bringing Jesus into the mix. When he persisted, there were death threats by some of the more zealous churchgoers, and even from one chunky high-school football player who thought that it might be best to beat the evil spirit out of him as opposed to having it expulsed during a traditional exorcism. Fortunately for Kelby, his old jock friend, Schramm, intervened.

Roovert Purdy had a different idea about how to deal with these things. Word had it that every day for a solid month he pulled in front of Kelby's parents' house and laid on the horn while holding the passenger door open in hopes of personally chauffeuring one perfectly possessed human being to his soul-salvaging digs.

Even though Kelby never mentioned my name as being the one who told him about the sightings of the strange albino-like figures (I didn't disclose anything else about my *othering* experiences), I was still concerned that being friends with him might lead to problems. Both of my parents suggested that I keep my distance so as not to be associated with such controversy.

There were still plenty of people that attended these get-togethers, although fewer people were going to Molewhisker's house to witness for themselves the seeming anomaly of the birds. (Those who didn't bother to check it out suggested that whatever was happening was just one of those strange things that occurred in nature.)

The last that I heard, Kelby's newest theory suggested that the white haired strangers with eyes like flaming torches were fallen angels of the apocryphal texts that had been cast into a fiery pit because they rebelled against God. Indeed, Schaufler had opened the gates of hell and the strange doings associated with his house could be explained by its foundation covering this infernal abyss. This prompted a new legion of gawkers to the devil's Victorian.

With Zerrill's disappearance and other matters weighing on my mind, I decided to take my parents' advice and distance myself from Kelby. Over the next few months I studied harder to improve my grades, hoping that I might get a scholarship to the University of Southern Illinois.

While studying at the desk in my bedroom one night, I heard a slight whizzing sound before feeling something come to a rest on the top of my head. I was surprised to grab a black paper airplane whose folded wings were marked with a sword in front of a swastika outlined in white. Turning around to see who threw it, I saw a young boy in a black beret standing at the door. Wearing a Boy Scout-like uniform with an armband that was emblazoned with the same Thule Society insignia, I recognized him as the kid who tossed all the paper airplanes at me in the mental hospital I had visited during a class field trip.

"Fake skin!" he shouted loud enough to draw the attention of my parents. Instead of them checking to see what was going on, two ominous-looking figures slowly walked into my room. One was the doctor from the mental institution and the other was my elementary school principal. Both were dressed in dark military uniforms, complete with black visor caps and polished high boots that resembled the ensemble worn by Waffen-SS officers in movies that I'd seen.

Zothyriantics

"I hope you like borscht soup," the doctor with the eye-patch smiled.

"With some black bread, perhaps," the sadistic principal added as he clenched my shoulder firmly with a crooked talon-like hand.

"So, according to the boy here, you are a prize catch," the doctor said. "One that we shall study in order to create a phantom army as a demonstration of strength for the hidden empire. We have known about your kind – organic robotoids – from expeditions by the Ahnenerbe to Tibet. Just like those created by adepts from the kingdom of Agarthi. Imagine goose-stepping tulpa soldiers followed by a blitzkrieg from sky-stormers of the Fourth Reich on foreign soil. A true Twilight of the Gods orchestrated by the true mastermind. Forget about the burnt remains that were found. They belonged to the green grocer... Bartholdy... the fuhrer's double. Not the black magician, himself. Certainly you have no objection to a little magical fascism."

The principal showed me the Bubinga "Whammer" paddle before grabbing my hair and pushing my head down.

"Now, before we board the U-boat out front that will take us to Neuschwabenland, would you kindly pull down those cotton briefs and bend over," the bitter fossil grinned sourly.

"I can't go to Neuschwabenland. I'm going to college. I don't even know where Neuschwabenland is," I uttered in a growing state of panic. "Neuschwabenland – "

The boy in the Hitler-youth uniform clicked the switch to illuminate the world globe on my desk and pointed to Antarctica. As the principle made ready with the wooden paddle, I heard a loud whacking sound and felt something strike my knuckles with enough force to make them sting. Looking up, I saw my sixth-grade teacher, Mrs. Rutledge, tapping a yardstick against her

287

palm. Glancing about the room, there was now no sign of the others. With an irritating smirk on her shriveled profile, empurpled lips shouted:

"Wake up and die right! We've barely peeled the butternut when it comes to the Zoths."

Gasping for breath, I awakened from the nightmare, but not before my flailing hands struck Midnight Meringue, who had been curled up next to me on the bed. After making sure that no one was standing there in the shadows of my bedroom, I pounded my fist against the pillow. The same recurring dream had been tormenting me for several days now.

Standing up on the bed, I peered out the window at the streetlight. Even though there was no German U-boat in the foggy driveway, I knew what I had to do. All my trouble began after I removed the doohickey from Molewhisker's house.

Molewhisker was sitting on a stool at his table, picking at the withered greens on a chipped plate with an oily pair of pliers.

It didn't take long for the distorted imagery in the afflicted mirror to change. Within seconds, the drab furnishings in the dining room underwent a remarkable transformation. I was now standing in a spacious cube that was bathed in soothing cobalt-blue lighting. Even with the continually shifting ornamentation, the ultra-modern décor blended together with a pleasing conformity.

Where Molewhisker had been seated, I was now standing before a delicately featured person that I recognized from the octagonal temple. Exquisitely crafted white plaits framed the perfectly symmetry of his alabastrine face. His draping was like a form-fitting stream of eddying dark purple that was in stark contrast to his eburnean flesh. When he looked up at me with a penetrating glare from his golden-hazel eyes, a subvocal thought bloomed in my head. The oddly familiar tonality was, "YWLLWY", which I somehow understood to be his name.

Placed before him on a tabletop whose surface appeared as gentle waves of shimmering gold energy was a scalloped white bowl that contained the most extraordinary salad one could ever imagine. It was like a miniature jungle that had sprouted with geometric precision.

Strangest of all, the botanical curiosities were rustling from a bewildering movement. Upon closer examination, these turned out to be minute virescent organisms in a variety of mammalian likenesses that were attempting to disguise themselves among the peculiar greenish shades.

Watching Ywllwy approach the salad was like observing a big game hunter on an African safari. He cautiously stalked the micro-zoological creatures with some type of multi-functioning tool that resembled a fork with a series of complex ejectors. With the culinary device's rotating blades, he was able to penetrate the luscious verdure. As he did so, variegated stems exuded olivine, orange and cerulean oozes. He consumed these viscous discharges along with scoops of the slashed flora and maimed prey. Threadlike tiny vines were also sliced and eaten with the chilled gushes (dressing?) by using the axially moveable appliance.

With my eyes riveted on all that was taking place in the bowl, I hadn't noticed that the stodgy butler had appeared near the table. Standing motionless in his oversized aesthetic, he appeared to be keenly anticipative of his master's needs while pursuing his trophy. Clipping away the tangled leafage, Ywllwy discerned through a layer of magnification that encircled the implement a miniscule arthropod that was suspended in some kind of glistening filaments. As it attempted to scurry from the sparkling webbing into the toppled vegetation, the spindly thing was skillfully lanced in its tiny emerald thorax by a pointed attachment on the culinary device. A clear fluid seeped from its quivering torso that Ywllwy sucked into his mouth with a thin metallic straw. When he offered me a bite of its sheeny trunk, the inscrutable servant with the slanted topaz eyes quickly slapped my hand away.

Having what appeared to be a violent reaction to what he just ingested, Ywllwy's eyes turned pale pink before the irises took on a fiery red hue. He stood up and brushed aside the servant, who bowed before backing out in the black tailcoat with the boxy tailoring. Ywllwy staggered towards me. With all the strength he could muster, he pushed me from the subdued bluish setting into one of those dilating black ellipses that always seemed to appear out of nowhere. Stumbling through the glossy opening, I found myself being impelled forward at an alarming speed through a tubular hallway. At first, my body was doing a comical dance as if stuck in a wind tunnel. When I trusted that I could remain perfectly balanced in the tingling zephyr, I relaxed my frame and let the current propel me along the smoothly winding corridor.

Heading right towards a larger version of Molewhisker's black hearse hot rod, I braced for impact, only to be gently 'braked' just prior to colliding with the colorful projection of the chrome-festooned spectacle that glided silently through the neon-splashed King Coney parking lot. Inside the phantom street machine, from the exaggerated grimace on a multicolored mask of a vividly freakish creature, a croaky voice bellowed, "*Schnickelfritz!*"

This was followed by an image of myself (twice my actual size) being struck on the knuckles with a yardstick by Mrs. Rutledge as I stood before the illuminated pale blue world globe on the desk in my darkened bedroom. From her shriveled profile, empurpled lips uttered, "We've barely peeled the butternut when it comes to the Zoths." To my utter amazement, the three-dimensional scenes weren't being projected onto a large movie screen, but, rather, the realistic imagery was occurring all around me. By what technological means could my dreams have been recorded?

Without any effort on my part, my body slowly rotated while my mind was being prompted for what was about to occur. Once again, I felt myself being pushed by the prickling surge of the corridor's silent effluxion, only, this time, it seemed like my entire body was tightly encased in some invisible sheathing as I moved at a disturbing velocity in the reverse direction.

A second later, I emerged from a liquid black portal into the soft blue luminosity behind the table where Ywllwy had been engaged with his salad. The bowl was now gone, but where it had been I noticed numerous snakelike white coils amongst the golden swirls. Taking a closer look, I realized that either Ywllwy's braids had been sheared or that they had fallen out for some reason (curiously, their intricate patterns continued to restyle themselves even when not attached to his head). In favor of the latter, silky eyelashes were also scattered about. Adding a morbid touch to the mystery, I counted ten manicured fingernails placed uniformly in front of the discarded plaits.

With a noiseless 'whoosh', the display was absorbed by the tabletop. Soon after, the servant strode into the room carrying a tray that contained a small wedge of white chocolate. I recalled having experienced this glazed treasure in my childhood, when the intensity of the ambrosial syrups flow-ing through the golden capillaries within lingered in my brain for hours. After setting it on the table, the butler remained standing there with his usual unexpressive manner. Finally, he inclined his head, indicating that the dessert was for me. As tempting as it was, I refrained from taking a bite (and not just because I was unable to fathom how to operate the 'fork' that was placed next to it), although I did think about taking it with me as some kind of evidence of the *othering*. Instead, I bolted towards what I hoped would be a very 'un-othering' door in the unkempt Victorian.

Every time I drove past Molewhisker's house, the place appeared to be abandoned. If Ywllwy had died, or, more likely, undergone some kind of radical transformation to "finisterrae" (the end of the world), then his distorted 'other' might have vanished with him. I wondered what happened to his servant, but, of course, I was mainly concerned about what might happen to me. Was it Ywllwy's expressed intention that I was to survive his projection into some trans-mundane existence after swallowing the fabled panacea? If so, how long would the mindform be sustained until eventually dissipating?

If this whole crazy business couldn't be attributed to some mental aberration – something that I still thought might be pos-sible – I began to practice magic with Trixie in her attic temple. Over a period of several months, she instructed me in the pre-liminaries of the Arte. What should have been a severely taxing curriculum of exhausting conditioning seemed to come rather easily to me, probably due to the inner connection that I had with Ywllwy. The starting points included breathing exercises, meditative postures (without being tied into a knot!), the proper use of consecrated weapons and banishing formulas. Next came mental gymnastics designed to enhance my iMAGInation.

Focused-will techniques demanded intense concentration. Due to the wandering nature of the mind, rigid training was required to keep me from relaxing my vigilance for even an eye blink. (At first it was extremely hard not to visualize the color green when Trixie told me not to think about it.) Also, so as not to be tricked of a great treasure, Trixie warned me to be specific when it came to the object of my desire. If the intent of the operation was mone- tary gain, one might find a grimy penny if a specified amount (or a close approximation) wasn't previously defined (and even if the working proved to be a success, the payoff might be granted in the form of something akin to my old packs of "Wackies" becoming increasingly valuable over time).

Nights were filled with experiments whose magical goal was self-deification. We investigated things like energized enthusi- asm, eroto-comotose lucidity, deliberate forgetfulness (relying on sigils alone to fulfill desires) and subjective synthesis – an integrated belief system in which the seemingly absurd require- ments of the old grimoires were strictly followed in order to disrupt normal brain mechanisms (filters). There were drills on how to deal with astral turbulence and tangential tantrums. We even cautiously approached mental processes that involved atavistic resurgence. This dangerous undertaking involved tampering with functions of the autonomic nervous system for the magical purpose of returning to the original source (or, at least, the subconscious regions that reptilian complex reversal allowed one to tap into).

Mainly, we focused on the tantric enhancement of scripted ceremonial magic, using hyper-erotic procedures to prepare the vessel for a conscious manipulation of the endocrine system and its ethereal counterparts. This was both to generate and collect valuable tantric essences. If we were to be entitled to the rewards of our magical endeavors, we would need to form a bond – an alliance that need not be of a romantic or 'significant other' nature – but one that involved the alignment of our astro-sexual rhythms. It wasn't about sexual desire. Tantra was a precise occult science.

After graduating, I moved in with Trixie, taking the doohickey and Midnight Meringue with me. Her parents had cut her off both emotionally and financially because of her "evil beliefs." With this new arrangement, I was able to help with some of the expenses and devote more time to our magical pursuits.

Over time, it was amazing to realize how the magical temple in her cramped attic could be transformed into a vast expanse. As we 'painted' the rituals to create the right atmosphere, the portal into the iMAGInal realm expanded. As glittering nights unfurled, we stepped into magnificent hypostyle halls whose papyrus columns were decorated with variegated colors. The piping of melodious bones could be heard as the fragrance of storax drifted from hanging censers. Within a magic circle on a tiled mosaic, Trixie was robed in iridescent gauze while lying on a divan of Arabian opulence.

Our experiences had extended into omnijective territory, where the relationship between imagination and perception were seamlessly interconnected, magically speaking. Fanciful whims and concrete reality were equal. There was no blurring – no divisions between the two. Our occult faculties had also facilitated an interface with intersecting parallel realities. Which caused me to wonder again: With the *othering*, had I somehow stepped on the edges where a higher vibrational realm and my ordinary, more familiar surroundings overlapped? Or was this *terra incognita* some advanced technology at play? Could it possibly be both? I still wasn't sure.

When not engaged in magical activities, we compiled a list of some of my more indelible early memories. We would frequently check this just to make sure that I hadn't forgotten certain things.

We also watched for other telltale signs of 'fading', such as losing my sense of touch and other unusual physical sensations. Trixie feared that Ywllwy might appear when I looked into a mirror. (Hopefully, she was only kidding.)

When I once again started doing only half of things and too many people accidently bumped into me (including Trixie on several occasions), we decided to take action.

I suggested that we perform the operation in the private cemetery, but Trixie quickly rejected the idea. This was because of a riddle in the *JEET* comic that she had unraveled. In the PaRDes tradition, before reaching paradise, there was a warning concerning a trick or illusion that was associated with the sixth gateway: "One must not say water, water when arriving at a sea of marble." Two kinds of water flowed from the divine abode, she emphasized. This puzzling quote made me think about the invigorating water from the spigot near the cemetery with its worn marble grave markers. Trixie explained that the water being referred to was the *elixir vitae*, whose wondrous properties would re-vitalize me. Instead of the cemetery, she thought that the abandoned hippie commune in the woods near the Moore's property would be better suited for the Working.

When the astrological conditions were favorable, we gathered our magic tools and weapons and headed for the country.

The flames of gelled alcohol cast shadows on the verd antique pillars that supported the High Altar. Upon its serpentine finish, a mirror of obsidian was angled to the sparkling void. As the aroma of bdellium and galangal drifted from black onyx tripods, the blue aureole of the lamps illumined complex diagrams that had been drawn at the cardinal points of a magic circle.

Once we were united with our perceived deities, a careful balancing act began to unfold. As the fire-snake (kundalini) was awakened and began its ascent from the base of the spine of the 'goddess', I continued to make a series of complex gestures with my fingers so as to further stimulate and magnetize the subtle power-zones.

As the energy circulating from the serpent-fire was being drawn up the cerebrospinal axis, paroxysms from 'Trixie's' lissome body shook the blessed chalk of the protective magic circle. During these orgasmic spasms, I noticed that a tick had fallen from a tree branch and landed near her navel. Due to the peculiar mental excitement brought on by the exhausting mechanics of the ritual, from the spiraling clouds of incense there appeared an image of Kelby as he looked when in the sixth-grade. He kneeled over 'Trixie's' writhing nakedness and tried to remove the tiny insect. Without hesitating, I reached for the magical duplicate of a Tibetan phurba (ritual dagger) and pinned down the unwanted thought with the well-scrubbed face before banishing it into a multicolored smear.

I resumed my sustained focus on the ethereal vortices; making passes over the sixth zone (Ajna chakra). While doing so, specks of energy like the dust of opals accumulated around the hot-point. Whether or not this was vitrified ojas or illusory dross, I wasn't sure? At the same time a daddy longlegs dangled from the altar stone. With a thunderous squeak, I heard the words, "Afraid? You are about to fall into the schmaltz pot!" The indigo flames of the jellied alcohol bellowed with ultra-mauve tints. This was followed by another specter that manifested itself from the fragrant suffumigations. I recognized the features to be those of Ollie's. The puffy-cheeked kid was holding a green "GO" sign as he drew closer with his eyes closed.

As the tick continued to crawl across 'Trixie's' glistening feminine curves, I was troubled by my negligence in not removing it. Before I could raise the dagger, a vision of a three-dimensional black-and-white cartoon armadillo materialized. It was "Darby", straight off a page of a *JEET* comic. As the critter quickly slurped up the tick with its long dark tongue, another cartoonish figure emerged from the forest.

This was the blurry farmer, "Flattop Emmett", from the same freak comix. Wearing denim bib overalls and brandishing a rifle, the comical monochrome apparition had a speech bubble hanging over its head that read: "Scram!"

At the sight of this, 'Trixie' began laughing uncontrollably.

Things were getting crazier as the "Silver Cirkus" guitarist, Topo Gigio, came into sight playing a scorching riff on his Telecaster guitar from the song *Treatises On Ludicrously Faked Sunsets.* (Had I made an error with a gateway of a 'Nightside' tunnel, I wondered?) Buried up to his neck in the dirt in front of the wiry rocker, the wavering mirage of "Dovie" smiled and said, "What's the riff, silly?" before fading away along with the specter of Topo.

With thoughts of cosmo-telluric discord pouring from the gateway located near the portal of Daath – especially of some emigrant with piercing topaz eyes that sought to breech the false sephira and enter into the human life-wave, I glanced at the asterism of the Big Dipper hanging in the sequined night as captured on the translucid screen. While deep in trance, strange hissing and popping noises issued from 'Trixie's' lips. In a voice that sounded like Nestor, only with a thick Bengali Indian accent, she uttered: "What about your Stray Dog?"

My mouth was burning from thirst. While attempting to activate the power-zone that I knew was fraught with danger, my attention was diverted by a rusty red spigot whose handle was self-pumping a stream of water just outside the magic circle. I collected myself, only to have my attention diverted by 'Trixie's' richly bedecked inviting lips. In her mounting rapture, she pleaded with me to kiss her wagging tongue, saying that it tasted like anise-flavored wine. Aware that any deviation from the tantric procedures would ultimately 'short-circuit' the ritual, I managed to refrain from doing so and, instead, continued to stroke the hot-point. With a series of luxurious moans, her shapely thighs undulated. Seeing that she was now wearing Playboy Bunny ears and holding a pair of pliers, I quickly shook this diversion tactic off with yet another banishing formula while tracing a glowing pentagram as the Operation reached its zenith.

Despite the expression of bliss on Trixie's face, I wasn't sure if the chemical wedding that occurred in her cranial vault had been a success. With this uncertainty, I observed the genital release of the *elixir vitae* as it was collected on a metallic disc talisman. With an unflinching gaze, I watched as the young mibster, Kelby, materialized once again. As my prized "Joseph's Coat Swirl" headed for the sixth archway in a game of "keepsies", just as he was about to cheat by slightly moving the bridgeboard, I banished him by tracing a pentagram with the anointed phurba, thus allowing my marble to pass easily through the cutout. As I assimilated the vision (finally realizing the chakra connection), I noticed several Boy Scouts watching from behind some trees. They didn't need to be banished, but judging by their shocked expressions, I knew that the erotic frenzy was one thing that they weren't prepared for.

On the way home Trixie tried to assure me that the unique properties of the essence had not been tainted. She had tricked the scheming creator of *JEET* by having us engage in the tantric procedures when the alignment of stars weren't favorable to allow any emigrants that remained suspended on the other side to slip through the cracks. (Chthonic worms are blind and much of the gibberish in the comix were also blinds intended to mis-lead us.) She was referring to those like the butler that I called Major Domo – an egregore that had been a thorn in the side of Ywllwy ever since his botched Operation. Trixie could only guess, but she suspected that such mental constructs were ex-pressly created by the denizens of civilization X for the purpose of serving them. The unfortunate things contained parts of their maker's own personality traits (and physical constitution) that were incorporated to make them more familiar.

However, Ywllwy's attendant was infected. Along with a distinctive physiognomy, it had developed a self-serving autono-mous existence. You could say that it truly was a demon servitor. It had gone to extraordinary lengths to enable others like it – those from an alternative 'universe' that certain occultists call "Zothyria" – to break through a particular Nightside gate.

Trixie said that, with its blurry status, this "buttinsky" was responsible for a lot of stuff that happened in my life; including my taking the personal item that I called the doohickey (believ-ing that none of us would ever discover the protective glyph that was ingeniously concealed in the multitude of ever shifting symbols). Once the doohickey had warmed up to her, Trixie discovered that the symbol would fully reconfigure itself at a specific time that was indicated by clues contained elsewhere in the object, and this matched perfectly with the one in Nestor's Polaroids. Besides its shielding abilities, paradoxically, the mysterious symbol also had psychoanalytic properties – bringing repressed mental conflicts to the conscious mind, such as the distressing thoughts of the "Zothyrian blunder" that Ywllwy had tried to bury over the years.

Major Domo had also arranged for Trixie and I to meet on the Notilus (with its mind-generated interior), and to find the issues of *JEET* that it also produced for its own agenda. The emigrant was probably responsible for the death of Ywllwy's female partner, and possibly even Ywllwy himself (if he had been poisoned?) because of the adept's vow to hide the forbidden (Atlantean?) knowledge that might result in other unwanted things gaining access into the continuum of earthly consciousness.

And what about Zerrill? Could his investigations into Ywllwy's life have had anything to do with his disappearance? This research might have also been detrimental to the servant's plans. In the clichés of so many whodunits, the butler had done it. It would probably gradually dissipate, Trixie thought, so there was really nothing for me to worry about.

Some of the town folk were still convinced that the old Victorian had been built over a hellish abyss where the Biblical fallen angels had been confined. Cashing in on this idea, flashy banners for the freak show at the most recent Mayfest trumpeted their most sensational exhibit: "The Phosphorus King" was billed as a terrifying demon that had managed to escape its chains until it was killed by a couple of deer hunters near an abandoned railroad trestle. Even though the colorful posters of the biological aberration on display looked like an obvious fabrication that was cobbled together from latex, treated animal skins and other fabrics, there were long lines of people hoping to get a glimpse of the thing. Listening to the spiel from the sideshow manager, I wasn't surprised to later learn that the person responsible for the exhibit was none other than Kelby.

At the same carnival, I ran into Nestor at a concession stand. Once again, I asked the dweeby beanpole about the symbol in his Polaroids. Although I didn't expect an answer, he told me that he had seen it in a copy of an old *National Geographic* magazine that his grandmother had kept. It was barely noticeable on a coffin in a photo that, according to the caption, contained the mummy of an unidentified pharaoh that archaeologists had recently unearthed in Egypt.

"Akhenaten?" I asked.

"Don't know the name, but he looked like a weirdo."

I was sitting alone on the eroded mourning chair in the secluded rural cemetery on an overcast afternoon. Shriveled, brittle autumn leaves covered a sunken stone path that twisted around weathered headstones and scattered pieces of blackened statuary. Among them was a newly placed marble slab. Etched on its surface were only two names: YWLLWY * ELXXLE, with the mysterious horizontal symbol incised in the sparkling crystalline beneath them.

"I thought I might find you here."

The sound of Trixie's voice caused me to flinch.

"Did you see the bone orchard's new addition?" I asked while gesturing to the polished slab. Bending over, I picked up a flaky bronze leaf by its stem and handed it to her.

"Pretend that this is a flower that you want to place on the grave."

With a confused look on her face, Trixie slowly walked towards the grave marker. She stopped a few yards in front of it and turned back towards me with an anxious, bewildered expression.

"I don't want to," she said while dropping the leaf.

"Yeah, I couldn't get too close to it either. At least until it decides that its okay... Like it did with Akhenaten when his tomb was finally discovered."

"So... no post-mortem residue," Trixie shrugged her shoulders.

"Yep, no corpse stew," I said.

"Who do you think did this?" she asked with roving pupils.

I detected a trace of concern in her voice.

"I don't know, but I saw that country woman that I told you about – Gertrude, I think is her name – leaving when I pulled up."

"Weird."

She paced for a few seconds with her eyes looking down at the leaves that crunched under her wooden clogs.

I peered up at the leaden sky.

"Today's an anniversary. I'm pretty sure that I was... externalized... on this magnificent hunk of rock," I said with a faint smile while rubbing the mourning stone's broken edges.

302

"We've been through this how many times," she said with a gentle, compassionate voice that was tinged with frustration. She then sat next to me and reached for my hand. "You are here. You have memories. And the Vee-Dub still runs… sort of. Isn't that all that matters? If you emerged from their minds… then, fuck, what about me… and all the others?.. And whose mind created them?" she gestured to the new marble slab.

"God's," I shrugged.

"Well, right now, that sounds better than getting into a whole ontological cluster-fuck," she managed a laugh while glancing about at the dreary surroundings.

I opened my mouth slightly while searching for the right words.

"You know, during… the last ditch effort… you were begging for me to kiss you… and I almost did", I said with a playful grin.

She gently stroked my hand. I could feel every caress.

"You can't get into trouble now."

She bit her lip while waiting for my reaction.

"Because there's no energy to short-circuit?" I joked; unsure what to say as I leaned closer and looked into eyes the color of that French liqueur that she was so fond of.

She pulled away a strand of glossy dark hair from her mouth.

"That… And, it's Addison's Day.

ABOUT THE AUTHOR

The Othering is the first novel by **Blair MacKenzie Blake.** His second novel is entitled *The Paragon Junk*, with *Grumble's Star* (the final book in the trilogy) projected for the spring of 2022. He is also the author of *Ijynx, The Wickedest Books in the World – Confessions of an Aleister Crowley Bibliophile, The Curious Diary Entries of Verity Pennington* (a short story), and is one of the writers of *Remember the Future*.

He has contributed essays to ten volumes of the anthology *Darklore* as well as to numerous esoteric-themed magazines, including *The CoSM Journal, Sub Rosa, Silkmilk* and *Dagobert's Revenge*. For over 21 years, BMB has been the writer/content manager for www.toolband.com and www.dannycarey.com.

He currently resides in Las Vegas, NV.

CPSIA information can be obtained
at www.ICGtesting.com
Printed in the USA
BVHW050857220322
632082BV00001B/56